TERROR TALES OF
EAST ANGLIA

TERROR TALES OF EAST ANGLIA

Edited by Paul Finch

TERROR TALES OF EAST ANGLIA

First published in 2012 by Gray Friar Press.
9 Abbey Terrace, Whitby,
North Yorkshire, YO21 3HQ, England.
Email: gary.fry@virgin.net
www.grayfriarpress.com

Typesetting and design by Paul Finch and Gary Fry

ISBN: 978-1-906331-30-6

TABLE OF CONTENTS

Loose by Paul Meloy & Gary Greenwood 1

The Most Haunted House in England

Deep Water by Christopher Harman 21

Murder in the Red Barn

The Watchman by Roger Johnson 46

The Woman in Brown

Shuck by Simon Bestwick 60

The Witchfinder-General

The Marsh Warden by Steve Duffy 78

Beware the Lantern Man!

The Fall of the King of Babylon by Mark Valentine 96

The Weird in the Wood

Double Space by Gary Fry 106

The Dagworth Mystery

Wicken Fen by Paul Finch 123

Boiled Alive

Wolferton Hall by James Doig 145

The Wandering Torso

Aldeburgh by Johnny Mains 165

The Killer Hounds of Southery

Like Suffolk, Like Holidays by Alison Littlewood 180

The Demon of Wallasea Island

The Little Wooden Box by Edward Pearce 196

The Dark Guardian of Wandlebury

The Spooks of Shellborough by Reggie Oliver 207

LOOSE
Paul Meloy & Gary Greenwood

Towards the end of May, East Anglian fields become luminous. Beneath the wide, unsettled skies, the soil at the edge of the fens and beyond brings forth, for some dark spring days, brief, dazzling ingots of yellow, stinking rape. And then, almost overnight, the crop is harvested, the lights go out, and profusions of poppies emerge like beads of blood welling from the raw, grazed earth.

The countryside is flat, littered with machine parts and the shells of outbuildings, windmills, pump houses and neglected railway lines. There are plenty of working farms, catteries, boat-builders, but it is the dereliction that seems to give the landscape an age. It leaves its history lying around like discarded rind.

Other abundant features are the water towers, great structures that bestride the fields and roadsides. The variety of their architecture is striking; some look like follies, with their turrets and fancy brickwork, others like alien war machines bristling with panels and aerials, others still like colossal viruses, built from diagrammatic specifications in text books, their elevated reservoirs like stylised concrete capsids.

So this land, inert, dreary, interminable to some; an inspiration to artists, horsemen, travellers, preservers of Tudor architecture, bucolic, antique and primal, keeps secrets and legends tight in the dark back rooms of drowsy pubs, the fire-lit tiled parlours of isolated farmhouses and the intricate quarters of the tithe cottages lining the drives of the ubiquitous studs.

It is seldom fragrant. The air carries the heavy odours of silage and ordure. Miles of churned manure; huge, slumbering pigs lethargic and deliberate outside their ranks of half-cylinder tin shelters; the scorched beetroot stench of the sugar factories and the miasma of hops fermenting in the breweries; that sudden, bright, dirty incandescence of rape.

And there are brutes at large in the fens, the fields, and the night-lone back streets of dark and secluded villages. Black Dogs and Big Cats, phantom beasts, elusive monsters. They have always been amongst us here, their burning eyes glimpsed across a yard, through dark windows, watching you from a remote horizon.

This is Old England and these are its legends, its Hob-footed thugs.

But now there is a new unease, a slow paranoia creeping through this old, measured shire. There is talk of a new beast.

And it is loose.

*

Dan was prepping wild mushrooms when Tomas came into the hotel's kitchen dragging two shoulder-high green rubbish bins behind him. Dan froze, a feathery, faun-coloured lobe of *Girolle* held between thumb and forefinger, slender chopping knife aloft in the other. He opened his mouth to say something but it was too late. Tomas tripped on the step, stumbled, lost control of the bins and staggered into the kitchen; the big bins, their lids clopping like pelican's beaks, wheels caked with mud and peelings from the yard, came after him. They toppled over and spilled their contents of sloppy flyblown silage across a wide area of floor and up the sides of the gleaming aluminium workstation at which the *sou* chef, Mike, stood chopping leeks.

Tomas steadied himself against the sinks and turned, white-faced and panicky, to look down at his handiwork. His left foot slid in some foetid okra and his knees buckled. He hauled himself upright again, and dared to look at Dan.

Dan stood up, the knife still in his right hand. Mike was shouting obscenities. The stench was phenomenal; Dan could see rills of tiny white blowfly maggots squirming like horrible, animated rice amongst the filth.

Tomas was weeping. His hands trembled and he flinched when Mike came round the counter and struck him across the back of his head with a partially chopped leek.

"What the *fuck* are you doing?" Mike screamed. Tomas let out a little shriek and cowered, scuffing backwards through the grot.

Dan stepped between Tomas and Mike. He remembered he still had the knife and placed it on the worktop. "It's alright, Mike," he said. "I think this is my fault."

Mike stared at Dan. His mouth opened, then closed. Then he said, "Your fault?"

Dan nodded. He was looking warily at Mike, aware that Tomas was watching him with a quizzical expression. Tomas wiped his eyes. "I'm sorry, Dan. So sorry. I was only doing what you asked."

Mike narrowed his eyes. "You *asked* him to bring bins into my kitchen? Are you insane?"

Dan let his shoulders slump. "No Mike, I asked Tomas to fetch me the green beans."

Tomas looked both confused but suddenly hopeful. "Yes, chef, green *beens.* I bring Dan the green *beens* he ask for. But I trip. So sorry, Dan."

Mike brandished the leek beneath Dan's nose. "The next time you ask this bottle washer to fetch you something, make sure he can speak better fucking English." He turned to Tomas. "I ought to throw you out with that garbage, you Lithuanian dickhead. I have absolutely *no* idea why the boss keeps you on. If it were up to me I'd've sacked you months ago."

Dan had to concur with Mike's opinion on the mystifying continuation of Tomas's employment. It was just a crappy little hotel on the borders of the Suffolk Fens but jobs were scarce and there were queues of people trying to get work there, especially with the recent influx of Eastern Europeans taking a lot of the menial jobs.

Tomas shook his head, made begging gestures with his clasped hands. He looked like he was shaking lucky dice. "No, no, chef, please don't. I try hard. I try harder now. Please don't sack me. I have to have job."

"If you've got to blame anyone, blame me, Mike," Dan said, his tone resigned. "I should have made sure he understood."

"Yeah, you get a verbal warning. Any more of this and it goes on record. Then I get rid of you, too." Mike was shaking his head. He said, "An inspector comes in now, we're closed down." Then he looked up, said "You're a lucky boy. No head chef, no hotel manager today. Fuck knows where the boss is. You're lucky I'm so reasonable, Dan."

Dan sighed, "That's me, Mike. Born lucky."

Mike stepped away, put down the leek and dragged his apron over his head. He balled it up and chucked it on the counter. He looked down at the bins. "I'm going into town. You really need to clean that up."

Dan nodded and he and Tomas watched Mike strut out of the kitchen.

A waiter came in and stopped dead. He wrinkled his nose.

"I hope that's not the special," he said.

Tomas laughed.

Dan stared at him until he stopped.

*

When Dan got back to his room the first thing he did was throw himself facedown on his bed and fall asleep. He dreamed of being chased through the hotel corridors by green bins, their lids clopping

3

up and down, pegged with big brown teeth like a horse's. Streamers of rotting vegetation caught in the hinges flew behind them like pennants as they trundled after him. He could smell their breath and hear the flies that swarmed in their feculent guts. He whinged in his sleep, rolled onto his side and made futile gestures with his hands. The bins raced along a corridor and as Dan turned in his sleep, so he turned to look behind him in his dream and was horrified to see that Tomas was riding in the leading bin. His face was an exhilarated rictus, hands clasped so tightly on the rim of the bin that his knuckles were white. A leek rose like a thick, pale hardon from within the bin level with Tomas's waist. Dan stumbled, turned into a stairwell and ran down into darkness. At the bottom was a dead end. He spun around as the bins reached the top of the stairs. They were backlit by the dreary 40-watt bulbs that dangled from grimy cords along the corridor. Their lids rose and fell. Tomas was gone. Dan cried out as the first bin launched itself down the stairs.

He awoke with a strangulated squeak. The dream had ended with him watching a golden stoat skulking in a tree while he gave birth to a baby the size of a two-year-
old that turned out to be made of rubber.

"Fuck," he said. His heart was pounding. His legs were entangled in a sheet that felt like a giant, over-moistened Rizla.

Someone was banging on his door. Dan groaned and sat up. His slid his legs off the bed and tottered across his room. "Al*right!*" he barked.

He opened the door. Tomas stood in the hall, fist raised. He gave Dan an unfastened kind of grin.

Dan blinked, still half asleep. "What?"

Tomas withdrew his other hand from behind his back. "I wanted to thank you, Dan," he said. "You save my job."

Dan looked at the offering Tomas held in his hand. Half an ounce of Amber Leaf and two tins of Carling hanging from their plastic loops.

"Oh, that's really sweet," Dan said. Tomas nodded, eyes watery with unspoken and overwhelming non-sexual love. He lifted his gift towards Dan, smiling.

"Now piss off," Dan said, and shut the door.

*

The next day Dan caught himself chucking stuff around the dry goods store. He let his shoulders slump and sat down on a bag of flour. He remembered an incident shortly after Tomas had started

4

working at the hotel. He had found Tomas rooting around in here, searching fruitlessly for the 'curly flour'.

"Cauliflower, you twat," Dan said to himself. He found a grin from somewhere. He looked up at the shelves that lined the narrow store. He had come in here for oatmeal and had ended up succumbing to an ill-tempered tantrum when a bag of basmati rice had plumped onto his head and burst. The horrific confetti analogy hadn't been lost on him and he had responded by grabbing handfuls of the stuff and flinging it around the room. Dan felt his eyes sting. He took a deep breath and stood up. He had rice in his hair and down the inside of his whites.

As he turned to leave, the door slid open and Tomas walked in.

"Ah," he said, and turned to walk out.

"Hang on, hang on," Dan said. "Come in here and close the door."

Tomas froze, then slowly turned and pulled the storeroom door shut.

Dan sat down on the flour bag again and gestured for Tomas to find something to sit on. Tomas made a quick sideways step, his eyes never leaving Dan, and sat down on the edge of a crate of breadmix. He clasped his hands between his knees in the folds of his chequered apron. His eyes were wide.

Dan looked at him and sighed. "Tomas," he said, "I've been a right cunt to you recently."

Tomas started. Then he narrowed his eyes. "You have?" he said.

"Yes, Tomas. I've been moody and objectionable. You try your best. That's all. I wanted to say sorry."

Tomas leaned forward. The flimsy crate slid into a parallelogram beneath his backside, threatening to splinter. He rocked back again, arms flung wide. His boots gritted in the spilt rice. Dan sighed.

"You are unhappy?" Tomas asked.

Dan raised his eyebrows and peered at Tomas. Tomas's face was open and frank. "I'm not myself at the moment, you could say that." Dan said.

"We *are* friends, yes?" Tomas said.

Dan continued looking into Tomas's face. They had rooms in the same shared house in the grounds, they worked the same hours in the same kitchen, they sometimes drank in the same pub, but Dan realised that he had never once had a conversation with Tomas that had ended without him giving him an order.

"Yeah, we're friends," he said.

Tomas beamed. "So, Dan," he said, the crate lurching beneath him, "you tell Tomas what problems are and see if he can help!"

5

"I don't think there's anything you can do about my problem, Tomas," Dan said, "But thanks anyway." He stood up and untucked the front of his whites to let a shower of rice empty onto the floor.

Tomas was undeterred. "I have always thought of you as my friend, Dan."

Dan tucked his shirt back into his trousers. "Okay," he said, his tone guarded.

Tomas nodded, his chin jutting with a kind of conspiratorial sincerity. "I can sort it out for you." He winked.

Dan made a weak sound in the back of his throat, neither a phoneme nor a cough. "All right, Tomas," he said, "I've been seeing one of the girls from Front-of-House, Kasia, the Polish one. She's pregnant. She wants to keep it and get married. Her brother works on one of the farms here. They came over together to find a better life, just like you, except this English bloke knocked her up. Her brother was a lumberjack back in Poland. He's huge and he's going to kill me. So, Tomas, what have you got?"

Tomas sat back on his crate and gazed at Dan. "That is big problem," he said, his expression grave.

"Yeah," said Dan. He reached up to a shelf and pulled down a bag of oatmeal. "You reckon you can do anything?" His tone was mildly sarcastic but any humour he felt, however dark, evaporated when Tomas said, "Probably not, Dan. I've seen the size of the fucker, too."

*

"You're absolutely sure?" Dan said.

Kasia sniffed, wiped her eyes. Her long black hair was held back in a ponytail, which accentuated the paleness of her skin and the striking structure of her cheekbones.

They were sitting opposite each other in a booth in Burger King. Kasia's hands were clasped around her Sprite. Steve's burger was untouched, still swathed in its greasy paper. He glanced down at a blue mayonnaise sachet and thought how it looked a bit like an elongated condom wrapper. He sighed.

"I want to keep it, Dan," Kasia said. She looked up into his eyes. Dan felt drained.

"I can't stop you," he said. He felt unmanned, as if his undercarriage had been ripped off in a terrible fanny-related incident.

Kasia's expression hardened, any light of hope draining from her large brown eyes. "You don't want to be with me, Dan?"

6

Dan studied the backs of his hands. She was a looker, that was for sure, and a bit of a *character* in the sack, but this was always meant to be a bit of fun. How could he have been so stupid? He'd just been trying to have some fun, to inject a little excitement in to his tedious, stifled, *exhausting* existence. And he'd even managed to fuck that up.

"*Dan?*"

He was jolted out of his ignominious reverie. "Huh? No, look, Kaz, it's not that I don't like you ... "

"Oh, I know you *like* me, Dan. You *like* to fuck me. What else?" Kasia's Sprite cup made a disapproving, icy tutting sound as it compressed in her fist.

"I like spending time with you," he said feebly.

Kasia stood up, flinging the half full cup at him. It hit him in the chest and dropped into his lap. The lid popped off, impaled on the spindle of its straw, and Spite and ice cubes soaked his crotch.

"Kazimierz will be *so* pleased to hear our news," she shouted, and stormed out.

Dan watched her go, feeling the cold soak through to his nuts. His face felt pinched in towards his nose, as if all his features were puckering with disenchantment and embarrassment. He remembered Kasia telling him about her brother. A corporal in the Polish army, arm wrestling champion and lumberjack. A great big monster hewn from Eastern European granite. Pulling up sugar beet in a field in Suffolk from six in the morning until six at night just to keep an eye on his little sister's welfare. She told him once that *Kazimierz* translated as '*fearful destroyer*'. How cool was *that?*

Dan felt his burger mash in his fist.

*

They were scared of the man in the corner.

Huddled as far into the rear of the truck's container as they could get, the dozen or so men and women, along with the four children, all stood and swayed with the truck's motion. There were no seats in the compartment; those on the outside of the group clung to the wooden slats that lined the interior of the container. Their hands, marked with the grime of their passage, the detritus of living hand to mouth for weeks on end, gripped the wood as tight as they could; several of the men had nails that were blackened not through dirt but through dried blood where they had split and torn.

The women, too, looked tired and worn. A few wore headscarves pulled tight to contain their unkempt hair, the cotton cloth biting into their scalps. Like the men, they bore the signs of living on the road; spots clustered around their noses; their clothes and boots were muddied.

The four children, aged between eight and twelve, looked worse of all Each of them had sharp features, cheeks and jaws sharply delineated through their taut, hunger born skin. Their eyes were dark and sunk into shadowed sockets.

Neither man, woman, nor child, however, took their gaze from the figure in the corner. He squatted, opposite them, returning their stare through a lank fringe of dark hair that covered the top half of his face. A thick beard that ran from his upper lip to the base of his neck covered the lower half. He rested his chin on the top of his knees that poked through the torn jeans he wore, his arms wrapped around his shins. His hands, as thin and bony as those of the children before him, poked from a cloth jacket that had one epaulet hanging from a shoulder. His feet may as well have been bare for all the covering the old slippers provided; the soles had already worn through in several places and his right big toe poked out from the front.

Though the others were unkempt and unwashed, they had long become used to the smells of their own bodies.

The man in the corner stank.

His was the stench of something having died alone and afraid in the dark. The thick, cloying smell of urine and faeces, hung about him. Something around him festered and rotted, decaying in his presence.

He had joined them a couple of days before. Their driver, whom they knew only as Alex, had stopped one evening, not long after passing through a large town, pulling his truck into what turned out to be a deserted factory's car park. He had let them out of the truck, urging them by means of sign language to stretch their legs and perform any bodily functions. As they wandered around, never straying far from the truck, Alex had stood and smoked a cigarette, looking out past the factory.

Long since abandoned, the building was little more than a shell. The windows had been either broken or stolen; the wooden frames they had been set in sharing their fate. The huge chimneystack stood at an angle.

Beyond the car park that was overgrown with patches of weeds and determined grasses, a chain link fence stood or lay in pieces, long since rusted beyond the point of being functional. Sloping up and away from it, the grass was broken by a few rocks that jutted out into the air like swimmers gasping for breath. The edge of a forest, dark and uninviting, sat at the crest of the slope and it was from here that the traveller came.

He loped out of the woods, a small bundle of belongings on his back, and crossed the car park in just a few strides. Alex met him halfway as his passengers crowded around the tailgate of the truck, watching the newcomer.

One of the men, an older man, swore under his breath and spat to one side.

Alex and the man said nothing; the man merely handed him a small package stuffed full of notes. The broker who had arranged this last minute tag-along had said the traveller was desperate to leave and would pay any price. A quick flick-through showed the price Alex had set had not been too high. Alex grinned around his cigarette, stuffed the wad of notes into his jacket pocket and jerked his thumb in the direction of the van.

The others had watched the transaction take place and as the stranger moved toward the truck, had called to one another, bringing those who had wandered off back. The tallest and eldest of the men in the group stood between them and the stranger, who stopped, his beard splitting into a rancid smile.

"No," the man said, first to the stranger, then again to Alex. "No. No travel,"

Alex looked from one to the other. "You don't want him in the back with you? Can't say I blame you, mate, he stinks like fuck. Trouble is, he's a paying customer just like you and your lot." Alex stepped up to the large man and jabbed him in the chest with his finger as he spoke. "Besides which, it's my truck. I say who gets in it, and I'm saying he's in. You don't like it, you can stay here."

The man stared at Alex for a moment before flicking his gaze over to the stranger. He turned, eventually, and climbed into the truck with the rest of the group. With a rattle, Alex pulled the shutter down and headed for the cab.

Throughout the rest of the journey, the travellers had remained as far away from the stranger as possible. When they stopped, they filed past him and left it as long as they could before they climbed back in. The ferry crossing had been almost unbearable; locked in the back of the truck, unable to get out, they had endured a full day in the cooped-up environment, breathing the stench of the stranger who, for the entire journey, had squatted unmoving in the corner.

The sounds of the port were a welcome signal to them when they landed, though they remained still and quiet, fearful of being discovered at the eleventh hour. Voices from outside – Alex speaking with someone as they walked around the vehicle – were raised but only with laughter and everyone, even the stranger, relaxed when the truck pulled away once more.

Hours later, tired and hungry, the travellers rocked against each other and the walls of the container as the truck came to a stop. The cab door opened and they heard Alex jump down on to the roadside. A moment later, the shutter rattled upwards, letting in the weak evening light.,

"Welcome to England, ladies and gents," he said, standing back and waving them out.

The stranger launched himself out of the truck and hit the ground running, sprinting off the edge of the road and over the small wire fence that separated it from the field. Within moments, he was gone.

One by one, the travellers filed out, the men helping the women and children out of the container and down to the ground.

"Nearest town's about three miles that way," Alex said, pointing south. "Best of luck," He pulled the shutter down once more and locked it.

"He is trouble," the eldest traveller said, pointing into the field. Alex glanced over in that direction. "The man. He is trouble,"

"Like I give a fuck, mate," Alex said. He walked back to the cab, climbed in and drove away.

The traveller looked out over the field, trying to catch a glimpse of the stranger before he turned away and joined the others in walking towards a new life.

*

Kazimierz Mazur had known this was going to happen. In truth, it was his fear of it happening that had uprooted him from his village in Poland and brought him to England in the first place. His fear of some kind of harm coming to his beloved sister Kasia in this land of predatory, greedy and Godless men. His large fists trembled as he held them beneath the cold tap at the sink in the kitchen of the dilapidated house he shared with eight other migrant workers. He rubbed at his knuckles in an attempt to remove some of the dirt ground into them. He looked up and contemplated his reflection in the dark glass of the window above the sink. His broad, plain face glared back at him.

Tonight he would take a walk, cross the fields and find the pub where the man drank. Tonight he would avenge his sister's honour.

Kazimierz reached into the sink and pulled out a carving knife. It was blunt and the blade was loose in the plastic handle, but it would suffice, given enough force. Kazimierz clenched his huge fist around the handle and slid the knife into his belt.

*

He hated this place. The smells were all wrong, the lights too bright and the noise incessant. Shouts and screams were constant as was the dull thud of music that rampaged out of every pub and club on the street.

He huddled in a corner of an alleyway, crouched beside a large bin, staying out of the lamplight from the street and the crowds that rushed by. His fingernails, dirty and greasy, picked at the thick beard he sported, idly pulling the remains of his last meal from the whiskers. He breathed slowly, trying to remain calm beneath this barrage of alien din.

The town wasn't large – he'd been able to see that as he approached – but he had considered skirting around it, heading into the fields surrounding it. There was no point in risking anything now that he had come so far and was so close. It might add a little more onto his journey, a few hours, but that was nothing compared with how long he'd already travelled.

He'd ignored his own advice and wandered into town. It was the first time he'd paid no attention to his instincts for God knew how many years but he found himself skirting the main road of a small, but busy, town. He barely registered the looks of other people as they passed him; the wrinkling of the nose, the way they guided their children away from him, or how they crossed the road at his approach.

It was early evening and many shops were closing up as the pub trade started increasing.

He sat in the corner, squeezing himself between the wall and the bin, and realised that, for the first time in years, he was hiding; hiding from the world outside the alleyway, hiding from a world he didn't understand.

He was scared.

That thought, that sudden realisation, should have spurred him into activity, sent him out fighting the unknown, as it would have done back home. But now, in this strange place ... now he was scared, and he despised his own fear, the stink of it.

He stood up. He would find his brother tonight and then take back what was his, what his brother had stolen and fled the country with while he languished in Lukiškės prison. He had been left powerless, and now he intended to take his power back.

The man turned and walked the length of the alley, towards the racing lights and hideous noise.

*

Dan was the last to leave the pub. Because of the hours he worked at the hotel he normally finished around half-ten and had negotiated a dispensation with Kev the landlord. There were always a couple of pints waiting for him after hours in exchange for a sneaky supply of backhanded meat for the barbecues in the summer. There'd been a lot of venison burgers and sausages this year. He heard Kev lock up behind him and turned and walked straight into a brick wall.

Dan looked up, winded.

"Hello, Dan," said the enormous man blocking his way.

Before he could say anything, Dan was grabbed by the throat and dragged around the side of the pub. The car park was empty; fields stretched away in every direction, the edges of the turned earth gleaming like strips of foil beneath the full moon.

Dan was thrown against the side of a wheelie bin, his knees buckling but he was held against the flank of the bin by the pressure on his throat. He wheezed, trying to speak, to beg this man to stop his assault, but knew without any doubt he was about to get a bad beating. There was no likeness in their features, nothing of her dark, almost refined, beauty, but Dan knew this was Kasia's brother, knew it before Kazimierz spoke and pushed the point of the knife into his ribs.

"I'm going to cut your balls off, you bastard!" Kazimierz spat in Dan's ear. Then he drew back a fist, the blade of the knife curled in towards his own body and smashed Dan in the solar plexus. Dan collapsed, wanting to scream with the sudden awful void of pain that opened inside him. He didn't know whether he'd been stabbed or just punched, but there was nothing but an airless darkness beneath his breastbone. He'd never felt anything like it.

Kazimierz stood over the boy, the knife held point-outwards again and considered kicking him to death instead. No, he thought. Not death. Kazimierz was no cold-blooded murderer. He'd been a soldier once. Now the boy was defenceless he felt some small pity. One of the reasons he'd been glad his sister had left Poland was because of the reputation she was starting to get in the villages; if she wanted to come here and fuck stupid boys then he was done with her.

Kazimierz put the knife back in his belt and knelt by the boy.

Dan looked up, his eyes wide with fear and pain. It looked like the man was about to speak but wasn't able to utter a word because in an instant he was gone from Dan's side as something came out of the darkness at the edge of the car park and hit him so hard that he flew ten feet across the concrete.

Dan struggled into a squat, still clutching his belly, and watched in horror as something bounded over to the stricken man and began

12

tearing at him with enormous, brutal jaws. It looked like a huge dog, maddened and full of violent strength. Kazimierz was thrashing, trying to grapple with it, but the dog's jaws were latched on his throat. Dan stood on trembling legs, still bent almost double by his spasming guts, and shuffled forwards. He halted in his tracks as the dog lifted its head and glared at him. It snarled, blood flecking its muzzle. Dan froze.

It wasn't a dog, it was a fucking *wolf*.

The monster switched its head back to business; Dan could see – almost high-definition bright in the moonlight above the car park – the expression on Kazimierz's face as he lay pinned beneath the claws of the beast. His fists beat at its muscular flanks without effect. There was a moment when they were eye to eye. It was a pause of terrible finality. Kazimierz's arms dropped to his side. Dan could hear the low rumble of the beast's growl. And then, in one final figurative act of courage, a soldier's fighting resignation to his irrevocable fate, the big man threw his arms around the monster in a crushing embrace and pulled it onto him.

Dan cried out as the beast's jaws closed around Kazimierz's windpipe and ripped it out. Terrified, revolted, Dan turned and hobbled away trying to block out the sounds of wet, exhilarated tearing.

*

Dan made it back to the hotel. The pain in his abdomen had relented a bit but it still felt like a truck had hit him.

He staggered up to his room and let himself in. He collapsed onto his bed, his head reeling. What had just happened? One minute he was expecting a kicking, or worse, and then a horror film had started shooting in the car park. He rolled onto his side and groaned. He felt sick. He'd only had a couple of pints but he felt them rising, pushing up in a nasty froth from beneath his slowly relaxing stomach muscles. He got off the bed and stumbled to the bathroom. He knelt in front of the toilet and tried not to breathe in the acrid stink of cheap bleach and piss. After a few minutes the nausea subsided. He stood up and ran some cold water into the sink. He splashed it on his face.

He heard someone knocking at his door, but still hung his head over the sink, his eyes closed. He tried to steady his nerves by regulating his breathing but the horrible dull ache in his belly felt like a rock compressing his lungs,

Shaking water from his hands, Dan finally turned and went to open the door.

It was Tomas.

He stood, wild-eyed and weeping, in the corridor. He was filthy, covered in dirt, scratches and blood. He was naked but for a pair of filthy old underpants and a strange belt of twisted leather around his waist.

"I'm sorry, Dan. So sorry," he said, and collapsed. Dan caught him and dragged him into the room. He had left, Dan noticed, quite a trail of dirt and blood behind him in a wavering streak along the tiled corridor back towards the stairwell.

Dan shrugged him off into a chair and stood brushing earth off his shirt and jeans.

"What have you done, Tomas?" he said in a weak, tired voice.

Tomas stirred, looked up at Dan and lifted his hands in a gesture of hopelessness. "I only meant to scare him for you, Dan."

Dan nodded, looking down at Tomas. He felt a strange and enervating sense of inevitability steal over him. These bloody foreigners were always going to be trouble. The talk in the pubs, the blind paranoia, the mistrustful hostility towards these eastern European workers, was inescapable, rife across the region. Dan had always tried to distance himself from it, from the extremes of ignorance and lazy racism, but here it was, sitting in his room, openly displaying the madness, the insurmountable *foreignness*, of their dark, unrefined differences.

"What have you *done*, Tomas?"

Tomas cringed. He reached down, his hands going beneath the small of his back, and untied the belt. He lifted it and held it up for Dan to see. It was a dirty, greasy-looking strip of material. It resembled dog-chew stretched to go around a man's waist.

"This belonged to my brother," Tomas said. "I stole it from him before I came to England. He is a gangster, Dan, a very dangerous man. He used this to give him power, to control the villages around our home. When he went to prison, I stole it so I could use it. I thought if I was careful it would serve me, but it's so strong, so evil. I have made a terrible mistake."

Dan didn't even bother speaking. He just stood staring at Tomas, and felt a huge fury rising inside him.

Tomas went on: "It's a wolf strap, Dan. It's made from the skin from the back of a hanged man. It gives the wearer the power of the wolf."

Dan stared at the belt. It seemed to give off an aura, a pull. Something indefinably powerful. Something *potent*.

Tomas threw the strap onto the coffee table. He wiped his hands on his bare knees.

14

"At first, Dan, I used it to provide meat for the boss. We did a deal. He didn't know about this, didn't know how I got it, but I hunted for him, brought him deer, rabbits, pigs from the surrounding farms. He asked no questions, Dan. It made me feel so alive. But never this. I've never used the strap to hurt anyone. I just wanted to help my friend."

Now Dan knew where all that meat had come from. Thousands of pounds worth of the stuff. Bleeding and raw in the freezers, appearing as if by magic since Tomas had been working at the hotel. What a hook for continued employment despite his ineffectiveness as a chef.

"It's so powerful, Dan, full of my brother's evil. I can't control it. I've killed a man." Tomas's voice broke, and he buried his head in his hands.

Dan looked down at the strap. Primitive power, magic, whatever, he knew what he'd seen. His guts still hurt where that bastard had hit him. Thanks to Tomas he'd probably avoided being cut up, maybe even emasculated.

"It's all right," he said. Tomas sobbed.

"I'm a killer, Dan." He snorted a sinusful of snot.

"You were just trying to help," Dan said. "Thanks."

Tomas looked up through his fingers. His eyes were red. "My brother's coming for his wolf strap, Dan."

"What?" Dan said, distracted.

"I got a letter from my mother. My brother escaped from prison last week. He'll be coming here for me. He'll kill me and take the strap. He'll use it to commit terrible crimes here. He wants it very badly, Dan. I'm so scared. I've been stupid."

Yes, you have, thought Dan. "How will he know where to find you?"

Tomas shrugged. "My mother wouldn't have told him, not unless he threatened her. But I don't think he'd do that, not even in his greatest rage. He wouldn't need to. He'll just follow the pull of the wolf strap. It will be calling him."

*

Outside in the dark hotel grounds the man crept towards the house. As he approached so his senses became more acute. He could feel the pull of the wolf strap, so imbued with its power had he once been, and its proximity, its calling, aroused the latent beast within him. He could hear voices, could smell his brother's sick sweat. His mouth flooded with saliva and he spat a thick rope of drool onto the grass between his feet.

15

Almost on all fours, he bounded up to the door and crouched there, panting. His hands scrabbled at the handle and found the door to be unlocked. He slid inside, into a communal hallway with stairs leading to the left of a narrow corridor. With caution, alert and throbbing with the need for power, he crept up the stairs, turned onto the landing and made towards the door at the end.

*

Tomas froze.

Dan looked at him, asked, "What?" But there was really no need for an answer. The look of terror on Tomas's face told him everything he had to know.

He turned to face the door to his flat.

"He's outside," Tomas said in a small and broken voice.

*

The man paused, lifted his face towards the ceiling and sniffed. He had come miles for this, had suffered indignities and discomforts, hunger and thirst, but worse than any of these, he had suffered his rage. The fury that had eaten away at him leaving him feeling dense and wasted, like a collapsed sun.

He crept forward and reached for the door handle.

And was thrown off his feet as the door wrenched inwards and the beast fell upon him.

He screamed, trying to get away, making it only to his knees and dragging himself towards the darkened stairwell. He looked back, feeling awful pain in his legs and saw the beast tearing at his exposed thighs and buttocks. He screamed again and collapsed onto his belly, his chin jarring against the tiled floor.

He tried to roll into a ball but the wet muzzle of the beast bore into him and tore a chunk from his shoulder. It snarled and snapped and the man screamed again, high-pitched like an animal, as the flesh, the muscle, was rent in a strip from beneath his right eye down to his jaw line. Incapacitated by shock, the man lay prone, gasping for air, his eyes wide and white in their sockets, trying to understand how he could have been so wrong about his craven, worthless brother.

"Tomas," he said, and then the beast was over him and he could smell its bleak and savage stink, and felt the arteries in his neck burst beneath the fangs of the beast, and had time to see it twist its huge shaggy head as it wrenched his throat out, and then he died, with his brother's name on his blood-frothed lips.

16

He watched from the doorway as the beast tore the man to shreds. He was shaking with fear, and the horror of it, but felt a strong sense of relief that now it was over.

The beast paused, its front legs buried in steaming loops of intestine. It switched its head to look back, its muzzle rippling as it let out a low, rattling growl.

He stepped back and started to close the door, his heart racing, hands trembling in crawling, mortal terror, but then he heard the clatter of the beast's claws on the tiles and a loud crash of glass shattering.

He peered around the door, looked along the length of the short corridor and saw that the beast had gone. With slow tread, he walked around the corpse and followed the bloody paw prints to the window which overlooked the yard at the back of the house. He put his hands on the sill and squinted across the moonlit fields.

Tomas smiled.

There would be talk of a new beast, now.

And it was loose.

THE MOST HAUNTED
HOUSE IN ENGLAND

Go looking now for Borley Rectory, once famous as the Most Haunted House in England, and you'll find barely a trace of it. In fact, you'll be lucky to find Borley village, though that at least is still intact. It occupies a remote location on the Essex side of the border with Suffolk, but it doesn't advertise itself much, mainly because the villagers have long become irritated with the constant presence of sightseers and 'ghost tourists'. Though there are a few piles of moldy bricks where the Rectory once stood, and an overgrown path known ominously as the Nun's Walk, nobody will guide you around the site. No-one will even acknowledge that it has a disturbed past, but rumours persist that it did have and in fact that it has a disturbed present as well.

According to folklore, the hauntings at Borley long predate the construction of the Rectory. The main culprit it seems was a nun called Marie Lairre, who was strangled to death in 1667 by her lover, a male member of local nobility, the Waldegrave family, and buried there in an unmarked grave. In the tradition of many ghostly English tales featuring ill-fated nuns, Marie's unhappy spirit was said to have roamed the wooded site afterwards for many centuries, and by 1863, when the Rectory was built on the same spot by the Reverend Henry Bull, the place was already shunned by locals. Inevitably, the ghost transferred its activities to the building, but whereas previously the only phenomenon was that of a mournful shade seen walking alone at dusk, the occurrences inside Rev. Bull's new house were significantly more frightening.

To begin with, the apparition of Marie Lairre was now seen a lot more clearly, wandering the corridors with her eyes closed and hands joined. In addition, a spectral coach-and-four would be driven right across of the interior of the Rectory, passing through walls as if they were not there. There were sighs, groans, shouts, screams and a plethora of poltergeist activity with objects thrown and doors and windows opening and closing of their own accord. Somehow, Henry Bull was able to withstand this supernatural chaos for 29 years, but when his son, Harry, became the incumbent cleric in 1892, stories about Borley Rectory had spread far and wide. Harry could not even find servants who would work there, and after he died in 1927, it took an entire year for a replacement clergyman to volunteer his services. This was the Reverend Eric Smith, who along with his wife, stated quite firmly that he did not believe in ghosts – which, needless to say, was soon to change. The haunting increased in intensity. Demonic laughter and spine-tingling whispers augmented the usual screams and shouts; objects – some heavy, like candlesticks – continued to be thrown, but now at houseguests rather than against walls. In 1929 the newspapers took interest, the 'Daily Mirror' printing a story about the house. This attracted the attention of Harry Price, the charismatic head of the National Laboratory of Psychical Research, and it was Price who put Borley Rectory on the world's paranormal map by launching a long investigation and producing all kinds of astonishing evidence which seemed to prove beyond any doubt that there was an unexplained presence in the building.

Despite Price's regular attendance, the Smiths abandoned the house that same year, and once again it was 12 months or so before anyone could be found to replace them. This time it was the Reverend Lionel Foyster and his wife Marianne; a brave but unfortunate couple who were to find themselves on the receiving end of the most severe manifestations to date. Marianne was repeatedly struck and slapped by unseen hands. Crude handwriting began to appear on the walls, begging Marianne for help but never explaining why. The Foysters could only take so much of this, and fled the house in 1937, leaving Price and his team to camp out there for an entire year, gathering more and more evidence. But it was around this time that suspicions were aired by some of Price's fellow researchers, who felt that Borley Rectory was almost too good to be true. The results that Price tabulated knew no end, and some of them were truly spectacular – bottles of wine transforming into bottles of ink, house-bricks photographed suspended in mid-air, séances which generated a wealth of pseudo-historical data (and one unnerving prophecy, which forecast that the building would be destroyed by fire).

After Price's investigation finished, the house was renamed 'The Priory' and was leased to a certain Captain Gregson. He was the one who experienced what was possibly the most disturbing incident in the entire history of Borley Rectory. He was crossing the yard one evening when his two dogs both stiffened and began snarling. Gregson could see nothing, but heard the sound of heavy footsteps approaching. The dogs began yowling bizarrely, apparently driven insane by what they could see, and tore away from their master, never to return. Gregson was still in residence when, in 1939, a paraffin lamp was knocked over and, as was forecast during that earlier séance, the building caught fire. Nobody was injured but as *the structure collapsed in roaring flames, eyewitnesses pointed to tormented forms in the heart of the conflagration, one of them a woman in the guise of a nun.*

Of course, the matter did not end with the destruction of the Rectory. In 1943, a dig close to where the building once stood, led by Harry Price, uncovered the grave of an unknown woman who might well have been Marie Lairre, but by this time the war was on, plus Price's reputation was in some doubt, so it was less of a sensation than it might have been. Odd occurrences have continued into modern times. The local chapel and other houses in the village are supposedly the site of ghostly activity, though paranormalists are rarely granted permission to investigate them.

All kinds of explanations have been given over the years: faulty plumbing creating weird sound effects, voices being heard through the sewers from other buildings nearby, village pranksters and even Price and his colleagues perpetrating a fraud. It is clear now that a definitive answer will never be reached, but one thing is certain – the site where Borley Rectory once stood is an eerie place. Many who visit it even today talk about its forlorn and desolate atmosphere, and of a constant sense of the unseen.

DEEP WATER
Christopher Harman

Detective Sergeant Trench had brought the damp cold September in with him. He sat down on the sofa before Peter thought to ask him for his gleaming wet coat and pork-pie hat with its ring of droplets around the rim. His heavy grey face had the sheen of lead. His voice bounced off the exposed stone walls as he said he had no news, positive or otherwise. By then Peter had stopped interpreting the wide crack of Trench's mouth as a dependable smile and his own shivers weren't all due to the thermostat malfunctioning.

He drew the belt of his dressing gown tighter. He'd remained standing and caught his pasty morning face in the mirror over the mantelpiece. A wayward tuft of grey hair resisted his attempt to flatten it.

He'd rung some of the names listed in Celia's address book late last night. No help, and cloying, the expressions of concern. At about one he'd called the police and Trench himself had taken the call. Whisky at the dining room table until around three. He'd retired to bed as unconsciousness hit him like a relentless incoming tide.

A horrible awakening. He'd risen through fathoms, in his ears a muffled distorted tolling from the bells of sunken Dunwich churches. Panic, lungs bursting, the bells shrill, then he was sucking in morning light. The bells went on, chivvying him downstairs. Crisis over. Celia back, pressing the doorbell button over and over. Must have forgotten her key. Desperate to get inside and out of the rain to explain herself.

But it had been Trench at the front door.

Getting up off the sofa, Trench's coat creaked. It had a cracked, rubber-like appearance resembling gutta-percha. He ran a long finger up the piano keyboard then lifted the framed picture off the teak wall unit. Peter and Celia at a ship's rail, Peter dark-haired, Celia slim. Behind, mountains sloped to the sea. "A fjord off Norway. Honeymoon," Peter said. God, always the bloody sea. In the layered town of the ship he'd been constantly aware of what lay beneath its foundations. Their marriage had commenced over an abyss.

Trench picked up a shiny porcelain length, stippled and patterned with lines; no snake this, with its saurian neck frill, its fins, its

21

beetling brow and little arms with spread fingers. "Any reason why she might disappear? Any problems? Has she seemed herself lately?"

"Yes, as far as I can tell. We lived separate lives." He added quickly, "Amicably though." The electric hiss of rain filtered his voice. He sounded detached, a recording. He tried to instil more body, more obvious tension, into his voice. "She was always busy. In her office upstairs – or out researching, talking to kids in schools. She was active in the coastal artistic community."

"Has she spent the night away from home before?" Trench ran his long fingers over the razor shells embedded in the pargetted fireplace surround.

"Yes, goes to London to meet her agent and publisher. Tells me beforehand."

Trench peered into the goldfish bowl. Tails quivered excitedly at the attention and tiny mouths complained at the outrage of the glass barrier. You wouldn't like it out here, Peter thought.

"Working on anything was she?" Trench asked.

"Always, and always sea-related." 'Fishy' had been unfittingly frivolous on his tongue-tip. "Everything from great classical legends to folk tales of the East Anglian coast. Adapts them for children. The sea's her métier."

"Not yours?" Trench said, his crack of a mouth hardly moving to articulate the words.

"No," Peter admitted. "Hardly needs to be with the job I do."

Trench moved to the hallway, his gait an odd mince, one step before the other, like on a tightrope. He wore the grubbiest, tiniest plimsolls; they could have been purloined off a drowned child. Peter followed Trench to the front door and waited in the porch as Trench stepped out into air packed with rain. Low cloud dissolved the upper reaches of Sizewell power station. Leiston was squared-off lumps of dirty ice. Black puddles on the drive looked deep enough to swallow Trench whole. Saying he'd be in touch, he pattered over them and vanished through the open gateway in the flint wall and into the lane.

The phone was ringing as Peter closed the door. He felt a spasm of hope, an urge to rush out and call Trench back. He might never have to see the man ever again.

It was Elise. Her voice lit a match inside him that fought Trench's lingering chill. Elise hadn't gone missing – that would have been unbearable. "No news," he said. Her disappointment and sympathy were all for him. She and Celia had never met.

Peter and Elise agreed it was best not to meet at the cottage or her flat in Saxmunden. Peter suggested Dunwich and a time, and

22

they rang off. Rain layering the window glass cast an underwater light into the room. When the phone rang once more he grabbed it for more of the comfort of Elise's voice.

Hollow knockings, as on submerged pipes. An enormous gulping reminded him of the drinking-water dispenser outside his office in Woodbridge. His repeated "hellos?" didn't prompt a reaction. No heavy breathing or abuse. Peculiarly ill-timed, your miserable thrill, he might have said – but why reward the sicko? He restricted himself to an acidly uttered "You need professional help" and slammed the receiver down. He'd enough on his hands without encouraging a hate campaign. He picked up again, rang Cultural Services and belatedly explained his absence from the office that morning. Mike's sympathy and dismay rendered his voice almost unrecognisable.

Peter switched on the lights. Stravinsky on the stereo wakened his brain, but not his body. He felt dirty, encrusted. He ran a bath and would have lingered in it but for his appointment with Elise. Steam curled like a sea-fret. Sleepy rather than enlivened, he got out. Clear drip trails striped the condensation in the cabinet mirror, making him partially present – the rest in a place of negligible visibility.

He drove under an ocean of cloud. More fields would have lagoons before the day was out. The rain came on heavily and Theberton was dissolving castles and follies in a fish tank. Out again, through Middleton then Westleton. Dunwich at last. He was regretting it. Over-cautious meeting this far away; enough to raise suspicions in itself.

The café was part of a complex of former fishermen's huts a few yards short of the beach. He'd gone to the museum first. The staff knew Celia. They'd looked dazed and slightly shifty taking in her disappearance, and this man claiming to be her husband.

Sliding into his seat opposite Elise, he flinched at his face reflected in the window; bloated, warty with beads of rain. "You look terrible," she said helpfully. His face would recover though – and his body had looked acceptable in the bath. He'd got trim after stage-door Johnnying Elise after the concert three months ago in the Jubilee Hall in Aldeburgh. There had been some freebie tickets for staff in Cultural Services. Elise had played the flute like something out of mythology, land-based – not one of Celia's ubiquitous Nereids. Elise hadn't fled with eerily beautiful giggles at his approach, nor from his embarrassingly fulsome comments on the performance. He confessed he'd been a music teacher himself before the dead hand of arts administration dangled a big salary on a hook. She'd taken the bait, and the next day they'd dined on cod and chips in the *White Lion Hotel*.

The Dunwich café was less refined. Peter needed a sugar-hit and piled his scone with jam. Elise had a sundae. Peter described Trench. "Not a ball of fire. Too wet for a start. Dripped all over the sofa. Treated the living room like a museum." Cold air off the window was a weight on his back. Elise stared past his shoulder: "The longer she's gone ..." A ladder of furrows was propped between her brows.

"What? The worse things'll look?" Elise's role was to buck him up, not look for gloomier scenarios. She seemed to realise this.

"She'll turn up," Elise said, going too far in the other direction. The tea urn whistled derisively. Peter crashed his cup into his saucer; he was lucky it didn't shatter like a shell. He ate the last of his scone and pushed aside his plate. His silence was too much for Elise; she looked for something to say and found it. "Think she knew – I mean knows? Could that be it?"

Peter shrugged. "It'll come out if that detective keeps digging. I'm hoping she'll pop up again before that happens. It's less than twenty four hours. Let's give the woman a chance."

They left and walked beneath the crumbling sand cliff. It had stopped raining. In the distance, a clean white block and dome of Sizewell power-station were like a fat figure one and a nought. Elise chattered on and off. Peter grunted, and looked past her at the sea which was like a boundless blackboard dusted with chalk.

On the drive back, cloud cover was faintly luminous. In dripping villages residents stepped around huge puddles. A rainbow bent down to Sizewell, visible between massive rain-washed hedgerows. He stopped at Thorpeness and noted every car in the sea front car-park. Jazz on the radio; wide-spaced cymbal brushes kept in time to the frothing collapse of wavelets on the beach. He watched the sea for ages. It seemed to look back at the watchers in their cars.

He drove south, heading to Aldeburgh. On the beach, Maggi Hambling's 'Scallop Shell' sculpture was like the iron-gauntleted hand of something drowning. He headed inland under bloody tyre tracks staining the clouds. The pink colour wash of the cottage flushed darker in the low sun's rays. Celia had long since stopped voicing her wish for a place overlooking the sea. Her modest royalties didn't stretch to one and he hadn't told her that his latest promotion meant his salary did. But it wasn't going to happen. Whatever else might keep him awake at night it wouldn't be the surf whispering of airless gulfs and things content to live in them.

Vaughan Williams' *Pastoral Symphony* was solid ground under him that evening. When the phone rang he got up too quickly and a

24

head-rush threatened to capsize the room. He grabbed the stunted mast of the stair newel post with one hand, the receiver with other.

More concern, more earnestness. Trevor Wishart's questions prodded him. He had to stick in his own like a knife between the man's ribs. "Has she seemed bothered by anything recently?" *Like I'd know.*

A brief hold-back before Wishart said, "Deflated when I last spoke to her." Not physically, Peter reflected, though he'd stopped wishing for that. "A difficult gestation, the current project. Has she mentioned Seagrim to you . . ." In that tailing off, Wishart guessed she hadn't.

"No," Peter confirmed. She never discussed work in progress any more than she discussed work finished. And Peter never asked. She'd always known he'd preferred fiction with characters, not archetypes.

"The story's not for the very young. Teens are another matter. I gave her a scenario I'd thought up and she said it made Seagrim too blatantly a villain. Well he is, I said, considering what he did in the original tale. Do you want to hear all this?"

"Interesting," Peter allowed. "But perhaps another time."

"Yes, of course," Wishart said at that dash of cold water. Peter said he'd keep him informed and goodbyes were quickly concluded.

He retreated to Vaughan Williams' protecting hills and meadows. Elise had musician friends in the Chilterns and had spoken of moving there. Another point in her favour, not being enamoured by the sea.

Later he turned on the taps before remembering he'd already had a bath at lunchtime. But under present circumstances two in one day wasn't the height of self indulgence, it was medication.

*

The next morning Peter parked by the yacht club on Slaughden Road, which ran south out of Aldeburgh. From the top of the high shingle bank he could see the winding Alde Estuary on one side and the steeply shelving beach on the other. Sunlight shattered on the blue banding of the sea. In the distance a walker hurled a stick and a barking black blob hurtled after it along the shoreline. A cluster of fishing rods thrust out over the surf like spindly fingers. Peter recalled the early days and his and Celia's beach-combing for cornelian and amber. She still liked to walk here. He'd objected recently when she'd lugged grotesque pieces of driftwood into the cottage.

25

The aural scintillation of masts and wires faded as he trudged heavily down to the shoreline. A far-off figure was ghostly, winking out and appearing again like a cursor on a screen. Walking under a gull-less sky emptied Peter's head of all but an awareness of the dark vertical in the distance. It solidified, and his heart pattered as quickly as the dog taunting the milky advance and retreat of the sea edge.

This wasn't Celia's hiker's stride, though it could hardly be a ripple either, unless the bright sunshine was producing the effect. Whatever the true nature of what he was seeing, Peter halted. The ripple resolved to a quick fussy tightrope gait that had bemused him on their previous meeting.

"Mr Belloes!" Trench's voice boomed and disintegrated like a great crashing wave.

"Anything?"

"Sea, shingle, sky." Flat, bottle-top eyes, lashless, lidless. Not a scrap of empathy in them. "That's not to say she isn't here." He looked out to sea and Peter felt released.

Celia killed and dumped out at sea did he mean? Misdemeanours, yes, I'm guilty of a few, but not that one. Trench shouldn't unnerve him. He was a monochrome clown. His mackintosh looked inflated by a bicycle pump. The grubby plimsolls, the hat with its white cracks and salt stains. If the police viewed Celia's disappearance seriously they would have sent someone serious. Had Trench asked to be assigned the case, having taken the initial call? Did it work like that? Peter didn't like to ask.

Whatever the case, Trench was wasting his time here.

"Well, keep me informed," Peter said. Trench didn't have the option not to, but the form of words was a means to end the encounter and let Peter take his leave.

His feet chewed the shingle as he climbed the three great steps of the beach to the high bank. He glanced back and down; the sea's rising voice demanded it.

Trench hadn't moved, apparently oblivious of the surf whitening around his ankles. His thin legs were pressed together like an under-fin stuck in the sand. His watching was the enormity of the sea until Peter was shielded from it behind the high bank.

As soon as he was home he went straight up to Celia's office.

There was a stale smell from a piece of stained Styrofoam packaging. Peter couldn't recall the last time they'd eaten together. Celia didn't cook unless she had to. He pressed a switch and the storm lantern hanging from the ceiling spread out a muddy sulphurous light. No obvious note left for him amongst the papers littered on the ship's oak table. She'd have left one downstairs if anywhere. He powered up her computer. Her emails weren't password protected. No need as he never came in here.

The latest was from Trevor Wishart, and dated two days before her disappearance:

Celia, see attached sketches. Seagrim's victims reduced to bone pictograms left on the beach. A marine metropolis (I've a few others – the sea's a big place!)
   Best,
   Trev.

Peter opened the attachments. Beaches, each with a white fragmented design laid down like the work of some ambitious pavement artist with only one colour on his palette, bone-white: a broken-winged gull, an unlaced boot, a ring, a comb with teeth missing. There was a city of filigreed bridges, colonnades and towers wreathed in rainbow shoals. An emerald sky; the sun a bronze penny amidst creamy combings of blown glass. The tipped wreck of an enamelled and silk-sailed barque. Gilding the lily, those gems set in already gorgeous coral beds. All a lie. Peter knew the truth of the sea. A gradation from twilight to murk to blackness and colossal pressures. Pollution a minor crime to set against the suffocating horror of it. No cities, just slimy deserts inhabited by clawed, scaled and fanged things which existed in order to eat.

He hated the room. Too much like a cabin in a sunken vessel. A pocket of stale air. Dull dry shells on a shelf; fragments crunched underfoot. Black netting draped a wall. He switched out the light. A beam of sunshine remained; dust floated like plankton.

Going downstairs was like rising to the surface. He needed to wash the silence out of his ears. Britten's *Four Sea Interludes* had brought the sea to heel before now, and he wondered if he'd missed in previous hearings those subterranean rumblings below the bright surfaces. Malcolm Arnold's *Sea Shanties* for wind quintet failed to lift his mood; an inch behind his eyes rotting sailors danced the hornpipe. Music always medicated him better in public places and he rediscovered that later.

He drove through light rain to the 'Barn'. It overlooked the Alde Estuary and had been derelict until its conversion into a small theatre and concert venue. Elise had booked his seat a fortnight ago.

One work was sea-themed and he would have preferred none to have been. In the event he was entranced by Takemitsu's *Towards the Sea III* for alto flute and harp. 'Towards' was the operative word; he heard no immensities, no violent surges, just oystercatcher calls, the breeze playing on the surface of the wide estuary outside, whispering in the reed beds. Ageless and sinuous, Elise's body was her instrument, the alto flute no more than the mouth-piece. A shiver ceased to be pleasurable. He turned around in his seat and saw that the entrance door hadn't been opened to let in a latecomer. He refocused on the ranks of heads and shoulders before him. His heart tolled silently.

Celia was midway along the row, three or four ahead of him. The fact that she always professed to hating classical music added to the intense wrongness of her presence here. Her mousey curls were near flattened, as if a localised cloud-burst in the drizzle had found her. In the green gleam of her waterproof was the roundness of shoulder that had lately so dissatisfied him. Yes, definitely her. She leaned a little. He doubted the oak pillar significantly spoiled her view of the stage. So was she drunk? No, not Celia, whatever pressure she was under. Not snoozing either, too intent on making a point – too intent on Elise?

He'd no reason to believe Celia stared fixedly at her, let alone with anything like loathing. His guilt was projecting that. The simple fact remained that Celia lived – and that was good. So what was the sensation in his chest – like a current of cold water – elation or anxiety?

The Takemitsu ended and clapping drowned out the torrent of questions in Peter's mind. It was the interval and he was the first to leave his seat. Outside, he gulped air and watched audience members stream out. He recognised some of the set who regularly turned out for concerts at the Snape Maltings complex, which floated on reed beds a mile away. Celia wasn't amongst them. Remaining in her seat, was the idea of speaking as unthinkable to her as to him? Knowing he had to overcome that, even if she couldn't, he went back inside.

A handful stood in the aisles. One or two solitaries studied their programmes. Celia was no longer present. Elise was. "Peter?" she said, peering as if he were under a rock.

"Thought I saw Celia." He shook his head, baffled.

"Where?"

An unbelievably stupid question. For a second he was as short-changed by Elise as he had been by Celia. "Here," he hissed, a mask of tension over his face; he wiped it off with a downward movement of his palms. "Sorry. Three rows from the front – or she was. Hang on ..." There was a door close to the stage. She could have got out that way.

Elise had followed his gaze. "I've just come out of there. There's only been me and the gang."

He'd missed her slipping out the front way. There was no other sane explanation. He moved against others filing back to their seats.

No sign of Celia's car in the car park or diminishing into the distance. When he was back inside Elise pouted sympathetically. Nice lips, showed to good effect when poised over the aperture of her flute and not quite touching it. Peter shook off the observation.

Was he relieved or frustrated? "Can't have been her, after all. Wishful thinking," he said with a slight cynical spin on 'wishful'. "You don't need all this," he said, sheepish. "Sorry. Again. Good luck with the next bit."

"Don't worry. Music's different. Another world."

A bit like Celia's then, Peter thought with a touch of envy. Another woman in the seat now – or was it the same one? The waterproof discarded at her feet? Similar hair shape and colouring – and her hair may have dried off. How drenched her hair had been – as if she'd swam across the Alde Estuary to get here.

Elise introduced him to the other players and in the crush of departures he didn't get to see the woman's face. He declined Elise's invitation to join them for drinks at the pub in Snape. He'd have been dour, preoccupied company.

*

The house was chilly, the air damp. The radiators were barely warm; the thermostat or timer needed fixing. The place didn't look lived in; it needed a woman's touch. Celia had never provided that, ensconced in her cabin under the eaves like a winkle in its shell. As he drew the curtain on the suffocating blackness in the living room window, the phone rang. Anxious to hear a voice he snatched up the receiver.

Knockings echoed. A sporadically repeated low *glooping* sound was suggestive of the release of great shapeless bubbles of air. A bony snapping, a flurry of water and in his mind's eye silvery fins flashed away.

"Celia? Just talk to me will you?"

Nothing, only the sea spitting and groaning in some recording she must have made.

"What's going on? Was that you at the Barn? This just isn't your style ..." A distant roar, as of surf, was growing. He drew the phone from his ear, dropped it into its cradle, almost convinced sound was about to become substance and jet water out of the earpiece. The growl of dialling tone would have been a reprieve had not the ocean continued to blast and heave above him.

The walls swirled as in a whirlpool. Peter grabbed the stair rods. Celia had a phone in her office. A damp stone of dread in his chest left little room for his heart with its beat blurring like submerged bells.

The stairwell was cramped and stuffy as a vent. Ancient anguish of the sea, coming from the top of the house, drowned out the whines of the centuries-old staircase as it took his weight.

No light under the door. What state of mind was she in to sit in the dark amidst the seethe and splash and thunder of waves? There were depths to Celia he'd known nothing of. He switched on the landing light to prepare her, turned down the door handle and pushed.

In the room there had briefly been a light, a tiny one, over by the window. Darkness now, which Peter hit the wall switch to dispel. Though the storm lantern cast only a dull orange illumination, Trench shielded his eyes though they remained round and wide. His bulbous body was cupped in the scallop chair by the front window. That little light must have been a pencil torch, deftly, and bizarrely, concealed under his hat as by a magician's sleight of hand. No embarrassment in his immobile face at being caught reading one of Celia's notebooks. Reading or not, his presence here was an outrage.

"What's this?" Sea sounds washed around Peter. "How did you get in?" He looked at his watch. And the *time*. It was after ten.

Trench's bottle-top eyes stared and Peter withered inside as if he'd uttered an impertinence to one vastly superior and he'd suffer the consequences. Well, policemen unsettled him at the best of times – and these weren't.

Trench had raised the book to his left eye, as if the other, an almost abnormal distance away, were blind. No left to right movement of his eyes as he read to the accompaniment of sea sounds overflowing from the hi-fi speakers.

"'The ocean is the world. In its empires and dominions are mountains and forests and plains and chasms that drop to deeper and deeply inhospitable realms.'" Incantatory words and the crushing relentless weight of crashing waves drugged Peter. He sat heavily at the desk. Trench went on, "'There are beneficent liquid goddesses; shell-armoured warlords; scaly potentates. And in the deeper unlit places there are deities beholden to no-one ...'" Peter reached to the cassette player and ejected the tape. Trench laid down the book.

"Loves the sea. So many do. After all, it's where everything started ... or *nearly* everything. They stare at it from their cars. At the end they're buried there ... or should I say *sprinkled*. Some can't wait, and go there before their time."

A macabre turn and if he was hinting at Celia's suicide he could be wildly wrong. "Thought I saw her tonight – at a concert in the Barn. She left before I got a chance to make sure." He chuckled bitterly. "I'd've been surprised if it was her. I mean, she doesn't even like music."

"How do you know? You don't seem to know much about her at all."

"More than you do," Peter said, standing his ground with effort. He couldn't imagine the unprepossessing Trench on personal terms with anyone sufficient enough for him to know them intimately. *Besides, he shouldn't be passing judgement, he should be investigating.* "Are you going to look into the possibility she's in the area, playing at God knows what?"

Trench got up and the open jaws of the scallop chair vibrated, hungry to grip him again. He proffered the notebook to Peter. "Read. There's all you need to know about her." It felt like placation, taking the book from Trench. His bones warmed as the man went down the stairs. He opened the book, read –

" 'The waves my ceiling

The sands my floor

The fish my courtiers

The darkness my law' "

– snapped the book shut, breaking the spell of Trench's quiet suggestion which had stuck in his head like an irresistible command. In the window the lone street lamp glowed orange in its wreath of mist like some cloudy photo-luminescent jellyfish. No sign of Trench outside. Come to think of it, he hadn't heard a car drive off, though he hadn't been listening for one with so much washing around his head like flotsam and jetsam against a stinking harbour wall. He searched the cottage, came to the front door and bolted it. He went to the piano and dropped both his forearms onto the keys to make the loudest, angriest cluster-chord he could. It worked; some of his tension died away with the sounds.

*

The next morning in Aldeburgh the clear arcs of the windscreen wipers constantly refreshed colour-wash facades, enriched the redness of old brick. Veins of white water ran in the roadside gutters. Locking his car on the promenade he heard the sea's deathbed rattle against the shingle, the laughter of gulls.

He bought groceries in the Co-op, then dashed into the newsagent. 'Drunken Beach Party Shame' was the headline in the diamond wires of the sandwich board outside. Nothing in the *Eastern Daily Press* about Celia. No point in stepping up the search and alerting the public if there was more than an outside chance Celia was in the land of the living.

Queuing in the bank in the High Street, Peter stared through the smoky rain at the aquarium, visible at the end of the narrow thoroughfare of Neptune Walk. Large wooden aquamarine-painted boards covered the windows or had replaced them. It could have been the discreet frontage of a sex shop, but for the peeling depiction under the guttering of fins and jaws and, coiling around the words *Sea World,* thin tubes with bulging eyes. He'd yet to go in – he'd yet to see anyone go in.

Now someone did. Rounded green-waterproofed shoulders shone with rain; salted brown hair was wetly plastered against the skull. Those sensible sturdy shoes were for cliff paths and awkward shingle.

Peter rushed outside, splashed across the car-lined road.

Beyond the door, an underwater silence. Nobody in the kiosk. Ahead of him a dank, green-shaded passageway between tanks. Water beaded glass. Puddles here and there, evidence of a slow leakage – no punters around tramping wet footwear.

He called Celia's name and fish looked out at him, as if they'd heard, from their twilit, olive green or tawny domains. Long translucent whiskers twitched under a rock on an otherwise featureless sandy beach. Two immense crabs, coarse-shelled and tasselled like handbags, paused in their conflict, claws raised. In an English country garden, underwater to its treetops, a fat fish looked up from the grass it was nibbling. In further tanks fish spied from caves and half-dissolved caramel castles. Things flitted, too quick to see, into follies and ice-cream temples. Smooth green muscular tubes switch-backed, and off to one side, behind several thickness of glass, someone stepped out of sight.

"Celia," he called out and ran gingerly on the treacherously wet floor. There was only one way forward. He turned a corner and glimpsed behind layers of glass and distorting volumes of discoloured water the faint gleam of waterproofed fabric. Another turn – and again the hunched figure – gliding, gone. The place was like a fairground hall of mirrors. He knew that hair, darker years ago, a flow and bounce to it like in the adverts, but even lately it had not been this lifeless drab seabed-brown. Her precipitous physical decline couldn't be all down to him.

A barnacled lobster claw waved him on like a fist. A fish with big pale eyes and a mouth too full of fangs to close, tempted him with a worm wriggling on the end of the dorsal spine sprouting from its brow.

Another corner and a sheen of green vanished around the next. Closer now, he felt trepidation. Hovering in formation, perch watched him. He was ready to flinch back around the next turn but there was no Celia to face.

No way forward past the tall tank ahead of him. It contained an upright sprig of supple, slender bodies. They stared, round expressionless eyes like buttons on heads smooth as skinned onions. Ribbon-like fins rippling down their flanks maintained their alert upright positions.

Suddenly, dropped jaws revealed hitherto invisible mouth lines. Hungry for him, all of them – savagely intent. He felt compelled to get out from under those gazes. He realised it was Celia he really feared meeting here, these fish just surrogates.

He returned to the entrance. If there had been a side exit through which she'd slipped, he'd missed it. What state of mind was she in? Until the situation was resolved he was determined that Elise should be as physically absent from his life as Celia was pretending to be.

Over Columbian coffee in the Cragg Sisters Tea Room he rang Elise, his bewilderment spilling out without preamble. "Twice now – the Barn, the aquarium. She's up to something. Wasting police time might be the least of it." He didn't want to name fears stirring like things on the glutinous seabed.

Elise tried to quell the flow with repetitions of his name. She suggested Dunwich again.

"No, not if she's keeping tabs on me. Bad enough that Trench is. I have to keep telling myself it's a good thing. I mean, she's not dead in a ditch."

When he got home Peter went up to Celia's study and switched on her computer. He opened earlier emails from Wishart. So much to-ing and fro-ing on the nature of an imaginary being. Wishart, just last month:

I can see the merits of your new take on Seagrim – physically elusive, a matter of monstrous hints. Not evil, just way beyond puny questions of morality. The girls/women pass into another state of being when he's got them – yes I can buy that. And considerate of Seagrim to represent and sum up their earthly essence and identify them to the bereaved by the layout of bleached bones. But for story purposes I think he needs to be identified as the enemy and you should resurrect your story idea of the hero who sets forth in the slender hope of rescuing his wife before she is irrevocably lost and returned to the beach as artfully arranged bones. See attached for witch who gives him lungs to breath water, the Nereids who try to seduce him. See also giant squid battle. Mr Jones and his chest of gems and precious metals – our hero's for the keeping (if he gives up and returns home). The net that drags him for miles in a slimy stew of shells, flapping gasping fish and sundry wriggling things. The underwater quakes and tsunami when Triton blows his horn. Collapsing cities. The stepped fissure in the sea floor down which our hero ventures to confront Seagrim in a final battle. His victory and the release of Seagrim's victims from their enslavement in fish bodies. Reconciliation with his wife in a deep sea cave, the air almost depleted . . .

Peter ignored the attachments and switched off. He thought, *I'd go to retrieve Elise, not the damp wretched shape in the aquarium.* Was a mere artistic disagreement an element in a personal crisis Celia had been undergoing, and which he'd been totally oblivious of?

*

The A12 to Woodbridge felt as inland as Birmingham. His office in-tray had fattened. There were emails and all of them could wait damn near indefinitely. Leaving, he was hooked in the corridor. He wished he had something clear-cut to confide. All bare forearms and tiepin, Mike was awkwardly sympathetic. He was on surer ground evincing impatience with the police. Whatever Peter felt in regard to Trench, it wasn't impatience. Something predatory in Trench's watchfulness, a confidence, as if he knew the whole matter would resolve to his satisfaction if not Peter's. Driving back, Peter blinked at swift oncoming headlights, like luminous globular eyes in the late afternoon murk. Magenta clouds stretched from the coast like fraying bread dough. He felt like that, attenuated, all thought, no substance.

At the gym in Aldeburgh the punch-bag nodded agreement. The plasticized leather was like Trench's coat, his tough grey skin. He hit it hard. On his back pressing weights a few minutes later he was a thoughtless machine – that was until someone passed behind scattering droplets that stung his eyes, blinding them to everything but colour. A shiny green. A waterproof. "Hey!" he shouted, dumping the dumbbells onto the blocks at each side.

He was up and running as the waterproof darkened in the entrance to the changing rooms.

The cubicle doors were all ajar and he'd have checked them all but for another glimpse of shimmering green, passing amoeba-like through the open door to the pool. He ran to catch up.

A droop of a man stopped mopping the pool's concrete margin. The place was otherwise deserted. Chlorine hit Peter's sinuses, prickled his eyes as he stared into the turquoise water.

"Not open till six," the cleaner said warningly, as if Peter looked set to plunge into the pool clad in his tracksuit.

"Where did she go? A woman came through just before me."

The man resumed mopping. The mop had a head of wet, bleached-brown and tangled rat-tails which audibly sucked and slavered over the concrete: Peter stopped looking at it. "Just now? Don't think so," the mopper said, unsettled, and with a glance about him he knew was unnecessary. There was no alternative way out or in. Peter walked the margin as much to give himself time to think. Water smacked its lips at the tiled wall. He paused, stopped thinking.

A darker shade in the thick lens of the water. His vision pierced down to a slow-swirl of green fabric. At its nucleus, a crouching on the pool's floor. As Peter watched, unbelieving, separate panels of green were floating apart like great plates of seaweed. His mind dived, he choked and stepped back. The mopper's mop stopped slapping as Peter staggered past.

Outside he gulped air. Not Celia, not anyone or anything but the strain he was under. On his way to his car he studied the flowing clouds rather than confront the memory tangled at his feet: flowing green material, faded rat-tails framing a face bitten to the bone.

There was no need for morbid imaginings. He'd find Celia, physically well – if not mentally.

He drove to Leiston fast. Dark clouds were shot through with lemony light; to the west they were bloodied sops. He ignored his ringing mobile phone; he wanted to get home and lock the doors. He reconsidered. It might be Elise, better still it might be Celia, even to harangue him. He'd relish her panto transformation into a bitter sea-witch. He slid the car into a lay-by and put the phone to his ear.

It was Trench. Rough sea and wind blew around his voice which sounded enclosed, like in a conch shell. "Come to the beach where we met the last time."

Peter did a three-point turn on the empty road and headed back to Aldeburgh. Some revelation was afoot: a lightness in him was indistinguishable from dread. He parked by the yacht club. To the south the Martello tower was a tall black cake. Protecting him from the sea, the high shingle bank was like an oatmeal stage curtain, ominously imbued with what was about to unfold. He climbed to the top.

Below the lowest great step of shingle, Trench looked barely in contact with the beach. He was a narrow oval, a fish seen end-on, motionless, waiting for a morsel to show itself. With white fingers, the surf clawed close to his feet. A diminution in the grey meagre light might obliterate him entirely.

Peter crunched down the shingle. Closer he saw innumerable pale shapes at Trench's feet in a circumscribed area of sand. He thought of the Seagrim tale. Trench was pondering too; no chin to cup, he spread tubular fingers and thumb beneath his wide mouth.

A great twisted funnel? A tornado? Small bones extended as long as a forearm from the narrow curled point, like a spit of tiny islands. Peter couldn't speak. *Animal bones. Let them be animal bones.* Trench directed Peter to stand alongside him and it became clear what the shape represented. It resembled the renowned Japanese woodblock print 'The Wave'. Clean white separated bones delineated its taper from wide base to curled-over point with its frayed line of spray. Now the separate collection of tiny bones at the base of the wave made sense. Man-shaped, they were perpetually on the point of being engulfed. The wave seemed a visual representation of a threat of implacable and inescapable revenge.

Had Trench read the emails, the entries in the notebook relating to Seagrim's dreadful memorials? Time to come clean if he hadn't – clean as these bones which weren't Celia's. Nobody had reduced her to this.

"There's a tale she was working on ... "

"I know it."

"So what's her game?"

Trench's unblinking eyes were as empty of human feeling as old pennies from an ancient sea chest. "Game? This is no game." The crack of his mouth might have suggested it was.

Did he know about Elise? Had Celia told Trench? Were they together against him? But what of the bones, hundreds of them. Not Celia's. Not human at all. Animal or fish bones, otherwise the beach would be humming with police, stooping, photographing, measuring, sampling. If Celia had placed them here – what next?

He quelled an urge to violently kick at the bones and destroy her work. She should forget him and Elise and channel her anger more productively.

He stepped back as a skein of water smoothed over the sand and ruckled around Trench's disgusting plimsolls. You could fit a fish sideways into that long crooked crack of a mouth. Peter didn't doubt

Trench knew everything, and murder didn't come into it, but the man was seeming a greater mystery than the bones.

"Tell her to get a life," Peter said, turning away and walking. Hard going, climbing the yielding shingle steps of the beach. His legs shook. The ease of the waves patiently plashing on the shoreline mocked his stumbling.

Move inland, that's what he'd do. Put the cottage up for sale – that would draw Celia out of the shadows. Probably wouldn't have to wait that long. He imagined her as some fanged sea snake in a crevasse, waiting for the right moment to spring out and strike.

Back in the cottage Peter went through every room until he was convinced he was alone then picked up the telephone. Elise didn't need to know about the bones. Too disturbing. The whole murky business must be reducing his stock in her eyes. A resentful, possibly mad wife in the shadows. The creeping policeman Trench. Shuddering at the thought of either of them making contact with Elise, he put the receiver back into its cradle. He went to bed and hoped he'd sleep.

The lone street lamp bobbed as if to lure him like the lighted organ on the filament poking out from the forehead of some grotesque deep-sea dweller. Rain streaking the window cast vertical shadows which twitched on the wall like tube worms. The bed drifted back and forth. He switched his bedside light on, nauseous. He drank water from the bathroom tap. The sea, two miles distant, murmured in age-old resentment and hunger. In bed again he sank into the sound, deeper and deeper. The blackness was total, as unbreathable as water. He woke, gasping for air, opened his eyes wide to drink in the bedside light. He got up. In the mirror his skin was fish-pale and putty soft. He looked drowned and revivified.

*

Midmorning the next day, as dark clouds lurked far out at sea, he jogged on the raised path around Aldeburgh marsh then headed for the gym. He was a physical being again, capable of action. An hour later he drank coffee and ate an energy bar from the vending machine. Outside, rain pebble-dashed him as he ran to his car on the promenade. Beyond dark-stained fishermen's huts, the surf rasped against the shingle like the coordinated sharpening of innumerable rusted knives.

Heading out of Aldeburgh along Leiston Road, he braked abruptly and edged to the kerb. He looked up at the cold strip-lighting in the police station windows and arrived at a decision. He'd admit his subterfuge; via Trench maybe it would serve as a prelude to a rapprochement with Celia. He'd be making amends–or at least appearing to.

The desk sergeant made notes and Peter strode out again ten minutes later light-headed, disembodied. The streets tipped like decks and he was more breathless than jogging and the gym had made him. Trench hadn't been present. The pink-cheeked young man had checked a screen, then murmured to an older colleague. He'd turned back to Peter, vindicated. Celia's disappearance hadn't been logged on Sunday night, and there was no officer called Trench in Aldeburgh, nor in the wider Suffolk Constabulary as far as they could tell. They would make further enquiries.

You won't find him on the staff establishment, Peter thought. He felt a grim relish. Trench was too plain odd to be employed in any capacity. Pure accident that his anxious initial call had wormed its way to Trench – and the man had taken sick advantage. The real police would be onto Trench soon, despite the fact that the teenage fellow at the desk had looked at Peter when he'd described the bones on the beach, the Seagrim tale, the wife stalking him, as if he were one of the lost souls who gravitated towards seaside resorts.

He drove back into town and on to the yacht club on Slaughden Road where he climbed the shingle bank and walked along it. No sign of last night's twisted rug of bones down below. The police should have taken them, the high tide shouldn't have, nor should Celia, and definitely not Trench – to whatever he called home. Peter pictured a hovel, damp, peeling, windowless.

A kite bobbed on a trampoline of air. A dog barked at the sea, knowing something its master didn't. Further along the shingle bank the rusted burger van looked abandoned there by an abnormally high tide. At the window his description made Trench seem a fabrication. The vendor surprised him. "Yeah, I've seen him. Few evenings ago. Joggers and dog walkers are usually heading back to civilisation at that time. But he was going down to the sea. Had a torch to light his way." He made a finger and thumb against his forehead. "Next thing it had gone out. Leastways I couldn't see them."

"Them?"

"Yeah, this woman with him. Frumpy. Green waterproof."

"Yes," Peter said, adding pointedly, "my wife." Not even a residual indignation on her behalf. The seller looked embarrassed, either at his unflattering thumbnail, or he was thinking he'd unwittingly uncovered an affair. Rain suddenly beat on the van's roof. Peter was drenched before he got to his car. He drove home and rang the police as soon as he got there, repeated what the burger seller had said he'd witnessed. He didn't need do anything else. The police would be onto Trench soon.

The dark carpet was like oily floodwater. Wavy horizontal white stripes on the bare stone walls could have been salt stains left by an outgoing tide. The silence was worse when the rain let up. Piano sounds would have mitigated it had he been able to un-stiffen his puffy white fingers. Wrong to think listening to others playing on CD would be easier. Vivaldi was dry, rational until slow pizzicato strings described hard claws tiptoeing across a striated sandy floor. Bach's contrapuntal lines entwined in his head like smooth tubular growths.

He rang Elise, not intending to tell her of his deductions, his victimisation. He had in mind an un-furtive, unapologetic meal out later. "Ring back when you're free," he told the answer-phone. Out, rehearsing for a concert or teaching; a free spirit, not an office hours drudge. He felt calmer, thought most problems in the world were solvable by staying indoors. By the time he'd dozed and soaked in the bath most of the afternoon had gone.

At six, ignoring the corpses of fish in the freezer, he stir-fried field produce and ate in front of the TV. He felt secure until ocean filled the screen. The aerial view prompted a swimming sensation in his head. If he hadn't already been sitting down he would have had to. The camera panned back and here was the pebbled beach and policemen looking overdressed on it. "... a bizarre find," the female voice-over said. "And nothing that could have been left by the outgoing tide – according to local fisherman Bert Spode. In other news ..."

He switched off. There was no other news and he could guess what the bizarre find had been.

His coat was cold and clammy from his earlier drenching. Outside the cottage he could smell the sea, fish and seaweed rot, salt; the centuries-long meal of the coast could have advanced two miles to the flint wall of the front garden. One day the house would be a dissolving folly in a vast wall-less fish tank.

Rain drummed the car roof, lashed the flint wall and feathered the lane as he sped onto it. He drove to Saxmunden, hammered on the door of Elise's flat until neighbours emerged to complain. No, they knew nothing about a concert or anything else she did. Peter drove to Aldeburgh, parked by the yacht club and noted the line of vehicles on the high bank – marked cars, a white windowless van.

He climbed to the top of the bank. Below, the surf glowed white at each fall onto the sand. A cluster of lights and activity, almost a merry-go-round of busy shapes, and not one of them would be Trench.

Peter ran down the shingle, dodged between bodies, was caught and strong-armed away as he was about to burst through the tape barrier. "I've got to see," he gasped. "Bones, aren't they? I've seen them like it before. Arranged into a representation of something."

"If there is you can read about it in the *Eastern Daily Press* tomorrow."

"You think?" he said, glaring. A woman officer drew him up the steep shelving of the beach until they were level with the police vehicles. She took his name and address; he insisted she did, then told her of missing Celia, Trench. "Your colleagues are already onto him."

The burger van was still present, but below the high bank on the track by the estuary. The man swam into view in the small lit side window. Peter asked for a burger. "Nearly out," the man said, handing one over. "Those coppers have been packing 'em away since three."

"Incredible isn't it," Peter said, eating fast. "Bones, they're saying. Bones laid out in a picture. You wouldn't credit it."

"You're telling me. I was ear-wigging one of the plods. Bones – all detached. Said they were set out like a clarinet or flute, rib bones like the keys over the holes. Weird. Human bones, one of them said. I'll tell you one thing – I won't be lingering after the police have gone."

Peter's legs felt full of cold air as he walked on to order his thoughts. Once he was past the police vehicles he climbed the bank again. Police activity resembled a subdued beach party. It shrank behind him as he approached the Martello tower. Black ocean overhead, the stars like luminous plankton on the point of vanishing. One had fallen to the beach. It bobbed, a white firefly. Peter climbed down the beach and was soon close to the water. The point of light brightened. Peter realised it was approaching. Trench's shape was apparent for only a moment before the light disappeared under the brim of his porkpie hat. "Hey! Over here!" Peter shouted hoarsely over his shoulder to the capsule of lit bodies he was wishing were closer.

In a medium that seemed other than air, Trench was movement only, not a running motion so much as a rapid quiver. Peter could summon no running motion himself; sand transmitted cold up through his legs. Turning, the beach turned with him so Trench was unavoidable in his relentless approach. His legs were a single muscular fin. His empty sleeves pulsed. The hairline crack of his mouth had became a gape filled with finger-length, inward pointing fangs. The hunger in the flat grey eyes was almost routine.

Sucked in air felt as thick as water in Peter's swelling lungs. He fell onto his back and the beach tipped up, leaned over him in a solid wave and buried him in blackness.

Instantly he was awake again, stretched out on his back. The stars had gone. He knew why: he wasn't on the beach. He was in his bath. A drab orange-green light stained the walls narrowly enclosing him. He must have dozed – not that there had been any risk of drowning. The water had drained away. The utter silence seemed an alien invasive medium. He needed music.

A minimal, almost non-existent effort and he was upright and stepping over the edge of the bath. The walls had the texture of rusted iron. No door, no end wall in which to contain one. Not his bathroom, he realised. Whose? He was bewildered but mutedly so: emerging outside he felt no physical symptoms of stress. Was he dreaming?

Ochre pitted pillars rose and merged into heights of powdery olive greenness. There were thick humps of upright, partially buried rubber tyres. A massive barnacled anchor. Chain links you could shoot a torpedo through. Thick yellowish stems rooted in the drab flooring he saw were long limb bones. He walked, weightless, his body without sensation, a vehicle doing his bidding for the moment.

At a low liquid laughter of released air bubbles, he swirled around.

An open-fronted stacking of oil drums, rust-bruised and veined with seaweed, made for a vaguely throne-like structure on which sat a massive shape of darkness. Peripheral rippling appendages kept the thing upright and stirred an encompassing cloud of sediment. His fear would have been great had he felt physically present.

Amidst rubbish at the foot of the oil drums, a pair of round grey eyes stared. He'd have called out 'Celia' but for their context in the head of a smooth scaled and serpentine green body. The face toppled sideways and out of sight, and he saw it had been a reflection in a tarnished and elaborately framed mirror, as from the stateroom of some long-sunken luxury liner. A tapering suppleness flickered away into the darkness.

Heartbeat and breaths were as good as undetectable, and gave the lie to what he was seeing. His body knew where it was, and was unafraid. He'd go back to what he knew. He'd lie down again, sleep again, wake again in the human place he knew.

The bath had become an open white tomb. On all sides smooth scaled bodies leaned into it. It was a feeding trough. A frenzy of tearing and flashing teeth such as to give the pulled and ravaged thing lying inside a semblance of life despite the contrary evidence of white bars of ribs, porcelain wrist bones.

41

One devouring head after another bobbed up. All looked at him like those fish in the dead-end tank in the aquarium. Nose-less, smooth scaled faces. Needle teeth trailed pieces of flesh. Again something tugged in the simple features of one, something in the shape of the mouth.

No glass barrier now, but their interest in him had been satisfied. One by one they resumed feeding.

He walked away, his feet making no clouds on the sandy floor. He wore no clothes, nor was he naked or in any state in between. He knew why. A membrane separated him from reality and physical sensations; he only needed to break through.

The deep bubbling laughter began, like a mockery of his dimly felt determination. He executed a drifting turn until the shape on the oil drums was before him. The great murk of its upper reaches was now dissipated somewhat by a small globe of intense light overhead. It shone from the end of a spine sprouting from the thing's forehead like a prow, and illuminated the angular line of the mouth, the cruel, round and staring eyes which were surely older than stones. Muffled pleading and begging filled Peter's head as he approached.

But then the light went out and he must have missed his way.

As the darkness thickened he wanted to be pursued. The floor sloped whichever direction he took. He'd have cherished the tickle of innumerable light bites, or even, if his body allowed him to feel them, the obliterating awakening power of massive jaws.

But he felt nothing, saw nothing and heard nothing. He believed he was walking and knew in the rumour of his heart he was entering the sea's deepest abyss.

MURDER IN THE RED BARN

I n 1827, the so-called 'Red Barn' at Polestead, Suffolk, became the scene of a very grisly murder, which, for various reasons, would go down as one of the first cause célèbres in British criminal history. It has all the features of a stage melodrama, and also possesses a strong supernatural element which, even today, defies full explanation.

William Corder was a farmer's son, who was said to be handsome and charming, but also a rogue. Despite his refined outward appearance, he had been involved in several felonious activities, primarily fraud and forgery; his childhood nickname had been 'Foxy' owing to his untrustworthy disposition. In 1827, Corder commenced a sexual relationship with a certain Maria Marten, a noted village beauty, though one who evidently distributed her favours widely as she already had children fathered by other local men. When she fell pregnant again, this time as the result of a dalliance with Corder, she decided to seek respectability and asked for his hand in marriage.

Corder was apparently happy to oblige, but then told Maria he'd learned that the local parish authorities were seeking to prosecute her for her wanton ways, and said that he couldn't possibly marry her here in Polestead as it would be no good for his reputation. In the presence of her mother-in-law, Ann Marten, Corder arranged to meet Maria later that week at the Red Barn – a dilapidated structure, so named because it had a roof of reddish clay tiles, located about a mile away from the village – from where they could elope to Ipswich.

Maria did as Corder asked – she packed her bags and went off to meet him, and subsequently was never seen again.

A short time later, Corder returned to the village alone, stating that his wife had gone on ahead of him and that she would come back and live with him when the controversy about their marriage had quieted down. However, exactly the opposite happened: local folk gossiped continually about the mysterious disappearance of Maria Marten, and at length, feeling threatened, Corder moved away.

Ann Marten was now very concerned for her daughter-in-law. She claimed to have had a series of bizarre dreams in which the blood-soaked spectre of Maria led her to the Red Barn and pointed dolefully down to a corner of its interior. Ann pestered her husband

43

so much that he finally went and dug there and, to his horror, uncovered a mutilated corpse buried in a sack.

What followed was, for the era, some rather smart detective work by the local constabulary. The body, though badly decayed, was identified as Maria Marten from a broken tooth, and the twofold cause of death was established as a gunshot to the abdomen and a dagger-thrust to the eye. A chief suspect – William Corder – was also quickly identified, as a green handkerchief found twisted around Maria's neck was recognised as belonging to him.

A man-hunt began, which eventually located Corder in London with his new wife, Mary Moore. When arrested and interrogated, he at first denied the crime, but the evidence was stacked against him. Not only had his handkerchief been found on the body, but it seemed that his reason for taking Maria out to the Red Barn in the first place had been bogus – no prosecution was pending against her for alleged immorality. It had been nothing more than a lure.

When returned to Suffolk for trial, Corder's explanation was that he and Maria had quarrelled in the barn, and that she had committed suicide because he'd said he was leaving her. In response, the prosecution insisted that Corder had never intended to marry her, that she possibly had some hold over him because of his criminal activities, and that he had sought to rid himself of her once and for all. There was also talk that Corder had murdered Maria's sole surviving child – because this youngster could no longer be traced – though no charges were brought in this case.

Despite the curious piece of evidence concerning Maria's ghost leading her parents to the grave-site, the jury chose to believe the prosecution. Corder was convicted and sentenced to be hanged and dissected.

Shortly before his execution at Bury St. Edmunds in 1828, Corder confessed his guilt. But his death was not easy. The drop from the gallows did not break his neck, and he was seen to be struggling and jerking at the end of the rope. The following day, his corpse was taken to Cambridge University, where various students and physicians witnessed the remarkable sight of his dead limbs twitching and dancing to electric currents. He was then subjected to a public post-mortem, and his skeleton removed to the West Suffolk Hospital as a teaching aid, before eventual cremation in 2004. One final ghoulish outcome was the removal and tanning of Corder's skin by the surgeon George Creed, who then used it to bind the case-notes.

Later sequels to the story concern belated suspicions about the mother-in-law, Ann Marten's role in the affair, and rumours that she may have been involved with Corder herself, having *participated in the murder of her daughter-in-law, and then turned on him when he married Mary Moore, inventing the story about the ghost in the barn. Another tale connected the murderer with a famous actress of the era, Caroline Palmer, who later appeared in a play based on the case, while yet another implicated London's infamous serial poisoner, Thomas Wainwright. Such sensationalist possibilities – though apparently unfounded – maintained the public's interest in the case, and it became a popular subject in penny-dreadfuls all through the 19th century.*

THE WATCHMAN
Roger Johnson

S imon Wesley stubbed out his cigarette and asked, "Are you familiar with Woolton Minster?"

"Woolton in Suffolk?" I shook my head. "I know of it, of course, but ..."

We turned to George Cobbett, who was scraping the bowl of his pipe. He looked up.

"Woolton? Yes, I've been there. A handsome church, mainly Norman. There's a very fine west window, and some remarkably grotesque gargoyles. One of 'em, right at the top of the west front ..."

"That's the place," said Simon, "though you must have visited it before the war." (George nodded.) "In 1944, a German bomber on its way to Norwich got into difficulties and had to jettison its bomb. The thing landed right in the Close. Remarkably, no lives were lost, but the west front of the Minster was destroyed. The window – yes, it was a fine one – was shattered, and the gargoyles were pulverised. It was a sad business, but it brought me into the story."

*

You see (he continued), I was assistant to Sir Martin Runciman, who supervised the restoration work when it finally started. The building had been patched up, of course, but it wasn't until 1951 that they could afford to do the job properly. Money was short, and funds came in slowly, but at last we were able to begin.

Fortunately, there were plans and photographs to work from, and we aimed to make that west front look just as it did before – or very nearly. We used the same Barnack stone, and the window was fashioned as near as could be to the original, though somehow the glaziers didn't quite manage to reproduce the colours. I don't know: there's something about mediæval glass ... It was a miracle really that the window had survived the Reformation, but Adolf managed to achieve what William Dowsing and his chums had failed to do.

Anyway, we did good work. You must go and have a look at the church, Roger. It really is very handsome.

The only real difficulty was over the gargoyles. You'll remember, George: there were three of them at the west. Oh, dear. I'll have to describe the place. That west front comes to a peak, about eighty feet high. The porch doesn't project, and there are no towers there; the building is roughly cruciform, and has a sturdy, fairly low central tower. The church is almost entirely Norman, with an apsidal east end, but the west window is – or was – a very nice example of a fourteenth century Tree of Jesse.

At each corner of the gable was a gargoyle – grotesque enough, to be sure, but not uncommonly so. You can see similar figures on many churches: rainwater pipes carved into demonic shapes, with the water coming out of their mouths. But the thing in the middle, right at the peak of the gable, was something else.

Strictly speaking, it wasn't a gargoyle at all, but a statue. It was extraordinary. The only thing I've ever seen like it – and remember: I only saw it in photographs – was the so-called Baphomet of St Bris-le-Vineux in Brittany. It had bulging eyes under thick brows, a heavy moustache, and huge hands that gripped the edge of the roof. And it had female breasts. A very strange and sinister creature indeed. It was crouched, as if ready to launch itself into flight. Yes, there were wings too, folded behind, so that you couldn't see them properly from the ground. There were the traditional goat's legs, and small horns, and the teeth were bared in a rather disconcertingly confident grin.

Well, there was much discussion among the Church Council, and with the Bishop's agreement it was decided to replace this particular demon with a statue of St Michael. That would be more fitting, they said, especially as the Minster is dedicated to St Michael and All Angels. They got John Elen in for this; it was his first major public commission, and he did a fine job. The saint, in armour, is standing, legs astride, looking up, and holding his sword hilt-upwards in front of him. It's hardly what you'd call *avant-garde*, but that's not what was required. It's a very impressive conventional – no: traditional – work of art, and somehow it gives quite a different aspect to the building.

Our work was finished towards the beginning of 1953. A new history of the Minster was published, written by the Vicar – a decent fellow, who was something of an antiquarian – and commemorative copies were presented to Runciman and me.

I've got my copy here: *The Collegiate Church of St Michael and All Angels at Woolton*, by the Revd Edmund Wheatley, M.A. There are photographs of the west end before and after the war, so you can get some idea of what sort of a job we did.

Wheatley and I got on very well together, and before the end of the restoration work, when Runciman had gone off to supervise another project in Shropshire, he suggested that rather than stay on at my hotel in the town I should move into the Vicarage, which

47

stands on the site of the old Deanery, just south of College Gate. This was very agreeable to me, as you can imagine, and we'd often sit up of an evening, chatting about antiques, or music, or ghosts – or just reading.

Now, while the work was going on there was a watchman stationed in the Close – to protect my men's implements, mainly – and after Evensong Wheatley always used to come with me to his cubby-hole and have a few words with him. This was sheer good nature on his part, you know, because the church plate – some of it pre-Reformation – was kept pretty safe under lock and key in the vestry.

Bob Chater, the watchman, was a big man: an ex-Bombardier, sociable and cheerful. I wondered occasionally how such a person could cope with the solitude of the job, and was rather taken aback when I discovered that he spent the quiet hours in teaching himself classical Greek. That's by the way, though. Bob would take three or four turns around the Close – at no set time: we agreed that was best – but mostly he'd sit in the little room built into College Gate, with a lantern and his books and a flask of coffee.

I might add that the room had been the janitor's lodgings in the middle ages, and Wheatley told us that it had been used again early in the nineteenth century, when the resurrection men were at work. Still, Bob wasn't likely to meet anything quite that gruesome, we thought, and it became something of a standing joke when we said good-night for the Vicar to add, "Keep an eye open for the body-snatchers, Bob."

Body-snatchers, eh? ... Yes, well –

It was early one March morning, a Tuesday, when I was woken by a hammering at the Vicarage door. I thought perhaps it was an urgent call on behalf of a sick parishioner, so I was surprised when Wheatley came into my room and said, "There's been an attempted burglary at the Minster. No, it's all right – nothing's been taken. But Bob Chater's here with a rather curious story, and I'd like you to hear it."

He waited while I got into my dressing-gown and slippers, and we went downstairs to his study, where he already had coffee brewing on the gas-ring. Bob declined a cup, but accepted a shot of whisky. Then he gave his report.

"It's a dark night, sir, as you can see – dry, but very cloudy – and about ten past three I decided to take a walk around the Minster, my third tonight. I started at the west end, opposite my sentry-box, and went round the south side, and everything was fine. Then the east end – nothing. And then I started along the north wall, and as I

48

cleared the chapter house I saw a light in the vestry, as it might be an electric torch, where there oughtn't to be a light at all.

"I don't know, sir, but somehow I never really expected burglars here, since everyone in the town knows that I'm on duty in the Close of nights. Still, I knew it couldn't be anyone who'd a right to be there. Any of the clerical gentlemen, or you, Mr Wesley, would have come and had a word with me first. Now, I don't usually carry a stick, as you know, so I had to be very cautious. I put my ear to the vestry door, not knowing what I might hear. I certainly didn't expect to hear what I did: it was a man's voice, sobbing! With fear, too, I'd stake my oath.

"A rum do, I thought, and ever so gently I tried the door-handle. The door was unlocked. I screwed up my nerves, and suddenly flung back the door and stood in the doorway, with my fists clenched, looking as menacing as I could – not knowing what I was up against, you see.

"Well, there was a man there, all right; just one, crouched over by the other door, the one that leads into the choir. As soon as he heard me, he looked up, and his face was grey. There was fear in his eyes, sir – real fear. And now there was another shock. He said, 'Thank God!' – just like that. 'Thank God! A human face!'

"Things were going too fast for me. I said, 'Of course I'm human, my lad – and just in time, by the look of things.' (For I could see that he'd already started to break open that big safe of yours, Padre.) 'What did you expect?' I said, '– a ghost?'

"And at that his eyes opened wide, and his jaw dropped as if he was going to scream. I walked over to him, and I saw that he was hanging on with both hands to that iron ring that's the handle on the choir door – hanging on as if for fear of his life – and he seemed to be twisting it in his hands, trying to open it.

" 'You stop that!' I said. 'Your night's work's done, my lad!'

"Then the movement stopped, and for a moment I thought he was kicking his heels against the floor, because I could hear that hollow sound – you know? But it was a harder, sharper sound than he could have made, because he was wearing rubber-soled boots; and anyway I could see now that his feet weren't moving. Yet I could still hear the noise for a moment. Then it faded away.

"Well, I was curious, sir, as you can imagine, so I collared this fellow. He was quite small and lithe, like you'd picture a cat-burglar to be, but he was so broken up that I could see he was no match for me.

" 'Now,' I said, 'you're coming along to the Police Station. Robbing a church is a very serious offence.'

"I'll swear, sir, that he was actually relieved. 'God, yes!' he said. 'I'll be safe there. Just take me away – I couldn't face *that* again!'

" 'Face what?' I said, and on the way over to the Police Station he told me. Very strange! I left him with the law (and they'd like you to go over, Padre, as soon as convenient, to see about preferring charges), and then I came back here straightaway.

"What he told me was this:

"He was from out of town, and he'd heard about the church plate. Well, it's no secret, is it? He'd found out where it was kept, and all on his own he planned to steal it. He knew that I was there – and that's no secret, either – so he hadn't tried to come in by College Gate or Dean's Gate, but had climbed over the high wall to the north-east, the one that gives on to the gardens in Wells Street. I said I thought he looked like a cat-burglar, didn't I?

"He seems to have had no trouble getting into the Close and across to the Minster – he knew just where the vestry was – or in picking the lock on the door. He found the safe all right, and noticed that the door into the choir was closed but not locked. That didn't bother him; not until he'd actually started to break open the safe.

"Then he heard the footsteps.

"Quiet at first, they were, but clear – ghostly, you might say – and they were coming towards him from the other side of the choir door. They grew harder, and stronger, and heavier: more – more *real*.

"Now, I should judge him to be quite a brave man, and perhaps violent too on occasion; but he wanted to know what the opposition was like. The footsteps still sounded some little distance away, so he switched off his torch and stuck it in his pocket, and then he opened the door a crack and looked through, into the church.

"What he saw made him slam the door shut and hang on to the handle for dear life, wishing that he could lock it. He was too frightened to call for help, and I really don't know whether it was in order to attract attention or simply from fear of the dark that he switched on his torch again. That, of course, was the light I saw, and when I burst into that room, he says, he was never so glad in his life to see another human face!"

I couldn't stand this. Bob Chater certainly knew how to build up suspense.

"What the devil *did* he see?" I said – shouted, almost.

But Bob's face was very serious.

"You must remember," he said, "that he only saw it for a moment, and in poor light, but he says he never wants to see anything like it again. As to describing it, he was – what's the word I want? – he was incoherent. It looked like a man, he says, but it

50

was big, really big. Ten feet tall or more, he reckons. And it was grey; and, as I say, it looked like a man, but it didn't *move* like a man, not quite. And it was coming towards him, as if it knew just where he was, and what he was.

"So he clung to that door-handle, and he could hear the man – or whatever it was – coming closer, right up to the door. Then he could feel the handle moving in his hands, against all the strength he could put to it; and he was sobbing with fear ... And then – well, then I came in."

My mind was full of questions, all unasked. I turned to Edmund Wheatley, trying to frame some words; but they didn't come, and they didn't need to, because I could see excitement and something like understanding in the priest's face. Without a word, he stood up and went over to one of his book-cases, at which he peered, shelf by shelf, until he had found what he wanted. It was a smallish red-bound volume, which I guessed to be about a hundred years old.

"This," he said, and his voice was very restrained, "is a curious little book which I bought some while ago at an auction. It's the work of Dr Davey, one of my predecessors, and was privately printed in 1847."

As he opened it, I could see that the title page read: *Quaint Historical Anecdotes and Legends of Suffolk, compiled and re-told by the Rev. John Davey, D.D.*

Wheatley and I kept in touch, you know, even after he retired from Woolton; and a few months before he died – that would be in '76 – he gave me that same copy of the book. Here it is, and this is the chapter that he read to us that morning. It's quite short, and if I may I'll read it to you now.

The Guardian of Woolton Minster

> Woolton is a small and rather decayed town which stands a few miles from the coast to the north of Leiston. The chief glory of the place is the Minster Church of St Michael and All Angels, which will be well known to the antiquary and the ecclesiologist. For details of this fine building, however, the reader must consult a guide book. We mention it here because to it attaches a curious legend, which we have collated from several sources. The reader will appreciate that we have used our imagination somewhat in the telling of this tale, but be assured that the essentials have been followed faithfully.

In the days of the fourth King Edward, there dwelt in the town a merchant, one Thomas Drinkall, or Drinkale, who was neither pious nor amiable. He respected neither God nor man, for his creed was that Wealth is Power, and being both wealthy and powerful he believed it wholeheartedly.

This Thomas led for many years a life without crime but without charity, until on a day he found himself bereft of his wealth and consequently of his power, for his two ships, bearing between them the greater part of his fortune, were lost at sea in a storm of præternatural fury. He was forced, in order to meet his debts, to sell much of the property remaining to him in the town, and was thus reduced to a state that to him at least represented poverty. As the reader may surmise, however, Thomas Drinkall was not the man to accept such a fate. He foresaw months, perhaps years, of hard toil before his trade could again flourish; and truth to tell he was no lover of hard toil. He quickly resolved, therefore, to steal what he would not gain by honest labour, and to set himself up in some place far away: Norwich, perhaps, or better, the thronged streets of London.

Now, the house of Sir Giles Flambard, whom he did not love, was nigh impregnable, and only one other house in Woolton held so much treasure for the taking: the House of God, to wit: the Minster Church of St Michael. For the moment fate seemed to conspire with the evil man, for he recalled that his father had been Sacristan at the Minster, having charge of a key to the church. At the old man's death, Thomas had through mere indolence retained this key rather than return it to the Dean and Chapter. Now he thought that perhaps his indolence was vindicated. He determined to "strike while the iron was hot", and to rob the church the very next night.

Meanwhile, he prepared himself by procuring a farm-waggon and a light load of hay, for he intended to leave Woolton as soon as might be in the character of a lowly freeman, which guise should, he thought, protect him from footpads upon the way. He muffled the wooden wheels of the cart and the hooves of his solitary nag, and provided himself with a number of large sacks to contain his spoils. Night fell, and the

52

Angelus sounded, as if urging him to his task. The merchant waited for as long as he could restrain his impatience, until he was sure that the townsfolk were abed, and then he took his horse's reins and set off towards the Minster.

Fortune remained with him, for the night was neither too dark nor too light. Steadily, but without haste, he led the horse along Market Street, past Fish Street and Rosemary Lane, and at *The Golden Cross* turned right into Gracechurch Street towards the Minster Close. He did not directly approach the great gate, but as a precaution led the horse and waggon into Crown Alley, where they would not be seen by the Watch. Then, be it never so gently, he forced the lock of the wicket-gate and entered the close.

In those days there was an old man, a pensioner of the College, who kept watch in the Close by night, which is to say that he sat in a little room by the great gate and drank small ale. Thomas Drinkall went quietly to the door of this room and rapped gently upon the wooden boards until the old man peered out. Then, swiftly and silently, Thomas struck at the wizened neck, rendering the watchman unconscious, and caring nothing whether or no he had snuffed out the frail glimmer of life. He bundled the body back inside the room and softly closed the door upon it; then he turned to face the mighty west front of the Minster.

High above, at each corner, the gargoyles' faces stared in silent reproach, jutting as the old watchman's face had jutted upon its long skinny neck. Thomas looked up, at the vast window, and over that at the largest dæmon of all: the great grinning figure whose bulging eyes seemed to regard him with scorn and whose huge hands gripped the ridge of the building that it had guarded for more than three centuries. The merchant averted his gaze from this stone watchman and ran silently to the dark safety of the west door.

His father's key fitted snugly into the lock, and turned, ponderously, but with little effort, until the bolt sprang from its socket. Gently he drew out the key and replaced it in his belt, and then grasped the huge iron ring that served for a door-handle. Again a slow, heavy turn, a slight creak, and the latch was free. As quickly as he dared, he pushed at the door, and shortly there was a space wide enough to step through.

The merchant gathered up his sacks and slipped inside the porch, pushing the great door to behind him. It was quite dark, but he had no difficulty in finding and opening the smaller door into the nave; here there was light enough, for the moon was now clear of the clouds and shone through the arched windows of the south wall, while far ahead the candles burned upon the parish altar of All Saints. As his eyes became accustomed to the eerie half-light, Thomas could distinguish the great golden crucifix and the golden candlesticks grouped upon either side of it. Now, he felt, he was committed to his sacrilege, and soon he stood before the altar, stuffing the cross into a sack and putting candlesticks in after it. The sweat fell from his face with mere exertion, for the weight of these holy treasures was considerable. He must not, he thought, be over-greedy, else he would be unable to carry his booty away! With this cheerful reflection he passed beneath the pulpitum towards the Chantry Chapel of the Flambards.

Here he was faced with riches unsuspected, and his evil heart rejoiced. Eagerly he filled a second sack, and began to stuff treasures into a third, bending or breaking those that were too large. At length he opened a fourth sack, delighting in the merry clatter of gold against gold, and it was at this moment that another sound came to his ears: footsteps, hard and heavy, stalking inexorably along the nave from west to east.

His first thought was that the old janitor had recovered and had perhaps alerted the Watch. That would indeed be a blow! He quickly determined, however, that the steps were those of but one man, treading firmly and surely. One man might be dealt with, he thought; for had not he, Thomas Drinkall, trailed a pike in the wars? Swiftly he took the great cross from the altar and secreted himself by the arched entrance to the chapel, thinking to have the advantage of surprise.

Nearer and yet nearer came the stranger, seeming to know exactly where to look. The footsteps echoed solidly and deafeningly among the great pillars, accompanied by a slight creaking that suggested a man in armour. Yet, strangely, there was nothing metallic about the footsteps. Thomas thought that his brain would give way before the hard, reverberating sound. He lifted the cross as he heard the steps approach the chapel, with no diminution in their speed or their volume. Truly, the newcomer seemed to lack all caution. The merchant's arms were tiring quickly, for the big crucifix was very heavy, and the sweat streamed from his brow. He set his teeth, and as Nemesis stalked commandingly into the chapel he shut his eyes and swung the cross down with all his considerable strength.

The cross struck a hard surface and merely glanced off, throwing the merchant off balance. With remarkable agility, he jumped to his feet again and prepared to deal another blow.

He never did, for he saw now what manner of being it was that towered over him. He let the cross fall from his hand, and, overcome by the dæmonic horror of the thing, he slumped to the cold, hard floor. Then the other bent down over him and began to do certain things.

————

The next morning the Sacristan was appalled to find the old watchman lying dead in his little room, with the mark of a blow upon his neck. Hastily he summoned the Dean, who with some half-dozen of the Chapter followed the trembling Sacristan to the great west door of the Minster. It was unlocked. They stepped into the church and were at once confronted with the desecration of the parish altar, for the candles were snuffed and the precious ornaments missing. Now the Sacristan seemed to take leave of his senses: he let forth a cry of anguish and ran straightway to the high altar in the choir, sobbing with relief when he found it untouched. More sedately, the Dean and his fellows went to the Chapel of St Botolph, off the north aisle, but it too was undefiled. Then they crossed the nave towards the Flambard Chapel. At this time was distinctly heard a metallic *clank* from the west end of the church, as if some heavy iron object had been dropped by the great door, but so intent upon its purpose was the little band that no one stopped to wonder what it might be. At the entrance to the chapel they paused momentarily and then boldly entered.

Not for a little while did they remark the sacks upon the floor or the golden and bejewelled ornaments that lay scattered about, for something else demanded all their attention. The man who lay dead in a pool of his own blood might have been friend or foe, neighbour or stranger, for he was quite unrecognisable. The eyes had been torn from his head and the heart from his breast. There was another wound also, of which it were better not to speak.

As the priests and the Sacristan, shaken and wondering, passed out through the great west door, they saw the thing that had been dropped to the ground. On the lowest step, covered with gouts of drying blood, lay a mighty key. Warily they looked up, to see the grey stone figure of the guardian dæmon leering down at them. The grinning jaws of the statue and the huge hands that gripped the edge of the roof were dark with blood.

*

"There's another paragraph or so," said Simon, as he closed the book and set it down in front of him: "just a few lines in which old Davey draws a moral. Very sound, no doubt."

He accepted a cigarette from me and drew on it gratefully. "Well," he said, "you've heard my story. Have you any comments?"

George pulled at his grey moustache, pondering. Then, after a pause, he said, "You told us, I think, that the gargoyle – the statue – was completely destroyed by the bomb?"

Simon nodded, soberly. "That's quite true."

"You also said that there had been no loss of life."

"That was the official report."

"Ah. The report would refer, of course, only to human life. Normal human life."

As I was considering this, a thought occurred to me, and I said, "How strange – how very strange – that it should happen there, of all places!"

George looked up, quizzically, and Simon raised an eyebrow.

"Don't you remember the dedication of the church?" I said. "St Michael and All Angels! Ironic, don't you think?"

I heard a suppressed chuckle from George, and then: "I never get your limits, Johnson. There are unexplored possibilities about you."

I frowned at him, and said, "Don't quote Sherlock Holmes at me, George. What do you mean?"

The old man's face and voice were serious as he answered: "There are Angels of Darkness, you know, as well as Angels of Light."

THE WOMAN IN BROWN

Raynham Hall near Fakenham, in Norfolk, is the ancestral home of the Marquesses of Townshend. Today, it is still in the ownership of the Townshend family, but it is also the haunt of a particularly ghoulish spectre widely believed to be the lost soul of a former resident, Dorothy Walpole, who was wife to the Second Marquess and who died in 1726 from smallpox.

The ghost, which has been reported on many occasions, is said to take the form of a woman in a brown dress. On some occasions she is vaporous, but at other times so solid that she might initially be confused with a real-life person. The most disturbing aspect of this phantom figure is usually only noted if the witness meets her at close-quarter – for her skin is like parchment and her eye-sockets are empty.

Several witnesses have been persons of illustrious name and reputation. For example, when George IV was Prince Regent, he slept in the State Bedroom at Raynham Hall, only to be woken by the ghastly figure standing alongside him. He was quoted afterwards: "I will not pass another hour in this accursed house; for I have seen what I hope to God I may never see again." The author Frederick Marryat, a former naval officer and close friend of Charles Dickens, was surprised on the main landing of the house by a spectral form in brown, which he said leered at him in nightmarish fashion, frightening him so much that he actually fired a shot. He insists that he struck the figure but that the bullet passed clean through; a search of the landing the following day revealed it embedded in a nearby door.

And yet, disquieting though these incidents are, there is no reason known to history why the ghost of Dorothy Walpole should be so maleficent.

There are various competing versions of the events that led to her death. One holds that her husband was unkind to her, having discovered that she had engaged in a pre-marital affair with a roguish nobleman. Another insists that her husband was much older than she was, and that she simply did not love him. A third claims that she was never happy because she felt that her in-laws were withholding money to which she and her children were entitled. But none of these explanations seem massively tragic when compared with the devastating events that have led other ghosts to wander the halls and manors of old England.

A slightly more eerie possibility – as suggested in William Dutt's 'Highways And Byways of East Anglia' (published in 1901) – is that the Brown Lady of Raynham Hall is not the restless spirit of a deceased person, but the manifestation of something that has never lived on the Earth, and that it was active when Dorothy Walpole herself resided at Raynham, having accompanied her when she first moved from her own family seat at Houghton. In this respect, the fearsome apparition could be regarded as a kind of family banshee, though only in one instance has the Brown Lady apparently presaged a death in the house: that of John Townshend, the Fourth Marquess, in 1863.

As a footnote to this tale, the Brown Lady of Raynham Hall has the distinction of being one of the most convincingly photographed ghosts in the paranormal pantheon. In September 1936, photographer Indra Shira was documenting the interior of the house and taking measurements on the oak staircase, when he spotted a glowing form descending towards him. On his shouted instruction, Shira's assistant – who later claimed to have seen nothing – activated the camera, and the result was an astonishing and now very famous photograph which first appeared in 'Country Life' the following Christmas. It appears to show an elegant but semi-translucent woman in period dress standing near the foot of the staircase. The image has been the subject of intense analysis over many decades, but most experts are still of the opinion that it is genuine.

SHUCK
Simon Bestwick

Maggie dipped her brush in the water jar, hovered it over her palette and looked past her easel to the sunset bleeding red across the wide flat Suffolk landscape.

Brushes, paints, an unbroken view from her little stone cottage's garden. Now she only needed ability. *Any fool can paint in oils*, Martin said once; *watercolours take a* real *artist*. Martin with Carol, his pregnant new bride. *Bastard*. Her hand tightened on the brush. *Calm*. She breathed out, looked up at the October sunset.

"I'm happy now. Free." *Remember your mantra*. "Om me padme hum …"

Something caught her eye – a flicker of black to her right, where the jagged hedgerows crossed the green fields. She looked; nothing. A crow, a bin liner caught in the hedge. Nothing important. She looked back at her easel, then her palette.

Start with green. She dipped the brush in the powdered paint, began painting the fields. But the sun was sinking; the light would soon be gone, and there was no guarantee tomorrow's sunset would equal today's.

They'd forecast rain tonight. She hesitated, then touched in the skyline and cleaned the brush. Blood-red first, for the sunset's heart; orange to surround that, then lilac, purple, lemon-yellow, mingled with clouds tinged gold and umber. She despaired of capturing it accurately, but still, she tried.

A second black flicker to her right. Her eyes went to where the ground dipped slightly to a ditch. No, nothing. A crow, a binbag, imagination.

Black. A little black paint, a smaller brush and she could add a gallows to break the skyline; it'd look good against the red sun, especially with a body hanging. A couple of crows, too, maybe; one circling above, the other pecking at the corpse.

Goddess, that was *morbid*. Back to the sunset. The light was almost gone.

Black flickered again at her sight's edge; too close, too big to be her imagination, or a crow. She spun and saw a black-clad man running at her, a knife in his hand.

Madman, addict, rapist. They existed even here. Maggie ran – get in the cottage, lock the door, call the police – but his hand

60

caught her curly black hair and pulled. Pain and white, flaring light. He put the knife to her neck.

They stood, still, scared breath whimpering in her throat.

"Are you alone?" he said. She opened her mouth; he jerked her hair again. She cried out; tears started from her eyes. "Don't lie. I don't want to, but I'll kill you if I must."

If I must. Clear-voiced, well-spoken. Educated. But he still had a knife to her throat. "Yes," she said, "I'm on my own. Please don't ..."

"Shut up. Get inside."

"Alright. Alright. Just don't ..."

"Move." For a second, she thought she heard fear in his voice, but that couldn't be right. It was her, should be afraid.

*

Inside, he shoved her away and pointed to a chair. "Sit. Don't move."

"Alright. Alright." She hated herself; the quavering voice, the inability to think of anything other than doing as he said in the hope he'd leave her alive.

"Try anything and I'll kill you."

"Alright."

He slammed the door. The key was in the lock; he turned it, then shot the bolts at the top and bottom across. "Stay," he said again. "Are you on your own?"

"Yes?"

"No husband?"

"I'm divorced."

He smiled. "I can tell. You look the type."

Maggie bridled. "What's that supposed to mean?"

"Careful." He raised the knife, pointed it at her face.

"I'm sorry." Hating the words and herself as she said them.

"Good. Meaning bitter. It really does show."

"I'm fine," she said, but knew the words were coming out through her teeth. "I'm over it."

"Of course you are," he said mockingly. "Nobody else? Friends? Relatives? Boyfriends? Girlfriends?"

"No."

"Any animals? Cats? Dogs?"

"No. Nothing."

He pointed the knife at her. "Stay." He was very pale, and the knife seemed to shake a little, too. Wouldn't stop him stabbing her, of course; might even make it more likely.

61

"What are you looking at?"

"Nothing." She looked down. Heart thumping. Remember your mantra. Calm. Calm. She whispered it to herself: "Om me padme hum, om me padme hum …"

"What was that?"

"Nothing."

He looked at her for a long moment, then turned away. "Shut up, then."

She fell silent, kept looking down. A few seconds passed before she nerved herself to peep back up.

He was looking round, taking stock. It was a good sturdy little place, her cottage; whitewashed on the outside, a good couple of hundred years old and still standing strong. Downstairs there was only two rooms: the big living room they were in now, and the small tidy kitchen off to the side. Upstairs, a good-sized main bedroom, two small bedrooms and a tiny bathroom. They might have been a mile away now for all the chance she had of getting to them. Not that there'd be much point. It wasn't as if there was a shotgun up there.

"Is there a phone?"

"Yes." She nodded at the corner.

"Mobile?"

"Yes."

"Where?"

"My bag. There." She pointed to where it lay on the floor.

"Good." She saw him better now; he wore jeans, trainers, a fleece – good quality, expensive, brand names – and had a small leather bag at his side. "Pick it up and throw it to me." He pointed the knife. "At my feet. Nothing clever."

She did as he said. He picked up the phone, pocketed it, then went to the landline and sliced through the cable. Then he went back to the front door and crouched there. He dug a fistful of herbs out of the bag and ran to the big living-room window, rubbed them all around the frame, hard, till they shredded and fell to the carpet. A strange, astringent reek filled the room. He bolted to the second, smaller one in the front room and did the same. Halfway through he flung the herbs aside and dug out another fistful.

He finished the job there, then ran back to the door. For a second, he stopped to stare out through the front room window, where the last red light gleamed in the distance, the sky outside deep blue, almost black. "Oh Christ," he said. "Oh *Christ*." There was naked panic in his voice, and a kind of spoilt rage; a child who'd never realised before how wrong his games could really go.

And he was a child, really. Couldn't be more than nineteen; twenty at the most. If Alex had lived, this could have been him. His face was pale, smooth, porcelain, with light blue eyes, wavy fair hair. He was beautiful, she had to admit it, despite the danger.

He scrambled to the door, rubbed the herbs along each side of the frame, then along the bottom. Fast. Panicky. His hands were shaking. No, she hadn't been wrong before. He was scared. Lost. A little lost boy, far from home and alone in the dark. Lost, but violent with it. He glared at the door as he worked, bit his lip; tried to rub the herbs along the top of the frame but couldn't reach. He whirled towards her.

"Stool," he snapped. "A stool or a kitchen chair. Now!" He jabbed the knife in her direction. It shook.

He even sounded like a child. Didn't make him any less dangerous, of course. Despite it all, she felt sorry for him.

"Where?" he shouted. Spit flew from his mouth; she felt it hit her cheek.

"The kitchen," Maggie said, pointing. "In the kitchen."

"Stay where you are," he said, and ran through. A clatter and crash.

Now, she realised. This was her only chance. *Get out now.*

She jumped out of the chair and ran for the door, grabbed the handle. It wouldn't open. *No. No no no no no no no.* The key. The key. He'd locked it. She turned it, pulled again.

It still didn't shift. *No no no no no.*

He bolted it, you stupid bitch, said Martin, clear as if he'd been there. *Can't you get anything right?*

She reached for the bolt, and suddenly the room went still.

She knew. Knew without turning to look, but she did anyway. The boy stood in the kitchen door. A wooden kitchen chair hung from one hand; in the other was the knife. It suddenly looked very big and very long. Not that it needed to be; she'd read somewhere, some paperback thriller, that there wasn't a single vital spot on the human body more than five inches below the skin. Or was it four? She didn't know. It might not even be true. Didn't matter now. All that mattered was the knife, the boy's utter stillness, his eyes' cold, utter emptiness.

He let go of the chair; it clattered on the floor. He didn't let go of the knife, though; he gripped it tighter and raised it, stepped towards her.

"Please," she heard herself say, stepping clear of the door. "Please. Please."

Stupid bitch, said Martin. *Stupid, weak bitch.*

He advanced on her. Didn't speak. Just watched her with those empty eyes, mouth pressed to a tight white line. This poor lost boy. This poor lost boy who was going to kill her.

"Please ..." she said.

Outside, a flicker of black – she looked out through the window but saw only the dying glimmer of her last sunset.

The boy closed on her –

"Please – "

And something smashed against the front door, so hard it almost tore off its hinges.

Maggie screamed, couldn't stop herself. The boy turned and stared at the door. A high-pitched, screeching howl sounded outside, and whatever was outside smashed against the door again.

"Christ!" The boy ran back towards the kitchen, grabbed the chair and yanked it to the door as the howl sounded again. He snatched the herbs up from the floor, leapt up on the chair and raked them back and forth along the top of the doorframe. The howl rang out once more, and the door jerked and rattled again, but not as hard this time.

The boy scrabbled around inside the bag. "You!" he napped at Maggie. "Get upstairs." He threw about half a dozen little bunches of herbs in her direction. "Rub these around the window frames. Is there a fireplace up there?"

"No. Yes. Yes. There is one, in the spare room ..."

"Rub them around that as well. Then it can't get in."

"It?"

Outside there was a howl, and movement – heading round the side, towards the kitchen.

"*That*, you stupid cow." When she didn't move right away he shouted: "Do it fucking now if you want to live," grabbed the bag and sprinted for the kitchen.

For an instance Maggie thought again of flight – pull back the bolts, turn the key in the lock – but the howl remained in her head and the sight of the door bulging inward under the impact stayed there too. At least the boy was some kind of known quantity. From the kitchen came another howl. Maggie grabbed the herb bunches and ran upstairs.

*

She did the bathroom first, rubbing the herbs around the edges of the big frosted glass pane and the smaller inset window, perching on the bath and the toilet to reach all the way round before scrambling into the spare room with the fireplace. It was only a gas fire – hadn't

64

been used for a real one in years – but she rubbed the herbs round the frame anyway.

That's right, Maggie, said Martin. *Do as you're told like a good little girl. You're too stupid to do think for yourself.*

"Fuck off," she snarled, and ran to the window. No, none of that. Negativity. Anger. Bitterness. They didn't help, emotions like these.

"I'm better off without you," she said, dropping a shredded bundle of herb and deploying another. "I'm free now. I'm happy. I'm not letting you make me angry – you and your fucking new girl, you bastard …"

From downstairs, the howl again. Something thumping against the walls below. She ran into the next spare room. The window there was a tiny triangular one and it took only seconds to rub the herbs around the frame. *Then it can't get in.* She ran through into the main bedroom.

Christ, why had she saved it for last? It was the biggest of the lot. Do the easiest first. The bottom of the frame, the sides as far as you can reach up. Then she pulled the chair over from the dressing table, stood on it and did the rest, and the top of the frame.

There was an inset window here as well. She jumped down off the chair and rubbed at that –

And with a wet, rubbery *slap*, something vast and black with snarling teeth and one red, blazing eye flung itself across the window.

Maggie didn't scream this time, just sucked in a shocked gasp of air that stuck in her lungs and wouldn't come back out again. She stared at it and it stared back.

Leather black skin; coarse, shaggy black hair. Its arms were almost impossibly long. Some kind of ape or monkey? But she'd never seen one like this; it looked about man-sized, but its ears were pointed, triangular, and its face – its face jutted out in a doglike muzzle full of long, sharp teeth. And its eye – the single eye glowed, like an ember in the charred coal of its face. It sniffed at the window, pulled back, snarling; she heard the snarls through the glass. Then it pushed its muzzle up against the window and she saw its face spread, flatten and distort, as if boneless, the snarling teeth stretching out into an impossibly wide grin.

The thing shook its head back and forth, sliding its face along the window-glass. Then it pulled back from the glass, the muzzle springing back into shape, and howled again. The window rattled in its frame, and Maggie could have sworn she felt the wind of its breath. Abruptly, it pushed itself away from the window, out into space, and was gone.

A soft thump from below. Then another howl. Seconds of silence, then the banging and rattling started coming again – this time from downstairs, from the kitchen, she thought. The back door – but there was no sound of splintering wood, no crash and un-muffled howl as the thing gained access. It was holding. The boy hadn't been idle; whatever he'd done to the front door, he'd done to the back as well.

So it couldn't get in, at least for now, but it wasn't going to stop trying. Even if it didn't gain access, what were her chances, trapped in here with the boy?

"Om, me, padme, hum," she murmured as she backed away from the window. "Om, me, padme, hum."

"What the fuck are you jabbering about?" The boy lounged in the doorframe. His face was still damp with sweat and his hair hung lank with it, but he was smirking. "What's that? Some hippie New Age bullshit you picked up? Think you know something, do you?" He shook his head. "You know nothing. Nothing. You don't know a thing. Me, though …" His grin widened, then faded. His face went blank, and he motioned with the knife. "Get downstairs."

*

Outside, the thing snarled and paced; a flicker of black slid past the window. The boy motioned her to a chair. "Sit."

She did as he said. Keep on his right side, then she might find a way to reach him. There was good in everybody. She had to stay calm. "So what happens now?" she asked.

"Shut up." He motioned with the knife. "I'll tell you when you can talk." He glanced at the window. The hunched black shape rose to fill it; Maggie couldn't tell if it was on all fours or standing slightly hunched. Its snout looked longer than it had upstairs. But then she'd only glimpsed it. Foam fell from its open jaws and the lone red eye burned steadily. No white, iris or pupil – just an eye-shaped piece of red light that stared hungrily through the window at the boy. The head tilted slightly and the eye studied her. The tongue lolled. More drool fell.

The boy tittered, stepping aside from the window. "He likes you."

The thing wasn't moving. It just stared at her. She held its gaze for seconds, couldn't look away. A couple of times she forgot the boy was there. "Can't you at least pull the curtains?" she pleaded.

"What did I just say?" He took a pace towards her, raised the knife. The beast stopped looking at her, turned to study him instead. The boy smiled, lowered the blade, stepped back. "But no. Best

66

leaving them open. We've sealed the house against him, but Shuck's a cunning bugger. Aren't you, boy?" He turned to the window and grinned. His smile stiffened and wavered for a moment when he found the thing's – Shuck's? – red gaze on him once more, but he got it back. "We're in here and you can't get in. And come the morning, you'll have to go away. And I'll have another day to find out how to deal with you. And I will, boy. Oh, I will."

He turned back to Maggie. "Alright," he said. "You can talk for a bit. Got a name?"

"Maggie."

He smirked. "Yes, I thought you might be. My name's Joseph. *Not* Joe. Joseph."

"Okay."

"So, Maggie. Have you got any cigarettes?"

"No. I'm sorry." Don't apologise to him. *God, you weak bitch*, said Martin. Shut up, Martin, you're not trapped in here with him and that thing outside. Sometimes you just have to say what you have to say and do what you have to do in order to get through.

You've never done anything else, you pathetic cow.

Oh to hell with you, you and your little new wife –

"No," said Joseph. "Of course you don't. You're probably a vegetarian as well, aren't you? Or god help us all, a vegan. I bet you're big on the virtues of tofu and spelt pasta, aren't you? Organic food." He looked up and laughed. "My God. You have dreamcatchers." And yes, she did; there was one, hanging before the front room window. "CDs of whale music and Gregorian chanting, meditation music? I can just imagine. And you think you know something. When you know nothing." He gestured to the window. "I'll bet that none of the fatuous New Age books you've read touched on this, did they? Nothing about Shuck in Khalil Gibran's writings, is there?"

She swallowed. "What is it?"

"Well, now thereby hangs a tale. Hullo!" Shuck had slipped away from the window. There was padding and snuffling from near the front door, and then it moved away. "Pacing around, testing the defences. Still, they should hold till morning. Wolfsbane works well for that. Seals entrances against him. He can't get in unless one of us is silly enough to open the doors or windows." Joseph dragged up the chair he'd stood on to 'seal' the front door, turned its back to her and sat astride it, chin and folded arms atop it. "And I don't think even *you'd* be that stupid. Would you, Maggie? With me, if you behave yourself and don't do anything stupid, you might just stand a chance of survival come the morning. With old Shuck, you won't have a prayer."

67

"What is it?" she asked again.

"Shuck," he said. "From the Anglo-Saxon, *scucca*, meaning devil, or demon. Never heard of Black Shuck? Old legend in these parts. A devil dog, like the Wisht Hounds or the Welsh Cwn Annwn, or – well, pretty well every part of these islands has a legend like it. Black Shuck, though – he was the scariest of the lot. Big as a Shetland Pony, for one thing. There's a story he once burst into the churches at Blythburgh and Bungay and killed several members of the congregation. Huge, black, with a single glowing red eye. And then there's the Shug Monkey. Surely you've heard of the Shug Monkey?"

Mutely, Maggie shook her head.

"Good God. You really *are* self-absorbed, aren't you?"

"I've had other things on my mind. I've …"

"Spare me, Maggie dear. I'm really not interested. The Shug Monkey. Said to haunt Rendlesham Forest. A large creature resembling a monkey or ape, but with a pronounced doglike appearance to its head. Sound familiar?"

Maggie found herself looking towards the empty window.

"Yes. Exactly. 'Shug', of course, comes from the same root as Shuck. The Devil Monkey, basically. Black Shuck and the Shug Monkey get their names from the same source, but the relationship's even closer than that. They're one and the same beast. Shuck – as I call him for short – is a shape-shifter. Dimensions, proportions – he can alter them all. Dog, monkey, it's all one. But it goes further still. You know, I'm sure, what a familiar is? Oh come on, you must know that."

"Witches," she said at last.

"Well done, Maggie. There's some sense in that feeble little brain of yours, in amongst all the twaddle. Yes. Witchcraft. And I'm sure you believe the witches were just harmless old wise women, persecuted by the evil Church. Well, there's a little truth there. Or you believe it was just scapegoating – victimise the weird, the strange, the unusual, the outcast. The unconventional. And there's a grain of truth there, too. But what if I told you there were really those who could fly through the air, strike their enemies dead, turn invisible, and conjure up pretty much whatever they wanted using what most people would call black magic? Hmm?"

Maggie just stared at him, blinking. *He's mad.* For the first time, she began to wonder if she really was in more danger from Shuck than from the boy.

"Oh yes. The witch's familiar. Usually an animal of some sort – a cat, a bird, a toad. Or something else. Of course, while that creature might have looked the part of a cat or bird, or whatever, it

68

was really nothing of the sort." Joseph jerked a thumb towards the window. "Shuck. Or other creatures like him. They may be all but extinct now. He may be the very last of his kind. But creatures like him were the source of the witch's power. Symbiosis – you've heard of it?"

"Two creatures," she said. "They have a relationship where one does something for the other, but they both get something out of it. Like those fish – pilot fish." She struggled to remember. "They pick the bits of food out of shark's jaws, stop it going rotten and causing disease – "

" – and get a free meal for themselves. Yes. That's just one example, of course."

"So what does that thing get out of the deal?" Maggie asked. Humour him. "I can see what the witches got out of it. But what did Shuck get?"

Joseph smiled. "Clever girl. There's hope for you yet. Well – old Mother Nature's very big on balancing things out. Don't you find that?"

Keep him talking. He's enjoying himself here. Less dangerous. "How do you mean?"

"Consider: here we have a creature that can do things denied to almost all other animals. So she strips it of the intelligence to use those talents properly."

Maggie jumped as that howl sounded out back; Joseph looked up, then shrugged, turned back to her.

"On its own," he went on, fully in lecture mode now, "Shuck is just a wild beast, capable only of random acts of mindless destruction – which is why he's been hunted almost to extinction. He has power, but no will. No control. In conjunction with a human host, though, that power is directed and focused. You're familiar with the story of the 'witch's mark' – a blemish on the body that marked the witch's contract with the powers of darkness?"

Maggie nodded, but she needn't have; he'd forgotten she was there. "In fact it marks the bond between Shuck – or one of his kind – and his host. He draws nourishment from his host, and in turn does all he can to provide for the host and extend its lifespan. Symbiosis." Now he looked at her. "And I found out all about it, Maggie. The facts, not the myths and the legends. The facts. No hocus-pocus, just symbiosis." He grinned and almost looked like a little boy now – a little boy playing grown-up games. "There's a reason that the witches and warlocks were always the strange ones, the weirdoes, the outcasts. Shuck's kind have power, but no will. Where better for them to go than those with will, but no power? The perfect match. Made in heaven."

"And what about you?" Maggie heard herself ask. "Is that what you are?"

Joseph's face went blank. *The wrong thing. I've said the wrong thing.* The knife gleamed in his grip. Then he breathed out.

"Never say that to me again," he said. "Do I look like a misfit, an outcast? No. Not that my father recognises that. He's a very successful man. I don't quite... have his aptitude for business. But he'll soon see I've got other abilities. When he sees Shuck."

Maggie glanced at the window again. It was black outside now; the night was heavy with cloud, blotting out the moon and stars. She thought she saw a flicker of red out in the dark.

"I was out at Rendlesham," he said. "In the forest. I'd found out how to track one down. And I found him. Maybe the last of his kind. And it should have worked."

"What should?"

He glared. "The symbiosis, of course. We should be bonded together now. But something went wrong. I don't know what. But I will work it out. And I'll fix it."

"He turned on you?"

Joseph glared again. "Careful," he said through his teeth. "He pursued me. And that brought me here. Somewhere I could barricade against him, just until morning. He'll be powerless in the daylight, you see. And then I can put things right."

Shuck howled. The door crashed, juddered in its frame. The beast slammed against it, again and again and again. There was a sound of splintering wood.

"No ... you little bastard!" Joseph rooted in his bag, came out with a few loose sprigs. A moment later, Maggie let out a cry as Shuck appeared outside the window and hurled himself against it. Astonishingly the glass didn't shatter – it seemed to wobble instead, like some sort of plastic, and Shuck rebounded, only to gather himself again. Hissing snarls sounded from the night outside.

Joseph threw the sprigs of wolfsbane aside. "He means business, I see." A long sigh escaped him. "I'm sorry, Maggie. I'd hoped to avoid this."

Her throat seemed to close up. "What?" she said. But of course, she knew.

"The wolfsbane won't hold him for much longer. He's very determined. If I had more, of course, we could strengthen the protection, but I don't. He'll break in here long before it gets light. Unless I use something stronger to keep him out."

Her eyes shifted to the blade in his hand.

"Blood," he said. "Sacrifice. A little something to distract him 'til dawn."

She got up, stumbled backwards. "Please," she said again. "Please."

"It's nothing personal."

"Please," she said again, and hated herself – hated herself for having nothing else in her arsenal, for having to beg, for the frightened, whining note in her voice. "Please."

"Please," he mimicked. "Please. God, woman, do you know how bloody pathetic you sound, you weak bitch?"

She tried to run past him for the stairs, but he caught her hair again and tripped her. Her cry was cut short when she hit the ground; it knocked most of the wind out of her, and what it didn't, the kick he gave to her stomach did.

"Stupid bitch," he said, and reached down.

*

Maggie was never sure exactly what happened in the few seconds that followed. She might have passed out for an instant and had the briefest of dreams – didn't dreams only last a few seconds in real life, however long they seemed? Or perhaps it was a hallucination. Certainly it was a way for something – be it part of her or something else – to show her what she needed to see.

"You stupid cow," Martin said. "You stupid, worthless cow."

Carol giggled at his side, huddled up against him. A vicious little girl with a swollen belly.

"You bastard," Maggie said thickly. She lay in a pale circle of light; Martin and Carol stood at its edge. All around them was darkness; a darkness that clanked and breathed. "She's young enough to be your daughter …"

"Shut up," said her father.

"Dad?"

"I said shut up. You never were any use to anyone."

She blinked, and he was Martin again.

"Weak," he said. "Worthless. Not a brain in your head. Not much of a cook or a housekeeper, were you? And that really only left one thing, didn't it? Giving me a child." Suddenly he was shouting at her. "And you couldn't – even – manage – *that*, could you? Could you, you pathetic worthless bitch?"

"I tried … we tried … Alex …"

"Alex, Alex, always bloody Alex. That was the best you could do, wasn't it? A scraggy little premature birth that lived three days – three fucking *days*, was that the best you could do?"

Maggie realised she was sobbing. Bastard, bastard, bastard – she thought of razors dragged across his eyeballs, salt poured into the

71

ruins, a blowtorch to his face. Oh Goddess, no, that violence inside her, that evil. Make it go away, make it go away. Drive it out. Om me padme hum.

"And then all the rest. All the miscarriages. Half of them didn't even make the full month. That was the best you could do. You couldn't do the one thing a woman's put on Earth to do, could you? Worthless. Absolutely, totally, utterly fucking worthless."

Bastard, bastard, bastard. No, fuck the mantra. The rage was real, necessary. She'd told herself it was gone, it wasn't there anymore. Spent. The divorce had involved a few cross words, nothing more. But it'd been a lie. A lie. She wanted him in this chair, tied up, forced to watch while she took away Carol, took away his new wife and the child she carried with knives, with fire and sharp things. She wanted him suffering all that – slowly, over days, even weeks – before she even *started* on him.

"And still you went on clinging to me, like I was still supposed to stick with a fucking deadweight like you. Well you can fuck off. I found another woman, a real woman, a woman who knows how to treat me. A woman who'll give me children. And you? Still a deadweight around my neck with your alimony payments. Why don't you just die, Maggie? You're useless, worthless, a failure at everything. So as far as I'm concerned – " his voice changed, and for a moment it was Joseph there, then it became Martin again, " – Shuck can have you. So why. Don't you. Just crawl. Off. And. *Die*."

Maggie howled. Oh, the rage, the rage she'd denied. How bitter it was; how sweet it tasted. I want you dead. Both of you. All three of you. You, her, the unborn bastard. Die. Die. Die. I want your children to die in front of you, you bastard. Martin, Dad, Joseph, all of you. Why don't *you* crawl off and die? Not me. You. You. *You* …

*

"You!" she shouted, and was awake again, back in the cottage as Joseph leant down with the knife in his hand. His groin was close enough – she punched him in it, thrashed aside from him as he doubled forward and gouged the blade into the carpet where she'd been.

"Bitch!" He got to his feet. His eyes were emptier than they'd ever been, his white, wet face twitching and writhing.

When he'd become a lost boy she didn't know, but lost he *was*. He'd always been. Nothing she could do about that, even if she guessed they both understood what it was to be branded stupid and

72

worthless by the one you looked to for reassurance. It was him now, or her.

Something caught her eye. A glimmer of red outside the window. Shuck. He was staring through the glass, but not at Joseph. At her.

And the look on his face – even though there was nothing human about him or it, she thought she understood that look and what it meant. She thought she understood Shuck in a way that Joseph, for all his cleverness, had failed to do.

Something bumped her leg; one of the low tables in the living room. There was a heavy crystal vase on it; she snatched it up.

Distantly, she heard Joseph laugh.

Well, laugh now, you sad, vicious little boy. Because this isn't what you think, and even if I die, so will you.

She drew her arm back and threw the vase, but not at Joseph. She hurled it at the window behind which Shuck loomed.

Joseph's head jerked round; his mouth sagged open into an appalled, comical O as he saw the vase arc through the air, and he leapt for the window in a doomed attempt to stop it. The vase met the window in a shattering of glass, and from outside Shuck's howl blasted into the room.

"Get him!" Maggie screamed. "Take him and kill him, tear him to pieces …"

"You bitch," shouted Joseph, and he lunged at her.

She brought up a hand; the knife went through the palm and out through the back. She screamed; he snatched the knife free to strike again, but never did. Something flew into the room; something vast and black and shaggy-haired, something with a single, blazing red eye, something that fell upon him and bore him down.

Maggie fell to the ground, covered her face and listened to the screams. "Away," she gasped, "take him away."

Joseph's screams vanished, fading, as he was snatched from sight.

Maggie uncovered her face. She couldn't move her hand. It was numb. There was blood all over the carpet, and the window was shattered. But of Joseph there was no trace. No trace at all.

Except for the screams that came from outside.

When they finally died away, there was another sound; padding feet or paws, drawing near. And then, hoarse breathing.

After a long, paralysed moment, Maggie reached out her arms and whispered: "Come to Mummy."

*

73

Morning.

The sun shone over the cottage and lit the fields beyond. A breeze crept in through the shattered window. Still huddled on the living room floor, Maggie wondered idly if they'd ever find some tattered, illegible remnant of a human carcass out there, or if Shuck had disposed of all the evidence.

"He made a bit of a mess here, didn't he, baby?" she said after a moment. "Have to clean it all up later. When it's darker. I don't expect we'll have any callers today. This is an out of the way sort of place."

She looked down and smiled tenderly at the black shaggy shape that she cradled in her arms. Shuck was, at the moment, no bigger than a small dog. "I like you when you're this size," she said. "It suits you. It's portable. Unobtrusive. I think it's a good shape for you to have. At least when other people can see you."

She stroked his head with her left hand – healed now, unmarked. His eyes were closed as he suckled at her. Not at her breast, but at a point a few inches below it, where a small dark blemish, rather like a birthmark, was starting to form.

"He was almost right, wasn't he?" she said. "But he was wrong about one thing. It isn't will that you don't have, is it, Shuck? It's imagination. And he didn't have much of one either." She smiled. "But I do. Later on, we'll clean up this mess. And then we'll see what I can imagine for Martin and his trophy wife. And after that, my sweet little Shuck, we'll see what we can come up with next."

Still stroking Shuck's head, Maggie began to laugh. It was a giggle, only with a sharp, jagged edge to it.

A little like the cackle of a fairy-tale witch.

For Hannah Dennerly, who asked the right questions.

74

THE WITCHFINDER-GENERAL

Our modern perception of Matthew Hopkins, the infamous Witchfinder-General of the Civil War era, has been strongly influenced by the 1968 horror movie, 'Witchfinder General', starring Vincent Price. While the events in the movie were heavily dramatised – to the point where they bear little relationship to the facts – Price's actual portrayal of Hopkins is eerily reminiscent of the ice cold personality known to historians.

The real Matthew Hopkins was, in every way, a cynical opportunist taking advantage of a period of chaos and fear. An unsuccessful lawyer from Manningtree, in Essex, he discovered his ability to root out 'witches' in the year 1645, when he forced a confession from elderly Elizabeth Clark in his home town; Clark, broken and exhausted, went on to accuse 32 other 'witches', most of whom were sent to the gallows. Over the next two years, Hopkins would roam across East Anglia, denouncing, interrogating and ultimately causing the execution by hanging (and in a few cases, burning) of at least 400 people, the majority of them old women, a career for which he was amply rewarded.

But Hopkins was not alone in this criminal enterprise. He could never have propagated his terror without the connivance of many rural communities in England's eastern counties, who were all too quick to take him at his word that the Devil was among them. No-one seems to have stopped to ask themselves why, if Hopkins was the foe of genuine witches, he himself was not subject to curses and maledictions. And this lack of rational thought is the mystery at the heart of the Matthew Hopkins story. In the tumultuous years of religious strife following the arrival of the Reformation, England had punished its fair share of heretics, but compared to her European neighbours she had been slow to take up the pursuit of witches. The medieval English Church had not even believed in witchcraft, teaching that it was silly superstition. And yet for some reason, by the 17th century, particularly in eastern England, all of this had changed – and to such a bewildering extent that lives were suddenly forfeit.

One explanation lies in the Reformation itself. When the Catholic Church fell from grace in England, to be replaced by the more austere Protestantism, its elaborate prayers and rituals were dispensed with. As such, in East Anglia in particular, where Protestantism took the form of hard-line Puritanism, a latent fear existed that holy services which did not involve magical Latin incantations, ministers who had not been officially ordained, and chapels lacking the ornate paraphernalia of religious worship were a poor defence against the forces of darkness – and so maybe harsher methods were called for.

Another explanation lies in the Civil War itself. Waged from 1642 to 1651, between the armies of Parliament and the English Crown, this protracted bloodbath didn't just turn brother against brother and father against son, it tore apart the established fabric of English society. Suddenly no-one held authority anymore. Not only that; the country's legitimate forces were decimated in a series of colossal battles, which led subsequently to banditry, pillage and, in many areas, full-scale anarchy. Though every corner of the kingdom had its own ideas about whom their lawful ruler should be – East Anglia, birthplace of Oliver Cromwell, had largely opted for Parliament – there was a constant air of suspicion and fear. Who knew what mayhem the next troop of soldiers would bring? Who knew if neighbours could be trusted – were they reliable friends, or spies for the enemy? Such an atmosphere of mistrust provided a platform for a man like Matthew Hopkins to set himself up as a strong figurehead whose iron will and depthless knowledge could not be questioned.

But even by the standards of the era, the atrocities that Hopkins perpetrated are quite astonishing. On his instigation, there were mass-executions right across the region, with sentences often passed on the flimsiest of evidence. In Bury St. Edmunds alone some 68 people were hanged at Hopkins's word. Chelmsford witnessed the amazing spectacle of 19 formerly respectable townswomen being hanged at the same time on the same gallows. Though torture was illegal in England, Hopkins managed to get around this by binding his suspects tightly and subjecting them to days of exhausting interrogation, 'running' them to keep them awake. Some unfortunates were 'swum', an ordeal during which several drowned, while others were examined for witch marks – teats by which they would feed their familiars; this usually involved warts and moles being probed for hours with daggers and needles. Though there are no accounts of anyone being racked, branded or scourged, it is little surprise that many still broke and confessed. The sums Hopkins was paid – £15 for cleansing King's Lynn, and £23 at Stowmarket – may seem paltry to modern ears, but in the 1640s they made him a wealthy man.

However, Hopkins wasn't to have it his own way indefinitely. In 1646 a respected vicar, John Gaule, raged against his activities from the pulpit, questioning both his expertise and his motives.

Unnerved, Hopkins wrote a pamphlet in response, which for a man of such powerful personality was surprisingly weak and unconvincing in its attempts at self-justification. Perhaps sensing that his days were over, Hopkins retired to private life. It would be nice to be able to report that he was then hunted down by vengeful Roundheads, as he was in the movie, or even, as rumourists have held, that he was grabbed by a village mob, accused of witchcraft himself and drowned in a pond, but the known facts, sketchy as they are, suggest that Hopkins died in his bed in 1647, possibly from tuberculosis.

THE MARSH WARDEN
Steve Duffy

In the absence of any particularly convincing personal
experience of the phenomenal, I take the liberty of presenting
the following anecdote for your pleasure, having had it at first
remove and been assured thereby of its verisimilitude. It is
appropriate at this juncture for me to add these few details, so
familiar to those who know the protagonist of my story as a friend
and fellow-scholar, which may help 'fix' that shy, retiring
individual before your mind's eye. Picture an amiable, balding
gentleman of some fifty-five or sixty years, pipe-smoker, whist-
player, academic, and ornithologist; the last-named of these
eminently agreeable occupations is perhaps of some significance,
for it was in the pursuance of this particular diversion that our Mr
Rushall (as he will herein be named) set out, one blazing summer
now long since past, to explore the marshlands of Essex, the old
smugglers' haunts that lie between the mouth of the River Crouch
and the estuary of the Blackwater. From Shoeburyness he tramped
to Foulness Point, and thence to Burnham-on-Crouch, and was on
the look-out for a place at which to break his journey when he came
across the village of – call it Sambridge Flats, not far from
Southminster.

A pleasant corner of a pleasant county, to hear Mr Rushall tell it:
the church, an unexceptional late Norman edifice; the single street
of dwelling-places, post-office, general stores, once so familiar a
sight in old England and nowadays (alas) so seldom encountered in
these days of the motor-van and the kinematograph-palace; the
charmingly rustic fortified Hall, thirteenth-century, much obscured
by foot-thick, untamed ivy and the encroaching foliage of two or
three massive old oaks; and the local hostelry, a solid three-storey
building at the edge of the village, corners-on to the church and the
Hall, which went by the name of *The Marsh Warden*.

Mr Rushall enquired as to the possibility of a room at *The Marsh
Warden*, and was told that he could choose from half-a-dozen, trade
being what publicans are pleased to call 'slack' at that juncture.
Indeed, later that evening, having taken the most commodious of the
rooms on offer and come down bathed and changed for dinner, Mr
Rushall seemed to be the sole partaker of the landlord's, a Mr
Hinckley's, hospitality. He dined adequately off reasonable beef and
an acceptable claret, and, on retiring to the lounge bar, offered his

host a Trichinopoly by way of showing his appreciation of the meal. Mr Hinckley, a dark-browed, heavy, somewhat introspective individual, accepted the cigar with thanks, and the two men struck up a desultory but not uncomfortable conversation. "You're not from these parts, I think?" ventured Mr Rushall at one point, detecting an unmistakably urban aspect to Mr Hinckley's deep low voice.

"No, sir: I'm from the East End originally, Canning Town, but my father used to take us to Canvey and to Southend when we were but children, and I always wanted to come out here to live if I could manage it. When the old fellow died, he was the best-off, best thought-of businessman in his Lodge, and left the lot to me: I sold the business at a profit, and bought up *The Ram's Head* in Benfleet; lived there for fifteen years, almost, and when the wife passed on I sold that – at another healthy profit – and took up this place." He smacked his palm on the dark oak panelling of the lounge, as one might pat the flanks of a prized brood mare. "Yes: just over three years at *The Marsh Warden*, now."

"Very pleasant place, too," hazarded Mr Rushall, sipping his whisky-and-soda.

"That it is, sir: I won't say Sambridge is the easiest of places to settle in to, not by a long chalk, but the folks hereabouts won't do you a bad turn if they can help it, and that's not always the way in a small village. I'll say that much for them: queer, solitary souls they might be, but there's no harm in 'em, for the most part."

"Jolly good," said Mr Rushall, glancing around the deserted lounge, "er – rather abstemious lot, aren't they? Taken the pledge, or something of that nature? Or doesn't it get busy until later in the evening?"

This was obviously not the thing to have said, for Mr Hinckley's brows came down abruptly, and he rose from his chair and made a pretence of dusting down the pump-handles at the bar. "Quiet these nights," he muttered, his back to Mr Rushall, "you'll excuse me now, sir if I get on with my chores."

"Oh dear!" said Mr Rushall to himself, as his landlord retreated to the saloon bar, his place behind the pumps taken in a few moments by the barmaid, "sore point there, I think. I wonder where all the customers are, anyway: I'd have thought a pint of beer and a hand of dominoes would be just the thing on a lovely summer's evening such as this. It can't be anything in the nature of a quarrel," he continued, rambling as was his habit along his leisurely train of thought, "our host seems well enough disposed towards his clientele, even if they aren't exactly beating a path to his door tonight. Well, perhaps things will look up once I call it a night;" for it had been a hard and dusty day's travelling, and Mr Rushall was disposed to do no more than leave orders with the maid for an early breakfast and retire for the night to his room, which was large, well-appointed, and furnished after a comforting and solidly Victorian fashion. He made his evening toilet, gratified at the pristine condition of towels and bed-linen, only a little disappointed in the water in the jug beside his basin, which seemed to him to have stood a little too long for absolute freshness. This was a detail, however, and one which in no way marred the deep and satisfying slumber which soon overcame him, and which lasted unbroken till just after seven the next morning.

The day was once more hot and sunny, and it was with a keen anticipation that Mr Rushall came downstairs for his breakfast, which it pleased him to have served on the low wooden table in the grassy yard at the rear of *The Marsh Warden*. He addressed himself to the eggs and bacon with relish: the bacon was agreeable, properly crisp and flavoursome, but the eggs he thought a little questionable, and this impression he communicated to the maid, only to be informed that they were "today's, sir; fresh from Jackson's hens only this morning."

"Be that as it may, I think you'll find there's something amiss with them," demurred Mr Rushall: "here," pushing his plate with the barely-touched eggs on it across the table, "try them for yourself and see if I'm not right."

The maid took a forkful of the offending egg, and was forced to concur with Mr Rushall. "They do seem a little off, sir," she said, having politely disposed of the disagreeable morsel behind the coal-shed: "very sorry, I'm sure. Can I get you anything else?"

"No, no: really, nothing, thank you," averred Mr Rushall, not wishing to put the girl to any trouble; and at this juncture, Mr Hinckley, the landlord, appeared from behind the hedge at the far end of the yard and enquired whether everything was to his guest's satisfaction.

"I'm afraid the eggs are funny, Mr Hinckley," the maid informed him: Mr Hinckley took his turn to sample the dish, and his face twisted in disgust as he closed his mouth upon the fast-congealing mess. "Do you know, Mr Hinckley, the taste – it's not unlike that smell from – " began the maid, as one who throws light on a mystery previously impenetrable, only to find herself interrupted with perhaps undue force by her employer.

"That's enough, Betsey – cut along to Jackson's farm now, and tell him his eggs are off. Tell him I shan't be wanting any more of them either, until they're fit for anything but the swill-bins."

"Very good, sir," called back Betsey in retreat, and Mr Rushall was left alone with his host.

"Busy already, eh?" our friend enquired, and was by way of answer led across the yard and through the hedge to a largish field or enclosure, run completely wild with dense and riotous undergrowth.

"Here's my work at the moment, sir, which it has been this past fortnight," explained Mr Hinckley. "I've been here three years, and it wasn't till last month I ever realised this land went with the Warden, can you believe that? I thought it was Church land," gesturing to the far side of the plot, where the north wall of the graveyard was just visible above the weeds, "but no, I went through the deeds with my solicitor, and he showed me how it was mine after all. Make a decent patch of garden, once it's clear." This last proviso seemed eminently warranted: the ground was absolutely choked with every variety of weed and creeper, and a fortnight's work on Mr Hinckley's part had succeeded only in driving a path of about four feet in width through towards the graveyard wall. Nor could it be said that the air in that particular portion of the grounds was altogether congenial, filled as it was with that peculiarly rank smell of cut-down nettle and bramble in a damp and sunless place. Hardly envying him, Mr Rushall wished his landlord well of the forthcoming day's labours and set out for a day's bird-watching, the particulars of which need hardly detain us here.

The day was well on towards evening when he returned, tired and happy (as the saying goes), and in need of some substantial refreshment. The meal provided was well-enough prepared, and for the most part palatable, but again Mr Rushall found occasion to summon Betsey, the maid, and draw to her attention to the somewhat unwholesome nature of the salad with which his main course had been served. Apologies again, and once more a prompt removal of the offending dish; but in Mr Rushall's mind a plan was forming, which stratagem called for his summary withdrawal from *The Marsh Warden*, as soon as suitable premises elsewhere in the vicinity might be engaged. Still thirsty from his day's exertions, he called for a pint of the local ale after his dinner, but – once more according to an emerging pattern – found very definite cause for grievance in its taste, which to Mr Rushall seemed to share in that indefinable unpleasantness present in both his morning eggs and his suppertime salad. In no little measure displeased, he made the matter known to Mr Hinckley at the bar, and received from that gentleman an immediate apology, a fresh bottle of Bass fetched from the supplier's only that morning, and an invitation to come

81

outside to the back yard and drink it, all of which restitution he accepted after his essentially kindly fashion.

"Look here, Hinckley," he said, once they were outside, "I don't mean to make a fuss unduly, but you won't deny that there have been one or two instances in which the service has fallen somewhat below – "

"I'm aware of that, sir, and you have my apology on it, and something more," said Mr Hinckley, gesturing in the direction of the hedge enclosing the patch of waste at the rear. From behind that hedge as he spoke there emerged a tall dark gentleman of military bearing whom Mr Hinckley introduced as Dr Steadman, the local physician. "Let him give the verdict, sir," said Mr Hinckley, in his direct way. "If Dr Steadman says the place isn't fit, then I shall repay all, and bear the cost of putting you up somewhere else into the bargain."

"Well, Hinckley," said Dr Steadman slowly, "you place me in an interesting position. I shouldn't say the place was unfit for human habitation, but on the other hand I can certainly understand why your regulars are giving you something of a wide berth. That well, or whatever it is – are you sure you haven't disturbed something there? Something seeping into the water table?"

"The well?" said Mr Hinckley, in some surprise. "I only uncovered that just this afternoon, no – but you're right, it's where all that stink's coming from, I reckon." Indeed there was a smell, and Mr Rushall recognised the rank odour he had smelt that morning in the enclosure; only now it seemed to pervade the whole of the rear of the hostelry, redoubled, more penetratingly unpleasant.

"Which well is that?" enquired Mr Rushall, and was led through to the enclosure in the last of the evening light, to be shown by Mr Hinckley the circular stone lid of what appeared to be some kind of well or cistern, built slightly up from ground level close against the graveyard wall and with a much-faded engraving on its top side. The stench in its vicinity being all but unbearable, the men accordingly retreated to the yard, there to discuss the matter further.

"Well, Hinckley, irrespective of what Dr Steadman says, I should be inclined to place the source of your problems at the bottom of that well," said Mr Rushall. "In my opinion, some impurity is finding its way into your water supply, and I must insist that any preparation of food or drink in your kitchens be carried out using only boiled water if I am to remain on the premises."

"Just as you say, Mr Rushall," agreed the publican, with a dark and troubled brow.

"But then there are the cask ales," interjected Dr Steadman. "I really don't see how the well or the water supply could have affected them, you know, and they've been giving you trouble the longest, haven't they, Hinckley? How long now, since your customers have been staying away?"

"A week now, more," admitted the landlord grudgingly. "But – "

"Yes?"

"T'weren't only the beer, you see," said Mr Hinckley, sitting down on a bench and looking up at the two men with what seemed a very honest confusion in his face. "T'were when I first told 'em about the bit o' land out back there. Things were said, and – I don't know – they stayed away ever since, for the most part: I can't make any sense of it. Then this thing happened with the smells, and stuff starting to taste not right, and – " He covered his face briefly with his hands; and said hollowly, "I don't know, sirs, really I don't. You try and make somethin' of a place, think you've come out ahead over the years, an' then a thing like this comes along ..."

"Come now, Hinckley," said Dr Steadman briskly, slapping the landlord's back in a comradely manner. "Once clear all this business up, and your customers will be back in droves, don't doubt it. For the meantime, I should think Mr Rushall's advice very well worth sticking to – boiled water for all your drinking and cooking, and in my opinion, bottled Bass only – not that I suppose there's any more of the Bass to hand, eh?"

Mr Hinckley departed for the bar, seeming somewhat gratified at Dr Steadman's words of encouragement, leaving that gentleman to murmur to Mr Rushall, "And if he can't shift it, whatever it is, you're welcome to dine with me tomorrow night, you know. Just across the way there, two down from the Hall."

They were interrupted by Mr Hinckley's return from the bar, bearing three bottles of Bass, and with a new vigour to his stride. The remainder of the evening they passed in more or less idle conversation, at first outside in the yard, and later, the miasma from the enclosure mounting with the fall of night, indoors.

The next day Mr Rushall once more spent at his birdwatching, repairing homewards to *The Marsh Warden* in order to change for dinner, to be taken at Dr Steadman's as discussed the night before. He was disappointed to find the smell stronger if anything, and hurried over his dressing: the only glimpse he caught of his host was from the bedroom window, as he looked out across the garden to the enclosure wherein Mr Hinckley was labouring with scythe and mattock. As Mr Rushall gazed upon this scene – the bulky form of the landlord struggling amidst the foul exuberance of the weeds – and meditated on the perverseness of the regulatory instinct in mankind, he noticed an agitation in the undergrowth close by the well, as if something or somebody was attempting to part the weeds and clamber out into the low evening light. A moment more, and the movement resolved itself into the sturdy, familiar form of Bob, *The Marsh Warden's* mastiff guard dog. He set up a brisk agitated yapping, leaping up at his master's legs and snapping at the vegetation through which he had plunged as dogs are wont to snap at flies and moths, and Mr Hinckley paused from his endeavours a moment to lead him back to his tethering-post by the back kitchen door. The dog howled once, and from his listening post at the open window Mr Rushall heard a solid impact, as of a working boot on well-packed meat, a brief yelp, and then no more.

Mr Rushall enjoyed an excellent dinner at the house of Dr Steadman, and formed a most agreeable impression of his host, a man (in his judgement) not given to wasting words but who was instead that rarer thing, someone able to converse sensibly on any subject of real interest. The talk continued through the meal and on into the evening, and towards half-past ten Dr Steadman got up to open a new half of port. "Here, try this: you'll perhaps prefer it to *The Marsh Warden's* vintage, these days."

"*The Marsh Warden*, indeed," said Mr Rushall ruminatively; "yes, I rather think Mr Hinckley is having a lean patch of it at present, what with his cellar-stock turned to dishwater and his clientele all fled. I almost seem to be a jinx on the place – perhaps I should have left after all."

"None of your doing," said Dr Steadman briefly. "Hinckley was warned by half the village and by the vicar in particular not to go meddling in Hob's Acre, and it seems they knew what they were talking about."

"Hob's Acre – is that the enclosure behind the pub, there? Where Hinckley found the well?"

"It is. The vicar, Dr Martin, did his very best to dissuade Hinckley from opening it up, but as Hinckley said, it's his property, and the vicar be blowed. Serve him right in a sense, now he's found something nasty in there. As to what it is, though – "

"Yes – I wanted your opinion on that, rather – can it be wholesome? That ghastly miasma, night and day? I don't mind telling you, I shan't be staying there much longer at this rate."

"Quite wise, in my opinion. You can always put up here, you know: there's a guest bedroom you're welcome to, and the woman comes in and does a very palatable meal, as you know. But *The Marsh Warden*: I shouldn't wonder if Hinckley will have to quit it himself over the next couple of days. The girl Betsey gave her

84

notice today, you know: she left this evening, so Hinckley's on his own now with just the dog and the one guest."

"Just the dog, I'm afraid – I've made up my mind on the matter. I shall be moving out tonight, if you'll have me on such short notice." For Mr Rushall really did not see why he should be forced to put up with *The Marsh Warden* and its various insanitary aspects any longer.

"Very well: it's settled, then. I've taken samples of the water from Hinckley's taps, and looked into his food preparation and so on – I can't find anything definite, but I must say I think you're best out of it for the time being."

The two were discussing the best way to break the news of Mr Rushall's decision to his landlord when they were interrupted by a rage and a fury of barking from the direction of *The Marsh Warden*. Mr Rushall identified without difficulty the tones of Bob the guard-dog, and adjourned with Dr Steadman to see what was the matter, thinking as he crossed the empty street that the incident might even serve to distract Mr Hinckley from the impending departure of his sole remaining guest. As they rounded the building and entered the yard at the back, the barking rose to a perfect madness, breaking into a weird strangled shriek before stopping dead of an instant, leaving the night in absolute silence save for the echoes of that final howl. The two men were joined at that moment by Mr Hinckley, who had seemingly been seeking solace for his woes on the shelves and in the bottles of his public bar: he reeled slightly as he stood in the lighted kitchen doorway, and he blinked at Mr Rushall and Dr Steadman as if failing to recognise them. "What's the matter out 'ere?" he croaked. "Who's been interferin' in my back yard, frightenin' my dog?"

"Look here, my good man – " began Mr Rushall, but Dr Steadman was more practical.

"You're drunk, Hinckley," he said, grasping him by the arm and dragging him over to the wooden table on which Mr Rushall had breakfasted the previous day. "Sit on that bench and don't get in the way, while we see what your plaguey yapping dog's got himself into. You haven't been setting gin-traps in there, have you? It sounds as if he's been caught up in something." The doctor waved a hand in the direction of the enclosure.

Mr Hinckley proving incapable of answering, the doctor set off through the hedge into Hob's Acre, shining ahead the torch with which he had thoughtfully provided himself before leaving his house. Mr Rushall, not wishing to remain in Mr Hinckley's company under the present circumstances and unaccountably unwilling to follow his new friend into the enclosure, went inside to

85

collect his belongings, and on emerging with packed bags into the yard once more, was confronted by the spectacle of Dr Steadman dumping on to the wooden table a dark and heavy bulk which, on further examination, proved to be the lifeless body of the mastiff, Bob.

Mr Hinckley by this time being heavily and stertorously asleep, the two men bent over the dog and themselves examined it for clues as to the manner of its demise. They both noted that the smell of stagnation and decay was very marked and advanced, over and above the odour now endemic to the rear of *The Marsh Warden*, and that the dog's coat was sopping wet as if it had been totally immersed; Dr Steadman drew attention to the extraordinary bloating of the stomach, as if decomposition were already in progress with the animal not five minutes dead. "I found it in the midst of the weeds and the suckers," said the doctor, wiping his hands on the bar cloth from over Mr Hinckley's shoulder, "I had the devil's own job dragging it free; I suppose it must have got caught up amongst them and strangled itself. Boo! Nasty thought. Nasty place; let's get Hinckley inside and leave him to it." And having left the landlord stretched out on a wooden settle in the lounge, they repaired back to the good doctor's house and passed the remainder of the night free from all further alarms.

The next day was, if possible, hotter than any yet that summer, and Mr Rushall was disinclined to spend it roasting on the mud-flats in search of sundry avian miscellanea. Over breakfast he announced his intention, first of dropping in on Mr Hinckley and putting on a more formal footing the events of his departure the previous night, and then of visiting the parish church for an audience with the Reverend Dr Martin. "For," as he said, "I've become rather curious about this Hob's Acre. Why was the vicar anxious for him to leave it alone in the first place? Did he know something about it that Hinckley didn't? I'll be quite discreet, but I should think I'll be able to wheedle something out of him – I'm told I can be quite persuasive when I want to be."

Be that as it may, Mr Rushall was thwarted of the chance to practise this latter gift upon his quondam host. He banged on the front door of *The Marsh Warden*, he went round to the yard and shouted in through the open kitchen window, but of Mr Hinckley there was no sign – only a twitching at a bedroom-window curtain, which was not repeated while Mr Rushall watched. "Probably ashamed to show his face after last night," decided Mr Rushall, and wrinkled his nose at the stench wafting across from the enclosure, worse this morning than at any time in the previous two days. As for Bob the unfortunate mastiff, it seemed that some rude disposition of his remains had been made: if not by his master, then by whoever else had passed that way the night before. The dog's body had been removed from the table, and Mr Rushall noticed a faint trail of greenish-black slime, such as may form on the margins of a stagnant woodland pond, leading back in the direction of the gap in the hedge round Hob's Acre. "Dumped it down that old well, I suppose," thought Mr Rushall, "just the thing to sweeten the smell after a day or two. Dirty beast!"

Mr Rushall's luck improved at the vicarage. Not only was Dr Martin at home and receiving guests, he was able to furnish his visitor with a full account of the extraordinary history of Hob's Acre, which I shall take the liberty of summarising for the reader's benefit. It seemed that the field in question, being on the north side of the graveyard, had been used as the burial-place for those who died outside the auspices of the Church, suicides and other scapegrace unfortunates. One in particular, a Jonathan Hobbs, was said to have given the field its name, "but," as Dr Martin explained, "the spelling seems to indicate that a correct attribution might place the blame a little deeper than that: on Hobbs' father, so to speak."

"You mean his father was a suicide, too?"

"I mean that little or nothing is known of Hobbs; little, that is, beyond certain rumours that he had entered into a compact of the most unwholesome kind, and that compact with the Father of all wrongdoing," replied Dr Martin, peering at Mr Rushall over the top of his spectacles. "The land was his, and it is said that he spent more time in the enclosure than in his own house: especially after dark, it seems. He was supposed to have spent whole nights out there, sitting on the wall of the graveyard and talking to somebody – no-one knew who, or cared to get near enough to find out. In any case, Hobbs was found dead in his enclosure one morning in 1644, and the account in the church register says that his body was entirely black: 'black with the magnitude of his sins,' as my predecessor has it. What sins they were, I am afraid the chronicler omits to mention in any great detail; however, we may speculate that they must have been of a singularly heinous nature to produce such a marked post-mortem reaction."

Aware that the vicar's relation of this tale was not entirely unmixed with a certain academic levity, Mr Rushall enquired delicately after the reasons behind Dr Martin's reluctance to cede Hob's Acre to Mr Hinckley.

"As to that, it is a matter of public hygiene as much as anything," explained the vicar. "The land was used at the time of the Plague as a burial pit, and I am assured that the pestilence has been known to linger in the soil through many hundreds of years. My advice to Mr

Hinckley was that he should avoid if at all possible any disturbance of the earth, which I trust he has seen fit to act upon."

This news engendered in Mr Rushall a degree of alarm for his own well-being, having regularly partaken over the last few days of *The Marsh Warden's* food and drink, and he set before Dr Martin an account of the discovery of the cistern hard by the graveyard wall.

"Is that so? And Dr Steadman has been informed of this? I see. Well, if he can find nothing, I daresay there is no great risk to the general health; however, I may say that I find your decision to remove from *The Marsh Warden* well founded."

Well founded, indeed. As Mr Rushall prepared for his evening meal that night at the doctor's house, he congratulated himself on his perspicacity on absenting himself from such an unsavoury lodging. "Plague pit, indeed! And to think I put up there all unknowing: it only goes to show. And the other business: I must tell Steadman about that, too, though I daresay he's a trifle too hard-headed to swallow it." For as we have seen, Dr Martin had also laid before him such details as were at his disposal of Hob's Acre's more fanciful aspects, which details Mr Rushall passed the time after dinner in relating to his host.

"A plague pit: how very unpleasant," commented Dr Steadman. "I suppose that's why they used it as a kind of dumping-ground for all the undesirables they wouldn't bury in the churchyard, then?"

"Not according to the reverend gentleman," averred Mr Rushall: "apparently, it was used as a plague pit because of its bad name hereabouts, rather than the other way around. There are traditions, supposedly, connecting it with certain occult practices which predate any local outbreaks of plague, you see."

"Occult practices – well, well. Black magic, is it?" said the doctor, lighting a cigarette and exhaling. "That would explain the locals' staying away, quite as much as the business with the plague. They're a rum lot hereabouts, you know: practical as you like about most things, but rub them a certain way about anything along those lines and they're as skittish as you please."

"Remarkable, is it not?" assented Mr Rushall. "But there's more: it seems that even after Hobbs' demise strange things were afoot in his acre of land. The records show that a full year after they put old Hobbs underground, the locals were staying away from that corner of the village, convinced that he – or something he had called up, at any rate, though they don't explain precisely how that part of it worked – was still abroad in Hob's Acre, and there were people falling ill and even dying. Believe it or not, they actually called in Matthew Hopkins, the Witchfinder-General, but he seems to have done no more than 'swum' a few unfortunate old women and departed with his usual twenty shillings in his purse and a job half-done behind him. It was after that that the land was closed off: it really does seem that they were afraid that something was in there which was – well, which was better left to its own devices, if you like."

"Well, there you are, then," commented Dr Steadman, as he rose to fill Mr Rushall's glass; "let any of the regulars at *The Marsh Warden* catch wind of a thing like that, and they'd as soon drink fire and brimstone as any ale of Hinckley's."

The conversation ranged on from that point; broadened and grew more diffuse, with each instancing some curious and inexplicable incident from amongst his recollections which in turn drew a like response from the other. It must have been after midnight when the two were standing out in Dr Steadman's little patch of garden, smoking and admiring the moonlight view of the quiet little village before retiring. Mr Rushall had just turned to the doctor and was in the act of opening his mouth to say goodnight when, exactly as had happened the night before, the silence was disturbed by a barrage of noise from the direction of *The Marsh Warden*. Only on this occasion, the disturbance was not the barking of a dog.

"Good gracious – what on earth – " Mr Rushall strove to adjust himself to this aural assault; Dr Steadman, in keeping with his more active disposition, lost no time in idle speculation. He started across the road, calling back over his shoulder, "That's no mastiff – that's Hinckley, and he sounds in a bad way. Come on after," and he was vanishing around the side of the public house before Mr Rushall had cleared the garden gate.

"Horrors of drink," reflected that gentleman uncharitably, panting along in the doctor's wake as the lusty yelling of Mr Hinckley redoubled in volume. "He's been at the stock again –oh, my goodness, what a reek!" For the smell, bad enough that morning, was now all but unbearable. Mr Rushall paused a moment to wonder why it was that so bitter and pervasive a miasma should be so very localised – for he had caught not a whiff of it in the doctor's garden – and was roused again to his senses by the sound of breaking glass. As he came into the yard, he saw that the doctor had smashed a pane of the kitchen window, and was feeling for the latch on the door alongside. "Have to do it," he explained tersely, "poor old Hinckley sounds as though he's having a fit in there. *There* we go – " and he was inside, Mr Rushall bringing up the rear.

Once within, the two split up in search of the unfortunate publican: Dr Steadman took the upstairs, while Mr Rushall rummaged through the public bar, the snug and the saloon lounge without finding any trace of Mr Hinckley, whose cries had ceased abruptly and somewhat worryingly upon their entrance. He was on the point of following the doctor up the stairs when he noticed that the cellar hatch behind the bar was open. "Down in the cellar, I shouldn't wonder," thought Mr Rushall; "drunk as a lord and jumping out of his skin. Well, here goes: down the steps and never mind a candle. Ugh! Nasty and dark, and the smell worse than ever. No light – matches; here we are. *If* they strike – it's quite bad air enough to stifle them, I should say. Ah! Yes! Well, nothing out of the ordinary, seemingly. But that stink – the place is quite evidently unfit for habitation. He'll have to get out of it now, wherever he is – no man could bear it for more than a few minutes." For down in the cellar the smell was indeed at its most penetrating and disagreeable – an open London sewer could hardly compete with it in point of vileness and persistence.

Mr Rushall turned, and made for the steps back up to the bar, when his foot slipped on a patch of moisture on the otherwise dry cellar floor, taking him by surprise and sending him sprawling. The match he held aloft was of course dropped and extinguished, and as he strove to regain his footing, he found the floor, of flagged stone and packed earth, giving way in a manner wholly inexplicable to a kind of loose wet sand, such as one might find on an estuary bed at low tide. Mr Rushall, in no small measure alarmed by this bizarre turn of events, flailed and scrambled for a foothold in the dark, and felt instead his body actually sink into the oozing, sucking sand. He kicked out desperately, wriggling forwards in the direction of the stairs, and found his passage still further hindered by coils and hooks of weed amidst the quicksand that caught at him and ensnared him afresh, dragging him down into the muck and the stench 'til to breathe was all but impossible.

With a frantic effort he thrust clear of the slime his head and shoulders, drew gulping, sobbing breaths, and yet was once more hauled under by the cruel rapacious weeds – they seemed to have a life all their own, so strongly did they grab and choke, drawing him inexorably to the mouth of some soft and unimaginable pit, where but seconds ago had been cold flagstone and the promise of security. He tasted a cold and filthy vileness in his mouth and gagged uncontrollably in disgust; he heard the gurgling rush of the quagmire as it closed above his head – who knows? perhaps for the last time.

Mr Rushall was not an especially strong man, nor was he perhaps in the peak of physical condition, but he knew instinctively that to surrender to the mire and to the weeds was to die, and in such a situation even the weakest may find reserves whose existence they had barely, if ever suspected. With an effort positively Herculean he

90

surged upwards and forwards, grasping blindly in the darkness, and felt his right hand close upon rough wooden planking – the bottom tread of the staircase! He seized hold of the tread as if it were the last anchor in a world cut loose from all its moorings, and by virtue of this fulcrum was able at last bring his weight to bear on something more solid than the muck in which he floundered. Now he was able to haul the whole upper half of his body free – a second tread – a third, a fourth – and now he was scrambling up the stairs on his hands and knees, terrified for his life and for his very reason, not pausing 'til he had slammed shut the cellar trapdoor and collapsed exhausted on the floor behind the bar.

He was insensible for a period of some five or so hours, regaining consciousness only as dawn was beginning to lighten the skies above the village of Sambridge Flats. Dr Steadman had carried him upstairs to his old room on the first floor of *The Marsh Warden* and set him on the bed to rest, and as Mr Rushall started out of his sleep with an exclamation of horror, the doctor took his shoulders and pressed him down again.

"It's all right," the doctor said in his quiet way. "Poor Hinckley's past helping, I'm afraid, but you'll do for now. It was a close thing, though, I think – I don't suppose you'll be wearing those tweeds again," gesturing to the chair-back over which hung the torn and filthy remnants of Mr Rushall's suit.

The story, once Dr Steadman judged his patient ready to hear it, was brief and categorical. He (the doctor) had gone upstairs and discovered Mr Hinckley lying in his bed in a second-floor room, dead and black and bloated: "Just like the mastiff of the night before, you remember. I tried to revive him, but it was no use – if I hadn't heard him yelling and carrying on just seconds before, I should have thought he'd been dead a week or more. Next thing, I heard a dreadful rumpus from down in the bar, so I came down and found you spark out behind the counter – what happened?"

Mr Rushall recounted – not without frequent pauses and pleas to be believed, all facts to the contrary – the circumstances of his adventure in the cellar, and Dr Steadman listened intently, chain-smoking as he did so his pungent hand-rolled cigarettes. At the conclusion of his extraordinary tale, the doctor stood up from his chair by the side of the bed and crossed over to the window.

"There it is," he said, his back to Mr Rushall; "you've said it yourself. I thought as much, but I couldn't see my way to believing it, but now – we shall have to clear things up before we call the police, that's all."

"Said it myself? Said what?" enquired Mr Rushall. "Do you suppose the same sort of thing that happened to me in the cellar happened to Hinckley in his own bed?"

"I don't know what I suppose," said Dr Steadman, turning to face him with a wholly indescribable expression; "there are the very clothes you wore to dinner in my house last night, looking as if they'd been dragged the length of the Thames estuary when all you've done is walk across the road and go down into the cellar in them. Then there's Hinckley – his bedclothes all full of the most revolting muck and slime and filth, marks on his hands and wrists and round his neck as if he'd been bound like a cow in the shambles, and the condition of the body – my God, man, as a doctor I tell you frankly I've never seen the like. Except perhaps once –" and he broke off, turning again to the window with a shudder.

"You mean the dog – " began Mr Rushall, but the doctor shook his head.

"No," he said, after a time, "this was in the War; the retreat from the Salient at Ypres. I was leading a party of walking wounded back to the field hospital, and the way went past a crater where the sappers had exploded an enormous charge – to breach the German positions or some such, I suppose, months, years before. The crater had filled up with rainwater, and worse than rainwater – you must remember there were bodies everywhere, the burial squads were working flat out and couldn't recover more than a fraction of them – and floating at the edge of the water was a corpse – well, it might have been a month old, perhaps even more than that. I – I won't go into any great detail about it, but it gave me a turn such as I never hope to have again, and my nerves were all shot for weeks afterwards – you think you're immune to it, but there's always something that will get through, I think. And the smell – "

"Good Lord," interrupted Mr Rushall, starting up to his feet, "the smell – last night – don't you notice? Haven't you noticed it?"

"Yes," said the doctor, turning once more to face him, and seeming to return to the little Essex village pub from some immense remove of space and time, "the smell's quite vanished now. It's been gone since it started to get light there in the East."

*

We need not overly trouble ourselves with the details of the formal inquest into the demise of Mr Hinckley. Dr Steadman prepared all before the police were summoned, and the appropriate conclusions were drawn by all concerned. The publican not having been seen by anyone since the resignation of his maid and the subsequent death of his dog, the time of death was eventually fixed precisely twenty-four hours too early, at a point almost immediately following Mr Rushall and Dr Steadman's midnight intervention in the mSatter of the mastiff and Mr Hinckley's subsequent collapse into a drunken stupor. The exceptional degree of post-mortem putrefaction observed by the coroner was attributed to the summer heat and the inadequacies of the local mortuary's refrigeration facilities, and the cause of death was officially set down as apoplexy.

Very likely such matters as these are by nature patchy and inconclusive; be that as it may, I fear I am unable to write *finis* beneath the affair of *The Marsh Warden* as decisively as did the court of inquest in its own, more material way. Mr Rushall was unable to uncover any further information concerning the late Jonathan Hobbs or his pestilent acre of land, and the precise nature of the retribution meted out in the case of the unfortunate Mr Hinckley must remain forever a matter of conjecture, as must the identity its perpetrator, if indeed identity it had.

Retribution, I say, but for what crime? What wrong had Mr Hinckley done, that he should meet with so bizarre and unpleasant an end? One is forced to assume that the law by which such matters are judged must remain forever mysterious to us, and its dispensations must needs appear barbarous and arbitrary to we unenlightened. Perhaps Mr Hinckley was a precipitate and a careless man, or perhaps he was a mere unfortunate, happening upon the wrong place at the wrong time. And perhaps, more pertinently, it makes no great difference either way; and with that thought, I lay aside my pen and wish you goodnight.

BEWARE THE LANTERN MAN!

In 1809, a boatman called Joe Bexfield, who operated one of the Norfolk wherries (sail-bearing cargo craft) along the River Yare, on a stretch between Norwich and Yarmouth, had finished his shift and moored for the night at Thurlton Staithe. He called into the nearby White Horse Inn for a drink and some food. During the course of the evening, he suddenly recalled that he had left items of value on his wherry, and announced his intention to return to the mooring even though it was now dark and a heavy mist shrouded the marshland. One of his work-mates advised against this, pointing out that he'd seen odd lights outside which could only mean that the Lantern Men were abroad.

Bexfield, scoffing at this old wives' tale, wandered off into the murk – and never returned. His body was found a week later, floating in the Yare at a place called Breyton. The cause of death was eventually given as accidental drowning.

These are the known facts in the case – but then the fancies take over.

Bexfield's colleagues remained convinced he had been accosted in the mist by a Lantern Man, one of the most feared goblins of the East Anglian fenland. Known by a variety of other names – Hinkypunk, Hobby Lantern, Will-o-Wisp, Shiner, Jenny Burnt Arse, and very popularly, though it's now a name that means something else entirely, Jack-o-Lantern – this mysterious being was a firm fixture in old East Anglian folklore, and was genuinely believed to be the cause of countless unexplained drownings in the fens and broads. Its exact physical form was unknown. Some witnesses described it as a hideous, twisted old man, some as a shadowy figure which was never completely corporeal, but all agreed that it carried a flickering light – a candle or fire-brand – the purpose of which was to lead astray any lost wanderers to the point where they would fall into deep water and drown.

Well into the 20th century it was considered unwise to carry a light when traversing the lanes of rural East Anglia late at night, as this would attract the Lantern Man, who would be enraged to see another flame, and would come rushing from his marshy lair to do mischief. Likewise he would be attracted to singing, whistling or lively conversation, for he could not abide to hear joviality in his dreary domain.

Even today, much of East Anglia contains vast acres of flat farmland rather than villages, towns or other conurbation. These areas are largely unlit at night, meaning that narrow paths and even country lanes can be treacherous; so imagine how it was in an era when much of this landscape was still under water. Imagine how it was when thick frets poured in from the North Sea to render the night even more opaque. It would be quite easy for travellers to blunder into bogs and mires. In fact it would be surprising if this did not happen. So why did the myth of the Lantern Man proliferate, and why were so many deaths attributed to him?

The answer would seem to lie in 'ignis fatuus', a curious flickering flame, which darts about here and there and is a genuine phenomenon of the marshland. Its cause appears to be the oxidation of methane and phosphine from rotting vegetation. Phosphine ignites on contact with oxygen, which in turn ignites the methane. The result: wavering balls of light all over the bogs; easier to see, of course, when it is dark or foggy.

However, this very scientific solution to the mystery is a rather dry and unexciting one, and not everyone accepts it, preferring the notion that once night falls, spooky mist-forms are abroad in the flat lands of East Anglia, carrying 'corpse-candles' for the sole purpose of leading the unwary to their doom.

THE FALL OF THE KING OF BABYLON
Mark Valentine

The thick dark water sucked greedily at the oars each time they dipped into the river's jaws, as if it was reluctant to let them go. He could tell by the way the boatman pushed hard against them that the current was offering him no help at all. It was as well that they did not have far to go. It was only a few minutes since they had left the banks of the city, and already the tall warehouses on the other side glowered above them. The towers of Babylon, he thought. Dark-bricked, dimly-lit on the bank side, with barred windows, and with foundations and lower chambers sunk deep in the ooze of the river, they were more like outgrowths than buildings.

The night was moonless and clouded, and the wind was riding in from the black marshes to the south. There had been heavy rain for days, and the river was broad and high, bloated. Its deep bed mud had been stirred up, and had darkened and soiled the waters. He sniffed at the rich, loamy miasma that had been released. The moisture in the air, squatting just above the water, seemed to stick to his face like a grease, in silvery streaks.

They thudded against the old quay: it consisted of slabs streaked with green spittle like a sick man's tongue. There were a few great rusted iron rings: much bigger vessels than this had once tied up at the side. The boatman grunted and held the barque almost steady in the water, though still the river seemed to grip at it, as if it wanted to pull it under. His passenger looked up at the dank wall: there was a narrow set of rungs, dripping with green weed and oily moisture. He swung himself out onto one of these, and caught hold of the cold rail. The boat began to move away at once. But its passenger was quicker. With a swift twist of his limbs, he kicked out, and caught the boatman a heavy blow on the head. He followed it with another. There was a baffled cry, and a gurgling of the waters as the boat thrashed about, out of control. Then there was a heavy crash and a great jet of the green water thrust upwards, flicking over him. He watched carefully, licking at the rank liquid on his face: little sparks of light glinted in his dark eyes. Nothing came to the surface. The boat began to drift away, empty. Good, he thought: I won't be needing you again anyway. Already he could feel his skin longing, and the river and its mud summoning him. Just a few more tide-hours, just a few.

He heaved: briefly, he was not sure he could haul himself up further without his soles or his fingers slipping, but he clung on and gasped to the top and onto the dank slabs, filling his breath with their ripe stench. Then he scrambled to his feet. He had business in Babylon.

*

That was what they called it, this mudbank of a place, an island of sorts, a backwater within the Isle of Ely itself, cut off from the city when they diverted the river centuries ago.

It was a huddle of slimy buildings: the warehouses, twenty or so hovels, a few boatyards, the shed where they made osier baskets, and one pub. Some of its people were the ancestors of those who had always lived here, the original 'exiles'. The freemen beyond the water, that's what the city people had called them. Some of those families were still stubbornly clinging to the place. But most of the inhabitants had come later, drawn by its isolation, the way it was left alone, a law to itself, by the 'mainland', as they sardonically called the city. And so Babylon had been built outwards onto the spit of mud, and upwards, with ramshackle attachments to the older structures: and there were also tunnels and archways between buildings, so that even here, necessary things could be carried on clandestinely.

And Babylon had a King, or that's what they called him. The boss. He liked the title. Elias Smith, his real name, it was said: but it didn't do to use it. He wasn't worried about a crown or a throne, but he did want the power, and the deference. Nothing moved on this mudbank without him knowing about it. Nobody lived there without paying his taxes, and those were set at whatever rate he pleased.

In the city there was a bishop and a soaring cathedral, with its great lantern tower, the glory of the Fens. But here in Babylon, there was no church, no chapel: just the eel warehouse, a ruined ziggurat of red bricks. And at its very top, in his own vaulted chamber, there resided the King. You had to be conducted there: no set of stairs led straight to it. There were different iron flights for each floor, and linking corridors, and empty halls, which you were hustled through in a blur. You went back, if you went back, a different way. But rumour said that from a concealed door in the King's reception room, there was a chute, a steep chute that went down, down, straight into the Great Ouse. And at such force that nothing sent down ever surfaced again.

In the warehouse, above smouldering pits of slow-burning alder-wood, skinned silver eels were being smoked in long rows of round

97

gallows like dark chandeliers. The columns of flesh swayed and twisted in the draughts, as if they were still alive. There was an acrid smell from the embers and also, still, the deep dank odour of river mud, not yet burnt out of the bodies of the eels. The two together were almost overpowering. In the cellars, frequently flooded, and always dripping with damp and mould, were the slabs where the catch was first reamed of its gleaming skin. A streaked tin tub of eel heads stood in one corner: the black eyes still glinted in the dim light.

The King of Babylon owed a vast wealth to this gruesome river harvest. But he was restless this night. There was something wrong in his realm, he knew that, and although he could not say exactly what, there were signs. There hadn't been a catch in days. The women in the weaving-sheds were murmuring amongst themselves: they shut up too quickly when they saw him. The river was too solid: he did not like the look of it. And from over in the city, there was too much talk of a foreigner seen, staring across at Babylon, asking questions. He had a strangeness in his tongue, the King's spies said, and probably came from beyond the seas.

The King's heavy form paced about his high room, and he glared down from this eyrie to the darkened alleys and empty yards below, through the small panes of smeared grey glass. Like the bricks of his building, his face and hands were a blackened red. Abruptly, he turned away, and tugged at a bell-rope. A cracked clangour sounded. Boot-steps stumped in the stairwells and along the corridors. A young woman, with cropped hair, and dressed in rough black clothes, presented herself. She had a white scar on her left cheek. It gleamed silver in a face already a dirty pale, the colour of congealed candle-wax.

He stared at her. She lowered her dark eyes, and fidgeted.

"Who's in Babylon tonight?"

"Forty-two souls, sir. Eighteen down below, doin' the skinnin', smokin' and saltin'. Balin, patrolling the building, with Den and Pulver. Twelve in *The Anchor*: that's nine o'the fishing men, the potman, the barmaid, old Agar talking to 'imself. Then there's Mother Shearn in her cottage …"

"What's she doing?"

"Playing at cards, sir."

"Playing? Or reading them?"

"Couldn't tell, sir. Looked like playing though. She didn't have that funny look in her eyes."

But you do, the King thought, that's why you won't look in mine. Hiding something. He gestured to her to go on.

98

"Four o'the women in the basket shed. And then there's them two men you put on the wharves, looking out. That you didn't tell me, nor nobody about. But I spotted 'em. And then me, and you, see, sir, makes forty-two. "

He grunted. "Been everywhere?"

"Everywhere."

"Would you like to be skinned, Nix?"

Still she would not look at him.

"I have been everywhere," she repeated, slowly.

"Skinned, salted, smoked alive on one of the eel-gallows?"

"Everywhere," she murmured.

*

Mother Shearn did not tarry long in the brick hovel she called her home, where dirty lace tried to escape through cracks in the smeared windows. After she saw Nix's pale face glimmer in the grey panes, then vanish, she blew out the candle. She continued to count out the cards in their rows and columns, knowing them by touch in the gloom. She had been in Babylon longer than anyone remembered, and was rumoured to be the only one on the isle that the King, Elias, was afraid of: wisely, perhaps, she had never put this to any great test. Her face was silted and brown like the river's leavings.

She hunched over the cards for some time, then hastily gathered them up and stuffed them in a little pouch of frayed red satin, which hung from the thick leather belt at her waist. She wrapped a bundle of tawny shawls around her shoulders. Outside, she sniffed the dank night air. Her thick greasy nostrils seemed to suck in and sift the stench. Then she made a gurgling noise at the back of her throat, and shuffled towards *The Anchor*. Its door unleashed a babble, then swung closed behind her.

Old Agar was reciting to himself from the Bible again: he seldom did anything else. At least, it sounded like the Bible. There was a lot of muttering about the things to come. He barely registered her arrival.

A group of men in the corner looked up from their beer as she moved towards them. She thrust her face into their hoarse-throated circle.

"Eels is risin'," she said, quietly.

They fell silent for a few moments then started to mutter.

"Can't be."

"Naw, not tonight, Mother."

"Have another look at they cards o'yours."

"Get her a gin."

"Eels is risin'," she repeated.

Reluctantly they began to get to their feet, clumsily lace up the boots they'd eased loose, and climb into heavy, soils-streaked coats, gather up kit bags. From a corner, they took up nets, clubs and the shining gleaves, long, speared forks, like primitive weapons. Grumbling and spitting, they headed for the door.

She watched them go, and then signalled with a quick jerk of her head for a double genever. She felt the spirit graze her throat. Yes, they were rising, all right, swimming up from the silt and the mud, following some instinct old and blind. She knew that: she always did; whatever the instinct was, she could catch its dim echoes, like a coiling of green miasma in her mind. But this time there was something else she could not fathom. There was a cold gap. She could not tell when the rising would end, when they would return to the slime, to the river's depths. She shivered, drew her shawls closer about her, and signalled for another spirit.

*

The men trudged, then waded, down to the shallows where the boats were kept. They lurched and jostled against each other. They could already tell the hag was right: the smell in the air was heavy enough to get through the beer in their heads. They bundled the eel-tools in a pile on the mudbank and hauled the boats toward them on their sodden ropes. The brown slime stuck to their hands. The coracles seemed heavy in the swollen waters, were reluctant to come. They heaved harder, their boots sinking into the clinging clay. At last, with a jolt and a surge, the dank wooden shells began to move towards them. Ben Crawke got his in first, but the sudden impetus took him by surprise and when the boat bumped against his shins, his fuddled brain wasn't quick enough to react, and he toppled forward into the bottom of the boat. Cackles of laughter greeted his mishap, and were redoubled when Crawke screeched. The boat thrashed about in the water and in the dim light they could see his limbs flailing about comically. Why didn't he steady himself? He used to be able to hold his drink better than that. Still, it was worth watching. After they'd let him mess about for a few moments, still bellowing fit to burst the moon, one of the men stooped down quickly and caught up the trailing boat-rope, and another helped to try to steady the juddering. It took both of them to tug the boat back once again to the bank. And then Crawke's head emerged.

The youngest fisher, Thom, had been sent against his will to an elementary school in the city for a year or two, before he slipped away back to Babylon, where they didn't come looking for him again. One day he had been shown a book of myths which he quite liked because it had a lot of pictures of strange things in it, things that even Babylon did not possess. And one of these was of a woman with a head all covered in snakes.

Crawke looked like that now. Except they weren't snakes. They were eels. And they weren't just in his hair, like that woman's. They were on his face too. No, not just on his face; in it. Some of the men stumbled forward, as if they could help, seizing their clubs and the long barbed spears. Then the river current, which had been slow and sluggish, seemed to give a great surge, to rise up in a sudden swell, and the ropes dropped slack as the rest of the boats rushed to the bank. And then they saw the writhing within them, a great mass of the dark coiling creatures. It would have been the greatest haul ever made, something to boast about in *The Anchor* for years to come. Except that, it was all wrong: for the first, and last, time in their lives, they had no need to go out for the catch. It had come to them.

The river surged again, lunging at them. The strong waters sucked at their limbs. They tried to ground their boots in the mud, to grab hold of the mooring posts, even to clutch at the sharp, yellow-green reeds. Still, they were summoned into the depths. And when they finally gave way, they found out why the current was so fierce. It wasn't just the water that had sucked them under.

*

Nix crouched in a dark corner. She had five dark corners on the isle, where neither Balin nor Mother Shearn nor Elias Smith could know where she was. To get to this one, she had quietly moved aside a huddle of osier baskets, then a stretch of oilcloth, revealing an iron lid. This she forced up with a little knife she'd filched once from one of the fishermen: it had grey string round the handle for better grip. The blade dislodged the seal of grit and mud around the lid, and she heaved it up. Below was a narrow rung, and at the bottom of this a platform above a black channel of water. It ran under the warehouse and came out under one of the unused cellars. Even Elias did not know about this. When she was alone she did not call him the King, even though she belonged to him. She rubbed the scar on her white face.

They told her she had been born in Babylon, and so she belonged to him. There wasn't anybody else claiming her; that was for sure. But she did not call him the King because she knew, somewhere inside her, that there was another ruler of this isle, and always had been, and he would come again. Maybe somebody had told her a story about it once, maybe she had overheard a few things and put

101

them together, maybe she had always known it. But she was more certain of it even than the breath of the boss, Elias, when he took hold of her and pulled her close and stared at her. That breath was the thing she feared the most, because she could tell from it what would happen next. His breath, heavy, rotten, rank, seemed to enter her like poison. And then his venom worked in her veins, all the way through her. But when she later lay quivering, trying to secrete the poison, trying to get rid of it, she also called, far in the depths of her mind, called and sang – to the unknown king, to the one that she knew would one day hear her.

Her body in its black clothes tautened, so tight, so intense she thought it might suddenly change, in a flicker, into something else. Footsteps. Coming steadily towards her. Heavy, too, sending echoes into the tunnel. His? Elias? She felt something surge in her, a burst of hot defiance. Her fingers tightened on the corded handle.

*

He could feel the waters rising. Already they would be filling up the underground channels, surging into the vaulted chambers, clawing at the walls. The deep, dark stench of the water called to him: already he had offered it two bodies he'd found prowling about after him. They'd been distracted by some babbling young fisher-boy, who clung on to them, shouting about a face he'd seen, a face that was writhing. The boy would have more to talk about now.

But there was a greater urging in him too, more overpowering than the river. He knew she was here: the sense coursed in his limbs like a shot of silver. He waited. Then his eyes seemed to form the image of an iron disk, and draw his body towards the shadow of the warehouse with insistent force.

She heard the grating noise, saw the lid rise up. A face of white shone in the gloom, and then a form slid easily down and dropped beside her. She felt her body become even more tense. And then stared at his black eyes, stared hard, and saw her own reflected back. She was seized and thrust into the dark waters. They closed about her head. For a few moments she was blinded and numb. Then she kicked out, thrust herself forward, and at once felt her body become part of the current. Around her, forms moved in the water.

When they emerged into the cellar, her breath was soiled at once by the burning smell from the smoking gallows above them in the building, which seemed to permeate every streaked brick. She felt a plunge of fear, and she wanted to cry out. But then a hard rage seethed through her and her eyes gleamed in hatred.

102

Her companion touched her, and beckoned. Their dark, dripping forms moved lithely to a stair and quickly ascended. Flight followed flight, in a crooked route through corridors that glistened as they left behind them a trail of the black slime.

And there was his door. Behind it, the man who liked to be called the King of Babylon. Now the hatred was so fierce in her that she knew it would change her forever: her body could not contain that dark fire. She heard the bell shout for her from its bronze throat: she heard that name bawled, "Nix! Nix!"; she heard the threats that followed. Her fingers felt the silver scar upon her face. Her companion thrust her to the stone floor, and crouched beside her. Then, together, as if they were one being, they lunged, and burst through the door. There was a sharp, keening sound, and a barbed glieve thrust through the air toward them. They twisted with a wild instinct, and it clanged uselessly aside. It was raised again for another strike, but stopped: it was held before them, holding them at bay. But still within them, they felt that instinct surging strong.

Then the King saw the intruders' faces change. They seemed to pulse rapidly, to quicken and writhe before him. And the flesh began to turn colour. It had been white, like the skinned strips dangling from the gallows below. Now it was darkening, becoming brown, like the river water, rank green, like its weed, and finally black, black like its depths of mud. And the shape of their faces was changing too: becoming sleek, sharp, pointed; until at last he knew exactly what he faced, and stared into the utter glinting dark of the eyes.

Elias Smith, alias The King of Babylon, bellowed, and backed quickly into an ante-chamber. He spun an iron wheel in the corner of the outer wall. With a grating noise, a door swung heavily open. There was a large arched tunnel, like an open mouth, with a brick throat, sloping steeply down. He leapt into its maw, skimming its streaked surface, feeling the fetid air rising to fill his breath as he descended at reckless speed. Behind, he could sense the things slithering even faster after him.

THE WEIRD IN THE WOOD

*I*n December 1980, Rendlesham Forest in Suffolk was the scene
of perhaps the most compelling and at the same time baffling
UFO event in British history. What makes this 'close encounter'
so different from many others, is the apparent trustworthiness of the
witnesses: a bunch of US Air Force personnel who were stationed
at the nearby NATO base, RAF Woodbridge.

*In fact, the proximity to Rendlesham of numerous security
installations – RAF Bentwaters as well as Woodbridge, and on the
coast, Orford Ness transmission station, which during the Cold War
was the location for 'Cobra Mist', a long-range recon and
surveillance programme – adds a whole new layer of mystery to the
case. If some intelligent, extraterrestrial force was at work in
Rendlesham Forest that frosty winter night, was it a coincidence
that high-tech military hardware was in the neighbourhood?*

*For all this, the first sighting of anything unusual was not by an
American airman but by a local forestry worker, who on the evening
of December 26th spotted a bizarre, mushroom-shaped craft in the
sky above the trees, giving off a weird greenish light. The witness's
dog was with him at the time; it was allegedly disoriented by the
incident, and a day or so later he reported that it had died.*

*American security guards at RAF Woodbridge were the next to
experience something uncanny. Two of them, John Burroughs and
Budd Parker, entered the densely-grown pinewood in pursuit of a
curiously shaped, hovering object – possibly the same one the
forestry worker had seen, though this was described as being about
the size of a car and having a cone-like exterior. The twosome
followed it for some distance before it came to a halt in a clearing
about a foot above the ground, and there radiated a piercingly
bright light. Burroughs, Parker, and others who had now joined
them, attempted to approach but were held back by some kind of
unseen force-field, which caused their hair to prickle.*

*A third US serviceman, Sergeant Jim Penniston, later said that
he had come into physical contact with a craft of unknown origin,
and described curious inscriptions upon its surface, though he did
not think it was extraterrestrial. The object Penniston saw had
triangular landing gear, and when a search was made in daylight
the following morning, a trio of small indentations was found in the
ground and the branches of surrounding trees were seen to have
been broken and burned.*

104

British police officers were called, but felt there was nothing suspicious at the scene, though it had also been reported to them that local farm animals and other livestock had been strangely panicked and distressed the previous night.

Unsurprisingly, the US military were not at all happy to have such unexplained and sinister occurrences in the vicinity of their base, and the following night Lieutenant-Colonel Charles Halt took a number of men into the wood to make a thorough search. At first nothing seemed to be amiss, but in the early hours of the morning they were confronted by what appeared to be another alien craft: a floating, revolving pyramid, which throbbed with intense light and colour; they pursued it for some distance before it rocketed upwards and vanished into the night sky.

The accounts given by the various airmen who experienced these events are rendered even more believable by tape recordings of their radio exchanges, which were made at the time – though of poor quality, these are quite spooky (the men sound truly unnerved) – and by a report from the RAF radar base at nearby Neatishead, concerning a UFO tracked by their scanners.

Despite this, not everyone bought into the tale. Alternative explanations offered by skeptics have ranged from military personnel making errors thanks to having enjoyed their Christmas festivities too much, to foreign troops becoming disoriented in unfamiliar surroundings and mistaking the pulsing glow of the Orford Ness lighthouse, some five miles away, for unexplained lights in the forest. Others have argued that there are too many contradictions and confusions in the various witness accounts. However, UFO researchers take the Rendlesham Incident very seriously. Lt. Colonel Halt filed a detailed and convincing report with his superiors afterwards, which can't be dismissed easily, and though the Ministry of Defence insisted that national security was not endangered and that, as such, the matter was never officially investigated, there were later revelations that the MOD had built up a considerable file of evidence (that said, much of this was later made available to the public and was found to contain nothing new).

Regardless of the actual facts, many of which have now undoubtedly been confused with fantasy, the Rendlesham Incident, like the Roswell Incident in New Mexico, has taken on a life of its own. Enthusiasts regularly visit the area, their private investigations aided by a special 'UFO Trail' set out by the Forestry Commission.

DOUBLE SPACE
Gary Fry

It was the use of an errant double space that alerted Jim to what his wife got up to in his absence.

Jim had travelled to Suffolk by train, missing the manic crowds of London after setting off mid-morning. That was the luxury of being an independent writer, of course. Provided that publishers' deadlines were hit, you could work whenever you pleased and at your own pace. And with this latest contract – writing a history of printing in East Anglia – Jim had all the time he needed for a comfortable year.

If only *everything* in his life was so agreeable, however.

After checking into his hotel late afternoon, Jim dropped off his luggage – laptop, change of clothing, a trusted notepad and pen – and went downstairs to dine in the restaurant. He'd stay in this village near Ipswich for two nights and had arranged to visit a local printing company first thing tomorrow. This was part of a month-long period of research, gathering materials from interviews and observation. He loved his job; it was everything he'd ever wanted out of life.

Well, *almost* everything.

Jim received the email at about eight o'clock, after returning to his room after a few digestion-facilitating brandies. He and his wife were used to spending time apart, having done so many times during their twenty year marriage with few complications. More recently, however, Jim had sensed something awry in the trouble-free nuptial home. Since Meg had hit forty last year, she'd seemed . . . *uppity*, Jim thought the word might be. The usual recrimination-free trips he made around the country had become fraught with uncertainty. Meg was his typist, the person who made sense of his handwritten manuscripts. He relied on her a great deal, but not only professionally.

He logged onto the hotel's WiFi service using the password he'd been given at reception and received a number of emails from various sources: his financial advisor arranging an annual review appointment; his publisher confirming deposit of this quarter's royalties; a contact who'd identified some information about offset printing techniques in the late nineteenth century ... and here, finally, was the one he'd *wanted*: a missive from Meg, typically brief, and yet, like a poem, every word loaded with compressed meaning.

Hiya, have decided to take myself out to the cinema this evening – that new French movie. Perhaps we can speak on the phone tomorrow evening.
   Love, Meg.

Jim spent the next half-hour scrutinising every phrase. Even after washing and changing for sleep, he ran over in his mind the words his wife had used.
   ... have decided to take myself out ... that new French film ... Perhaps we can speak on the phone ...
   These turns of phrase were so uniquely Meg, they might be trademarked. He was intimately familiar with how she expressed herself, having lived with her all these years. There was no mistaking the casual, direct way in which she engaged with others ... with *him*.
   So why did he now feel as if something was wrong here?
   It wasn't just the fact that she'd used email to contact him. Meg had been a reluctant recruit to the modern world of electronic communication, preferring the more direct telephone or even handwritten letters. However, she'd recently begun dealing with technical aspects of his work in this way, finding computer-based word processing far more efficient. But given a choice, she'd much sooner speak or write in pen.
   And so she'd chosen to go to the cinema this evening – well, this was hardly unprecedented. Both she and Jim were movie fans, preferring the big screen treatment over anything a home DVD might offer. Often while away researching in some nondescript part of the country, Jim would also source a picture-house and see if he couldn't chance upon a rare classic or a foreign gem that might otherwise have escaped him.
   So Meg's absence this evening – the fact that she hadn't called on his mobile and had suggested speaking tomorrow instead – contained no grounds for suspicion. She might even have gone out with Brendan.
   Brendan and Jim went way back together, were fellow Oxford alumni. Both independently wealthy from inheritance, they'd always worked in the same field of publishing – experts in media and communications – but more recently Jim had powered ahead, getting a string of book deals and wider exposure. Not that he believed Brendan was envious. Indeed, the man – a bachelor – had been nothing less than gracious during his frequent visits to their

home. As a fellow resident of Maidstone, he sometimes took Meg out whenever Jim was away on business.

Nothing wrong with that at all. Why shouldn't mature adults function in that way? Besides, Jim had always suspected that the man had unpalatable sexual preferences. This was not something they'd ever discussed, but one day back in the nineties, Jim had found some decidedly risqué websites stored on his friend's PC. Brendan *always* used a computer. He loved them and had developed an idiosyncratic way of preparing his relatively minor manuscripts …

None of this was getting Jim anywhere. He had an early appointment in the morning and much to think about concerning his latest project. He should try and get some sleep. After glancing again at that email, he closed down the laptop, switched out his room's light and then descended into atypically bizarre dreams.

*

Large lettering, as tall as people, had appeared in his Maidstone home. These ran across the carpets, crisscrossing the ground floor and advancing up the staircase. Jim followed them, trying to deduce their meaning, but the words they formed were nonsense, with no spaces between to provide context … until he reached the master bedroom, where the letters led directly to the bed and abruptly ceased. Jim lifted his head. Although he saw the erratic, meaningless letters continue on the other side of the room, it wasn't these that claimed his attention. It was the two figures in the bed: his wife and Brendan lying side-by-side, like a *double space* between two sentences, and one Jim was now desperate to delete …

*

He awoke, sweating profusely. He'd rarely suffered nightmares in the past, though this last year had been burdened by nebulous concerns he was unable to define. He got up and entered the *en suite* bathroom, washing his face and examining himself in the mirror. His eyes were wrinkling, his hair greying. Then he recalled how his good friend Brendan had aged more gracefully, not unlike the ever-fair Meg

Jim returned to his laptop, booted up its hard drive, and examined that insidious email again.

Now he knew what troubled him about it – the use of a *double space* between its two statements:

Meg would *never* do that. Under his instruction, she'd become a rigorous stylist down the years. Even in a casual missive issued via a medium of communication she was unused to, Jim knew she'd adhere to this inviolable rule. It was a good habit. His wife would no sooner hit the space key twice between lines than she would misplace an apostrophe.

But Jim knew someone who *would* do this.

All Brendan's manuscripts were characterised by this annoying trait. Ever since university, he and Jim had exchanged works-in-progress, making comments on developing projects in a mutually beneficial way. More recently, Jim had been unable to commit to this process, but that was because of tight deadlines imposed by his mass market publisher. Surely Brendan realised he was still supported in spirit ...

After dressing while processing these dangerous thoughts, Jim made his way out of the hotel, skipped breakfast, and then began pacing along the village's high street to make his early appointment. His mobile phone weighed heavily in one pocket, but he focused instead on this part of Suffolk, its sweeping fields and rich vegetation. He'd always loved the county, second only to his native Kent. He had further trips planned in East Anglia over the next month.

This would be more time away from home, of course ... further opportunities for Meg and Brendan to ...

As Jim reached the premises of the printing company he'd come to research – JAMES MONTY, its sign read, and then: EST. 1786 – he removed his mobile phone and quickly dialled his home number.

His wife answered on the third or fourth ring. She sounded sleepy, as if the shrilling phone had just woken her. This at least implied that she'd slept in her own bed last night, but ... had she done so alone?

"Hi," he said, as brightly as he could manage. He didn't want her to suspect anything out of the norm. After all, he could easily be wrong about this, couldn't he?

"Oh ... hi," she replied, and if she sounded guarded, that might only be as she came round from deep sleep. "How are you?"

"Fine, thanks." He hesitated, but was then unable to resist pursuing his concerns. "I got your email. Did you have a good evening last night – at the cinema?"

"Er, yeah, it was fine. I ... I saw that new French movie, directed by Michel Paret. It was a ... searing indictment of institutional bureaucracy. Some great performances, too, particularly from the leads."

She sounded like a film review, and Jim pictured her memorising these details while reading a newspaper yesterday. But he must give her the benefit of the doubt; the only alternative was confrontation and that simply wasn't his style. Despite his profession and the role she'd always played in that, theirs had been a marriage of few words, with much held firmly under the surface.

"Great," he replied, but then imagined his wife dictating that message to Brendan from bed last night. The man was seated at the desktop PC they kept in the master bedroom, half-undressed, smiling as he typed and perhaps putting in that double space *deliberately*, as a subliminal clue to rebuke Jim for his independent success and to heighten the risk factor as he clicked Send, closed down the machine and finally turned to Meg …

The *bastards*, thought Jim, realising that his suspicions had to be true. He knew this in the same way he understood many things: with subconscious certainty, a hunch confirmed by subtle mind-games. Meg hadn't visited the cinema last night and Brendan had written that email to her dictation. That would also account for so many small perceptions Jim had suffered in the last year, things that had squirmed at the back of his mind, but which had taken no tangible form … until now.

His wife was having an affair and Brendan was the offender. Jim would bet his professional reputation on it.

After more small talk, during which he gave nothing away, Jim hung up and then did the only thing he knew how to do well: went back to work.

The proprietor of *James Monty* was an aged man with an infectiously dark smile and playful sense of humour. The business was a family affair, handed down across generations since its inauguration in the eighteenth century. The owner had many sterling stories and much information to relate, including intimate knowledge about old-fashioned printing devices. He even demonstrated a few in a display room reserved for visitors, presumably intended to impress upon clients *James Monty*'s heritage and quality.

When Jim noticed a plaque mounted on the wall, he thought about his wife's final words over the phone. She'd asked what time he'd be home tomorrow. And if that hadn't confirmed her guilt – she'd presumably ask Brendan to leave long before Jim's return – nothing else had. Jim had told her that, with a "strong following wind" (a favourite phrase of theirs), he hoped to be back by dinnertime, though in truth planned to reach Kent by lunch. That

110

was surely the only way he'd catch his wife and her duplicitous beau *in flagrante*. And just what he'd do about it, he was unable to fathom right now.

The owner of *James Monty* was telling Jim about the words inscribed on the wall-mounted plaque, a little of that dark humour heavy in his voice.

"It's supposed to be a curse. The idea was that if you added this phrase at the foot of any printed missive, its recipient would come to an unpleasant end."

Jim leaned forwards, looking more carefully at the words, which appeared to be written in Latin. Before he could assess the wisdom of the act, he produced the notepad and pen he'd been using to jot down key quotations from his interview today. Again he pictured Meg and Brendan in the throes of subversive passion … and then said to his companion, "Is it OK if I make a note of this alleged curse?"

"Provided you don't intend to use it for nefarious purposes."

The man was joking of course, his sinister humour failing to relent. But Jim ignored that and went about recording this fascinating piece of hokum. It would make a good entry in the book he'd been commissioned to write.

Later, after bidding goodbye to his host and straying back through the village for his hotel, Jim realised how unhappy he'd been made to feel today. He'd tried to combat the truth by working hard, the way he'd always done. He was a professional, whose inherited wealth and modest income had provided well for Meg, allowing them both to live to a decent standard. Okay, so there'd been few fireworks in their marriage, but that was simply the kind of people they were. Similarly, they'd chosen not to have children, focusing instead on aspects of life that bringing up a family would compromise: fine films, the opera, literary festivals and more. Their sex life had faded years ago, but there was more to a happy existence than *that* …

Wasn't there?

After hurrying to his hotel room, he opened his email server and readdressed that insidious message.

… take myself out … this evening … speak on the phone tomorrow evening …

These phrases burned in his mind, but not as much as that one item of punctuation, the treacherous *double space*.

His brain reeling, Jim stooped to the laptop and then deleted one of the two spaces. He recalled his dream overnight, the way his wife and Brendan, together in bed, had interrupted a meaningless string of letters scattered around his home. Removing one of the spaces – the one on the right – seemed to correspond with eliminating half of this illicit pair: the man, laid in Jim's place, his loathsome face awash with post-coital pleasure.

Then, after responding to the email with hurriedly typed words – "Tired today; think I may be coming down with something. Will soldier on and return as planned tomorrow … Jim" – he added the cursed Latin phrase he'd learned about earlier: discreetly, huddled in one corner, almost unseen.

*

The following morning, after a reassuringly dreamless sleep, Jim regretted his behaviour of the night before. This wasn't because he felt foolish about dabbling in such nonsense as curses, but because he'd tried to alleviate his anxieties in an irrational way. However, he knew he must confront his problem head on. He'd never been that kind of person, always fearful of physical friction, but on this occasion, the moral right was surely on his side.

After a solid breakfast, he packed his goods and headed for the railway station. East Anglian countryside drifted by, laden with age-old secrets. He considered the distant past and how even relatively modern towns like Ipswich, Chelmsford and Brentwood had attracted a fair amount of apocryphal, outré material … Upon reaching London, however, with its hissing underbelly of hurtling technology, such fanciful ideas fled Jim's mind, and he soon found himself dwelling not on curses but the very real evil of extramarital affairs. He was determined to catch his wife and oldest friend "at it", as coarse folk phrased the act these days.

His Maidstone home was in a secluded, leafy borough which rarely attracted trouble … well, not from outside close personal relationships, anyway. All the same, Jim had often wondered what furtive truths lurked behind closed doors in this neighbourhood. Once the taxi had stopped, he paid the driver and climbed out, about five doors down from his house. Then he marched swiftly for the property, pacing inside as if he was just another happily married man, back from a long day in an office.

But his life had never been anything like ordinary. His career often took him away from home, driven by a preoccupation with – if he was honest – interests hardly appealing to a sexually mature woman. Jim had sometimes wondered whether he'd concealed his interpersonal difficulties behind marketable obsessions, but it wasn't the right time to ponder this now. He had his wife to confront.

He found Meg in the lounge, her eyes glistening with tears she immediately tried to shield. Was this because she was genuinely upset or because of truths she wished to keep from her husband? Either way, he kept his distance, wary of forgiving her if she placed her slender warmth in his arms, something that always reminded him of what he simultaneously desired and had always been quietly afraid of.

"What … is it?" he asked, dropping his luggage to one side, hearing his treacherous laptop thump on the carpet.

"The p-police have visited," Meg replied, with a directness that made Jim feel as if the news was something she'd be unable to conceal even if she'd wanted to. "It's … it's Brendan. He's … he's …"

"Dead," said Jim, and felt his legs give a little at the knees, a weakness arising more from incipient middle-age than shock.

Five minutes later, cradling his wife on their couch, Jim heard the whole story. Apparently, an associate of their friend had found the man in his bedroom, tied up with cables and wires extracted from his home PC. The websites onscreen had revealed deviant interests, perhaps accounting for the way he'd died – in a shameful act of erotic asphyxiation.

"Were any other websites open on the computer?" Jim asked, once Meg had revealed all she clearly intended to.

"Others? What do you mean, Jim?"

His wife sounded defensive. Perhaps the police had asked similar questions, perhaps even ones about her whereabouts the last few evenings. If Brendan had accessed Meg's email account from his *own* computer the other evening, she must have been at his house at the time. Indeed, a woman didn't need to stay the whole night to enjoy whatever sordid fantasies she'd long been suppressing, and which had become problematic only after hitting forty recently.

Jim didn't think cross-examining his wife further would help; it might even make her as suspicious as the police surely were. If officers had found Brendan's PC logged into Meg's email server, this would explain their arrival here earlier. And if they'd also read Jim's intercepted message, they'd certainly want to speak to him next.

But what could he tell them? That he'd sent his friend of many decades an ancient curse from Suffolk? They'd laugh at him. It was absurd. And although he couldn't help associating his deletion of that double space with Brendan's death later the same evening, Jim could hardly take it seriously himself … Whatever had happened,

113

he must remember that he was the aggrieved person here, and that this would lend him courage as the police made their enquiries.

That night when he tried talking to Meg, she grew uncommunicative. Each of his questions, well-meaning on the surface, had been underscored by a humiliated sentiment. Later, as she slept with her back to him, Jim thought: *What did Brendan have that I don't? I'm the successful one, the one with book deals. Are you so shallow as to prioritise his surface charms over professional success? Did he do something for you I've never been aware of? Do I even know you at all?*

These and other thoughts haunted him like demons, like a slow-developing cancer. He didn't sleep well that night. He kept imagining Brendan, alone in his house and seated at his computer. The man had just used Meg's password to monitor her online communications. Jim supposed even illicit lovers got jealous. Then, to alleviate tension induced by solitude, he'd accessed websites too lurid to contemplate. Jim had seen similar images before, but some maternal voice of disapproval had dismissed them as puerile, corrosive, unwholesome … And then his fantasy had endorsed this view: the modern device had rebelled against its user, cables and wires performing acts on him he'd previously relied on Meg to fulfil. But it had gone too far this time; the sexual frisson engendered by risk had turned to stark horror. Jim's friend had died in his bedroom, the victim of an ancient curse woven into a new form of communication. The computer's cables and wires had squeezed all the life out of him.

*

The day after, Jim felt perky. He brought Meg breakfast in bed, despite knowing she wouldn't have an appetite. It was nonetheless enjoyable watching her force down the food; this removed some of the hurt he felt. His wife was also unable to ask why he looked so pleased after his closest friend had died in tragic circumstances.

Jim knew that Meg couldn't have been at her lover's house the day Brendan had received that cursed email. She was cunning, an unexpectedly convincing actress, but all the same, he thought it unlikely that she'd be able to feign ignorance after witnessing the terrible magic Jim had set in motion. Meg shuffled around the house for days, pretending that it was her husband who ought to be grieving, while surely fearing the police's next arrival. When detectives finally visited, they took Jim aside and asked a number of pertinent questions, after which Jim realised they had no record of the email he'd sent from East Anglia. This was, after all, in his wife's inbox, and not Brendan's; the dead man had simply had the misfortune to intercept it, as Jim had known he would.

And so the deed was over: neat, clean and without sequel. The funeral was a solemn affair, with more unknown women in attendance than Jim or Meg could account for. The husband smiled acerbically while his wife's face ran an irrepressible puce. Later, after getting home, Jim tried something he hadn't been keen to pursue for years. In their sullied bed, he attempted to make love to Meg … and this proved an unqualified success. He was even a little more forceful than usual, and his wife, it seemed, liked this.

And so their lives continued. Meg grew more dutiful in a number of ways, both professionally and domestically. She typed up manuscripts with dogged determination and carried out housework with subservient haste. A few weeks later, when Jim announced his departure on another research trip to East Anglia, his wife appeared bereft, as if she'd greatly suffer from a break in their newfound love and exciting nocturnal activities.

"With a strong following wind," he told her, enjoying every moment of his renaissance self, "I'll be back very soon."

Meg smiled, defeated deep down, yet now compellingly addicted to him.

*

At least there'd be no interference on this trip from cursed email. Since the death of their close friend, Meg had sworn off operating a PC. Jim had said nothing about this, endorsing her use of an electronic typewriter to prepare submissions for his publisher. He scoured every page she produced for double spaces, but never found one. All that had happened was unfortunate, but it nonetheless bore a poetic symmetry which appealed greatly to Jim's need for ordered chaos, for manipulative control.

Norfolk was magnificent, a rich tapestry of golden fields and turning windmills. He observed tractors cutting straight furrows through sheaves of upright corn. In Norwich, he admired the grand cathedral, the views from its elaborate windows resembling medieval paintings. He visited the Broads, skirting great lakes and fine rivers, each littered with yachts and boats. He was staying in an area between Wroxham and Horning, in a smart country cottage he'd rented for half-a-week. He'd interviewed many local people about the way printing had reached such isolated communities, acquiring much strong material for his forthcoming book.

Nevertheless, on the eve of returning home, something began to trouble him. He'd spoken to his wife on the phone the day before and she'd sounded trustworthy and devoted, eager to have him back. These were encouraging sentiments, but all the same, Jim felt unsettled. Even a few glasses of red wine in the late evening did little to calm him. Rain fell against the cottage's windows like heavy droplets of blood.

Or *ink*, he thought with disconcerting intuition, but quickly dismissed the thought. He ran a bath, and after stripping to render himself vulnerable, he believed for one treacherous moment that the waiting water was as black as liquid about to be deployed by some printing device … He dismissed this notion, too, and then soaked his body for an hour, until the wrinkles on his fingertips look like smudges from a newspaper.

He had to stop thinking this way and get a good night's sleep. After dressing in pyjamas, he slipped beneath the bed sheets, feeling hesitant about staining their crisp whiteness with his damp body: another foolish idea he suppressed at once. Then he switched out the light and plunged the room into an inky realm of nothingness.

His dreams when they came were nebulous and frightening, involving figures, hardly solid enough to succumb to gravity, drifting him towards him in liquid-like patterns … When he awoke with a start, Jim felt uncomfortable, disorganised. He washed in the bathroom, suffering no further fears about marring his skin with any ineradicable substance. After dressing, he returned to the lounge and saw his half-empty bottle harbouring only red wine, which could never be loaded into a pen for writing. He blamed consuming this for disturbing what should have been a pleasant evening and then gathered together his gear to head outside.

He got no further than the front door.

Astonishingly, today's post had already been delivered …Well, Jim *assumed* the letter on the floor had arrived this morning, despite the fact that it was caught under the property's doormat. He might have inadvertently kicked it there yesterday, after returning from conducting interviews in Great Yarmouth. At any rate, he stooped to retrieve the envelope and immediately tore it open.

It was from Meg. He identified her use of language immediately. And the letter proved to be a heartrending confession.

She'd handwritten it on a piece of paper he recognised, the same as those in his trusted notepads. He'd just begun another, having filled the previous one with notes he'd left with her to decode … But instead of that, she'd clearly set her mind to another task.

Meg revealed in the letter everything about her affair with Brendan, how a period of weakness, probably associated with the encroaching middle age, had led to her succumbing to the man's lascivious advances. He'd come on strong to her and she'd yielded, though she made no excuses for doing so. For about a year, she'd felt old and used up, but a number of tawdry, sometimes humiliating nights with Brendan (she went into few details) had reminded her of the value of personal security over the base pleasures of lust. She ended by saying that she was truly sorry and that she loved Jim greatly and hoped he'd forgive her.

Jim's first thought in response to this passionate, handwritten account was concerned with its pleasing lack of double spaces.

Nevertheless, now feeling more powerful than he ever had in his reticent life, he found himself admiring his wife's honesty. He understood why she'd sent the note here, while he was away on business and would have time to think over her words with no interference. He also respected her for not conveying her thoughts via an electronic device. Computers were inherently duplicitous, he reflected, their deletion keys allowing for manipulative artifice. A handwritten account, by contrast, implied spontaneous sincerity, invoking a previous era when life had been less crafty, and its communication not subject to so many nefarious concerns ... Meg had even used a page taken from one of Jim's old-fashioned notepads.

Jim turned over this sheet, wondering whether his wife had added anything on the other side.

And saw the *curse*.

It was inscribed in his own handwriting, of course; this was the same sheet he'd used to jot down the Latin phrase in Suffolk. His mind began racing. Could the curse be cast just once? If its powers were renewed, however, how would *he* be made to suffer? And did he really believe that his old friend Brendan had been killed by anything other than taking a sexually deviant game too far?

Jim opened the door and headed out, crumpling the page in one hand before dropping it behind him. He'd made the journey here by car because the Broads were not served well by railway networks. He climbed into the vehicle, triggered his wipers to clear the windscreen of mercifully clear-looking specks of liquid, and then started driving back the way he'd come days earlier.

If his wife's letter had been delivered yesterday and he'd only just discovered it, might this account for the weird visions he'd experienced in the last twenty-four hours? These images continued to dog him, twitching in the corners of his eyes, causing the lake along one side of the car to shimmer like a pool of darkest ink. Rain fell like black bullets lashing the trees all around, as if etching each trunk with indecipherable text. In his rear-view mirror, multi-coloured blotches of water wriggled down his back window, but this was surely just an effect of uncertain light this afternoon, setting words and phrases alive in Jim's uppity mind.

Then he saw the *figure* emerge from a hedge way behind him.

As an undergraduate at Oxford, he could recall taking an interest in all intellectual matters, even issues outside his chosen disciplines of history and literature. One subject that had fascinated him was psychology, especially material about perception and memory. He recalled a technique called the Rorschach test, which had involved ostensibly random patterns of ink presented on a page; these were supposed to summon material from the subconscious, releasing deeply repressed concerns.

And if that was true, what should Jim make of what he now saw lurching along the winding country lane in his wake?

It looked like nothing other than a mass of ink, collapsing and reforming, squirming and splashing. It was surely about the size of an average-sized human, and occasionally bore the form of such a figure, before separating anew, its limbs evaporating as if they were wet flames, the head shimmering like a pail of liquid after an aggressive shunt. If it left in the road a number of blotchy footsteps, these vanished too quickly for the accelerating Jim to observe … by now he was able to see nothing behind him other than the pursuing creature, as it grew larger and larger.

Soon it was near enough to touch his racing vehicle. Then it skittered around one side of the car, sticky hands – or whatever it used in lieu of such appendages – feeling along its flanks … the windows … and then the bonnet …

Jim, snatching his face forwards with terror and a need to steer along the winding road, saw on the windscreen a patch of glistening darkness bearing what resembled moist fingers. As the thing flexed against one wiper and then shuffled glutinously onto the glass, rain mixed with its blackish substance, the dilution causing it to sluice and spill. And when Jim reactivated his wipers, he saw this part of the creature whipped away, like a typographical error elided by some ruthless copyeditor. For one stupid moment, Jim experienced joy – he'd *beaten* the terrible, half-formed entity – but soon realised this was only half the story.

The rest of the figure reared up in his peripheral vision.

Clinging to the side of the car with what served as its remaining arm and a pair of dripping legs, the head and body now resembled ink scattered in a ferocious wind. The rapid speed of Jim's vehicle did much to challenge the creature, making the largest ragged hole in its sorry excuse for a face stretch and tear. Then what passed for its eyes opened wide, and Jim noticed that it looked like … his *oldest friend Brendan.*

But surely that was only the Rorschach factor, dredging material from Jim's brain like some pernicious demon.

All the same, he now thought he'd forgive his wife anything, would even apologise to the spirit this latest invocation of that wretched curse had summoned … He didn't feel powerful any more, just weak, humbled, guilty.

With a strong following wind, he heard Meg whisper in his mind, *you'll soon be home where you belong.*

Jim pressed his accelerator to the floor.

His friend Brendan had been undone by an electronically generated *double space*, and his punishment – asphyxiation by a computer's cables and wires – had reflected his modern predilections.

For Jim, however, the source of retribution, accidentally cast, was more old-fashioned … yet no less sentient and sinister.

The thing, still clinging to the side of his vehicle – little more than a mass of ink gathered together by dark magic to assume the shape of a person – was eventually snatched away and sent reeling against a patch of vegetation, which instantly turned as black as the symptoms of some withering disease.

Jim tried to put as much space as possible between himself and the horror he'd just encountered. With luck, he thought he might even make it out of East Anglia before the thing regrouped and came – sloshing and gurgling with insatiable rage – to close him down again … But when he glanced one last time into his rear-view mirror and saw the reformed *thing* still loping wetly along the otherwise deserted lane, he realised that his native Kent was but a remote possibility and that a drowning here, among the mysterious Broads, was eminently more likely. He only hoped that whoever found him could distinguish fresh water from printing fluid, however much this dark agent might be washed from his helpless corpse.

Then, distracted from driving, he lost control of his vehicle – it left the lane and hit a river.

He grew delirious, not knowing which way was which. As liquid began subsuming him, his only wish was for nature to do its worst before something infinitely more terrible set its viscous hands upon him.

THE DAGWORTH MYSTERY

A very curious story comes to us from the medieval chronicler, Ralph Coggleshall, who was writing between 1187 and 1224. It concerns a series of events at Dagworth Castle in central Suffolk, and though it sounds initially like a straightforward case of haunting, it soon evolves into something a lot stranger.

In the year 1210, Dagworth was held by the Norman warlord, Osbern of Bradwell. It was a thankless task governing such a region. Though the great age of the Saxon outlaws had passed, the fens stretching around Dagworth were still a trackless, boggy waste, where any wolf's head – whether his crime be murder or tax evasion – could find sanctuary. And the reign of King John (1199 to 1216), was a particularly fruitful one when it came to the creation of such felons. Impoverished by his older brother's adventures abroad, bad King John was constantly devising new money-making schemes, most of which amounted to little more than pillaging his hard-pressed peasantry. Vast numbers of ordinary, everyday folk were left destitute, and resorted to a Robin Hood-type existence, living in out-of-the-way places and disrespecting the law. The result was that wildernesses like the East Anglian fens once again became a dangerous place for men of authority. They also became a place where it suited many purposes to invent scary stories in order to keep people away.

It was Osbern of Bradwell's lot to be lord of such a realm. We know very little about him except that he was a land-owning knight, though he must have been strong and efficient to maintain his position in such a district. By all accounts, his castle – though nothing remains of it today – was substantial, though as we'll see, its mighty walls were not proof against the mysteries, real or otherwise, of the fen country.

According to Coggleshall, the first indication that there were problems at Dagworth came when the laughter of a female child was heard in different parts of the castle late at night. Osbern and his staff searched the stronghold high and low. There were children living on the estate, but all were accounted for, and the source of the disturbance, though initially thought to be 'knavery', was eventually deemed to be supernatural. The fen-folk had a reputation in those days for being more credulous than most, but the first to flee the castle were guests whom the invisible entity had teased while they were lying in bed. The servants, all locally-born, stayed on, though the probability is that they were bonded and thus not permitted to leave.

The ghost, if such it was, soon became even more vocal. It began to converse with the castle occupants, though still in the voice of a female child – and here there is a very interesting and unusual detail. When speaking with Osbern and his family, the entity used perfect Norman-French, but when speaking to the castle servants it used English and with a distinctive East Anglian drawl. Even more mystifying, when a priest was brought in to attempt an exorcism, it conversed with him in faultless Latin and even showed knowledge of the Holy Scriptures. The priest, who is not named, was unnerved by this for he felt it indicated a powerful intelligence, possibly something evil. However, the entity insisted that it was not evil. It added that it was not even a ghost – because it was not yet dead.

This was totally confusing. In medieval times ghosts were accepted, but were regarded as heralds from beyond; messengers who were seeking to prevent others making similar mistakes in life to their own. The idea that this entity was not dead or, if it was, that it was unaware of such, was something completely new.

Up until this point the entity had refuse to name itself, but under questioning by a young chamber-maid, it said that it was called 'Malekin'. It explained that, though it dwelled among the faerie folk, it had once been a human child. It claimed that it had been stolen by the faeries when very young, while its mother had been working in a hayfield. Now it sought only to return to the corporeal world and be reunited with its family, though its captors had said that this could not happen until seven more years had passed. Until that time, the entity merely wanted to play. Its pranks and giggles were tolerated for some time afterwards, and Coggleshall described how Malekin even made a physical appearance in front of the chamber-maid, resembling a beautiful child dressed all in white, though after this – abruptly and strangely – no further manifestations of any sort were reported. It was as if the entity had simply ceased to exist.

All this does sound a little too unlikely to be true. One can't help wondering if Coggleshall, in the inimitable manner of medieval chroniclers, was embroidering a fanciful tale, but there are precedents for this kind of thing in modern times. Readers may recall the perplexing case of the Enfield Poltergeist, when, in a house in London in the 1970s, a disembodied voice engaged not only the resident family in prolonged conversations, but also visitors and even news reporters while cameras and tape recorders were running.

It is certainly impossible to draw any conclusions from the few facts we know to be true, but the Dagworth story was believed widely across East Anglia, where the term 'Malekin' soon came to refer to any kind of faerie changeling. One thing that makes this creepy tale stand out from others of that era is that it is non-instructive. It is neither a parable nor a fable; there hasn't even been an attempt to interpret its meaning. It is simply a blow-by-blow account of a weird and unexplained event.

WICKEN FEN
Paul Finch

"It's not that me and Carly don't get on any more," Gerry said over his pint of Oakham's. "I mean, in *some* ways we don't get on ... not like we used to. Hell, I don't know. After you've been married twenty-five years you get bored with each other."

"Bored?" Trevor replied. "With Carly? Mate, she's what ... forty-five?"

"Forty-six."

"She's forty-six, and whenever she walks down the road, there are still blokes eyeballing her with their tongues hanging out."

"Yeah ... because she's got blonde hair, a pretty face and big tits."

"Whoa!" Trevor glanced over his shoulder.

They were in a waterside pub called *The Kingfisher*. It was the hot and muggy end to a blazing July day, and the place was crammed; not just out in the beer garden and along the balcony overlooking the broad, but here in the taproom as well, rustic voices and gruff laughter echoing beneath the gnarled, smoky roof-beams. Not that they knew anyone here. Trevor and Gerry were Dagenham lads, currently sixty miles from home and 'getting away from it all'. It didn't matter if anyone overheard, but Trevor was discomforted these days when Gerry got into his cups and started discussing his own wife in that free, irreverent way.

"I know she's a looker, mate," Gerry said, elbows rested on the bar as he drained his tankard. "What're you having, same again?"

Trevor nodded, finishing his pint of Carlsberg.

"Yeah, I know she's a looker. That's why I married her in the first place. But once you've been handling the goods as long as I have, it all gets a bit samey."

Trevor supposed that might be true, but it was a shame to think of Carly, who was also a friend of his, and a very good friend of his wife, Josie's, in such crude terms.

"Tell the truth, mate," Gerry added, as he ordered two more drinks. "I'm not missing them at all."

Them, Trevor thought, interested. Them – as in Carly *and* Josie. He knew that his pal meant nothing personal by that. But it was increasingly Gerry's way that, whenever discussing whatever marital problems he imagined he was undergoing, and there seemed to be more and more of them, he tended to refer to 'their wives' rather than 'his wife', as if it was naturally the case that all men, Trevor included, should be going through the same kinds of midlife crises.

"I feel more and more that they hold us back," Gerry added. "You know … get in the way."

"Get in the way of what?" Trevor asked, not wishing to play devil's advocate but fascinated to know. He then apologised as a massive guy, his plaid shirt rolled back on meaty forearms, thick flaxen whiskers framing a beery red face, jostled against him at the bar. The whiskered guy made no apology of his own, nor acknowledged Trevor's.

Gerry noticed the incident but was too busy with his own thoughts to comment. He sank another mouthful of Oakham's. "We love them to bits … but after two decades married life is so *staid*. Is that the correct word?"

Trevor, who was a teacher, nodded.

Gerry, who was a mechanic and ran his own body-shop, pondered further. "I mean, we've been together so long everything's just routine."

"Isn't that what life eventually becomes?"

"Maybe for you. I don't consider I'm past *my* sell-by date yet."

"What else would you rather be doing?"

"Well … that lot, to start with." Gerry nodded past Trevor's shoulder to a nearby corner. Trevor looked around, and saw two girls beside the darts board.

They had their backs turned, but made a cute summer picture: one blonde, one brunette, both manes hanging wild and untamed, both figures slender but shapely. The blonde wore a t-shirt, a short denim skirt and Roman sandals, an ensemble that showed her sun-browned limbs to perfection; the brunette was in a sporty vest and denim cut-offs, 'Daisy Dukes' as Trevor had heard them referred to. She wore flip-flops and an ankle-chain with bells and stars; her legs were so smooth and tan you could have glazed them with honey.

"You want to …" Trevor said uncertainly, "you want to tap off with two …"

"With two lovely bits of stuff," Gerry replied. "What's not to like, eh?"

"You serious?"

Gerry sighed. "I suppose not. We can look though, can't we? At least they-who-must-be-obeyed aren't here to stop us doing that."

Trevor stole another glance. There was no denying it; the two lasses, who from this angle looked to be in their early twenties, had an aura. The sun slanting through the nearby window framed them in a golden glow, dazzled in their hair. If he'd come out now with some kind of pious statement to the effect that he and Josie, who had also been married twenty-five years, were still deeply in love and perfectly happy and never had any ups and downs, he'd be lying. They too had their problems, but didn't all married couples who'd been together so long? Certainly nothing had ever occurred that had set them so far apart that they'd gone looking for someone else. If Trevor was honest, he had occasionally – usually when he'd had too much to drink – wondered what it might be like to be approached by some, how had Gerry put it, 'lovely bit of stuff' – but at forty-eight and on a teacher's salary, he knew that was never going to happen .

"They haven't got blokes with them, either," Gerry said, furtively, like a man about to embark on a secret mission. "I've been watching them all evening, and they've been stood over there in that corner on their own."

"They'll just be on holiday, like us?"

"Or on the pull."

"We can dream, I guess."

Gerry's attention had now *fixed* on the two girls, his eyes adopting a predatory gleam. He was chunky lad – more chunky than was good for him, as Carly would often say – but the flat-cropped bristles on top of his head, the well-groomed moustache and trim goatee beard were still black rather than grey. His age-old Motorhead t-shirt revealed gym-toned arms covered with fashionable tattoos. In his macho 'wild beast' sort of way, he probably wouldn't be quite as unfanciable to younger females as Trevor, who, though he wasn't grey either, had only a mouse-brown mop and was tall and lean, with wholesome 'Stan Laurel' features.

"I'll not be a minute," Gerry said, a change of tone suggesting the mission had commenced. He slid from his stool and lurched across the taproom, wiping the beer from his hands on the back of his over-large tennis shorts as he approached the door to the Gents.

Trevor hoped and prayed that he wasn't going in there to do something *really* stupid – like buy a packet of condoms. But he needn't have worried: no sooner had Gerry vanished from view than the two girls also made a move, drinking up and heading for the nearest exit, the brunette's flip-flops slapping against the soles of her naked feet.

Trevor watched them covertly. He still hadn't glimpsed their 'boat-races', as Gerry would refer to them, but he didn't doubt they'd both be beautiful and kittenish. They walked with a lithe, practised sway. He noticed that both had painted toenails; the blonde's crimson, the brunette's gold. They oozed sexiness and, if he was honest, availability. It was no surprise Gerry had been hooked. Trevor looked around, and was taken aback that the rest of the gathering – which was mostly men, a lot of them rugged outdoor types – weren't also drooling after the objects of desire. He edged to the window and stared down the grassy slope to the moorings, where various leisure craft bobbed and tilted on the sun-splashed waters. The two girls were headed towards an impressive-looking boat at the end of a short jetty: an old style twenty-footer, a river-cruiser type done in swish blue-and-white trim. He'd had them pegged for students, but was probably wrong given the quality of that vessel. That would have cost a pretty penny just to hire.

Gerry reappeared about three minutes after Trevor had idled back to his bar-stool. "Bloody hell, have you scared them off?"

Trevor sipped his beer. "Went of their own accord."

"And you didn't …"

"What? Try to stop them? No, I bloody didn't. Look, Gez …" Trevor assumed his common sense tone. "We've had a nice relaxed first day, we've had a few beers, we can have a few malts when we get back on the narrow-boat. It's going to be sunny tomorrow. We can do it all again. Why mess things up?"

Gerry still looked disappointed. He strode to the darts board window. Trevor joined him. There was no longer any sign of the girls. The river-cruiser was also absent. Gerry blew out a long, wistful breath. "Bloody stupid idea, I suppose. Ah well … saves a shed-load of embarrassment. Let's have another round, if nothing else."

Happy to accommodate this lesser vice, Trevor returned to the bar and ordered two more pints.

"You're still wrong about Carly, though," Gerry said, perching back on his stool. "Blonde and pretty, I'll give you that. But big tits? Once, maybe. These days, she takes her bra off at night …" He pulled an ugly face. "Spaniel's ears, mate."

*

The landscape was so flat that Trevor could see in every direction for miles – at least he would have been able to, had the heat-haze not imposed limitations of its own. The endless green of softly rippling reeds finally blended with a sky the colour of hammered steel. The sun reflected intensely from the brown waters undulating past.

The narrow-boat was travelling slowly but smoothly, the chugging of its engine little more than a gentle throb beneath Trevor's sneakered feet as he stood at the prow, shielding his eyes

126

to peer along the broad; though he knew they weren't actually called 'broads', not here in Cambridgeshire – that was over in Norfolk. He thought this stretch was what the locals referred to as a 'lode', a kind of manmade channel connecting the natural waterways that networked this part of the county.

Trevor and Josie holidayed regularly in the Med, but even down there he hadn't known heat like this. He'd stripped off to a pair of shorts, but the sun was soon chafing his shoulders. Even the insects that swarmed these marshes in summer were stilled. If there were water-fowl around, and there should be every kind here – from bitterns and grebes to the rare black-tailed godwit – they were roosting among the sedge and bulrushes. There was no sound – none at all; it was almost eerie.

The ideal moment for him to sight what looked like a floating body.

In that disbelieving way familiar to folk throughout history who'd discovered corpses, he initially thought he was mistaken and then *hoped* that he was. Maybe it was just a sack of rubbish happening to resemble a torso and four limbs? Maybe it was a department store mannequin? But no – it was a body, male by the size of it, bobbing face-down. Trevor glimpsed what looked like a red t-shirt and a naked lower half. It was stationary in the water, but would pass them by a few feet to starboard.

"Gez!" he shouted over his shoulder. But Gerry was aft; he wouldn't be able to hear from so far back. Fortunately Trevor already had a pole to hand, with a hook on the end. He reached down, caught the corpse by its collar and lugged it towards him. It was heavy and awkward, perhaps snared on something underneath. He imagined thick bundles of weeds billowing up from the depths like ocean kelp, so platted and tangled together they were almost human in their outline: a central trunk swaying from side to side; even a head, a mass of green, spongy putrescence – possibly the upper portion of a log entrapped after decades, tresses of fronds coiling around it. And then the arms – more lengthy tangles of cable-thick weed, weaving back and forth as they reached up through the murk, not with ten fingers but hundreds: myriad mottled tendrils snaking towards the flickering sunlight.

When the body suddenly came loose, it turned over with such natural motion that Trevor thought the man might still be alive. But then he saw that where there'd once been a face there was now a jagged crimson cavity. The same was true of the chest. The guy had been hollowed out, gutted, reduced to a grisly shell by parasitic devils that had simply burrowed their way into him, voracious

127

aquatic monstrosities, their needle teeth rending and slashing, their spiny claws digging, tearing …

Trevor shot up from his bunk so quickly that even though the ceiling was several feet above him, he almost clouted his head. He sat there in the darkness, panting, the thin sheets plastered to his sweat-slick skin.

It was pitch-black. Beyond the partition wall, Gerry snored noisily.

Shaking, Trevor clambered from the bunk and fumbled out of his cabin into the connecting passage. Though he wore only a pair of underpants, he made his way aft, unbolting the doors and climbing up onto the rear deck.

An awesome silence lay across the benighted fens. The occasional *slosh* disturbed it as wavelets slapped on the hull, but that was all. There was no moon, so nothing was visible – but he could sense it, that vast waterlogged wilderness stretching out on all sides. The air was warm and damp, rank with wetland odours.

Then he heard the cry.

It came from far away – a huge distance across the sodden wastes, but it sounded distinctly female. Trevor listened out. It hadn't seemed like someone in trouble; there'd been no pain or alarm there. It was as though the woman, whoever she was, had been calling someone's name. Was it his imagination that the name had sounded like 'Trevor'?

That was ridiculous. He must still be half-asleep.

They were no longer moored beside *The Kingfisher*. After they'd left the pub, they'd opted to press on a little way, but the dusk had soon dissipated to darkness and they'd had no option but to rope themselves to one of the many stone quays located along the tussocky embankments. He didn't think they were *officially* in the fens as yet – more likely they were still on one of the River Cam's many sidings, but it was much of a muchness in this part of the world; to an outsider like Trevor, the distinctions seemed trivial. That voice though – okay, he was tired, not to say a little shaken by the nightmare, but he was certain he hadn't dreamed it. Before he knew what he was doing, he'd gone back down into the narrow-boat's belly and re-emerged topside, this time with mobile in hand. It had just enough juice left in it for a single call.

"Hello?" came Josie's voice, heavy with sleep.

"Hi, it's me. Everything okay?"

"Erm … yeah. Why are you … Trevor, why are you calling at this hour?"

"Sorry, I just wanted to check you were … you know, that you'd had a good time."

"I've had an excellent time." She sounded puzzled, and not a little vexed. "It'd be perfect if I could get a good night's sleep to round it off."

"Yeah, sorry ... I didn't realise what time it was. Erm, where are you?"

"Where do you think? Home."

He wasn't sure what he'd expected to hear in the background – rippling waterways, fen-fowl making night calls? None of that would have made any difference now. Just the sound of Josie's voice reassured him that she was exactly where she said she was. But it felt awkward to suddenly ring off after he'd woken her up. "You and Carly were going out, weren't you?"

"To watch *The Woman In Black*. And now I'm back. Obviously I'm back ... Trevor, it's two in the morning. Are you drunk or something?"

Trevor had never noticed before how sensual Josie's voice sounded when she was sleepy. She didn't compare much to Carly when it came to full-on glamour, but she was still an attractive girl; in good physical shape thanks to a strict diet and exercise regime, and with her dark brown hair, hazel eyes, delicate cheekbones and that pert, dimpled chin, she'd always been handsome.

"No," he said. "Well, yeah. But not *that* drunk. Just wanted to hear your voice, that's all." It sounded lame even though it was completely true.

"Sweet of you. But perhaps we can save it 'til tomorrow?"

"I thought you were going out again tomorrow."

"We are ... *Shrek* in the afternoon and *Wicked* in the evening. But that still gives you a few windows of opportunity."

"Suppose so, yeah."

"Okay. Speak to you tomorrow. You sure everything's all right?"

"Everything's fine. Love you." Trevor probably hadn't voiced those words with quite so much feeling for a considerable time.

"You too," Josie replied, sounding less sure. And she hung up.

The darkness snuggled around the narrow-boat as it rode the lapping waters. They still weren't on the fens, Trevor reminded himself as he watched the lights wink out on his mobile. But the sense of isolation in this place was tangible. Sixty miles from home – that was all; yet he'd have given a lot to be back there now.

*

Trevor didn't call Josie the next day. There didn't seem to be much point once the sun had risen and chased away the nighttime fantasies. In any case, his phone was dead. Gerry, who'd begun quaffing tins of beer as soon as they'd got underway again – around ten-thirty that morning – shrugged and said that he deliberately hadn't brought his own mobile. They were supposed to be on holiday; he didn't want bothering by "one of those monkeys back at the shop".

Of course they weren't really on holiday. Not in the true sense of the word. This was a weekend jaunt between Ely and Cambridge, taking in the fen country. It would be short and sweet, and the only reason they'd been allowed to do it was so that Josie and Carly could catch up on their West End shows. As a group, the two couples did almost everything together, but the men drew the line at theatre land, so this was an opportunity the women couldn't miss. Despite all this, Trevor still felt their wives would have enjoyed the narrow-boat, a cheerfully painted blue-and-pink affair called *The Sunny Dawn*. It was the last word in river-going comfort. Not only did it have a well-stocked galley kitchen, wherein he'd cooked an excellent bacon and eggs that morning (even if he did say so himself), its salon was roomy and well furnished and its cabins small but luxurious. In the event of problems, it had lifejackets on board, and an 'emergency kit' which appeared to have thought of everything: a compass, first-aid items, water purification tablets, stay-light matches, candles, a solar blanket and even a flare-pistol with three flare shells.

But it was the sedate pace at which the vessel moved that was its most appealing feature, especially on a scorching day like today.

"These are beautiful," Gerry said, "filching another beer from the cooler at his feet. "Ice-cold, I'll tell you." They were out on the rear deck, Gerry leaning lazily on the tiller.

"You want to go easy on those," Trevor replied, poring over the map. "According to this, we've got a couple of locks to get through yet."

Gerry shrugged, at peace with the notion, basking amid the scenery. Once again an expanse of gently swaying reeds rolled to every horizon; only a lone stand of trees, the odd barn roof, the occasional boardwalk breaking its lush uniformity. Unlike Trevor, Gerry had vaguely green credentials. In his youth he'd been a biker – not some hard-ass Hell's Angel, but he'd ridden a hog, worn tasselled leathers and listened to metal. He'd also, or so he said, camped out a lot and smoked a ton of weed. That didn't perhaps qualify him as a paid-up tree-hugger, but it meant he was closer to nature than Trevor, whose teen years had been firmly suburban and middle-class. Alternatively, Gerry's tranquil mood might just mean that he was already drunk again. He too had stripped down to his shorts, and the hot sun was visibly reddening his big, hairy body, not to mention his face. It seemed highly unlikely he'd bothered to put any lotion on, but Trevor wasn't going to say anything – he was Gerry's mate, not his mother.

As it happened, they only had one lock-gate to negotiate, and this they managed with ease. Beyond that they were into the fens proper; in fact, according to Trevor's map, they were now on the legendary Wicken Fen, one of the largest and most picturesque in the whole of the UK – though the only initial difference this seemed to make was that suddenly there was less water traffic to be avoided. They hadn't seen a great deal the day before – surprising, given the time of year – but now it was astonishingly quiet; even the *whooping* and *whippering* of the fen-fowl, of which there'd been a preponderance at sunrise, seemed muted.

"This is as good as it gets," Gerry said, eyes closed.

"Telling me," Trevor replied. It was now mid-afternoon: on all sides lay a golden haze. The water rippled quietly past. The sun-burnished foliage was so still it resembled painted back-drops on a studio set. Occasional clusters of trees crowded onto the banks, paths winding away through them into green shadow. The sedate pace, the soothing motion of the craft, the heat soaking through them – and of course the beer – were combining to lull both men to sleep.

"Bloody hell!" Trevor suddenly said, eyes snapping open. "Hey, wake up, Dufus ... you're the helmsman!"

Gerry snapped out of it as well. They were still mid-channel, chugging along in a safely straight line. Ducks skimmed by overhead, quacking.

They laughed, and cracked open more tins. "Where are we, anyway?" Gerry asked.

"Dunno." Trevor consulted the map again, but was enjoying the peace and ancientness of this place so much that it scarcely mattered. "How many turns have we made?"

Gerry shrugged. "Doesn't matter, does it? Probably come to another pub soon."

Trevor pursed his lips. "Not according to this. Look out for a windmill."

"A windmill?"

"Yeah. When we see that, we'll know where we are. There are as many hiking trails through Wicken Fen as there are waterways – we can't get lost for long."

Gerry pivoted round in his seat to scan the table-flat georama. "If it's anywhere in four or five miles we should be able to see it from here."

131

But no man-made structures came in sight. Even the occasional barns appeared to have vanished. Trevor put the map down and climbed onto the roof, to get a better view. They rounded another bend. Beyond it lay a kind of crossroads, channels leading off in various directions.

They each spotted the girls at the same time.

A small, grassy headland protruded from the left, and two shapely golden bodies were laid out on it. There was no doubt it was the same pair from *The Kingfisher*, even though they were face-down on blankets, their perfect peachy bottoms offered bare for the sun's kisses.

"Fuuuck me!" Gerry said slowly.

Even Trevor was briefly entranced; he stumbled down from the roof.

"Hey!" Gerry shouted. "Hey, girls!"

One of them, the blonde, glanced around from under her tumbling, tawny locks. She gave them a lazy wave as they cruised past.

"Get some clothes on, you saucy mares!" he laughed.

She made some comment to her friend, and a tinkle of laughter was heard.

"Fuck me," Gerry said again, as the channel curved and the heavenly forms passed from sight. "Stop this thing, I want to get off."

"If only we could," Trevor said, blowing fresh foam from a newly-opened tin, and he half-meant it. It had been a captivating sight, there was no point pretending otherwise.

"At least help me turn the bugger round!" Gerry leaned hard on the tiller. "Come on, Trev, this is the chance of a lifetime ..." The craft veered dangerously to the left.

"Gez ... what're you doing?"

"They're offering it, mate. You saw that as well as me. They want some company."

"Look, watch it, eh! You're going to run us aground!"

"Cut the engine or something."

"Gez, we can't just stop. This is a canal boat ... we need a proper mooring-point."

"Fucking bollocks!"

Trevor's good humour sagged as he saw how serious about this Gerry was; the big galoot straightened the craft up again, but gazed backward along the lode, crestfallen as the prize fell further and further behind. "At least let's find some open space ... we can pull a three-point turn."

"And like I say," Trevor replied tartly, "that'll run us aground."

Gerry rounded on him. "Anyone'd think you don't *want* to do this!"

"*I don't!* For Christ's sake, Gez, what about Carly and Josie?"

At first Gerry couldn't reply; he seemed to be struggling with some inner doubt. "A bit of harmless fun never hurt anyone," he finally said – he didn't look as if he believed that himself, but then he became excited and pointed left. "*There! Look!*"

A low section of brick embankment had emerged through the grass and sedge: maybe fifty yards in length, with occasional steel rings set into it.

"How convenient," Trevor said under his breath.

Gerry steered them shoreward eagerly. The quay was overhung by a canopy of willows. Behind those stood shadowy ranks of rowan and beech, gnats swarming in the sunlight shafting between them. They'd already followed the channel round in a near semi-circle, so, by Trevor's reckoning, the two girls were somewhere on the other side of the small wood – maybe fifty or so yards away, due southeast. Yet something about this place – and he couldn't quite pin it down – seemed wrong. The profusion of pondweed and marsh lilies, which he suddenly noticed half-choking this section of waterway, suggested that it wasn't used very often.

He scrutinised the map. "You know, Gez, there are no moorings at this point." Something scraped their underside as they approached the quay. He glanced again into the water. Thick reeds were trailing alongside the hull. "There aren't even any turns or side-channels, according to this map. That means we aren't on a public waterway and we shouldn't be here – probably because it isn't safe."

Gerry ignored him. He turned the key in the ignition, cutting the engine, and jumped ashore with the fore rope in hand. "Are you going to help, or what?"

Reluctantly, Trevor followed him onto the quay, taking charge of the central rope. "You realise this is, like ... the worst plan ever. We came out here to relax, sail from pub to pub, have a few beers ... not get into mischief."

"Listen to you," Gerry chuckled as he walked past. "*Mischief?*"

"What's wrong with just taking a boat ride?"

"It's a drag, that's what's wrong with it."

"It was *your* idea coming out here."

"That was before we got a better offer," Gerry said, tying them up at the rear as well.

"We haven't had an offer," Trevor protested. "Why would girls like that fancy us?"

"Dunno." Satisfied the craft was secure, Gerry climbed back on board, promptly reappearing with a fresh white t-shirt and a six-

133

pack of beer from the cooler. "Let's ask 'em." He made to waltz off through the wood, but Trevor grabbed his wrist.

"Gez, wait a minute … hey, just wait. Think about Carly."

"Do I have to?"

"Christ, mate … this isn't funny!"

"Neither is getting old and what was that word, *staid*." Gerry grabbed Trevor's wrist in return; his grip was tense and damp with sweat. "Look Trev, it's just a laugh, okay. And that's what we're out here for, isn't it? To have some fun, some R and R … nothing heavy, no strings. What Carly and Josie don't know about will never hurt them."

He grinned feverishly as he said all this – as if it was exclusively about gratification, as if there was no moral issue at all. Trevor, who'd assumed all the lusty talk in *The Kingfisher* had been just that, talk, was genuinely amazed. Gerry might be the more bohemian of the two of them, he might be the one with the slightly more chequered past, but he was still a respectable married man these days, who ran his own business. Okay, he liked a few bevies, he told blue jokes and had a stash of sleazy porn on his hard-drive, but that didn't make him unusual. He'd never done anything as reckless and, frankly, ridiculous as this before. Of course, it wasn't as if there hadn't been signs that something like this might have been on the way.

"Mate … you've got to get a rein on this," Trevor said slowly. "I mean seriously, you've got to grow up."

Gerry's impish grin faded. "And you've got to get yourself a new pair of slippers and a cardigan."

Trevor shook his head. "Okay … fine, I'm boring, I'm unadventurous. But I'm also happily married and I don't want to jeopardize it all for two marsh floozies."

"Marsh floozies?" Gerry chuckled again. He was still trying to make light of what he was doing here, most likely because somewhere inside he was feeling a little guilty. "You make 'em sound like flowers."

"Yeah … well go and pluck them!" Trevor stepped backward. "But you're on your own."

Gerry shrugged. "Suits me." He turned and headed for the trees, stopping once to look back, his expression determinedly unconcerned. "I'd say don't wait up for me, but I suppose you've no choice."

"Hah! Don't count on that."

Gerry muttered something under his breath and continued into the wood, pulling on his t-shirt after first using it to waft at the gnats. Trevor wondered if he knew how ludicrous he looked in

134

those tennis shorts, his big frame sagging down over the waistband. For all his tattoos and his gym work, Gerry was a still a middle-aged man with short, fat legs and an overly burly torso. He walked in the clumsy, plodding fashion of an ape pretending to be human. Those two nymphs would struggle not to laugh when he sat down and introduced himself.

"Hi, I'm Gerry Axewood from London. This is my mate, Trevor English ... oh, he's not here. Well, never mind, he'll show his face when he stops being shy. So how do you like my beer-belly? ..."

But in actual fact, none of this was very amusing. Trevor stood alone, perplexed at how quickly it had all happened. He gazed past the narrow-boat and across the water. Late afternoon sunlight flooded the dykes and reed-beds. The sky was still powder-blue, but the trees to his rear cast ever-longer shadows, reminding him that the day was waning. He didn't know how long he was expected to wait here, but they couldn't dally indefinitely. The boat-trip only covered thirty-eight miles and was scheduled to last three days and two nights. As such, there was plenty of leeway for them to proceed at their own pace, but they were still expected to book the boat in at the marina on the final day.

He wandered aimlessly along the bank, kicking through patches of bogbean and marsh marigolds, increasingly frustrated with himself that he hadn't been tougher – that he hadn't refused point-blank to stop here, that he hadn't insisted they keep moving. The more he thought about it, the more it struck him that it wasn't just a moral issue. They had to find their way through Wicken Fen before they could resume the trip. It covered at least two-thousand acres, and they didn't even know whereabouts on it they currently were. That said – he glanced at his watch. It wasn't yet six o'clock and wouldn't be getting dark for another two hours. He supposed there was no need to panic just yet.

He descended through a muddy hollow and rounded the exposed roots of an ancient, twisted willow, the multiple fingers of which trailed far out into the water, finally entering a narrow inlet – where he halted. At the opposite end of the inlet was the blue and white river-cruiser he'd seen at *The Kingfisher*. It wasn't moored or anchored – it appeared to be banked up amid a jungle of marsh-fern. Trevor peered at it, wondering what it was about the craft that now seemed odd. He advanced along the water-line, the ground squelching beneath his sneakers. The boat was tilted steeply to aft and starboard, as though it had run ashore. Had the two girls had some kind of accident? Only when he was very close did he realise that if they had, it could not have been in the recent past.

The boat was a derelict: rusted all over and crabbed with moss, its hull bashed and scraped, in some parts fissured clean through. Its upper woodwork had mildewed and rotted; all paint had flaked away. The glass panelling around the cockpit was grimy and broken. Marsh vegetation inundated the interior. And yet Trevor knew that this was the same boat he had seen at *The Kingfisher*. He didn't think it was; he *knew* it. Somehow or other this decayed relic, this gutted shell …

At once, the surrounding wetland seemed strangely still. All bird and insect life had hushed, as though anticipating an imminent dramatic event.

Trevor began to retreat, his eyes still rivetted on the wreck. At twenty yards, he turned and walked swiftly back the way he had come, his sweat-damp hair prickling. He didn't know what this meant, if it meant anything at all. He tried to tell himself he was mistaken, but again he *knew* that wasn't the case. Some coincidences were just too great. When he reached *The Sunny Dawn*, his heart sank to find that Gerry was not already there, even though he hadn't really expected him to be. Several minutes passed as Trevor gazed into the wood. Bright sunlight still speared through it, now latticed with early-evening shadows. There was no movement in there.

Eventually, reluctantly, he strode forward. He imagined Gerry on the other side, settled down on the small headland with the two girls – they must have welcomed him by now, else even as proud a guy as Gerry would have returned with tail between legs. Trevor pictured the scene: Gerry, all fat and sunburned, grinning like the cat who'd got the cream as the two minxes, shamelessly naked, shared their wine and cheese with him.

"If only Carly could see me now?" he'd say, trying to play down his Cockney accent. "Carly? … she's my wife. Yes, merely my wife …" He'd laugh. "That's so correct, *merely* my wife."

Carly and Josie were merely their wives, Trevor thought, baffled by the imagined conversation. Mere wives, that was all.

Mere-wives.

Had he heard that curious phrase before? He didn't know, but it sent a shudder through him. The trunks ahead opened, and he saw thick ranks of sedge, though a path looked to have been beaten through these, beyond which the waterway sparkled. This had to be the headland. It was strange; he'd have thought to hear their conversation by now – their *real* conversation. But there was no sound of voices.

He emerged into sunlight, proceeding warily. The sedge was dense, at this time of year chest-high and emerald green, filled with the radiant purples and yellows of orchid, iris and marsh pea. Crickets and swallowtails darted back and forth through it. But Trevor saw none of this. When he stepped out onto the open headland, he was tense, nervous. He truthfully did not know what to expect, but even catching Gerry in the act of having sex with the two girls would have been a relief.

There was nobody there. Nobody at all.

He ambled forward, bewildered.

The headland, if such a word applied – it was really little more than a spur of dry ground in the waterway's elbow – was about twenty feet by thirty, the size of the average suburban lawn, and was strewn with old rushes, which had dried out and been flattened as if someone had indeed been lying on them. He glanced around – and spotted Gerry's six-pack of beer, or at least the six tins, all lying separate from each other, none of them opened.

A splash caught his attention. He glanced at the waterway: large, concentric ripples spread across the otherwise motionless surface. A frog possibly? An otter? There'd be nothing unusual about that. But now Trevor noticed something else: a timber post, leaning sideways but jutting upward from the water at roughly mid-channel, splintered and jagged at its tip, with a rusty chain wound around it. The remnant of an old sign or tethering-pole, he surmised; a mile-marker or something. Either way, it clearly represented a dangerous obstruction, and yet they had sailed blithely past it. Now that he looked more carefully, he spied other potential hazards: an angled edge of rusted metal some three feet from shore. About the same distance from the opposing bank, the spiky branches of a lighting-struck bough protruding through the weed-choked surface.

How had they managed to navigate through all that unscathed? The luck of the drunken sailor? More to the point, this stretch of water was evidently not safe for recreational boating, so how had they blundered into it in the first place? Surely, in a well-managed nature reserve like this, all side-channels deemed unsafe would have been blocked off? In fact, Trevor knew that they were. He'd seen buoys floating at waterway entrances, chain-linked fences looping across them.

Such preventative fixtures could easily be removed, of course.

Another splash drew his interest to the far shore, where he fancied there was a brief flurry among the reeds, as if something had scuttled out of the water and gone quickly to ground. He stared hard, trying to penetrate the lush tangle with his eyes alone and having no success – but now feeling certain that another pair of eyes was staring back at him.

137

The obvious thing to do was call over there, to see if it was Gerry.

But Trevor did no such thing. Instead, he backed away. The sun was still some distance from setting, but it was now far behind him and the trees' lengthening shadows had reached the headland. The channel lay motionless again, pitch-dark.

He turned and headed back along the path. He'd wait on the narrow-boat. Lock himself in, if necessary – though why he felt the need for that, he couldn't really say. He was half way through the sedge when he heard a loud splashing somewhere behind. That started him running. A voice in his head asked if he shouldn't go back there, find out if it was Gerry; ask him what he was playing at. But another voice, a slightly crazier one, told him that he already knew where Gerry was – that he'd already seen him. Gerry had been wearing a white t-shirt that day, but it would be a different colour now.

Inside the wood, it was darker and cooler than earlier. Gnats and midges still flitted back and forth. He slapped at them as he stumbled along, sweat stinging his brow and eyes. He had a suspicion that someone was following him, but glanced back and saw no-one: just dark trunks and the odd beam of sunlight. He wondered with mild panic how long it would take him to untie the narrow-boat.

But why untie? Wasn't he going to be waiting for Gerry?

He didn't bother answering the question as *The Sunny Dawn* came into view.

His hands were greasy and shaking, and he fumbled as he tried to untie the aft rope.

"Shit!" he hissed, acutely aware of the silent woodland to his back. But this was bloody ridiculous. He didn't really know why he was doing it – the rope came loose and he lurched along the quay to the middle one – the last thing he wanted was to leave his best friend alone out here. But then it wouldn't be *so* outrageous. The fens weren't a total wilderness; they were dotted all over with visitor centres, ranger stations, bird-watcher hides. It wouldn't be difficult to get help and advice. People must get lost out here on their own all the time, especially in the dark. Surely there'd be protocols for such eventualities? And of course Gerry wasn't really out here on his own, was he – though that thought was no consolation.

The middle rope had been knotted tightly around its steel ring. Again, Trevor had difficulty working it loose. Again, he swore under his breath. Those two girls, whoever they were – how peculiar was it that neither he nor Gerry had so much as glimpsed their faces? It now seemed very intentional how, in the pub yesterday, the girls had been standing with their backs so firmly turned. He glanced up and over his shoulder.

Had a twig snapped in the wood? Had a leaf dropped?

All Trevor saw were the dim pillars of the trees and the even dimmer dells in between. Only faint remnants of reddish sunlight were visible back there.

He hurried along to the third rope, this one about six yards forward of the craft. His urgency to get away from here was becoming all-consuming. How had they finished up in this remote spot? Wicken Fen was not gigantic. Yet he pondered the blissful hours of idle, drunken boating. How far from civilisation had they somehow managed to travel? There was another sound behind him – and this one was real, not imaginary: a rustling of foliage. Trevor loosened the third rope, and pushed the boat away from the brick embankment, jumping across the narrow gap and alighting on its forward deck. Only then did he glance back, but if he saw anything, it was deep, deep in the wood, and it could only have been a heavy wad of undergrowth moving slightly in a breeze which for some reason he couldn't feel.

As he blundered through the salon and the galley, another thought came to mind. Suppose Gerry had got back here ahead of him? Suppose he was in bed right now with one of his conquests, or maybe both?

And they'd been in such a rush to get it on that he'd left his beers behind?

Trevor didn't think so. It was a near-comical image, like something from a 'Carry On' movie: middle-aged Gerry skipping through the woods, an eager dolly-bird on either arm. He didn't even bother to glance into the empty cabins as he made his way aft to the ignition-drive. The vessel was already drifting into mid-stream. He could feel it swaying. He also heard a scratching sound – as if something was bouncing along the underside of the hull. Tufts of pondweed, he thought; more loose branches. And then, as he climbed out onto the rear deck and turned the ignition key, he remembered the larger obstacles with which this stretch of waterway was cluttered. The scratching beneath his feet intensified; became a shrill squeal of twisting timber and tearing fibreglass, which seemed to run the entire length of the craft. *The Sunny Dawn* had lurched forward slightly when the engine churned to life, but still wasn't moving with any real velocity. Nevertheless, she now jerked to a halt, and Trevor was propelled violently down through the rear doors into the passage, catching his right temple on the steel lock en route.

The glancing impact was like a hammer-blow.

He wasn't exactly knocked unconscious, but for the next few moments was slumped on his hands and knees, dazed, trying to blink a hot stickiness from his right eye, and hallucinating that the floor was slowly tilting beneath him – though very soon it became apparent that this was no hallucination.

The floor angled upward so much that Trevor found himself sliding forward on the palms of his hands, and then tumbling, falling head-over-heels down the passage, past the cabins and into the galley, where he plunged face-first into the brackish water already swamping the cramped interior.

Spluttering and gagging, he re-surfaced and tottered to his feet. It was only thigh-deep, but it stank foully – not, as he'd expected, of mud and rotted verdure; but of petrol.

This revelation was shocking enough, but it was the craft tilting even further, listing sharply downward at the front, that had Trevor staggering again. The dark water continued to gurgle up around him, even as he struggled to balance. It was already at waist-depth, the light through the dusty portholes showing oily colours streaked in shifting patterns across its surface. Whatever object had torn through the hull had pierced the fuel-tanks. The stench was thickening, making it difficult to breathe. Trevor groped groggily around, wondering how he had made such an error, what this would cost – the enormity of his peril still not striking him.

"Gotta … gotta get out," he finally realised, the fumes dizzying his senses. Yes, getting out was all that mattered. If he could manage that, he was safe. He could make it to shore easily enough; he was a strong swimmer. But then he'd be out on the fens alone with darkness falling, wet and injured.

"The emergency kit!" he said aloud. It was here, in the galley – somewhere.

He plunged back beneath the acrid surface, opening one foot-locker after another, pulling out crockery and other useless junk – only to remember that the kit was actually in one of the higher storage units. Which meant it would still be dry. He gasped as he resurfaced, reaching up to the ceiling rack and immediately finding what he sought: a green zip-lock bag. He dragged it down, clutching it in both arms.

The water was still only waist-deep; whatever had holed the craft from beneath had now pinioned it in place – it wasn't sinking any further, so time was on his side. He still had to fight his way up the slanted galley, no easy task with its carpet tiles coated in pond-slime. But he made it. In front of him lay the cabin passage; that section of the boat was dry but tilted so precariously that he had to scramble all the harder. Directly ahead, faded sunlight filtering down the rear stair filled him with hope.

Only as he reached it, did a shadow block out the orange glow. Trevor looked up, mouth agape. His blood-streaked face blanched with shock.

The female form coming down the stair was an hourglass silhouette on the setting sun. He glimpsed shimmering brown tresses, droplets of water gleaming on the most beautiful body he had ever seen – perfectly shaped and curved, bronzed by more suns than any human had a right to experience.

His rubber soles gave way beneath him as he retreated, and he slid back down the passage, grabbing out with his right hand but unable to stop himself floundering backward into the flooded galley, where the air was now almost unbreathable.

He coughed and retched, plunging again to his midriff, but the intruder followed him without difficulty, sliding silkily down into waters now swirling with iridescent colour and reflecting in rainbow hues on the walls and ceiling.

"I ... I don't want this," Trevor stammered. "I never wanted this."

"You came here of your own free will," she said, in a voice achingly familiar.

"Not for *this*."

"Nevertheless, you came. What is a woman to assume?"

"I'd die before I'd betray my wife."

"A brave threat ... but why go to such a length?"

There was only a yard between them, and he saw her face clearly for the first time. Such beauty would have brought a lump to his throat had it not already been filled with phlegm. And yet – those hazel eyes, those delicate cheekbones, that pert, dimpled chin ...

"You're not my Josie," he blurted.

"True ... was she ever this lovely?"

"Yes!" Trevor shouted, rage growing with his despair. "But even if she never was, that doesn't matter. I've seen what you do."

"Not all outcomes are the same." She reached a gentle, sun-browned hand towards him.

"I don't want you!" He retreated again. "Stay back."

"I can be all that Josie was and so much more."

"Never."

"Or I can be significantly less." Her eyes sank and darkened, her flesh drooped. The golden tan faded to a greenish tinge.

"And maybe even less than that!" Trevor shrieked, tossing the emergency kit aside and pointing the flare-pistol at her chest. "Your final warning!"

141

Snarling and slobbering, the fungoid horror advanced, its mottled tendrils flailing.

Trevor sobbed as he squeezed the trigger.

The flame took them.

BOILED ALIVE

Today, King's Lynn is a busy market town and sea port located at the mouth of the River Great Ouse, on the Norfolk coast. It has had its fair share of hardship over the years, but is currently undergoing major regeneration schemes. It is really no different from many other towns in England, except in terms of its history – which at certain periods was exceptionally cruel. In 1542, the Tuesday Market Place in King's Lynn, nowadays a scene of common trade and friendly banter, was the location of an act so unimaginably brutal that it is scarcely possible to think about it without shuddering.

Death by boiling was a punishment that existed in England during the early Middle Ages, but which was never officially sanctioned by any government of the time. Reports of it actually occurring are few and unreliable. However, in 1532, in the supposedly more enlightened age of the Renaissance, Henry VIII – who on his accession was regarded as a affable and refined monarch – introduced Statute 22, by which murderers convicted of causing death by poison were to be slowly boiled alive. This was a truly diabolical punishment. Similar to burning, but not as quick, the victim was lowered by a rope and pulley into a cauldron of boiling water or oil, raised out again, lowered again, raised again, lowered, and so on until death. Fourth degree burns would result all over the body, causing terrible and prolonged agony before the ordeal was over.

In our relatively forgiving 21st century, it's too easy for us to be astonished that any society, even in olden times, would permit such sadism, but it's a simple fact that human life had markedly less value then than it does today; in an age with no professional police force, thieves and murderers were hated and feared because they preyed on an unprotected society, and justice was often confused with vengeance. The aristocracy – who controlled every aspect of life, and were believed to enjoy this privilege through divine right – felt no differently. They especially lived with a terror of poison, which was the main means by which assassins could reach them.

Henry VIII's action in introducing Statue 22 was prompted by a double murder perpetrated by one Richard Roose, a cook in the house of the Bishop of Rochester. Two persons died, and several other folk of rank and title were critically injured by the unknown substance that he administered. To see persons of such importance attacked so easily by a lowly cook must have made the rich and powerful feel very vulnerable indeed. It is perhaps inevitable that it saw the kneejerk imposition of an extraordinarily severe penalty.

Roose was the first felon to suffer this barbarous death – at Smithfield in London, in 1532. The second was Margaret Day, a servant in King's Lynn accused of poisoning her mistress – and the description of her execution is one of the most graphic ever incorporated into the annals of British law and order.

Day was repeatedly lowered into a vat of boiling water in the middle of the Tuesday Market Place. Her shrieks were said to be appalling, and even the Tudor crowd – which was well used to ghastly executions – was horrified and revolted. But worse was to follow. Day was soon scalded all over her body, but only expired when she swelled up and burst apart, her heart striking the wall of a nearby house.

This macabre event made such an impact that boiling alive as a punishment was never officially used in England again, and only the two cases mentioned here remain on record. This may be because the spectacle was so dreadful that courts could not bring themselves to impose it, but more likely it's the case that would-be poisoners were so cowed that they sought out different methods of murder. Either way, Edward VI, Henry VIII's young son, had no hesitation in abolishing the punishment in 1547, much to the gratitude of cooks all over England – they had become a rare commodity in the 1530s, for fear that someone might die as a result of a meal they had prepared badly.

Interestingly with regard to King's Lynn, there was a similar grotesque incident in 1590, when an accused witch called Margaret Read was reportedly burned at the stake in the same market square. Her heart too was said to have burst from her body and struck a nearby house; the exact place is now marked by a diamond engraved in the brickwork. Folklorists assure us that Read's evil heart was not yet dead, and bounced away from the stunned crowd, vanishing into the Great Ouse. This second story is less likely to be true, not just because of the bouncing heart nonsense, but because witches were rarely burned in England; usually they were hanged.

By contrast, Margaret Day is definitely known to have been boiled – that part of the story at least is authentic – but her heart exploding from her body also seems unlikely. Of course, as it's uncommon these days for criminals to be boiled as a form of judicial punishment, doctors are unable either to verify or dismiss the possibility.

WOLFERTON HALL
James Doig

I always used to scoff when I read the superstitious ramblings of medieval writers. The chronicles and annals of the period are replete with allusions to prophecies, portents, devils and miraculous incidents. According to the *Annales Ricardi Secundi et Henrici Quarti*, in May 1402 during a severe storm, the devil entered a church at Danbury in Essex in the guise of a Franciscan friar; he jumped three times over the altar before turning black in the face and making his exit through the legs of a terrified parishioner, burning him badly, and leaving behind the usual unpleasant smell of sulphur. A month later, a similar incident occurred at All Saints church in Hertford, where a hideous creature destroyed the clock tower, leaving marks like the teeth of a lion or bear embedded in it. In 1440 an anonymous London chronicler remarked on a great storm that broke over the city:

> whereof the people were sore agast, and afered of the grete tempest. And so it was spoken amongst the people that there wer some wikked fendes and spirites arered out of helle by conjuracion, forto disturb the peple in the Realme and to put theym to trouble, discension and unrest.

To my mind such accounts served only to highlight the child-like credulity of medieval folk, and it didn't surprise me at all that in more enlightened times the term 'medieval' has come to be a derogatory adjective used to describe something that seems outdated or antiquated, or just plain ignorant.

Now I know differently.

Let me ask you this: who is to say that there is not some truth to the way medieval folk comprehended the world? After all, how well have we moderns fared in explaining the nature of things? If we conceive of the universe as a gigantic jigsaw puzzle which scientists have attempted to piece together in recent centuries, wouldn't you say that many of the pieces are missing or just don't fit? There is profound uncertainty, a distressing lack of purpose, in our view of the universe and our role in it. Never before has there been an age where we have felt so isolated and alone. Medieval people had no such problem – they knew where they stood in relation to the rest of

145

the universe, and they knew intimately the forces, both malevolent and benign, which work within it. We have hardly an inkling.

My name is Hugh Terne – an unusual surname I am told. I once asked my father where it came from; he replied, rather vaguely, that it was an old East Anglian name, probably a rendering of Tearne or Tierney. My parents were solid middle class folk who early encouraged an interest in books and learning. My father worked for the Foreign and Commonwealth Office, and although he was conscientious and hard-working, the glorious diplomatic career he had hoped for eluded him, and his only overseas posting was a short stint across the Irish Sea at the embassy in Dublin. This was typical of the Ternes: a strong tradition of public service – generation after generation of soldiers, clergymen, teachers, and civil servants – with no one really distinguishing themselves beyond a single-minded diligence and an incorruptible loyalty to their superiors. True to form, as a boy I never gave much thought to my future, and was content to follow a desultory path to one of the same unremarkable professions as my forebears, a middle manager in one of the big government departments perhaps, or a history teacher at a sixth form college. What's bred in the bone and all that.

My outlook changed in my second year at Keele where I was engaged on a history major during the course of which I had failed to impress anyone, least of all my tutors. At the bar one Friday night I got a call from one of dad's colleagues who was working at the embassy in Paris – mum and dad had been killed in a car crash while on vacation in Normandy. Dad had turned out of a narrow road into the path of an on-coming truck – end of story. It was a terrible shock, one that plunged me into a deep depression and prompted me to reassess my goals in life. For the first time I became aware of the tenuous hold we have on this mortal coil and the folly of taking it for granted; I had been all vanity, believing that life – love, success, experience – would happen without any effort on my part. I changed my ways. I threw myself into my work and was gratified by the dramatic improvement in my results. My tutors began to take an interest in me. Medieval history was my particular interest, thanks to the schoolboy Latin dad had forced me to take at prep school and which I kept up at Keele – this was a distinct advantage because the average undergraduate history student knew small English and less Latin. By the end of my third year I was looking forward to a first and had determined to obtain a scholarship to pursue postgraduate studies. All I needed was a research topic.

My prospective supervisor alerted me to the Throgmorton papers which he'd found mentioned in the *10th report of the Historical*

Manuscripts Commission (London, 1896). According to the report the Throgmorton family archive was a substantial one with a near complete series of documents – deeds, receipts, accounts, agreements, memoranda, estate notes and valors – mostly unexamined and which were 'stored in bags and baskets and stowed in large chests'. This looked very promising indeed – the means to reconstruct the totality of the life and experience of a medieval family – in short, the perfect material for a Ph.D thesis.

A quick search in Cokayne's *Complete Peerage* revealed that the Throgmortons were one of the most venerable Norfolk families. Originally obscure yeoman farmers, they came to prominence in the fifteenth century through Sir Charles Throgmorton, a lawyer at Lincoln's Inn who died a judge of the Common Pleas. His son, Sir Geoffrey, enlarged the estate his father had created in their native Norfolk, and during the troubled years of the Reformation proved himself a loyal servant of the Tudor government. From these humble beginnings the Throgmortons became the most important landowners in Norfolk, with the family seat at Wolferton Hall. Pevsner claims that Wolferton is *the* paramount house in Norfolk, a splendid building built in the early seventeenth century by Inigo Jones himself. Today the ninth marquess of Wolferton resides there. I wrote to him and asked if could make use of the archive. He surprised me by replying via e-mail, expressing enthusiasm for the project and asking me to write when I would be coming. A room would be made available for me. Hunched over my aging Dell laptop, webmail open, at my draughty library desk, I whooped my thanks to the gods of good fortune – this was the life I was reaching for: a superior doctorate, a published monograph, a university placement. It all seemed within my grasp.

My luck continued apace and I obtained a decent scholarship at Exeter – my parents would have been proud. My supervisor was an aging, semi-retired academic who for the past forty years had been engaged on a major study of the Pilgrimage of Grace; so absorbed was he in drawing his life's work to a close that he steered clear of me, expressing a benevolent interest in my researches on the odd occasions when I ran into him. That suited me just fine – I wanted to be left to my own devices and I didn't want to be saddled with an over-zealous supervisor who would drag me into his or her office every few days to discuss my progress. I threw myself into the work with gusto.

The first months were taken up with time-consuming but necessary preliminaries: compiling extensive bibliographies of primary and secondary sources, both published and in manuscript form; writing exhaustive notes of the literature; making my first hesitant steps in the arcane arts of palaeography and diplomatic, subjects I'd had limited exposure to as an undergraduate. I also started work on the early history of the Throgmortons, charting the rise to prominence of Sir Charles Throgmorton, the patriarch of the family and the first Throgmorton described as 'gentleman' in the records. I came across some tantalising snippets which suggested that this title was perhaps undeserved; indeed, there was some evidence that in 1452 Sir Charles obtained the manor of Wolferton through a forged deed and forcibly removed the rightful owner, one Thomas Shackleton. Shackleton took the matter to the court of Common Pleas, but Charles's legal skills and influence won the day and Shackleton was left homeless and destitute. That wasn't the end of the matter, however. An indictment survives in the King's Bench records in the Public Records Office in which Charles took out an action against Shackleton for 'spreading false prophecies and rumours and causing disturbances'; evidently Shackleton had posted copies of a prophecy on the gates of Wolferton church predicting the demise of the Throgmortons. According to the indictment Shackleton had a reputation for dabbling in 'necromancy and other black arts', and his threats were taken seriously. However, nothing more is heard of the matter, except for a small notice in a slim eighteenth century history of the family to the effect that Shackleton subsequently went on pilgrimage to the Holy Land and was never heard from again.

By the time I was ready to tackle the Throgmorton papers it was early December. As the Marquess had instructed I wrote to him that I would like to come within the week. His reply reached me a few days later, once again in electronic form (there was something ironic about the heir of this ancient family using email – surely he should be using quill and parchment!). He expressed his regret that he would be unable to meet me – he was spending the winter abroad and the house would be partly shut up. A skeleton staff would remain at Wolferton to oversee the estate during his absence and settle me in. I must admit I was a little relieved that the marquess would be away: his absence meant that I would have few distractions and that, in effect, I would have the run of the house.

And what a house it was!

Early in December, I took the Intercity to Norwich and a coach to Walsingham. From there it was only a brisk two kilometre walk to Wolferton. It was a bright, blustery day with cloud shadows racing each other across the patchwork fields. Sheep dotted the meadows and the sky was alive with a paper-storm of gulls, blown inland by the wind. The leaves were gone now, passed back into the earth, and the trees stood bare and distinct against the pale sky. The hedges were bare of berries, but the odd thrush still hunted in the gnarled hawthorns, hoping for one last morsel. The wind buffeted me along the narrow lane, snapping at my coat. Before long I came to a tiny hamlet – little more than a cluster of stone cottages, a church and a green – and there, just beyond it, was my destination. The magnificent entrance, flanked by lodges with niches and urns, looked down across an ornamental lake with a great fountain of marble satyrs and cherubs, and a green lawn that unrolled like a great carpet until it reached the feet of Wolferton Hall, an imposing building of red brick and stone dressings. Columns of bay windows, now shuttered, glared at me across the park land. It looked an austere house, standing alone in the centre of a great corridor of bright green, flanked by ranks of silver birch and oak, like guarding sentries.

As I approached, following the long ribbon of the driveway towards the house, I saw that I hadn't been forgotten. A lone figure stood on the steps, one of the servants no doubt, a one-man welcoming committee. He was a slightly bent middle aged man, neatly dressed, scrubbed jowls gleaming in the sunlight. He introduced himself as Riding (no Christian name was forthcoming) and told me that he was a retired schoolmaster from Walsingham who was employed by the marquess to look after the house and see to its maintenance while he was away. He took my bag and led me into the house.

"With his lordship away we don't normally use this entrance – the house is shut up, you see. In future you should use the servants' entrance around the side. I'll give you a key when you've settled in."

I followed him into a darkened hall. With the shutters closed it was shrouded in gloom. Pale afternoon light spilled through the gaps revealing shadowy mounds of sheet-draped furniture, stucco frames, Ionic pilasters, friezes of masks and garlands. In the centre of the ceiling, far above me through the gloom, was a gigantic Throgmorton coat of arms, a great crowned griffin on a throne, with smaller panels of equally impressive plasterwork arranged geometrically around it. The panels showed scenes from the family's exalted past – famous battles, tournaments, ceremonies. Most of the scenes I could identify from my own knowledge of Throgmorton family history – there was Sir Charles beside the king at the Battle of the Spurs in 1513, Sir Edward triumphant at the Great Tournament at Nantes, Sir Charles II falling gallantly at Naseby in 1645, Sir Geoffrey III being admitted to the Order of the Garter. Other scenes were more obscure – one appeared to show a funeral procession, a solemn group of men escorting a dead man in some kind of bier; next to it was another curious tableau – a young man, clearly terrified, being pursued by a rather nasty looking character, skeleton-thin and hollow-eyed, some kind of medieval depiction of death I surmised.

I only had a brief glimpse of all of this before Riding led me through a mahogany door and along a dim corridor. We came to a warren of rooms and passages and staircases which I took to be the servants' quarters, or whatever passed for servants these days – perhaps there were none at all. The place appeared to be deserted and our footsteps echoed on the flagged floor. From somewhere deep within the walls the heating system ticked and banged. My room was on the second floor, a convenient distance, Riding explained, from the attic where the archive was kept. It was a pleasant room, small and cosy with a small gas stove, a colour television, and a brick fireplace. Most impressive, however, was the view.

I stood at the window and looked out over the great lawn and the fountain and further away to the thin scribble of road winding back towards the village, a distant island of smoking chimneys and roofs and spires anchored to the windswept meadows. Everywhere were sheep, traditionally the centre of Throgmorton affairs, and the basis of the family's wealth, thousands of them, sprinkled like rugs of snow. Cloud shadows swept across the landscape, skimming over the trees and hills like impossible birds. The Throgmortons had ruled this land for almost six hundred years; they knew intimately each cottage and hedgerow, each copse and flock and glen – this was a tiny, enclosed world, a microcosm of a feudal society built on fear and favour. But then I remembered the emails, the friendly exchange with the latest marquess – surely the old world of obligation, privilege and superstition was long dead, even if the bones of it remained. But if this was the remnant of a feudal kingdom, it was a kingdom without subjects – I could see rolling fields and wooded areas and cottages, but no people, not a soul in sight. It was as if, with the marquess away, not just the house, but the entire demesne had shut down for the winter. I looked around the grounds searching for a gardener or workman but there was no one. Over to the right a movement caught my attention, an inky, fleeting shadow like a crow passing over the sun; it came from a low, grey-stone building almost completely concealed by scrub and trees. There was no sign of any person or animal now. The building was covered by thick ivy and crimson jewels of blood glinted in the sun, presumably from the stained-glass windows.

"What's that old ruin over near the woodland," I asked Riding.

"That's the Throgmorton mausoleum," he said, joining me at the window. "It used to be a church. In medieval times the village was located over there, near where the woodland is now, but in the early sixteenth century it was moved brick-by-brick to where it is today."

"Really?" This was something new. "Why would they do that?"

"It is an obscure episode," he said. "But, as you see, the remains of the church are still there, and you can still see the crumbling walls and foundations of the original cottages, though they are mostly overgrown with scrub. No doubt you will find some record of it in the archives."

With that Riding drew me away from the window; he had work to do and he wanted to show me the attic. He took me up another flight of stairs, down a wide, panelled corridor and through a baize door. The attic yawned before us, a dark cipher, obscuring its secrets. And it was cold – there was no fireplace and from time to time a winter draught crept through the place. Riding found a way through a maze of obstacles and opened up the shutters. Golden light streamed in and blew away the shadows. The room was bigger than I'd first thought, almost as big as the hall downstairs – but it was crammed full of the flotsam of centuries of family life – cheval mirrors, fauteuils, chiffoniers, scrutoirs, tureens, mazorines, porringers, candelabras, picture frames, ceramics, tapestries. The *Antiques Roadshow* boffins would have had a field day. Riding called me over and pointed out a cluster of chests, trunks and boxes, untidily laid out on the floor as if tossed there like a handful of dice. Next to them was a massive oak bureau, its drawers and pigeon holes crammed with documents and papers.

"I'm afraid the papers are in a terrible state," Riding said, a little apologetically. "They have never been properly sorted or catalogued. You have your work cut out for you."

Indeed, it seemed that the only attempt at organisation consisted of rudimentary labels chalked on to the lids of some of the chests and trunks – 'Deeds, leases. Misc. unexamined, C14-18 cents.'; 'Norfolk manorial – Wolferton'; 'Comes Oxoniae'; 'Ecclesie de Wolferton', and so on. The drawers and pigeon holes of the bureau were numbered, but there was nothing to indicate what sort of documents they contained.

I looked at the archive with a mixture of excitement and dismay. On the one hand it was undoubtedly a rich source of material, on the other the sheer mass of papers was daunting. Riding was right. I was going to have my work cut out if I wanted to complete my work before the marquess returned in May.

I spent the rest of the afternoon in a state of acute despair. There was so much to do and I didn't know where to begin. Finally I decided to start on the bureau. It was a convenient place to work, and it seemed logical to put it into some sort of order before I turned to the chests. By the end of the day I had several bundles of documents neatly sorted and labelled, and I was relieved to find that my anxiety had subsided somewhat.

Over the following days I launched myself into the work, poring over scraps of vellum and paper covered in spidery Latin script – accounts, deeds, leases – carefully sorting them into year and type, setting aside those which weren't dated. I worked hard and to a strict routine, as I'd forced myself to do after my parents died. A normal day would see me start work soon after eight. I would take a short tea break at ten, and then work through until lunch. Usually I worked without a break in the afternoon, finishing around five or six, sometimes later if something had aroused my interest. I took lunch in the servants' kitchen with Riding, one of two other part-time staff and, when it rained, a couple of taciturn groundsmen. These were invariably solemn occasions with little in the way of conversation and I was happy to get back to the attic. Later I would have dinner in my room, or, if the weather was mild, walked the few miles into town and had a meal at *The Cock and Bull*. At night I stoked up the fire and settled myself in the armchair with a book, or cleaned up the transcriptions I had made during the day. The wind was always wild, hunting about the grounds, howling in the eaves; the sound would put me to sleep as I watched the ebb and flow of the dying coals in the grate, thinking about generations of Throgmortons, the history of their house, and how my life was intertwining with theirs.

Quite often, when I needed time to think or stretch my legs, I would wander about the house, along the dark panelled hallways, drifting from room to room, lingering in the mellow light of the fine drawing room or the domed parlour, dazzled by the magnificent library with its thousands of gilt, leather bound volumes, and the sumptuous ballroom decorated with bright floor-to-ceiling tapestries. But always I found myself returning again and again to the Great Hall and the stunning frescoed ceiling. The two scenes that had caught my eye on that first day – the funeral procession and the man being pursued by the curious scarecrow figure – continued to intrigue me. They didn't belong with the other, more detailed tableaux: there was something rough and ready about them, as if they hadn't been properly completed, like figures half-glimpsed in a dream. They were strange and mysterious depictions of, I was convinced, some sinister event in the long history of the Throgmorton family. But somehow they seemed familiar, as if I had

152

seen them somewhere before, in a book of art history perhaps, or more likely in something I had read about the house or the family.

I would have liked to spend more time exploring the house, but the archive always drew me, and I would spend hours in the freezing cold, rugged up like a bear, going through the bundles of papers. Most of the documents concerned the fairly dry business interests of the medieval gentry – land transactions, legal disputes, flock maintenance and so on. Occasionally something of particular interest revealed itself. At the end of the first week I stumbled across an account roll dated 1507 that detailed the expenses of relocating the village of Wolferton two kilometres to the west. Here was the evidence Riding had hoped I might find. While the roll itself offered no explanation for the extraordinary episode, attached to it was a scrap of vellum, evidently torn from a local chronicle, which gave the faintest hint of what may have happened:

> *Anno Domini M°cccccii [1503]: circa Incarnatio Domini et mensis Pasche diversis locis Wolferton' visum fuit malignus spiritus, que corda populorum mirabiliter perterruit. Unde vulgariter dicebatur*: terrible dayes schall befall us.

The crude and ungrammatical Latin said that between Christmas and Easter 1507 an evil spirit was seen in various parts of Wolferton, which wonder sorely terrified the people; the rabble were saying: 'terrible days shall befall us.' It appeared that the appearance of some kind of malignant ghost had prompted the translation of Wolferton! I chuckled at that – the child-like credulity of medieval folk never ceased to amaze me.

Towards the end of the first week I discovered something which I found especially exciting – an old manuscript beneath a bundle of manorial accounts. It was little more than a couple of quires loosely bound together between battered leather covers almost black with age. Leafing through it I saw it was a book of prophecies in Latin and English. In themselves prophecies are nothing extraordinary – the moldwarp and the ant and all that Welsh rubbish that Shakespeare scoffed at – but this collection was especially interesting because it included one prophecy which could be linked to a specific local event – the dispute with Thomas Shackleton over Wolferton Hall in 1482. The text of this prophecy, written hastily on a flyleaf, was as follows:

> Anno 1482 billes were sette on the gates of Wolferton churche withe these wordes:

Betwix christmas and candelmas, a litel before lent,
The Griffen schall slay Schuckton, by his own assente,
And his bones schall be laid nethe the altar.
On Magdalene eve schall the dead arisen,
And many wondres schall be done in that place.
This schall the Griffen and hys whelps see everich night
In dreaming: under the horned moone,
Deep in the mystes colde brethe and the darker
Wode, there we schall mete agayn
Until the one schall come us bothe to fre.
__In Aeternum__

Like most medieval prophecies this was nothing more than
doggerel verse, of no literary merit, but the explanatory line at the
beginning proved that it was the prophecy Thomas Shackleton had
posted on the gates of the church. It seemed to suggest that
Throgmorton (the 'Griffen', after his coat of arms) would murder
Shackleton ('Shuckton'), or have him murdered ('by his own
assent') and have the body disposed of; the rest of it was obscure,
but I took it to mean that Shackleton would return somehow to his
'home' at Wolferton and cause strange things to happen
('wondres'). The last lines looked like some kind of threat, but
beyond that I had no idea what they meant.

I mulled over what I knew of this episode. Shackleton was
supposed to have disappeared on pilgrimage, but the only source
that preserves this information was the eighteenth century family
history which I knew to be untrustworthy, a rather turgid piece of
propaganda that casts the family in a glowing light, even fabricating
a pedigree for the Throgmortons going back to Noah himself!

*What if Shackleton's alleged disappearance on pilgrimage was
also a fabrication?*

The thought occurred to me in a flash, and suddenly a veil fell
from my eyes. The so-called 'prophecy' in fact expressed
Shackleton's fear that Sir Charles was going to have him murdered
– and indeed that is exactly what transpired! Sir Charles had his
retainers bump off the poor sod and dispose of his body; then to
cover his tracks he spread a rumour that Shackleton has gone on
pilgrimage to the Holy Land. After a few years those who still
remembered him would assume that he had met with a bad end. An
ingenious plot, I thought. Presumably the irony would not have been
lost on Sir Charles that Shackleton's prophecy had been fulfilled!

While I felt sure I was on the right track, I could find nothing
more about the incident though I spent the rest of the day looking

154

through the archive. Presumably the Throgmortons had systematically gone through the papers and destroyed any incriminating evidence relating to the issue (though, of course, the prophecy had been overlooked). Then one day during my second week at Wolferton Hall, an unlikely source of information presented itself.

Riding and I were lunching alone in the servants' kitchen, finishing off last night's roast pork. The large clock on the wall said it was ten to one. The minute hand clicked up a notch. Outside the wind was buffeting the windows and low clouds periodically concealed the soft winter sunlight. Riding was telling me about his family's long association with Wolferton Hall and the village, that, in fact, he was the third successive Riding to have been headmaster at the village school. He was a one-man repository of a vast store of information about the Throgmortons and it occurred to me that he might know of legends or folk stories that might shed some light on Shackleton's disappearance. I asked him if he remembered any old stories about the house or the Throgmortons which he may have heard over the years. His eyes lit up at once. Local folklore was a particular interest of his and he'd devoted many hours of study to the subject. There were dozens of such stories, he said, old wives tales and nursery stories – the usual fare that surrounds venerable homes and families – tales of ghosts, spectral processions and strange lights. There were other things also. He had dredged up a wealth of rumours and uncorroborated reports of hauntings and unexplained happenings at Wolferton, even a story that parallels the Strathmere Horror of Glamis – of a hideous creature of unnatural antiquity locked away in the crypt.

"Of course, most ancient families have a healthy stock of such tales," he said, "and little if anything can be read into them; but they are not without interest and they offer a window into the curious world of popular superstition. There was a time when I considered drawing them together into a volume, but the marquess insisted I drop the idea."

I wondered at this, it seemed a harmless enough interest, unless ...

"Do any of the old stories involve a character named Thomas Shackleton?" I enquired.

Riding thought for a moment, the corners of his mouth pulled down. "Not that I recall," he said slowly, "but there is a Black *Shuck* of Wolferton, which sounds a bit like Shackleton."

He sounded unconvinced, but I remembered the 'Shuckton' of the prophecy which I'd assumed was a semi-literate rendering of Shackleton.

155

"Who is Black Shuck?" I asked, hiding my rising interest. If Riding knew I suspected his employer's wealth and name was built on criminality and murder, I doubted he would be so forthcoming.

"He, or rather, *it*, is a well-known bogey in this area, a staple of nursery stories told to children to keep them out of mischief. My own grandmother used to tell me to watch out for Black Shuck, especially around this time of the year; it supposedly haunts the estate between Christmas and Easter. It's a strange legend in that it seems to conflate two different creatures of legend – sometimes it appears as a huge black dog, at other times as a kind of ghoul or wraith."

My mind was racing now. Didn't the prophecy mention something about Christmas and Lent? Perhaps the folk memory of Thomas Shackleton had been transformed over the centuries into a vengeful ghost, which would make sense given the circumstances of his death – surely that was how folk tales developed and evolved … or was I trying to convince myself of a connection that wasn't there?

"What's the origin of Black Shuck? Is that known from the tales?'

Riding disposed of the last morsel of cold roast pork and sat back in his chair, his heavy jowls glistening with grease. "No idea. But, you know, there is a curious sideline to the Black Shuck tales that you might find interesting."

"And what's that," I said, pushing my empty plate away.

"Well, the head of the Throgmorton family has for centuries gone abroad between Christmas and Easter, and that's a custom that continues to this day. The Throgmortons will have none of it of course," and here Riding lowered his voice, "but there are stories of a curse, that if the head of the family remains in the house a terrible fate will befall him."

I nodded, half to myself – after all, what was a family curse but an expression of ancestral guilt? Perhaps more than most families of such lineage, the Throgmortons could entertain the existence of vengeful ghosts.

But after lunch, when I returned to my room, my enthusiasm had waned. The tale, such that it was, was threatening to get in the way of the real work I was doing; I was forgetting the big picture. My job was to write a doctoral thesis based on cold, hard facts that would be published in the scholarly dark blue covers of the OUP, be positively reviewed in the right journals, and get me a postdoc at an Oxbridge college. That was the goal I had set myself. I couldn't afford to be diverted by a racy piece of journalism based on hints and speculation that may well be unfounded – I was reminded of those early traditions about Shakespeare – the deer-poaching, the screwing around with pub maidens – that still enticed biographers. There lay the road to perdition.

Later I returned to the attic, determined to finish sorting the papers so that I could start a more systematic trawl through the documents and complete my transcriptions of the more important papers. I continued to work until well into the evening; it was after seven when, with a satisfied sigh, I put down my pencil and gathered up my papers.

I was exhausted. My eyes were red and strained from squinting at crabbed medieval scripts and my head felt thick and heavy. I got to my feet and walked to the window, stretching my cramped muscles. The house was silent, and so cold – I could almost feel the ice creeping up my limbs. The only sound was the echo of my own footfalls on the hard floor.

It was a beautiful night. No wind, no movement at all on the grounds. The lawn was frosted with bright starlight and the lake gleamed like a black jewel. A shimmering carpet of moonlight unrolled across the park and here and there were pockets of milky mist. There was an air of expectancy about the scene and I found myself holding my breath, waiting for something to happen, as if this were the opening scene of a play. And indeed, as I watched I caught a flicker of pale light away to the left. Out of the darkness a group of men emerged, picking their way across the lawn towards me. Something tugged at my memory, a thread of recognition that I couldn't quite grasp, but I knew it would come to me, and that thought gave me a deep sense of dread. One of them carried a brand that cast a flickering yellow glow over the straggling procession. Two of the men were pushing some sort of large wooden barrow which contained the body of a fourth man A fifth man strode ahead of the others, turning occasionally to urge the others on with impatient gestures of his hands.

The procession passed beneath the house and I saw that the man in the barrow had a terrible head wound. There was a ragged hole gleaming bone white, shiny with blood, a lot of blood – it dripped from the barrow and left a dark trail on the grass. A man with an injury that severe could not be alive, but as the group passed on I could have sworn his head turned slowly in my direction, following me with eyes like coal pits. The procession moved on, heading towards the mausoleum, and soon it was out of sight behind the building, the flickering torch light bobbing like a will-o-the-wisp before it too disappeared.

And then, when the figures had gone, the scene clicked into place. I had seen it often enough on my wanderings through the house. I was witnessing a funeral procession, the very same as that portrayed on the ceiling of the Great Hall.

I continued to stare out the window long after the procession had gone. I watched the point where the men had disappeared but they didn't return. There was nothing except the still night and the watchful moon.

When I finally turned away from the window I almost stumbled from exhaustion. I went back to my room, tugged off my clothes, and fell into bed.

I slept badly. I was plagued by troubled dreams, or rather one dream that kept recurring: I was sitting at the bureau in the attic poring over some documents; outside it was raining heavily, but through the downpour I could hear a dog howling, one of the sheep dogs, I supposed, calling for its master. I ignored it as best I could and continued with my work, but as time passed I began to sense that there was something in the attic with me. I looked around the vast room, my terror growing, but I could see nothing but yawning darkness. Yet, in the certainty of dreams, I knew I was not alone – I could *feel* it, an ancient, black presence. Then, out of the darkness, came a noise – something scraping, scratching on the floor. Terror seized me. I couldn't move or cry out. And just as I sensed it reaching for me out of the darkness I awoke, drenched in perspiration. Each time I fell asleep the dream came again, the presence ever more threatening and malevolent.

It was with considerable relief that I saw the first grey light of dawn through the window. I fell asleep and was untroubled by dreams until I awoke around midday. I was still tired, and I felt on edge, as if something terrible was going to happen and I was powerless to stop it. The weather reflected my mood: black clouds had swept in from the Wash and rain spattered like gravel against the window.

I couldn't find Riding downstairs, but he had left out a cold lunch for me. I made myself a sandwich and walked through to the Great Hall.

As always, it was like entering a vast cavern, an Aladdin's cave of hidden treasures and sparkling shadows. The ceiling stretched away into gloom, incoherent faces stared down at me from the walls, sheet-draped furniture loomed like altars before me. I went to the windows and threw open a couple of shutters. The poor light struggled to push the shadows away, and in the half-light everything looked vague, half-formed, as though glimpsed through a fog. I looked up at the plaster ceiling one-and-a-half storeys above, and the hairs stirred on the nape of my neck. As I had thought, the funeral scene was a replica of the ghostly procession I had

158

witnessed the previous night – the same group of men, one carrying a taper, two pushing a barrow or bier or whatever it was, the commanding figure leading the group, urging them on, and the man with the gaping head wound, laid out in the barrow like a slaughtered animal. He was a rather sinister looking character; in fact, for the first time, I noticed that he was the same figure in the adjacent scene, pursuing the terrified man – skin stretched tight over sharp bone, eyes staring from deep sockets.

I didn't like to think about these strange events and what they meant. I had to continue working, to focus at the task at hand, and so I returned to the attic.

Anyone who has ever engaged in historical research will admit that most days are tedious and uneventful, and that an uncommon degree of patience is a useful attribute. There are times, however, when discoveries come one after another in quick succession. There is no logical reason for it, you just learn to accept it and hope that those days occur more frequently. That afternoon I learned a good deal in a short time, but these were facts I wasn't looking for. A deed of 1543 mentioned the tragic death of Sir Robert Throgmorton ten years earlier in the family mausoleum. In the preamble to an account roll of 1682 the faithful reeve, a man named Tarn (could almost be my own name I thought), had written a memorandum that his master's life had been cut short during a severe storm on the eve of the first Sunday in Lent, and commended his soul to God. In a letter dated 18 April 1753, the Bishop of Norwich sent his condolences to the newly widowed Elizabeth Throgmorton, and assured her that masses would be held for Sir Robert's soul thrice daily. There were other things also. The Household Books revealed that in April 1590 Sir Thomas Throgmorton paid two shillings to have the altar removed from the mausoleum. A fortnight later Sir Thomas paid another two shillings to have the mausoleum repaired; evidently seven tombs had been badly damaged by a person or persons unknown. There were more reports of damage and the mass *Contra Inimicos* was said daily in the church. The acts of vandalism only stopped when Sir Thomas had a new tomb built in the mausoleum, though there was no record of any family member dying at that time.

The mausoleum – that temple to Throgmorton mortality –was at the centre of things, the key, it seemed to me, to the whole bloody mystery.

Evening had set in early. Darkness settled over the land like a cloak. I went to my room, put on a warm coat and pocketed a torch that Riding had left for me, and went downstairs in search of answers.

Outside it was blowing hard and bitterly cold. The damp grass wet the cuffs of my trousers. Ragged clouds flew across the moon. Wolferton Hall loomed behind me, dark except for my room in the servants' wing. Somewhere an owl hooted, the cry swept away by a gust of wind; an animal, a badger or a vole perhaps, scrabbled in the wet earth.

The surrounding woodland had encroached on the mausoleum, high elms whose bare arms, animated by strong gusts of wind, clawed and scratched the roof. The building was fringed with high grass and weeds and the walls were covered with ivy. There wasn't much left of the original church, only a section of the nave, which itself had been substantially rebuilt some time in the past, the broken remains of a buttress, and a single winged gargoyle that squinted blindly towards Wolferton Hall. The tower and the transepts were gone and trees had overrun the yard. Shadows ebbed and flowed like deep-sea currents. I was glad I had thought to bring a torch. The yellow beam dipped over the old building and the surrounding trees. Beetles and spiders dripped in the light like rain.

As I'd hoped, the ancient oak door was unlocked. It swung open into pitch blackness. I entered the building and left the door open a crack. The torch beam swayed over parts of old monuments and tombs: effigies of knights, marble crosses, brasses, stone caskets and sarcophagi etched with Latin epitaphs. They filled the area of the old church that would have been the nave and aisles. Magnificent though they were, I gave them scant regard – these were not the tombs I had come there to see. I passed between them, shining the beam over the flagged floor before me. The wind howled outside, whistled through cracks and niches in the masonry.

At the end of the nave, some distance from the other monuments, as if it were meant to be separate from them, was a plain stone sarcophagus, roughly hewn and unadorned. I walked around it, playing the torch beam over the sides, searching for a name, an epitaph, a decoration, anything, which might confirm my belief that this was the tomb of Thomas Shackleton. There was no adornment at all, just the rough, grey-stone slabs; however the top slab was slightly askew, a few inches off centre, revealing a small gap in the top corner of the tomb. I directed the torch beam into the crack and peered within.

There was nothing. Nothing at all, except for the imprint of a skull within a drift of dust and cobwebs. Whatever had been entombed there was gone. Instinctively, I swung around, searching with the torch. The beam bounced crazily off the walls, catching part of a marble cross, the edge of a tomb, the hollow-eyed visage of an effigy. There was nothing, only a swirling curtain of dust. The

160

darkness was like a lead weight all around me. Dust and stale air, and something else, cloying and unpleasant, filled my nostrils. An urgent voice at the back of my mind told me to get out of there quickly.

Then I heard it – a quiet, furtive movement, magnified by the heavy silence. Something was dragging itself across the stone floor of the mausoleum.

Terror seized me. My heart went quiet, my throat clicked dryly when I tried to swallow. There it was again, a faint rasping sound, something pulling itself over the flagged floor – something hard, like wood – or bone.

The sound came from the middle of the old nave, between the looming sarcophagi. I swept the torch beam over the cold stone. Where was the hollow-eyed effigy I had seen a moment ago? I stumbled to the side and made my way down the aisle, eager to escape the mausoleum and whatever had made its home there. Up ahead grey light spilled through the open door. A fragment of moonlight sparkled on the gossamer thread of spider's web, lit up droplets of rain like precious jewels. I switched off the torch. Just I few more steps and I would be out ...

The door swung closed with a loud *clang*.

Darkness was all I knew, black as pitch. I fumbled with the torch. It sprang from my grasp like a live thing and clattered on the floor. Groaning helplessly, I fell to my knees, my hands scrabbling over the rough flags, searching for the torch. If I could only find it and reach the door... Suddenly I froze, my breath hitched in my throat. The air was pregnant with that suffocating smell again, heavy with the dust of ages. Black Shuck, Shackleton, whatever it was, stirred behind me. I felt its skeletal fingers touch my back, moving like a caress to my shoulders. It held me in its grip and turned me to face it.

It was there, in that place of the dead, that everything was made clear to me.

*

The next morning I left Wolferton Hall.

I thanked Riding for his help the previous night. He'd found me in the mausoleum sitting bolt upright against the side of a tomb, staring into the blackness. The chain of events was self-evident (so he told me later when I had fully regained my senses) – the door had swung shut; in my panic I'd dropped the torch, and lost in that terrible blackness I had temporarily lost my mind, imagined all sorts of strange things.

161

A sound explanation, I thought, but I knew that the horror was not in my head. It was real. I think Riding knew it too.

The first night back at Exeter was the worst. In the darkest hour of the night I smelled its sweet, cloying odour; heard the scraping of its horny feet across the panelled floor. I caught glimpses of it. Sometimes it appeared as a rotted corpse, a dreadful scarecrow shape, eyes like red cinders, knots of ragged black hair. At other times it was a massive black shadow snuffling and growling outside the window or padding around the room.

It has come every night since.

In Aeternum the prophesy had said.

Forever.

THE WANDERING TORSO

One night in the mid-18th century, in Norfolk's coastal village of Happisburgh, two farm labourers were waiting nervously on the corner of Whimpwell Street. They had a lantern, but as yet refused to light it. They also had weapons – pistols and cutlasses, which they clasped tight to their chests. One might be forgiven for thinking they were waiting to commit a crime, but in actual fact, though they didn't realise it, they were on the verge of solving one – at least partly.

The 'Happisburgh Spectre' had been seen on and off for several years in the village, and local folk were at their wits' end – to such an extent that nobody even ventured outdoors once darkness came. The unknown figure was always seen following the same route, walking slowly up the main road leading into the village from the direction of Cart Gap, passing the famous red-and-white striped lighthouse en route, and always carrying a bulging sack. Though the figure interacted with no-one – there had been no reports of attacks – it was so hideous to look at, apparently covered in appalling mutilations, that witnesses had fainted and even suffered heart-attacks. Many who had seen it, moved away, giving up their occupations and refusing to live any place where such a ghastly and relentless apparition was active. Whatever the ghost was, its presence soon became intolerable. Volunteers were sought to either confront it or follow it, to discover its purpose, and thus the two farm workers – their courage possibly fortified by alcohol – were selected to keep watch.

How many nights they waited for is unrecorded, but their patience was eventually rewarded. The spectre appeared, again walking slowly along the main route into the village. Somehow or other the brave lads held their ground while it drew closer to them, and only then – in the glare of a full moon – were they able to distinguish the true horror of its disfigurements. To begin with, the figure was not actually walking – it could not walk because it had no legs; it was gliding. Though it wore what appeared to be a seaman's costume, this had been slashed and cut repeatedly as though by multiple sword-strokes. One of these had sheared clean through its neck, for its head was dangling to one side, attached to the stump of its neck by a single thread of muscle.

163

The farm workers were now so horrified that one of them fled. However, the other remained at his post and when the terrible form passed him by, began to furtively follow. The figure continued, apparently oblivious to the fellow on its tail, only stopping when it reached the village well, into which it dumped the sack it was carrying. A second later it had vanished.

The following morning, the farm worker reported back to the other villagers, and the well, which was very deep, was examined. At length, another volunteer was lowered on a rope, and after poking around in the water with a pole, dragged out two old sacks. Immediately there was a choking stench of decay. Fearing the worst, he opened the first sack and found a pair of severed legs. In the second, he found a hacked torso with a head only partially attached.

When the remains were brought to the surface, it became obvious that not only had the unfortunate victim been dismembered with a sword, but that he had been shot several times as well. Despite extensive enquiries, the victim remained unidentified, though his rotted clothing appeared to be of Dutch origin. Some villagers recalled an incident several years earlier, when gunfire had been heard near the shore, and the assumption was that Dutch smugglers – of whom there were plenty along this coast – had fallen out among themselves.

Whoever the murderers were, they were never apprehended, but the ghost was laid to rest – at least in terms of its actual appearances. The villagers never drank from the well again – they were sickened by the thought that they had been drinking from it for so long, plus, on stormy nights it was said that odd groans could be heard issuing from it. When the well was replaced with a pump in the 19th century, the groaning supposedly ceased, though the horrific phantom was later referred to as 'the Pump Hill Ghost'.

In modern times, there is no trace either of a pump or well. Locals are still aware of the tale, though there have been no reports of a haunting recently.

ALDEBURGH
Johnny Mains

He had tried in vain to communicate with the Provost, but his letters remained unanswered, much to his frustration. Joseph took up lodgings in Dedworth Road and waited for the Eton 'half' to end and for the Provost to be at leisure. He had the money to wait, and could, if need be, stay until the end of the decade. He spent his time either 'loitering' around Eton or frequenting *The Five Bells* on Sheet Street. He thought he had become a very effective shadow, but it was all to no avail: the Provost had either been alarmed by his correspondence or was just someone who loathed going outdoors. Joseph thought that it might be a mixture of the two.

The day after the college broke for Long Leave he spotted him in the school yard, emerging from under the arch of Lupton's Tower, walking hurriedly, perhaps towards the school library, three heavy-looking tomes under his left arm. He looked elderly but he was still a big, sprightly man and appeared to relish taking his time.

As Joseph approached him, the Provost smiled cautiously, and seeing that the younger man at least *looked* like a gentleman, bade him good day.

"Dr Montague Rhodes James?" said Joseph, stopping in front of him. James's smile faded; his eyes betrayed a faint recognition; then became quizzical, almost wary.

"Yes?"

"My name is Joseph Payton, and I believe that you wrote about my father, Percival, in your story *A Warning to the Curious*. I beg of you, please tell me what you know." He stared at James hard.

The older man's face crumpled somewhat; he looked like he needed to sit down. "I'm sorry, I have no idea of what you refer to. It was a fictional story," he mumbled, fending him away with his free arm. Joseph tried to reach out to make him stay but James pushed his shoulder with surprising power. "You will leave me be, unless you would like for me to call on the porter!"

"Sir, call on the porter as much as you like. Perhaps he won't be as dismissive of my belief that *you* killed my father!"

They were harsh words, but they had the desired effect.

The Provost's eyes narrowed. "Where are you staying, young man?"

165

"I have lodgings with Mrs Humphries on Dedworth; they cater for a better class of client," Joseph said, breathing deeply and puffing out his chest.

Dr James appeared not to notice this display. "Very well. I shall call on you tomorrow. Have your landlady prepare an early breakfast."

"You will call?"

"Yes." Dr James walked off, his black gown billowing about him, until he was out of sight.

*

"I think we should start at the end," Joseph began, unfolding his newspaper and revealing the hardback which bore the name of the offending story. He opened the book where he had placed his marker, coughed, and started to read:

"'You don't need to be told that he was dead. His tracks showed that he had run along the side of the battery, had turned sharp round the corner of it, and, small doubt of it, must have dashed straight into the open arms of someone who was waiting there. His mouth was full of sand and stones, and his teeth and jaws were broken into bits. I only glanced once at his face …'"

Joseph had tears in his eyes. He blinked and one solitary trail of saltwater ran down his cheek. He shut the book carefully on his forefinger so as to not lose his place.

"When I was ten, my mother sat me down, patted my knee and told me quite calmly that my father had been found dead on a beach in Aldeburgh. He died a very savage and lonely death, but this I didn't find out until I was sixteen. I had asked the question of what happened to him, and my mother gave me these clippings from the *East Anglian Times,* dated 1923."

He passed over two small newspaper cuttings. The passage of twelve years had made the cheap paper brown and brittle.

TREASURE-HUNTER FOUND DEAD IN ALDEBURGH
The body of Percival Payton, from Hunstanton,
was found Thursday, April 25th...

Dr James handed back the first and glanced at the headline of the second. It was dated June 1923.

VERDICT OF WILFUL MURDER BY PERSON OR PERSONS UNKNOWN IN STRANGE CASE OF TREASURE-SEEKER

Joseph continued, "As you well know, your book containing the story was published in 1925. I would never have become suspicious of you, sir, had I not been given a copy of your book as a gift last year. The shock I received on reading the story was horrific. There, laid bare, the 'facts'. You were staying in the area during April when a man was found dead on the beach. "And ... th ... though it's a slight description," he started to stammer as he became more agitated, "when you say ..." Joseph opened up the book again, and skipped back through the story erratically until he came to the correct page. "'He was rather a rabbity anæmic subject – light hair and light eyes – but not unpleasing,'" – you describe him to a tee. He was a 'treasure-hunter' as the papers put it, and from what my mother told me, a pretty poor one – a few shards of Roman pottery and maybe the odd coin were the entire fruit of his labours. But he was enthusiastic about his pastime and a true lover of the countryside." He was rambling now. "He took many photographs – the camera and eight or nine plates were returned along with his body."

The old man's eyes never left Joseph's. Joseph seemed to notice for the first time and breathed deeply.

Then more quietly, "I have the photographs of a church and of a coat of arms that contains the three crowns of East Anglia. It was indeed in the porch of the church." From the back of the book he removed a heavy grain, cream envelope and, opening it up slowly, took out several photographs, some of which he laid out on the table in front of Dr James. Indeed there was the church; also a picture of two kindly-looking old men, one of them was the Rector, the other, presumably, the sexton.

"So," continued Joseph, quieter now, "the evidence is as follows: you were in the area at the same time as my father, you have ably described his looks and his occupation and you have also written that he had taken photographs of a church and had seen a coat of arms with three crowns on it. My father's name and the name you use in the book is only a single letter removed! You said yesterday that it was a work of fiction, but I must ask again sir, what do you know of my father?"

Joseph had two more photographs and he placed them gently and deliberately on top of the others. Dr James looked at them for a long while. He saw himself, from a distance; he appeared to be studying the newspaper intently in the reading room at *The White Lion* hotel. In the other, he was talking at the front of the hotel to two ladies, one of whom appeared to be handing him something. James thought it might have been a book, one of his own that he had been asked to sign.

"My father took these photographs; they are clearly of you. Tell me, what do you know?"

The silence was broken by Mrs Humphries who entered the parlour with a fresh tray of tea. Dr James nodded tiredly at her: his rest the night before had been non-existent. Joseph nodded his thanks after she poured, and as she left, reached inside his jacket and pulled out one final photograph. It was his father, Percival Payton, a candid shot taken several years before his death, sitting in the garden, a young Joseph on his knee.

Dr James reached down to his leather satchel, placed it on his knees and opened it deliberately, the metal buckles clanging as he undid the straps and folded the top back. He rummaged around and pulled out a rather substantial sheaf of papers covered with his almost unintelligible handwriting.

"These are the notes I made when writing *A Warning to the Curious*." He glanced at Joseph over the rim of his glasses. His tone was sincere but weary. "It was written on my return to Eton of course, but the sad death of your father was the catalyst for the tale and I am sorry that I used his passing in this way. It is unforgivable and I am truly contrite, this you must believe."

The old man knew that this was not enough. He glanced at the notes in his hands. The morning light made the pages glow. He continued.

"I was staying at *The White Lion* hotel with a good friend and his acquaintance; they would spend most of their time on the golf course and I, invariably, would spend my time walking long distances or sitting on the shorefront reading, according to my wont, detective fiction or 'thrillers', as I believe they are now called. In the evening we would meet for supper then retire to the reading room for brandy and a little conversation. It was here that I first met your father, and the tale is entirely correct at this point; he came in looking rather distracted, asked if he could make company with us, and after a while I engaged him with some small talk. He told me that he was an antiquarian and a collector of curios and, naturally, I asked him what it was in the area he was looking for. It was then that he told me the story of his meeting the reverend and the three crowns of Anglia, about which I hasten to add, I already knew. He also mentioned that a family were the protectors of the site of the last remaining crown. They had performed this task for many, many years and the last in their line had passed away not long before, maybe only thirty years or so. It was your father's intention to find this crown, dig it up and make his name, because from his appearance it did not seem, if I may be vulgar, that he was a man of means. All in the room were curious at this point, and we talked about the legality of any discovery ..."

"Were the family who protected the crown called Ager?" Joseph interrupted.

The Provost smiled briefly, and thought for a second. "No, they were not. Although I wrote about something based on a true event, as a writer of fiction I knew the story would never be believed as true. Legend is legend, and the crowns and their protectors are purely such. But should that stop someone from believing that they exist? And of course I was not the first to document the crowns' existence; they are a pertinent, if obscure legend. I must say though that whilst writing my tales I do not like to make things easy should a reader decide to take up the mantle and do a little ... research.

"We talked about the legality of your father's discovery and we all agreed that he would receive a substantial sum from the Crown if no claim was made by landowners. He believed the current landowner to be without relations, so would have seen the lion's share of any wealth. At the end of the evening we parted company, having agreed that it would be the find of a lifetime should he succeed, and we wished him luck. We did not ask to be involved in the hunt, although it *was* extremely interesting."

"When was the next time you saw him?" Joseph asked, taking Dr James's proffered papers and leafing through them.

"The next time I saw him he was dead on the beach."

Joseph looked up, startled, the colour drained from his face. "But the story says ..."

"Fool!" Dr James's anger was up. His neck was beginning to mottle; the colour crept slowly up to his chin. He breathed in deeply and closed his eyes. The anger dissipated in slow receding waves, when he opened his eyes again he saw that Joseph was staring at him with fury in *his* eyes.

"We were in the reading room, when one of the waiters came in to tell us that the gentleman we had been talking to a day previously was believed to be dead," Dr James continued slowly. "We were shocked, horribly so, and we rushed to the scene, which was quite some distance away but not so far that the news wasn't carried back to the village quickly. The night was beginning to draw in, and by the time we got there it was near dark. There were five or six people in attendance, carrying lamps. A doctor had been called and pronounced your father to be dead. We were not asked why we were there and in retrospect it was rather ghoulish of us to go, but with the information that we had, if it appeared that he was murdered, we could have been of some use."

"Did you attend the inquest?"

"No, we did not, but I will explain why in a moment. Your father was partially covered in sand from head to toe, and his mouth was full of small pebbles. His neck was broken, but I elaborated of course in the story further injuries to attain shock, create an impact. We waited for a policeman to attend; while there was a doctor in town, a policeman had to be raised from another village, and we were with the body for a further hour and a half.

"Once he arrived, of course, we were asked about our connection to him and we told the policeman all we knew. He was satisfied with our story, and why wouldn't he be? The remains were removed, and two days later we ventured to Cambridge and in time there was an inquest at which neither myself, my friend or his acquaintance were called to give evidence. I still have that letter if you wish to look at it. I remember placing a phone call that day and was told that our statements given were enough."

Dr James sighed, his face puffy and he removed his spectacles and wiped them with a fine cloth. "I don't know if your father found the crown and had been murdered for it or if the crowns remain the legend they always were. I sit here in front of you and I can only state, with every fibre of my being, that I was in no way responsible for your father's death, and I am truly sorry that I used and indeed blackened his memory in the way I did. While unforgivable, these wild accusations have to stop. I am a writer of supernatural fiction, that is *all*."

Tears spilled silently down Joseph's face. Dr James softened, reached out with his liver-spotted hand and patted the younger man's knee before squeezing it affectionately.

"I lost him when I needed him the most," Joseph said quietly, looking embarrassed. "I was very directionless as a teenager, most troubled, and if it wasn't for the dedication of my mother and my father's brother, I would be in a worse-off state than I am now." He didn't elaborate further.

Dr James reached into his waistcoat pocket and pulled out a slightly battered pocket watch. He flipped it open, and satisfied that not too much of the morning had been eaten up, snapped it closed. He got up, retrieving the manuscript and put it into his bag.

"While I don't deny that you've been through a very trying time, I have stated the facts to the best of my knowledge. It has been a pleasure to make your acquaintance, even though you made a very serious charge against me – but we all make mistakes and say things we don't mean when emotional."

Joseph looked shocked. "You mean that's it? That's all you have to say on the matter?"

"Yes," snapped Dr James, as if his comforting actions of only a few moments ago had never happened. "I have helped as much as I am able. If you need further assistance, please leave a message with the porter, who will pass it on."

With that, he left the room, bidding Mrs Humphries a good day on his way out. Joseph picked up the two newspaper clippings and slid them into the envelope along with the photographs of Dr James at Aldeburgh. Then it came to him, the simplest of plans, and he smiled albeit a little sadly. Montague Rhodes James was going to help him find out what happened to his father whether he liked it or not.

*

The car pulled up outside the hotel he frequented on every visit to Aldeburgh, *The White Lion*. Getting out, M.R. James breathed in deeply, the salt in the air making his nostrils tingle, and not unpleasantly. He waited as the driver retrieved his luggage from the boot of the car and then proceeded to walk into the hotel, Dr James following leisurely.

He had been in two minds whether to come to Aldeburgh; of course he had returned every year since the death on the beach, but it was Joseph's appearance that had rattled him so. He was aware of the letters that he'd initially been sent by the younger man and had read them, hoping that if he simply ignored them the nuisance would go away. It was extremely foolish of him to dress a real life story with supernatural overtones, never thinking for a second that anyone would put two and two together and *definitely* not the son of the deceased. What he had desperately wanted to say, but daren't as Joseph Payton would have been mortified, was that the stories he wrote, in the main, were merely whimsies, written while slightly drunk on good brandy and primarily for his colleagues, or, more recently, a select gathering of Eton whom he enjoyed transfixing with what he liked to call "a pleasing terror". He was satisfied with the external interest in his work, and his collections were very fine, but the fact of the matter was that it wouldn't bother him in the slightest if the public stopped buying his books.

In the end Aldeburgh's charms were too great to resist, they always had been. He thought back to the first time he visited and little had changed in the village since then. Ironically enough, he had struggled with the notion of writing about Aldeburgh in a short story in the first place, thinking that if he revealed its locations the magic would be lost. So he changed the name and mixed up the ingredients slightly, but for the discerning armchair detective it wouldn't take a lot to figure which little seaside village on the Suffolk coast he was talking about.

As Dr James was taken to his room, the receptionist told him that his friend, who would be joining him on this trip, was delayed by several days due to an aunt dying suddenly. Thinking that he would do well to whittle away a few hours after he unpacked, he went back downstairs and looked through the various books on offer in the reading room. The only thing that held any interest was a copy of *New Tales of Horror by Eminent Authors* – a book that Dr James had in his library, but was yet to read. He looked through the contents and his nose wrinkled when he saw Arthur Machen's name, but Richard Middleton and M.P. Shiel would soon make up for Machen's inclusion.

He took the book outside with him. The wind had picked up ever so slightly, making him glad that he had put on his jacket. It wasn't too oppressive weather though, so Dr James ambled across the road to the beach and hired a deckchair. Once he had found a suitably level spot, he began to read.

Several of the stories were utter tripe and obviously written by hacks who had no understanding of the finer points of the English language, but James, loath as he was to admit it, was completely enthralled by several of the stories – so much so that he didn't notice the presence standing next to him.

"Good day to you," the presence said.

Dr James looked up, dismayed, recognising the voice instantly. "What are you doing here?" he barked. "Trying to ruin my holiday?"

"No sir," Joseph almost sneered, "trying to find the person who *killed* my father." He was holding a deckchair and proceeded to open it. Dr James made no move to get up and leave.

"The truth, sir, is that I didn't know that you were going to be here, but I made an educated guess and hoped that you would be. It's fine, I'm not staying at the hotel, I would never be that impudent. I'll room at another place in town." Joseph sat down and made himself comfortable, putting his hands deep into the pockets of his long trenchcoat. He looked at the Provost steadily.

James sighed, closed the book and placed it on his knee. "So what do you plan to do whilst here? Apart from the obvious, of course. And where's your luggage?" Dr James was surprised by the acidity in his voice.

"I never take much with me when I travel. Clothes can be washed and dried before bed and before I rise. But if you really want to know, what I'll do here is make enquiries to try and discover where the 'Ager' homestead was, then go there and look

172

for signs of disturbance in the earth, and then take it from there. I'll try and get under the skin of whoever killed my father. My presence will hopefully shock his killer to try and come after me ..."

"And what will you do if he or she does?"

"I'll shoot them where they stand." From his right pocket, Joseph pulled out a Webley revolver. He didn't appear concerned by the look of shock that appeared on Dr James' face.

"And what happens if you make a mistake and you shoot the wrong person? You'll swing, mark my words. And I wouldn't lift a finger, not if you gunned somebody down in cold blood." Dr James let the book drop from his knee onto the sand.

"And if I shot you? There would be circumstantial evidence in my favour."

"Are you insane, man?" Dr James leapt up out of his chair and for the first time in a long time a searing bolt of pain ran down his leg, the result of an accident many years before. He gasped, clutching at it, sitting back down, looking at Joseph furiously. "If I haven't persuaded you of my innocence, then I am clearly talking to someone who has taken leave of his senses."

"He could have found the crown, and you being such an *antiquarian* could have killed him and stolen it from him. You're elderly and jaded now, granted, but go back a decade, you could have overpowered him. He was after all a 'rabbity anæmic subject'.

Dr James guffawed. "Oh, my dear boy." He lifted his glasses up slightly and wiped a solitary laughter tear from his wrinkled skin. "After your father died, I made one or two enquiries myself and discovered approximately what I believe to be the location of the 'Ager' steading. If you want, we can walk there and you can go forage to your heart's content. If you find something and it's the *mythical* crown, then you can prove that I am nothing but a foolish scholar whose love of fantastical stories has clearly gone to his head. But I will say this for the last time. I am an author of ghost and supernatural fiction, who was inspired by the story your father told me and then inspired by his death, as uncaring as that sounds, to write a work of fiction which was part-based on true events. I cannot apologise enough. But after I show you the 'Ager' place, I expect you to leave me alone. No more threats or posturing from you, please. Stay in the village if you wish or go back to your own home, but you will no longer intrude on my privacy. I will summon the police and you can tell them all the stories under the sun."

Dr James got up again, this time more slowly. He favoured his leg and his face relaxed when there was no pain. "We can walk along the beach for a while before we walk out of the village and go in-country for a few miles. It's a long walk, made longer by the way

173

that we'll go, but I thought you might like to stop for a moment where they found your father."

The words hung on the air, waiting for Joseph to snatch at them. He was up in an instant, the gun back in his pocket. "Come on then Provost, we've walking to do."

The wind had eased somewhat and half a mile further down the beach, Dr James realised that he had left the horror book behind. He hoped that it wouldn't get taken by the tide; he hated doing disservices to books, no matter their content. His leg was fine, it wasn't giving him any trouble as yet, even though they were walking on small pebbles, but he thought that by the time he reached the 'Ager' site, it might cause him considerable discomfort.

Twenty minutes later, Dr James stopped abruptly, looking intently at the Martello Tower and at the cut in the middle of the dunes.

"It was here. This is where he was found. I'll leave you with your thoughts for a while."

Joseph's answer surprised him. "No."

They continued to walk in silence, the wind became stronger. One sudden gust nearly caught Joseph unawares; he was slender and had almost no meat to his bones.

They left the beach and walked down a high-hedged lane; the wind here was dampened somewhat. Twisting and turning their way through the countryside, Dr James pointed in the direction of a small copse of woods on the top of a slight mound, about half a mile away.

"It's just beyond those trees. You'll be able to see why when we get there. There's a gap in them that lets you see the beach and sea beyond for miles in either direction."

And then they arrived – at a three-quarters ruined cottage, the roof of which had collapsed, taking most of the house with it. Thick brambles grew everywhere and seemed to protect the cottage from would-be intruders. The trees surrounding them swayed in the strong breeze. James sat on a wind-blown tree trunk about ten metres away as Joseph reached into his pocket and pulled out his envelope and from it, two photographs. He stared at them, then held them out at arm's length, and moved around in a circle until he thought he had come to the place the first photograph depicted. The wind tried its best to whip the photographs from the young man's hand, but he quickly put them back in the envelope and into an inside pocket of his trenchcoat.

"This is the place," Joseph said, with a look of cold determination on his face.

Dr James looked up at him, half expecting him to be holding the gun. But the younger man's hands were empty.

"You can go now, Provost."

"Very well. I hope you find what you're looking for. If you do however, I have no wish to see it, so don't come gloating." Dr James got up from his seat and walked away down the gentle slope, his left foot coming down on the corpse of a small sparrow – he winced as the bones crunched under his weight.

*

Dr James was adamant that nothing was going to ruin the rest of his holiday; he hoped that the book he had left behind on the shingle wasn't too spoiled, or had had pages torn from it. The wind was certainly picking up again, stronger than before, nearly pushing the Provost over on a few occasions.

Of course, Joseph would come back with nothing and James wondered how long it would be before the accusations began. And then there was the gun. The Provost decided that as soon as he got into the village he would call on the policeman and say that there was a rather unstable chap who was a danger to himself and to others. If there were questions to be asked, Dr James knew he could answer them – even if the situation was odd and might raise eyebrows. But in his favour was the esteem and probity his name carried; he would be believed, there would be no reason why he shouldn't be.

Passing the Martello Tower and continuing down the lonely stretch of sand, a sound whipped passed Dr James, carried with the strong wind. He stopped and cocked his ear. It was high pitched, disjointed and nearly vanished under the increasing roar of the wind but it was almost as if he was *meant* to hear it.

"I put it back! I put it back!"

Dr James turned around. In the distance he could see Joseph sprinting towards him; he was running very, very fast, no doubt being helped along by the severe gusts that would see several trees felled before the day was out. This far away, Joseph's face was an undistinguishable blob of white.

The wind blew into Dr James's face and again that same phrase, now sounding like a scream, was as loud as if it had been shouted in his ear.

"I put it back ... *OH GOD!*"

The sky, which was aphotic and angry before, had turned an inky black. At eye level there was still enough light to see, even though James's vision had become grainy and scratched.

175

Joseph was carried off his feet, along the beach, about a metre into the air. He went no further up, but it appeared as if he was levitating. Dr James looked on in horror as suddenly the younger man's body was folded back on itself, the heels of his shoes slamming into his head, spine snapping as easily as a dead twig. It sounded like a starter's pistol.

Then the wind dropped, jarring Dr James with its suddenness. Joseph fell to the ground.

Dr James began running as fast as his old body would take him, his leg screaming with pain, his heart trip-hammering in his chest, a bird fluttering its wings against its cage, trying to get out. The sky slowly reverted back to being grey and overcast.

When he reached Joseph, it was plain to see that the young man was quite dead. His neck was broken; head twisted around so much so his face was buried in the sand. His arms and legs were in positions unfathomable to the human eye. Bones poked out of fabric.

"Oh Joseph," Dr James croaked, sure that the violence was going to re-visit any second. "I didn't know that ..." He couldn't think of the right words to say, and to dwell further on it ... therein lay the madness which was only a whisper away from taking him. But whatever had been here wouldn't return unless whatever it was that Joseph had found at the 'Ager' place was disturbed again. Which the Provost firmly had no intention of ever doing.

His hands shaking violently, Dr James opened up the dead man's jacket and felt for the envelope which he eased out and slipped into his own. When Joseph was found, Dr James didn't want anyone to look at the photographs and go foraging. It wasn't lost on him that if he had found the crown when he had visited the 'Ager' place, he would have met his end as violently as Joseph had. He slowly limped away from the broken remains, an old man confused and shaken by the invisible line between his writing and the truly unknown. All the way back to the hotel he felt as if he was being watched by an unseen presence, and knowing that the executor of the carnage wrought upon poor Joseph Payton was the force that was bound with the last remaining crown of East Anglia.

Knowing that he shouldn't but feeling as if he *must*, he turned around to look back one last time and, standing over the body was a man in what had once been a respectable suit but was now almost rags. He was thin, "rabbity looking", as Dr James might have said, and his dark, broken mouth was hanging open in an almost soundless scream of hopeless grief. James turned from this and, despite his leg, now excruciatingly painful, began to run desperately over the shingle.

Arriving back at the hotel, Dr James immediately retired to bed, and when his friend arrived, several days later, Dr James simply spent most of his time in the empty reading room, drinking brandy and waiting for the holiday to be over, truly expecting that at any moment Joseph would be found and the link between James, the boy and the boy's father would be unearthed.

Once back at Eton, Montague Rhodes James decided that the trip to Aldeburgh was to be his last. Joseph's broken body and his father standing next to him haunted Dr James until he died, a year later.

THE KILLER HOUNDS OF SOUTHERY

Not all the demon dogs alleged to haunt rural East Anglia have supernatural origins. One popular story, set in the Cambridgeshire fen country and dating from the early Middle Ages, concerns a canine monster whose creation is explained in plausible detail.

First of all, it is important to remember that the fens of the Middle Ages were very different from those today, which are largely drained and used as agricultural land. It is no surprise that, back in the 1070s, the outlaw Hereward the Wake and his band of Saxon desperadoes were able to hold out against the armies of William the Conqueror for years and years: the fenland in those days was a vast, mist-begirt wilderness of marsh, broad and reed-bed, with occasional small islands, though most of these, and the pathways that led to them, were unknown to all but a local few.

On an unspecified date sometime after the Norman Conquest of England, a party of monks from the cathedral chapter at Ely commenced the construction of a new church on what in those days was called Southery Island (it is now a civil parish on the official border with Norfolk, though still only a village). However, the island was already occupied by a group of fen-folk, among whose number were concealed a band of robbers. These felons, who now feared their livelihood might be exposed, tried to frighten the monks away by abducting several of them, murdering them and dumping their bodies. The Abbot of Ely sent soldiers to arrest the murderers, but the vicious band simply melted into the marshland mist. When the Abbot appealed to his neighbour, the Norman baron of Northwold, for knights to assist, this help was refused. Northwold had many times sent his knights into the fens to hunt down miscreants, and few had returned alive. Instead, he delivered a pack of very savage wolfhounds to the island, and told the monks that these beasts would offer them adequate protection. The problem was that the monks had been living on a diet of freshly-captured fish, which the dogs could not tolerate. Eventually, driven mad by hunger, the pack went on a bloody rampage, not just hunting, killing and eating the local robbers, but killing innocent villagers, and then killing the monks as well.

Those few who survived, monks and villagers alike, fled Southery Island, leaving the murderous dogs marooned. With nothing else to eat, the pack finally turned on each other. The dominant bitch – a *large, powerful and truly ferocious specimen – was the last one left, though when all the other dogs were eaten and their remnants had rotted to carrion, even this monstrous creature succumbed to hunger.*

The villagers were the first to return to Southery. They found the last dog, mangy, half-starved and only barely alive. They took her in, fed her and tamed her, and in time she became a fine hunting-dog, fiercely loyal to her patrons. But when the monks returned to the island and continued work on their church, the dog was antagonistic to them. There were several incidents – both of the dog attacking lone monks and the monks attempting to poison the dog. On one occasion the dog went missing for several days. The villagers felt certain that she had been killed, but then she returned, apparently impregnated. This was a puzzle as there were no other dogs on the island, and here the tale becomes somewhat fanciful. It is never specifically stated but there is a clear, if implied suspicion that one of East Anglia's many ghost hounds – possibly Black Shuck himself – was the father.

In due course only one pup was born, though he was said to resemble neither dog nor wolf, but something in between, and that he grew bigger, stronger and fiercer than either. He too remained loyal to the villagers and disliked the monks. On the day of the new church's grand opening, he slunk through the reeds and attacked and tore out the throat of one of the knights guarding the Bishop of Elmham. In retaliation, he was hacked and slashed by the other knights. Fatally wounded, he limped off into the fens, where he eventually died.

The medieval church at Southery remained a ruin into the early 20th century, but stories told how right up until the time of its demolition, scorings would regularly appear on the stones of its crypt: the marks of claws and teeth, as if some savage animal were attempting to get at the monks' bones within. Even today, on May 29th – the date of the Southery Feast – the phantom hound is said to howl out in the fens, and anyone who hears him will die within the next 12 months.

LIKE SUFFOLK, LIKE HOLIDAYS
Alison Littlewood

He had complained about her luggage. Now that they were here, driving along the little lanes that wound past thatched cottages and centuries-old trees, he could still hear his own words; and he could hear the tone of them, grating and complaining. He had lost his job in the summer; she had been understanding, caring. He'd moved into her flat and had spent the time since looking after it and sending application forms into the ether. Now it was their holiday, one she'd paid for, and he'd had to lug her bags, one after the next, into the boot of the car. He'd almost wished they would vanish too, taking her lace panties and silk slips with them.

Darren sighed, pushed the thought away. The air rushing in through the open window was clean and fresh and bracing, clearing out each mildewed corner of his mind, except those words. Then he felt her hand on his arm, and he turned and saw her smile, and even the taint of them was gone: he was alone, just him and Angela, and no one else. Nothing else that could remind them of home or his own dissatisfaction, nothing to remind *her*.

"Head down to the coast, turn left, and straight on till Dawning," she said, and for a moment that made him think of some story he'd read when he was a child, when such things seemed worth doing: then it was gone. He followed the road, passing a low barn, a stolid chestnut pony in a field, a wooden-framed, pink-painted house with roses growing over the door, and he remembered what Angie had said to him when she'd booked this place. "I want somewhere perfect," she'd said, and turned to him and smiled her smile, the one that showed a dimple in her left cheek and the gap between her teeth. "*Perfect.*"

As if on cue, the sun speared down through grey-ridged clouds, making everything bright, making everything new. Another cottage appeared round the bend in the road, swathed in rambling honeysuckle. *Perfect.*

*

The place was everything she'd wanted. Darren had known it would be as they edged around the coast; in the distance he could see a clean white windmill, and further yet, a small neat house that seemed to tower above the surrounding trees like a place in a dream.

They passed a boating lake, turned back towards the ever-present sea, and saw Dawning Cottage. Darren turned onto the drive and cut the engine.

Their holiday home, like much of the village of Thorpeness, was small and contained and mock-Tudor in style. It was painted white, glowing in the sunshine, edged by crooked black beams. There was a low awning at the front, sweetly curving over the door, small gleaming windows that sparked back the light. There was a basket on the step, the neck of a bottle and a loaf of bread sticking out of it. Angie was out of the car in a second and Darren heard her exclamations. "They left honey and wine," she called out. "And the key."

Inside the cottage it was just the same, everything small and neat and beautifully made, nothing out of place. One window had been left open and bright yellow curtains shifted in the breeze, freshening everything. The sofas were cosy, striped yellow and white, spotlessly clean. There were shelves with seaside decorations – a wooden lighthouse, pale driftwood carvings. There were blue-washed walls with pictures of a boat on the sea, of wheeling birds, the same white windmill they'd seen outside. On a shelf was another basket, this time filled with pebbles; Angie exclaimed again, picked one up and turned it in her hand. "There are names on here," she said. "Look!"

Darren saw that she was right. Names had been etched into the grey stones, Clarissa and Annabelle and Penelope, all in a flowing script he could feel when he touched them. Angie cried out, plucked another from the pile, and Darren wasn't surprised to see her name on it – *Angela* – along with the rest.

"No Darren, then," he said, and she playfully punched his arm. Darren scowled. She didn't need to answer: of course there wasn't a Darren. This place had probably never had a Darren staying here in its life.

Angie went to the coffee table and picked up a book. Darren was unsurprised to see it was about interior design: saw the words *Seaside Chic* on the cover before she flipped it over, cooed over the wooden bathing huts and driftwood carvings shown within. For a second she paused over the image of a painting, a watercolour of a white windmill framed with rope; then she snapped the book closed. Darren blinked. For a moment he'd wondered if there was another picture hidden away inside that windmill, in a hidden room, two people standing in front of it and wondering …

"Come on." She waved a hand in front of his eyes. "You can't come to the seaside without seeing the sea. Let's go paddle."

181

Darren allowed himself to be led once more to the door, out of the gate and across the narrow lane to the beach.

*

The beach was pebble, not sand, and a little uncomfortable underfoot as Darren followed Angie down to the sea. It stretched in front of them, a shiny pale blue, at once endlessly moving and endlessly still, and at first he couldn't take his eyes from it. The pebbles, while rough, set up the perfect loud crunching of holidays, and the sea hissed under everything, hushing over and over.

"Come on." Angie was pulling off her trainers, sitting close by the edge of the sea, where the pebbles fell away in a steeper slope. She pulled off her socks too, stuffed them into her shoes. Then she stood and pulled a face. "Ouch." She grinned, to show she didn't mean it, and held out her hand.

Darren followed, standing on the steep ledge of pebbles and letting his weight carry him down, his feet sliding and sinking deep into the mass. The pebbles felt dry and rough against his feet, and cold, but he found he liked it. He grinned suddenly, pulled free of the stones and took her hand. They stepped into the sea together, gasping at the shock of it, laughing like children.

He looked at Angie. Her cheeks were pink, her hair swinging loose around her face. She put her arms around her waist, made a mock 'brrr' sound.

Darren slowly spun in a circle. He looked first down the coastline towards Aldeburgh, the little houses in the distance; back towards their cottage. Then he turned and looked north, up the coast. There he saw more houses, little woodlands, more of those pebbles. And there, shrunken by the distance but still rising like an improbable vision, big and grey and unpleasantly square, was Sizewell nuclear power station.

Ahaaa! he thought, and he didn't know why.

Then Angie reached down and splashed him with the perfect waves, a shock of pure clean cold, and he forgot all about the power station, and he turned and smiled and splashed her back.

*

That night they drank the wine and sat in the lounge, the television off, listening to the sounds that came in through the window. Somewhere nearby must be a tennis court; the intermittent *pock – pock* of the ball drifted in with the night air, and then the high sweet voices of children calling to each other. Darren surmised that one

182

was called Crispin and the other Jocasta, and he half closed his eyes and smirked. Beneath everything, the sea whispered; an endless refrain with no beginning and no ending.

Then he felt Angie's touch on his face.

He opened his eyes to see her face close to his, that single rogue dimple, the familiar gap between her teeth. In the next moment she was kissing him, and she tasted of wine, and he forgot everything and started to kiss her back.

Later they lay amid rumpled sheets and soft pillows and the bright scattering of rose petals that had been left across their bed. Despite himself, Darren slept long and deep. He didn't remember dreaming.

*

The boating lake was called 'the Meare', and the early morning sun set up a soft hazy glitter on its surface. "The boatmen are out already," said Angie, pointing. "Look!"

Not long afterwards Darren found himself in a red and white rowing boat, the oars in his hands, and Angie sitting opposite. He started to row and the water spread out around them. It seemed to stretch on for miles, and yet the boatman had said it was nowhere more than three feet deep.

In the distance was the white windmill, and beyond that, the tall tower of a house that loomed above the trees.

"It's the House in the Clouds," said Angie. "It used to be a water tower." She laughed, indicating some islands that lay in the other direction. "Let's head over there," she said. "I want to see Wendy's home."

Darren didn't know what she meant and couldn't be bothered to ask. The work was warming and the sun was too hot on his hair; his back started to prickle. He took up the oars and turned the boat. At least the islands would provide some shade. When they drew near, though, he saw that she was right: a little sign said 'Wendy's home' and another said 'Pirate's lair.' For a moment he thought he glimpsed, between the trees, the long lean body of a crocodile.

"Oh, how clever." Angie was grinning, showing her dimple. "It's like being in a story."

Darren smiled back. She was right, it was: and he tried to remember the way he'd felt when he'd read it, excited and enfolded in its magic, probably grinning the way Angie was now.

She nudged him with her foot. "What do you think?"

He glanced at his watch. "Time's nearly up. We'd better be getting back." He didn't meet her eye as he plunged one oar into the water, tilting them in his haste to turn the boat. For a moment he thought he felt the blade touch the bottom, caught a glimpse of something beneath the water; then they were around and he was rowing towards the boathouse, looking over Angie's shoulder at the places they had already been.

*

Thorpeness was pretty and spotless and bathed in light. It had a close-cropped golf course and well-kept tennis courts and little timbered houses with not a flower out of place. They ate at a pub where the quality of the food matched the quaintness of the exterior and the comfort of the chairs, and walked arm in arm across a village green. Darren found himself scanning the frontage of each house, peering across their lawns.

"What's up?" Angie said.

"Nothing." Darren shrugged, then forced a laugh. What he had been doing was looking for imperfections: straggly grass at the edge of a lawn, chipped paint perhaps, or a cracked window. And he was remembering the flat: the rotten doorframe that needed replacing, the bins that never could be pushed quite out of sight.

Of course, he hadn't been able to spot any bins, here. Or peeling paint; anything that was broken or misshapen or flawed. Not a single thing to spoil the picture.

"Why can't home be like this?" he asked.

Angie flashed him a smile. "It's perfect, isn't it? I knew it'd be just the place to –"

"To?"

"Nothing," she said. "Come on, let's get back. We could go out for a drive."

*

They drove to the House in the Clouds. Darren slowed in front of it, drew to a halt. The house was another holiday let; they couldn't just go in. It was tall, with rich clean paintwork.

"How did you know?" he asked.

"Know what?"

"About the House in the Clouds. About Wendy's home."

She laughed, punched him on the arm. "No idea. A guidebook, I suppose."

"We don't have a guidebook."

"Well, somewhere. Anyway, so what? This is perfect, isn't it?" She rested her arm on the open window and leaned out. The breeze pulled her hair this way and that.

Darren didn't answer. He indicated, slowly pulled away, skirted the village. He hadn't consciously done so but found he'd come full circle, back to the cottage. He stopped again, facing that endless sea.

"It's beautiful," Angie said.

Darren didn't reply. He only looked. He wasn't looking at the sea; he was looking at Angie. She met his eye.

"Perfect, isn't it," she said, and Darren realised she'd said it before, over and over, a broken record he couldn't switch off. But that wasn't the main thing in his mind: that was the sight of Angie's face.

"Where is it?" he said.

"Where's what?" She smiled prettily. It wasn't there.

"Your dimple. You always have a dimple, just one. Left cheek. It isn't there anymore."

"Darren, what the hell are you talking about?" She smiled wider, laughing at him. This time the dimple was back, but so was its twin; one Darren had never seen before. Now she had two.

Before he realised what he was doing, he reached out and caught her face in his hands, pinching it tight, turning her face. Finally, he let go. Now there were two livid red marks on her cheeks. She stared at him; she wouldn't stop staring.

"Sorry," he muttered.

"That hurt." It wasn't the words so much as her tone that made Darren catch his breath.

"I really didn't mean to. You looked odd for a minute, that's all." He roused himself. "But it's nothing. I really am sorry. I don't think I've been myself lately."

She stared a moment longer, then gave a sympathetic sigh. "I know," she said, "but it'll be all right, Darren. I promise." And she smiled a wide, over-bright smile, showing two matching dimples and a row of perfect teeth.

*

The next day Darren woke feeling refreshed, his body light with energy. He made tea for them both, kissed Angie's shoulder and dressed. "Let's go to the windmill," he said. They had passed near it on their drive yesterday, but somehow hadn't really looked at it. He glanced up at the wall and saw it in the painting there, small and gleaming. "Let's go," he repeated.

185

It wasn't long before they turned onto a narrow lane. They walked the rest of the way, Darren pulling ahead, until he saw it clearly for the first time. It looked as though a white windmill had been placed on top of a little house, complete with a little red sloping roof. They could read the 'Closed' sign from where they stood, but it didn't matter; Darren could see that it was just a thing, just a place. There was nothing *else*. He rubbed his eyes, felt Angie's hand on his.

"What is it?" she asked.

"Nothing. Nothing. I just thought – it could answer—"

"Answer what?"

He pulled his hand away. "I said it was nothing."

He turned and walked back to the car, remained sitting behind the wheel with his hand over his eyes until Angela joined him. Then he turned. "You see, nothing's really perfect," he said. "It's always the little thing – a flaw, some tiny fault, that *makes* them perfect. Don't you see?" He stared into her face. She smiled a nervous smile, tried a laugh. Darren looked at her face, the line of her cheeks, her lips; realised he was trying to see what was wrong with it. "I think I'm going mad," he said. He leaned forward, switched on the engine.

"Of course you're not. You're still adjusting, that's all. Just relax. This place – it'll do you good."

He sighed, glanced back at her. "Yeah," he muttered. And then, "maybe," although he knew, deep down, that she was right: she had relaxed into this place, doing what holiday makers should. It was what *he* should be doing. And he could feel its pull on him, its sleepy lanes, soft breezes, the gentle shush of the sea. He *should* relax, rest into it, let it lull him –

He shook himself, sat up straighter. "All right," he said. "But there's one more thing I need to look at first."

*

He drove back around the lanes. He'd drive a little and stop. Drive a little and stop. He felt Angie's gaze on him, but he didn't turn to her and didn't speak. He was looking over gates and into gardens. Eventually he headed south from the village, taking turns that didn't seem to lead anywhere.

"There's" – Angie pointed towards a tourist sign pointing out some attraction they were supposed to want to see and Darren immediately turned in the opposite direction. Now they were heading down a narrow lane, away from anywhere. It narrowed

186

further, then opened out; there was a pub in front of them. Darren pulled up outside.

"Are we going for lunch?" Angie's voice was too bright.

"Wait here." He got out of the car, walked towards the low building, mellow in the sunshine. Instead of heading inside, though, he skirted it, walked around the back. He crossed the perfectly gravelled car park and looked around that too, scratching his head.

"What's up?" Angie had followed him; strange he hadn't heard her footsteps.

"They're not here," he said. "They're not anywhere."

"What, love?"

He met her eye at last. "The *bins*," he said. "The bloody bins."

"What on earth do you mean?"

"There are no *bins*," he said, "anywhere." He waved his arm around the car park. "Do you see any?"

She shook her head. "I don't understand."

"Neither do I," he said. "But I will." He strode back to the car, feet crunching across the gravel, so loud he couldn't tell if Angie was following. He sat behind the wheel and waited. When her door opened and closed he didn't look around.

"I just wanted one," he said. "Just one. Where are the scruffy bits? Where are the bad areas, the dodgy streets? The places no one wants to be?"

He felt her peeling his hand from the wheel and stroking it. "Shhh," she said. "This is holidays, Darren. We aren't looking for those things, are we? We don't need them."

"But I wanted to see *one*," he whispered. Angie was silent in the passenger seat. He didn't try to explain, knew it wasn't any use; she wouldn't understand. Just one, he'd said, and that was all he wanted; one little trace of imperfection that would make paradise perfect; and he couldn't bloody find it.

*

Darren was dreaming. He knew he was dreaming because he was standing on the banks of the Meare and he was looking at himself. He was standing in the water, a long way out with the water spread around him, and yet it only came up to his thighs. As Darren watched, Darren dipped his hand in the water and tried to hold it out, as though to show him something reflected in its surface. It ran through his fingers and back into the lake. He mouthed a word. Darren couldn't hear it, but he knew what Darren had said: had felt his own lips move, saying the same word at the same time, the one that didn't seem to fit.

187

He opened his eyes and saw the rise of Angie's shoulder under the sheets. He started to reach out, then drew back. She wouldn't welcome him waking her. Silently, Darren slipped out of bed.

He found himself dressing and leaving the cottage, walking towards the Meare. Cool night air struck him in the face, waking him fully, but it was too late; his legs were carrying him the way they wanted to go. It would have felt ridiculous just to stop in his tracks and turn, start walking back again in the other direction, even though no one was looking.

He stepped onto the pathway that ran around the Meare. He couldn't see the windmill now, or the House in the Clouds; there was only the night waiting there, dark and silent and watching. The water shone like oil. The moonlight was out there, a white globe in the middle of the lake. Darren kicked off his shoes. In the next moment he had slipped into the water, smooth and easy as slipping between sheets; but the cold was enormous, grasping hold of him. He stood and the water came to his thighs. The dark line of it rose, sucking its way up his legs.

He shuffled his feet on the bottom of the lake, kicking up mud. It was only that, soft and slippery, nothing more. He looked into the water and saw only a blank surface. What the hell had he expected? He looked back towards the village. Even now, Angie might be awake. What would she think? Would she scream if she saw him in the doorway, this dark and muddied thing? He imagined the sound of it ringing into the night, everyone in the village starting awake, and felt an odd sort of satisfaction. He poked his feet into the mud a little more, felt it insinuate itself between his toes. Then he climbed out and shook mud from his feet and sluiced water from his legs, picked up his shoes and walked back the way he had come.

*

He got into the shower before she woke up, heard her 'good morning' as he lathered himself, rubbing heat into his frozen skin. The bright sound of it made his heart sink. Had nothing changed? Hadn't she?

Angie appeared in the doorway, smiled and put a cup of tea down on the shelf over the sink. She gave his body a wry 'maybe later' look, and disappeared.

He was unsurprised to find the tea was just right, reviving, smooth and strong and just the right amount of milk; quite unlike the way she made it at home. Perfect.

After they breakfasted, they walked down to the beach. Darren squinted against the bright morning, pictured himself standing out in

188

the water. He sighed, slipped a hand around Angie's waist. "I'm sorry," he said. "I've been – a bit – "

"You're under strain," she said. "Of course you are. It's only natural."

"But—"

"Let's forget about it." She leaned in and kissed him. It was a good kiss. "Let's just enjoy this, shall we?"

They walked together into the sea, barely stopping to take off their shoes. They sloshed about and headed down the coast, turned to paddle back again. "It's gorgeous," she said, and he looked into her eyes and knew that it was. The pebbles were good underfoot, rounded and smooth and oddly warm. Strange how quickly the touch of them had become comfortable.

That made him think of something. He looked up, following the coastline north. His smile faded. His mouth went dry. The great grey square of the power station had risen on the horizon, dull and solid and definitely *there.* Now it was gone. There was nothing to spoil the view at all. He turned and looked back at Angie. She smiled, bringing those dimples to her cheeks, the ones he had always loved: *no.* Not always. There was something wrong with the picture.

"What is it?" she asked, and he found he couldn't answer.

*

Back in the cottage he made her tea, had her sit on the yellow and white striped sofa and put her feet up. He did it carefully, dunking the tea just so, adding the right amount of milk. Then he spooned out the teabag, put his hand beneath to catch any drips, crossed the kitchen and dropped it into the bin.

He went to carry the mugs through; but something stopped him. He turned, slowly, and looked back at the bin. It was clean and silver and shining, with a black plastic top. He put his foot on the lever and it opened. The insides were black, too. Clean and black and smooth. He leant closer.

There was no smell; that was what he noticed. That, and the bin was empty. The teabag must be in the bottom but he couldn't see it. It was dark in there, black and dead as the space between the stars.

He put out a hand and reached in. He was careful not to touch the sides, though it was clean, must be clean; and his hand simply wasn't there anymore. He could see his arm, the hairs on the back of his wrist, and nothing more. He waggled his fingers. He couldn't see them, couldn't even feel them.

"What are you doing?"

Darren jumped, snatched his hand back and stared at it. His fingers were whole. He moved them, clenching and unclenching them in front of his face.

"Mmm, tea," she said, her voice happy, the voice of someone on holiday, the voice of someone who knew their life was perfect, who knew their place was perfect. Darren turned. She stood there with her two sweet dimples, hair curling around her face. Had her hair always curled like that? He couldn't remember. He closed his hand into a fist. Angie leaned over and picked up a mug, steam rising from it and into the air, took a sip and put it down again.

He took a step forward.

"Darren?"

He swung back his arm, raised his fist to the level of his shoulder. He didn't feel himself do it; only vaguely knew he had. Her skin, too, was perfect. Her eyes shone. The whites of them were very white. And then he let everything go, everything he felt, everything that wasn't right, the bad things and the disappointing things and the flaws in everything, and he slammed them into the wall next to her face.

*

Later he sat on one sofa and she sat on the other. They were watching television. Darren was cradling his hand; it still hurt. He felt he deserved to hurt. "I'm sorry," he said again.

Finally, Angie looked at him. "I told you I forgave you," she said, and she tried a little smile.

"I never – I don't know what happened." Darren said the words, but he knew it to be a lie. He'd looked at her perfect face and her perfect hair and her perfect world and he'd just wanted to change it; that was all. But then he said something that was true. "I didn't want to hurt you."

She nodded, looked sympathetic. "I know, Darren."

He buried his face in his hands. He could feel the clean air from the open window caressing his skin. He could hardly stand it. He looked up, just as the distant *pock – pock* of a tennis ball started to drift inside. He let out a moan.

I wanted it to be like this, he thought, *didn't I? Everything, my whole life. Like Suffolk, like holidays.*

"Darren?"

He looked at her.

"I just want to understand one thing." Her voice was the perfect combination of smoothness and softness and kindness. "It's just, when you hit out like that. What *were* you thinking? I'm not

190

blaming you; I told you that and I meant it. I just – " her eyes went dewy. "I just don't understand why anyone would ever, ever want to hurt anybody." She settled back in her chair and her voice went distant. "Do you hear that? The children are playing. Isn't it lovely?"

But Darren wasn't listening any more. He had risen and walked out of the room.

*

There was a knife in Darren's hand. He wasn't sure how it had happened, but it was there, and it looked perfectly sharp and clean, and its blade gleamed as he tilted it this way and that. The light flashed in his face. He gave a slow smile.

He closed his eyes and she was lying there, spread awkwardly on the tile. Blood splashed across the duck-egg blue walls, coffee table books, driftwood carvings. A gout of it marred the whiteness of a little white windmill. No: she didn't lie awkwardly. She was graceful, her limbs neatly arranged. She was smiling even in death. As he watched, she opened her eyes. "Why, Darren?" she asked. "Why would anybody ever want to hurt anybody?"

Darren opened his eyes and let the knife fall from his hand. *It's not her,* he thought: *it's me.*

He crossed the kitchen in long strides and opened the bin. Then he caught hold of the lid and wrenched it loose. Inside, the dark waited. It was there. He couldn't see into it. It breathed, and its breath was sweet. It was like the opposite of everything, the opposite of Suffolk: the thing that lay beneath the skin of the world.

Slowly, he kicked off his shoes. He lifted one leg high and stepped inside, sat for a moment on its edge. It shouldn't have held, should have toppled under his weight, but it did not. He looked once around the neat kitchen. If it toppled, it would make a mess; therefore it wouldn't topple. Outside, it was perfect. Inside – what?

He smiled a thin-lipped smile, pushed himself up, brought his other leg inside. It shouldn't have fit, but it did, of course it did; it went numb at once. And he remembered standing on the edge of a lake, looking into his own eyes, holding out a handful of water that ran through his fingers, offering an answer but seeming to provide none. As he watched, he mouthed a single word: called out his own name. *Darren.* He mouthed it again now as he clung to the edge.

Just one, he thought. *Just one little trace of imperfection to make paradise perfect, and it was there, all the time.* He just hadn't seen it until now.

191

He held on a moment longer and then he snapped his fingers open and let his body fall. He didn't close his eyes; he wanted to watch as the kitchen and the sunlight and all the beautiful Suffolk things passed rapidly out of sight.

THE DEMON OF WALLASEA ISLAND

E ven in the 21st century, the Essex marshes retain an air of timeless, unspoiled isolation. Difficult to explore except by boat, and famous for their creeks and mudflats, their tranquil villages and remote tidal inlets, they were long known to be the haunt of smugglers and pirates, and have been wreathed in tales of witchcraft all the way from the River Blackwater in the north to Foulness Point in the south.

At the very heart of this eerily quiet and beautiful region lies Wallasea Island. Sandwiched between the twin rivers Crouch and Roach, it looks more like a peninsula than a real island (though only bridges link it to the mainland), and is mostly used today – as it was in times past – for growing wheat and corn. It hosts several barns and farmhouses located far out among the crops, but little else happens there. Tourists arrive so rarely that the island is home to only a single campsite, which is not used a great deal.

It is a very peaceful place, and yet looks can be deceptive.

On the northeast side of Wallasea Island, there was once a ramshackle old farm called Tyle Barn. Though occupied throughout the 18th and 19th centuries and for at least half of the 20th, it was reputedly the haunt of an entity so violent and malignant that local folk insisted it was not a ghost but a demon. The details of its activities are sketchy; it is one of those myths that even today people in the vicinity seem reluctant to discuss. But it seems that even the buildings at Tyle Barn had a terrible aura. Farm labourers on the island didn't even like to pass the site in daytime let alone at night. Those unfortunate enough to have cause to enter it described a dreadful atmosphere of menace and misery, and a whispering, disembodied voice that would hiss at them in the harshest and most obscene terms. One visual manifestation was reported – though who by and when is uncertain – of a terrible form wreathed in fiery smoke, with what looked like wings folded behind its shoulders and horns sprouting from its forehead.

If all this sounds like the credulous folly of some old and primitive community, it's important to remember that in several recent reports of haunting – a good example being the case at Amityville in New York in the 1970s – devilish apparitions were described by witnesses, and their accounts were taken at face value by an awed public. (A noted demonologist who investigated the

Amityville case made a statement to the effect that apparitions with horns, hooves and other satanic paraphernalia were entirely plausible because, though they might not represent the actual appearance of damned or demonic souls, they were more than likely the result of negative energies drawing on the fears and imaginations of their victims).

The haunting at Tyle Barn became so serious that it finally resulted in a suicide. One of the residents, an old farmer – his name and the dates of his occupancy are lost to history – endured the malign presence for years and years. Whether this contributed to the failure of his health, his business affairs and ultimately his mental state, is unknown, but shortly before he took his own life, he told a neighbour that he was being driven to the point of madness by a bestial voice roaring at him to "Do it! Do it! Do it!"

What the Wallasea Island demon actually was or where it came from are open to question, though one interesting theory connects the island with the life of a famous witch.

The 18th century was the age of 'cunning men' – self-proclaimed warlocks, who, taking advantage of the relaxation in the laws against sorcery (the Witchcraft Act of 1735), felt free to create reputations for themselves as exponents of the mysterious arts. A female member of this fraternity – a 'cunning woman', if you like – was Mother Redcap, who, though she lived in London, spent much of her time in residence on Wallasea. Mother Redcap, whose real name was Jen Bingham, made her living as a fortune teller, but also had the reputation of being a midwife, an abortionist and even a poisoner. She was allegedly extremely ugly, and yet had a procession of lovers, some of whom she was suspected of murdering.

Again, that old question intrudes: was she really a witch, or was she just playing games to enhance her power and influence? Stories that she was seen travelling to her country residence on Wallasea by flying on a hurdle could only have added fuel to the debate, though how widely they were believed in the mid-18th century is uncertain. Mother Redcap eventually died of natural causes, but tales persisted afterwards that one of her familiars, an evil spirit which she had literally summoned from Hell, remained in the old East Anglian farmhouse. Nowhere is it written that she lived at Tyle Barn, but nowhere is it written that she didn't – and it isn't a difficult connection to make.

Nothing remains of Tyle Barn for modern investigators to look into. It was struck by a German bomb in the early 1940s (though suspicions have been aired that this wasn't a German bomb at all, but an action taken by the British government to destroy the hateful *place), and the rubble was finally washed away when a high tide inundated the area in 1953. All that remains now is Tyle Barn Marsh, a place of mist and stagnant bog pools, which are still, or so the folklorists assure us, to be avoided at all costs.*

THE LITTLE WOODEN BOX
Edward Pearce

Richardson didn't think of himself as a criminal. He had an eye for craftsmanship, especially in antiques, and though not an educated man, he also had a keen sense of history. It pained him to see objects go unappreciated that ought to be valued for the skill and care that had gone into making them, and it seemed outrageous to him when historic treasures were treated in a careless way that would damage them, or wear them out before their time. That was his undoing, really.

It was in a part of East Anglia known as the marshlands, in North Norfolk. The big skies and bleak, flat farmlands, dotted here and there with electricity pylons, have a strange quality of distance and indefinable sadness about them. Perhaps it is something to do with the emptiness of the country hereabouts, and the generally unkempt nature of many of the towns and, in particular, the villages. You can see a long way across the fields, and any tall object stands out for miles. This is perhaps the last part of England in which churches still dominate the landscape, much as they must have done in pre-industrial times. But then industry had never really caught on around here.

It was on a grey, wet and windy day, when the leaves were brown and shedding, that Richardson drove to the church. It was described in an old guide book of his as a particularly fine example of perpendicular architecture, and he was intrigued to find out what still survived, as even since the 1930s, when his book had been written, time and the activities of overzealous churchmen and restorers, to say nothing of thieves and vandals, have brought about a surprising level of losses in our churches. But as he pulled up on the grass verge outside the old stone wall, he saw that this church had great presence, at least externally. Its big, dark bulk was especially awe-inspiring against the overcast flat sky, and sat strongly and authoritatively in a churchyard which, for these out-of-the-way parts, was of an impressive extent.

On a board in the porch, a yellowing, plastic-encased notice announced:

This fine church is used regularly and is kept open as often as possible for the benefit of visitors. If locked, the key may be obtained from the Rectory immediately to the west of the church or from Mr. L. Byers at 2 Church Lane, the house with the blue door.

Tentatively, he tried the cold brown latch-ring of pitted iron. It lifted, and the great iron-studded wooden door slowly, reluctantly yielded to his touch.

Stepping inside, Richardson found himself in a magnificent, beautifully-preserved marshland church, big and empty. Sadly, there was no old glass, just clear panes, but the interior was a superb sight nonetheless. Much ancient wood was in evidence. A huge, beautifully-carved Jacobean screen, complete and in good condition, crossed the entire width of the nave at the tower end. Just inside the door a distinctive memorial tablet on the wall caught his eye. Star-shaped, it bore the inscription:

Iohannes Thurlstone, obit MDLXVII anno aetatis suae XLIV.
Spece ad lucem nec ad obscurum.

Above the wording were images of the sun and the moon, whilst below it were incomprehensible hieroglyphs and a curious, pyramid-like object.

His footsteps echoed eerily as he walked across the old stone floor down to the choir. Here there was an entrancing, if small-scale, array of carved stalls that were surely fifteenth century judging by their style and the skill with which the carvings on them were executed. Green men and strange beasts adorned the armrests, and the underside of the seats revealed the expected misericords of quaint scenes from medieval life. The expressions of the participants, and indeed the general feel of the carvings, reflected that superficially humorous but disquietingly unsentimental attitude to the sufferings of others that seems to characterise the England of the Middle Ages.

It was one of those churches that has all sorts of interesting odds and ends scattered around. There was a fair amount of wooden furniture, of indeterminate age, though the skilled eye might have detected a more recent origin to much of it than first appeared. More interesting were the smaller items, a profusion of which were lying about near the font, with its ornate cover. An old brass jug with incised decoration and a lid sat on the pedestal abutting the font base. Beside it was a very tall brass candlestick, of plain design but of some age and, presumably, value, and a surprising thing to find in an unlocked church.

Two big old chests lay on the flagstone floor by the screen, and there was also a wooden box of some kind, of seemingly ancient workmanship, on the floor on the other side of the font.

He picked up the box to examine it closely. It was about the size and shape of a toaster, was not heavy, and appeared to be made of some exotic wood – cedar perhaps? The wood had darkened and shrivelled slightly, but not enough to shrink the box away from its bindings, which consisted of a strip of deeply-patinated brass at either end. These strips were well-made with little curving arms coming off them, giving a pleasing appearance. A star, again neatly executed in brass, adorned the top. Finally, the whole thing was closed with a brass hasp.

The box opened surprisingly easily, and the interior colour and ever-so-faint fragrance confirmed that it was cedar. It was a simple but lovely thing. Clearly it was old – very old – and in excellent condition, apart from a scratch on one of the mounts which showed the yellow brass, and which had evidently happened very recently.

Outside the rain seemed to have eased off somewhat, but the wind had not, and it occasionally rattled the little clear glass panes in the windows, a disconcerting sound which took him a moment or so to pinpoint. Putting the box down, he went over to the windows to look, and on examining them closely found initials and dates – IR 1751 was one – carved into the soft stone of the window frames.

Early winter twilight was setting in, and with it came strange patterns of light and shade inside the church. Was that movement? He seemed for an instant to see something dark moving behind the screen. Looking sharply in that direction, it was clear that nothing was there. He dismissed it, but a minute or two later had the odd sense of seeing something: a man's figure, as if sitting in a pew, bearded and wearing a ruff, the whole thing monochrome grey as if carved from ancient wood. This really made him look closely, but once again there was nothing there, just a mixture of shapes that had perhaps made him picture, rather than see, a figure as he turned his head and outlines became confused. That was a strange thing to imagine, especially in such detail, but he had no sense of its being real and did not dwell on it.

He returned to the font to admire the treasures around it. They were not stacked in a tidy or careful way, but scattered about anyhow. He could just picture them being clumsily handled by the church's staff and visitors, and no doubt some delicate bit that had lasted centuries would eventually break off, and get lost. It did not seem as though anyone really cared about these wonderful antiques.

As if from nowhere, the thought came to him that it would be very easy to steal from this church. "But would it end there?"

followed on its heels. Richardson was not entirely scrupulous, but he was not beyond the reach of superstitious imaginings, and was uncomfortable with the idea of stealing from a church. Moreover, he had an ill-defined sense that there was some sort of background activity in this one, which was fine as long as you respected it, but if you did not – if you profaned it in some way – you might find that it was neither benevolent nor powerless, but would reach out and find you wherever you were and however safe you thought you may be.

The temptation, however, was great. The fact was – as he saw it – that he knew how to appreciate and look after delicate historical artefacts, and that clearly wasn't happening here. Here he was, the church was empty, and here was this wonderful box, which incidentally was not mentioned in the guide book, though the two large chests were. It was just starting to get knocked about, and it looked as though someone had recently found it tucked away somewhere and thought it might as well be put out in the church. It won't really matter to them, he thought, they obviously don't care about it, and if I took it home it'd get looked after and cherished. Besides, it's borrowing really, because I'm only be a temporary custodian of anything and I'll make sure it gets handed on to posterity in a good state.

No, it couldn't be left here, and he wouldn't get another opportunity like this one. It would probably take months before anyone even noticed it was missing, if they ever did. And there was a very good chance that someone else might steal it. He had to rescue it.

He stole the brassbound wooden box. It was easy. It went under his coat and he just walked out into the gathering darkness to his car. Nobody saw him; there was nobody about. He felt uncomfortable about it, but he took it just the same, trying but not quite succeeding in justifying it to himself. This was pilfering. No, it was theft. But he told himself that it was for the right reasons. He drove home with the box covered by a coat on the back seat.

Back at his house, he examined it in more detail. What was so special as to have suddenly made him feel he must have it, to have pushed him unexpectedly to just walk off with it? There was something compelling about the box which he couldn't resist. As a worker with metals – Richardson was a mechanic – he recognised fine work when he saw it, and this was of the best quality, but very much understated, just the sort of thing he liked. The brass-work on the outside really was very skilfully done, and the swirling, radiating arms were quite elaborate, giving the impression of reaching out, almost like ivy, and somehow enfolding the box in a protective way, as if guarding something. The work appeared simple, but the effect was surprisingly powerful. The only clue of any kind was a tiny character unobtrusively engraved on one of the hinges. It looked like a J, with a wider than usual T-piece across the top.

Inside, any lining the box may once have had was gone, and it was only on looking very closely that he could see how the plain, clean wood had been morticed together with great neatness and skill at the corners.

He put it in the back room with his other treasures. Richardson was an amateur antiquarian, and over twenty years or so he had amassed various interesting objects for less than their true value. Pride of place went to his Queen Anne bureau. This had turned up at a local auction. Miraculously, the dealers hadn't been about – there had been other auctions on the same day – and he had paid far less than he'd dared to hope. Various pieces of antique porcelain were staged around the room, including a beautiful early transfer-printed creamware jug in near-perfect condition, and his Chelsea Red Anchor plate bought at a car boot sale for pennies. Then there was the trooper's helmet from the English Civil War, still with its black pitch coating, and its companion sword, which he'd spotted in a local second-hand shop and convinced the proprietor were Victorian copies. He also had a taste for ethnographical items, in the form of various African shields and strange carvings.

This box was in a different league. Other than coins, he had no knowledge of medieval antiquities. They did not, after all, turn up often enough for you to get a feeling for them. Even so, it was clear from something about the workmanship of this box that it was very old indeed, the oldest thing in his possession. His other possessions were good, but this was something else.

*

That night, Richardson's sleep was broken. He knew what he had done was wrong, but also had the odd sensation that it could not now be undone. He could easily have returned the box to the church, but something told him there was more to it than that. His conscience, or something akin to it, troubled him, and he woke up several times during the night, once with the sensation of hearing his name, both first and last names, called by several voices in unison. This disturbed him and was not easily brushed away in the morning. They had not been comforting voices.

Richardson told nobody else about the box, but he wouldn't have done even if he'd acquired it in an above-board way. He was secretive about his collection, and others did not see inside the back room. He was not a talkative man generally, and at the garage where he worked, he acted no differently that morning to any other Monday. But inside he was not his usual self, and a sense of foreboding seemed somehow connected with his recent acquisition. The foreboding was justified. As he was working in the inspection pit, underneath a car, he heard shouted from above "Look out!", followed by a banging, scraping sound. Simultaneously he received a blow on his head, as if he had walked full tilt into a low doorway. Stunned for a moment, he realised that the car was in the pit with him. One of the front wheels had somehow slipped and the car had fallen in. Fortunately for him, the side of the car had then caught against the inside of the pit and stopped it from falling more than a foot or so.

"Are you all right?" He was able to answer that yes, he thought so, and the other two mechanics secured a chain to the car and lifted it away.

"Bloody 'ell, we thought you was in trouble then!" said one of them as Richardson, somewhat dazed, was helped to climb out of the pit.

"What happened?" he asked.

"Buggered if I know!" was the answer. "Nobody was anywhere near that car, an' it just seemed to slide in, loike it was skiddin' on oil, only there weren't no oil to skid on and nothin' to move it anyways".

He wasn't badly hurt. The manager offered to take him to hospital to be checked out, but he wouldn't go, nor would he take the rest of the day off. He did accept a twenty minute break with a cup of strong coffee though.

One further, disturbing event happened that day. It was when the others were outside, and he was in the workshop looking for something in a drawer, that he became aware of a strange, metallic squeaking. For a moment he was puzzled, then he looked up. The hairs on the back of his neck bristled in horrified fear. Above his head, at the far end of its rail where it had been returned after lifting the car off him, the great metal hook of the travelling chain was swaying, just a couple of inches or so in each direction, rather like the pendulum on a fast clock. There was no possible reason why it should be doing that. Immediately Richardson stopped what he was doing and stepped quickly away. After a few seconds the swaying ceased.

He continued his work for the remainder of that day in an odd haze of unreality, continually on the lookout, but nothing else happened to him. That evening he did not go out, but stayed in to watch TV, then read a book. For some reason he did not examine the box again. Normally he'd have brought any new piece into the sitting room to enjoy looking at for at least a day or two after acquiring it, placing it in different locations and admiring it from different angles. But now there was no joy for him in the possession of it, and his thoughts swirled about in a deep unease over the box, and on how he might return to the life he'd had only a couple of days ago. He needed to get rid of it – but how? And after the events of the day, he was alert for anything out of the usual.

It was particularly quiet that evening. There was no wind or rain, and the normal sounds seemed clear and magnified. As the evening drew on, the noises of the night, produced by the changing temperature of house as it settled down for the night, were full of sinister portent and ill-omen. At about half past eight, he distinctly heard the back bedroom door creak open. Throat tight and heart pounding, he climbed up the stairs as stealthily as he could manage. The door was standing open, but nothing out of the ordinary was evident. The box was in this room. He went in, switched on the light and looked at it from the doorway. There it was on the table, where he had left it. He didn't want to open it, or even go near it. He'd go back to that church the following morning, very early, and return it. That was all he could do.

Richardson closed the door carefully and returned downstairs. Not long after that, he went to bed, reading an Agatha Christie book to take his mind off things. He started to feel very tired. The day had drained him. He closed the book and turned off the light, and within ten minutes he was asleep.

If he hadn't been on his own, who knows what defence he might have had against whatever it was that happened next. But he was alone, and this told against him.

Richardson woke suddenly, sat up in bed and looked around in the darkness. He could see enough to tell that there was nothing there, but something had woken him. He could not think what it was, or remember anything of what he had been dreaming about, but he was filled with a sense of dread that someone – or something – was coming, was not far away, and, whatever it wanted, that it would not take 'no' for an answer.

In a state of near-panic, which he strove desperately to master, he got up, switched on the lights and tried to read. But it was not possible to concentrate on his book, and after a while he felt himself becoming drowsy. At the same time, the fear and worry receded and seemed petty, foolish. Once again he put down the book, switched the light off and lay down, and again he drifted off to sleep.

Again he woke up – or did he? He wasn't sure. Yes, he must be awake. And though there was nothing to be heard, he knew with horrid certainty that the unknown something, which he had sensed approaching earlier in the night, had reached its destination. It was here, with him in the bedroom, and if he opened his eyes he would see it.

The room was freezing, and a nasty tingling ran all along his spine and the back of his neck. He did not want to look, but he felt it drawing nearer to him. Slowly, unwillingly, he opened his eyes.

A misty grey form, more or less the size and shape of a man but with no distinguishable features, was beside the bed. It had a cold, merciless aura. Retribution was its purpose, and it would not be denied.

The grey shape raised an arm, beckoned and turned. Against his will, Richardson found himself getting out of bed and following it into the adjoining bedroom, where the box was kept. It stopped by the box, which he saw was now open, and pointed to it. He was impelled by some irresistible force to peer inside, and as he did so a tumult of voices became audible, seeming to come from a great depth. He sensed rather than saw indeterminate forms with raised arms and upturned faces, all shouting and laughing mirthlessly, in anticipation of ... what?

Richardson realised what as the increasing force pulled him toward the box.

"No!" he managed to call out as the box grew larger, seemed to engulf him, then swiftly drew him in like a swirl of smoke and consumed him.

The lid snapped shut.

*

Some days later the police broke in, but they could find nothing to account for Richardson's mysterious disappearance, and after some time he was declared legally dead. It turned out that he had no family, and his effects were eventually auctioned off. Remarkably, the box managed to make its way back to the church, where along with the other easily-portable valuables it has now been returned to the room where it had spent so much time locked away before its brief period out in the nave. How did it get back there? It happened to be seen by one of the churchwardens at the police station among the effects, and was recognised by him as having been stolen around the same time that Richardson had vanished. Pure chance, you will say. I think you must be right, as any other explanation is simply too preposterous to contemplate.

THE DARK GUARDIAN
OF WANDLEBURY

The Gogmagog Hills aren't really hills by the normal standards of Britain. Their highest peak is only 70 metres above sea-level, but, located just to the southeast of Cambridge, they are a dominant feature on the otherwise flat landscape, and it is easy to understand why an ancient fort, Wandlebury, was once constructed there – and used again and again by successive waves of conquerors – and why numerous mythical and ghostly stories have come to surround them.

To begin with, the name itself has esoteric origins. According to Geoffrey of Monmouth's 'Historia Regum Britanniae', written sometime in the 1130s, Gogmagog was a terrifying giant – a nightmarish, misshapen ogre – who rampaged through southern Britain, 'making great slaughter' on all who stood against him. According to Monmouth, Gogmagog was eventually killed by the hero Corineus, who threw him from a cliff after a day-long battle, and later had his corpse, and the corpses of other giants killed in the same campaign, buried in the hills near Cambridge, cutting images in the turf to mark the grave. This story was taken seriously in England until at least the 17th century, even though it was known that Gogmagog – or Gog and Magog, two separate individuals – were characters from the Bible, who also featured in early Moslem writings. In nearly all of these ancient annals, though their physical description is vague, Gog and Magog are recognised as dangerous foes who need to be destroyed; it was perhaps understandable that each new generation of scholars identified them with a particular enemy of their own period – the Jews saw than as the ancestors of the Scythians, the early Christians as the ancestors of the Romans, and so on.

Though nothing particularly terrifying is ever known for certain to have happened at the Gogmagog Hills, there have long been tales of unease connected with them, including one colourful legend from the age of the Norman Conquest.

Not long after William the Conqueror took possession of England in 1066, rumours circulated that Wandlebury hill-fort, which occupies a central position in the low range, had become the haunt of a mysterious black rider, a demonic figure who would cut down anyone who ventured there and was now terrorising the surrounding villages.

Whether this being was supposed to be a reincarnation of the monstrous Gogmagog is uncertain, but there was plenty of reason why the local population should suspect that the abandoned hill-fort held unearthly presences. After her devastating defeat in 61 AD, what remained of Queen Boudica's army sought refuge there, only to face siege and, ultimately, massacre at the hands of the Roman legions. During the Dark Ages, Vikings and Saxons fought continually over the prominent position, and it changed hands several times. If that wasn't enough, there were also stories that in days predating Corineus, wild pagan festivals had been held there, incorporating human sacrifices. Clearly, much blood had soaked the Wandlebury turf.

The medieval tale goes on to tell how a certain Norman knight called Osbert was stationed at Cambridge. He'd fought bravely at the battle of Hastings, but since then had come under the spell of Saxon England, one of the fairest and wealthiest kingdoms in all Christendom, and now felt guilty for the terrible deeds his people had done in crushing and raping this land. To make up for his own role in the destruction, he said that he would rid Wandlebury of its evil guardian, or die in the attempt.

He must already have won friends among the native English, because they attempted to stop him, telling him that earlier heroes – including mighty Saxon housecarls sent by Harold Godwinson and Edward the Confessor – had all failed in the quest. But Osbert was determined. Fully mailed and ready for combat, he rode up to the hill-fort at dusk, and was appalled to see the grisly relics of those who had gone before him hanging like trophies from the stunted, wind-blown trees. The dark guardian then sallied out to meet him; a towering, faceless figure dressed all in black – black mail and billowing black silk – and mounted on a fierce, black warhorse.

No parley was held and no quarter offered. Battle was joined, and it quickly proved exhausting for Osbert, who realised that he was indeed facing a supernatural opponent. Eventually both combatants were unhorsed, but the duel went on as they struck and slashed at each other. When Osbert was wounded in the thigh and had his sword knocked from his gasp, he feared that his time was up, and yet somehow he evaded his foe long enough to grab up his lance and lunge forward with it. The black rider was impaled through the middle. He fell onto his back, and Osbert leapt upon him, hammering the shaft through until his foe was transfixed to the ground and lay still. However, when Osbert attempted to unmask him, he discovered that nothing but empty mail and clothing lay at his feet.

Bleeding badly, Osbert made it back to Cambridge in time to be tended by the townsfolk. He had brought the black warhorse as a prize, only for it to later vanish from his stables, never to be seen again. Osbert was hailed a hero and a friend to the English, but the remainder of his life was not easy – every year, on the date of his battle with the black rider, his wound would open of its own accord and bleed profusely.

The story sounds suspiciously Arthurian to modern ears, but it is interesting that at no stage is the name Gogmagog mentioned, which one would have expected had the author been attempting to weave a fiction that he was trying to tie in with the surrounding locale.

As a footnote to the mysteries of the Gogmagog Hills, in the mid-1950s T.C. Lethbridge, who was director of excavations for the Cambridge Antiquarian Society, made a claim that he had found three gigantic figures carved under the turf on the hills, including one resembling a brutish horse. However, his methods were questioned by other archaeologists, and as letters from the 16th and 17th centuries refer to students from Cambridge cutting their own figures on the Gogmagog hills as a jape, it was not held to be a significant discovery.

THE SPOOKS OF SHELLBOROUGH
Reggie Oliver

S hellborough in Suffolk is the sort of place to which most English people would like to retire, but can't. Property in that select East Anglian resort is expensive and most people, at sixty five, do not have the requisite capital sum and index-linked pension. Of course, Shellborough is not to everyone's taste. English seaside towns tend to fall into two distinct categories, the vulgar and the sedate; and Shellborough is very much at the sedate end of the market. There is no pier; there are no amusement arcades or shops selling saucy postcards and sticks of rock. The beach is stony and dogs are forbidden by law to roam on it. Most of the houses form themselves into stolid bay-windowed ranks facing the heaving grey wastes of the North Sea. There are days on which its bleakness is all too reminiscent of Benjamin Britten's sea interludes from *Peter Grimes*.

But I wouldn't myself call Shellborough dull. The town has an excellent annual music festival and a generally active cultural life. For the less artistically inclined, there is a thriving yacht club and marina in the estuary of the River Shell, and on the sandy plateau of gorse-ridden heathland above the town there is a famous golf course of whose club I somehow contrive to be a member.

I should say that I am neither rich nor retired, but I run a pretty successful second-hand bookshop in the town and I live alone in a small flat above it. That is how I can afford to indulge my strange passion for pushing small white balls into holes. I justify the expenditure – the membership fees are exorbitant – on the grounds that quite a few of my best clients at the bookshop are fellow golfers.

There was one in particular whom I shall call Wentworth. It's a good English name and it suits him. He was in many ways typical of the kind of people who retire to Shellborough. He was on the small side, neat, grey-haired, balding, well-educated: an ex civil servant to his fingertips. Being unmarried and, presumably, childless he was in easy circumstances. I remember when he first came into my shop. He was wearing a Trilby hat and a silk scarf round his neck; he carried a walking stick. There was something old fashioned and dandyish about him. He smiled politely at me, even removing his hat.

Most shopkeepers can recognise the time wasters as soon as they enter their premises. I knew at once that Wentworth wasn't going to be one of them. He went straight to the fiction shelves and began to run his right index finger along the titles. I asked him if there was anything in particular he was looking for. He turned and smiled, obviously not bothered, as some clients can be, by having his browsing interrupted.

He said: "As a matter of fact, I have a rather soft spot for old fashioned spy thrillers. You know the kind of thing: Sapper, William le Queux, Dornford Yates, even Sidney Horler at a pinch. I'll go as far as Eric Ambler, but nothing too modern. James Bond I abominate."

"Not even Le Carré?"

I saw his face tighten for a moment. "No. Definitely not Le Carré."

"I believe you'll find a Valentine Williams a little further along."

"Ah! That sounds more like it. Mind you, I already have *The Man with the Clubfoot*. A favourite of mine."

"This one's called *The Yellow Streak*, I think."

"No. Haven't got that one. Sounds promising. Ah, here we are! Now then, what's the damage?" He picked the book off the shelf and looked for the pencilled price inside the front cover. He liked what he saw because I am a believer in low prices and quick sales. "I'll take it," he said, then paused and studied me. "Haven't I seen you up at the golf club?" I nodded. "What handicap do you play off?" I told him. "About my mark. We must have a game when you're next up there. The name's Jack Wentworth by the way," he said, and we shook hands.

As it happens, some days later, I was up at the club and saw Wentworth by himself in the bar. It was a windy February morning and the place was not teeming with eager golfers, but those who were there were in a little group at the other end of the bar from Wentworth. The distance between them and him seemed significant, but it was hard to say who was shunning whom. Wentworth looked relieved to see me.

"Ah, there you are, Martin! Care for a round?"

The weather was not ideal. A stiff, cold wind was blowing in from the North Sea which was just visible as a long grey line to the East above the green and yellow undulations of the course. Neither of us was at our best in these conditions.

You can learn a lot about a man from watching him play golf. Wentworth had a good technique and would address himself with ferocious concentration to the ball, discouraging all but the most laconic conversation during play. His approach shots were nearly always excellent; it was the putting that let him down. Once on the green, he would get what is called in golfing circles 'the yips', a sort of nervous condition in which the slightest distraction can put you off your stroke. I learned that once we had reached the green he was not to be talked to at all. Even the distant scream of a seagull could foul a four foot putt.

It was an odd thing for a man who otherwise had such an air of dapper confidence. I began to wonder about him. We managed to tie the game, however, and he seemed pleased with the result. As it happens, so was I. My competitive instincts are not pronounced, hence my profession. By the end of the game I was positively willing him to hole his putts, so obvious was his distress when he failed.

As we were walking back to the clubhouse he became talkative again. The wind was blowing even harder and clouds began to mass over the course. A few spits of rain stung our faces.

"You know," said Wentworth, "some people dislike this flattish, rather bleak terrain around here. I positively like it. You can see people coming from a distance for one thing. Not at all like Ireland. Ireland is mountainous and lushly green. Horribly green."

"You know Ireland?"

"I worked there once." A thoughtful look crossed his face. There was no-one about but us on this windswept scrubland: no-one except perhaps for a tiny figure in the far distance on the ninth green. Whoever it was was standing quite still and not addressing itself to a putt, nor even holding a club. Though the figure must have been at least a quarter of a mile away and it was impossible to tell even if it was a man or a woman, I could not rid myself of the suspicion that it was watching us. Wentworth did not seem to notice.

We entered the bar of the clubhouse in good spirits, and the prospect of a large whisky, courtesy of Wentworth, was inviting. A tall man in fawn slacks and a bright yellow cardigan was at the bar, his back to us. Even from behind he looked important. This impression may have been enhanced by the deferential attitude of the barman and the other members towards him. He had a full head of neatly cropped white hair.

He turned to see who had entered the bar and I noticed a look of recognition pass between him and Wentworth. I sensed that neither was pleased to see the other, but that, of the two, Wentworth was the more discomfited.

"Hello, Freddie," he said. "What are you doing here?"

209

"Didn't you know, Wentworth? I've come to live in these parts. I've bought Crow's Nest, the big bungalow on Crag Path. What are you drinking?"

Wentworth, reluctantly I thought, introduced me to his acquaintance. The man was called Sir Frederick Horner and apparently liked to be called "Sir Freddie", a combination of deference and familiarity which I found a little hard to take. Wentworth explained their connection by saying that they "used to work in the same department."

"You mean I used to be your boss," said Sir Freddie.

"Used to be. Not any longer," said Wentworth and I could tell that it had taken him some courage to say it. For a moment Sir Freddie's face darkened, but he maintained a kind of fierce joviality and bought us both large whiskies.

He was tall and lean, and, had his face not been the colour and consistency of a fairly mature beefsteak, Sir Freddie might have been a rather handsome elderly man. But I would never have taken to him: he had angry eyes and I soon recognised in him the obsessive urge to dominate any group in which he found himself. He would generally achieve this with charm and wit, but if he needed to do it by belittling somebody, he would not hesitate.

"So," he said, turning his formidable personality onto me, "you run the second-hand book store. Sounds a nice cosy billet. Ever done any proper work in your life?"

"I used to be in publishing."

"Ah! Might call on your advice there. I'm writing my memoirs. My friends have been begging me to for years. Finally I've given in." I was not looking at Wentworth, but I heard an intake of breath from him. "Don't worry, Wentworth," said Sir Freddie. "I shan't be mentioning you. As long as you behave yourself, of course!" And he burst out laughing.

Wentworth did not find the remark funny, even when Sir Freddie patted him on the back with a great show of friendliness. I was left feeling distinctly uneasy and drifted away from them as soon as I could. Ego radiated from Sir Freddie like heat from a blast furnace: I am never comfortable in the presence of such people.

As I was walking to my car in the club car park I heard footsteps behind me. It was Wentworth.

"Just wanted to thank you for the game."

"A pleasure."

"We must do it again soon. I might be on better form next time."

"Of course."

"Here's my number and e-mail." He handed me a card. "And you must let me know if you get in any more books by Sapper et al."

"I will indeed." It was clear that there was something else he wanted to communicate. I slowed the pace of my walk to the car.

"Were you aware that Sir Freddie had bought a house here?"

"Good lord, no! I don't know him from Adam."

"He was my boss for a while. In MI5. We're both ex spooks, you know."

"I guessed as much. I'm told there are a lot of retired spooks in Shellborough."

"That's why I was a bit concerned about him talking about his memoirs. I mean, one signs the Official Secrets Act and everything."

"Oh, quite. I expect it's just talk. People here are always telling me they're writing their memoirs. They very seldom get past Chapter One. Even when they do, they're usually far too dull to publish."

"His might not be."

"I doubt it. It's much harder to write an interesting life than to have one. A little known fact."

"I hope you're right. You might let me know if he starts to talk to you about publishers."

"I will be of no help to him at all. All my contacts in publishing are dead or exhausted. It's a young person's game."

Wentworth seemed relieved. He even shook my hand.

The following day Sir Freddie walked into my shop. He claimed to be interested in military history, but when I showed him what I had he said he had already read them all. Instead he bought a volume of erotic Japanese prints.

While he was paying for this he asked me how long I had known Wentworth. "Friends, are you?" He asked before I had answered his first question.

"Golfing acquaintances."

"Did he say anything to you about me?"

"He merely confirmed that you had been his boss."

"I was. In Northern Ireland. Did he say anything about that?"

I shook my head. He looked at me searchingly as if trying to detect if I were lying or not, then left.

As it happens, I was away for the next week, attending various house clearances and book sales in the Midlands. When I got back I found that I had a number of e-mails and phone messages from Wentworth, not saying anything, just wanting to be in touch. I rang him and explained where I had been.

"Ah, I see!" he said, sounding relieved. "I thought you were avoiding me, or Freddie had warned you off me, or something."

I reassured him. His anxiety puzzled me, but I agreed to meet him for a round of golf the following day.

Spring came early to Suffolk that year. The weather was mild as we set out on our round, and the light was fresh and milky. The streak of sea to the East had turned blue; even the gorse glittered. Wentworth was on much better form and by the time we had completed the first nine holes he was several strokes ahead of me. Nevertheless he remained quiet and concentrated, clearly determined to maintain his advantage. There were several players out on the course, but they did not seem to worry Wentworth too much. I did however notice one person at a distance who was not carrying a club and did not seem to be attached to any of the golfers. The figure was thin and slight with longish hair, and wore jeans and a T shirt so short that a bare midriff was showing. It looked like a young woman or possibly a prepubescent boy: more likely a female, though it was impossible to say for certain at that distance.

I did not draw Wentworth's attention to her, as I wanted him to remain undistracted, but her presence did seem strange, especially as I had the impression she was watching us. I tried to make sure that she, in turn, had not noticed that I was watching her, but once, when I was staring too long in her direction, she did a strange thing. She raised her arms and covered her face with her hands.

On the back nine Wentworth slightly lost his form and I began to catch up with him, but he maintained his grim determination and still sank a few good putts.

The seventeenth is a long par four and the tee is well within sight of the clubhouse. As Wentworth was about to tee off he stopped.

"Good God! Did you see that? Some fellow is flashing from the clubhouse."

"Really? Rather odd, even for a Shellborough member."

"No! No! Don't be idiotic. I mean, a flash reflecting the sun, Look! Someone's using binoculars from the clubhouse. Don't they know better than to do that? Could put a fellow completely off his stroke."

Wentworth was right. Someone in a bright yellow cardigan was standing on the clubhouse balcony and watching us through binoculars. Wentworth waved violently to attract attention.

"Hi!" He shouted. "Could you please stop that? You're in my line of sight!" The figure calmly put down his binoculars but remained motionless. "It's that shit of hell, Freddie Horner!" said Wentworth. The violence of his language surprised me. Wentworth had seemed such a measured, moderate person, a typical civil servant, I thought. When he finally made his tee shot he sliced it into a bunker, but recovered sufficiently to return to the clubhouse a stroke ahead of me. Sir Freddie with his yellow cardigan was in the bar.

I had the feeling that Wentworth might do something unwise, so I put a hand on his forearm to restrain him, but he said: "No need for that. I'm not going to make a scene."

He walked up to Sir Freddie and said quietly: "You really ought to know that pointing binoculars into the sun is not a very good idea on a golf course. It can put a fellow off his stroke."

Sir Freddie stared at him lazily for a while before he said: "Trying to make excuses for a badly sliced tee shot, are you, Wentworth?" Someone near to him at the bar laughed. I bought some drinks and Wentworth and I retreated to a table by the window. He and I talked about Sapper and William le Queux. By common, unspoken consent, Sir Freddie was not mentioned.

In the following weeks Wentworth took to dropping into my shop at odd times. Usually he was welcome, especially if he bought something, but I detected a certain neediness in him of which I was wary. I have chosen an essentially solitary life because I do not like either to depend or to be depended upon. Once or twice he would come when dusk was falling, just as I was shutting up shop and we would go next door to *The Shellborough Arms* for a drink. On these occasions he would often tell me that he had been for a lengthy walk along the stony shore as far as Alderness, five miles north of Shellborough, and back.

Our conversations were always about books or other neutral subjects. He barely let fall any opinion about politics or religion and he never talked about his life. I probed him once or twice with innocent questions, such as what part of the country he originally came from, but he always managed to avoid an answer. Clearly he did not want to have me as his confidant, and yet he seemed to need me, or rather my company.

Once, late in the afternoon, I was driving north along the bare coastal road to deliver a parcel of books for Dame Penelope Snell, a valued client in Alderness. A thick grey quilt of cloud hung over the sea and the stony shore to my right. Wind blustered, rain threatened and there seemed to be no-one about. Then I saw Wentworth tramping along the shingle, bent almost double against the wind, Trilby jammed firmly down over his eyes. He was walking towards Alderness with all the furious concentration he put into his golf. It seemed a curiously joyless form of exercise, a study in monochrome: grey sea, grey sky, grey man battling his way over grey shingle.

213

I stopped the car to watch him for a moment. There was, as I said, no-one but him about on that wild shore, and yet ... I got out of my car and looked again from a slightly higher vantage point. There *was* someone else, standing on the shoreline, some two hundred yards behind Wentworth on the Shellborough side, so that he could not possibly have seen her. It looked to be that girl again: the jeans, the bare midriff, the T shirt, they were all the same. And she was covering her face with her hands. I fancied though, that, through the prison of her fingers, she was watching Wentworth.

I was so struck by my vision of Wentworth struggling against the elements that I told Dame Penelope about it when I got to her house. There was just a chance that she might have known him. Dame Penelope Snell, yet another retired civil servant, had been something very high up in government, though I was never sure what, and did not care to ask. I think Penelope found me amusing and, had she not been over twenty years older than me, I like to imagine we might have been more than just good friends, but perhaps I am flattering myself.

"Wentworth? Wentworth ... Yes, I seem to remember," she said. "Didn't he used to be in Freddie Horner's outfit?" I nodded. "Yes. Freddie Horner, who has also emigrated to our shores, I understand."

"What exactly was Freddie Horner's 'outfit'?"

Penelope fixed me with a severe, but not unkindly stare. "That information, my dear Martin, is well above your pay grade. Freddie Horner was an extremely good officer, but a rather nasty man, as I remember."

"He still is nasty."

"His sort does not improve with age."

I would have liked to pursue this conversation, but Dame Penelope made it quite clear, in the kindest way possible, that our little talk was over. She had papers to study, cats to feed, letters to write, that sort of thing. She was still a very busy and important person.

Driving back under an even darker mantle of cloud I looked out for Wentworth, but both he and his watcher were not to be seen.

I played golf with Wentworth fairly regularly too and noticed that he was always at his best when Sir Freddie was not in the clubhouse. I remember on one occasion I had just parked my car next to the practise ground. Wentworth emerged from the clubhouse and waved at me, then he stopped dead. I looked round and saw what he had seen. Sir Freddie in his familiar yellow cardigan was on the practise ground, sending a row of golf balls into the hole with military precision. He turned and saw us just as he had finished sinking yet another.

"Hello, you two!" he said. "Going for a little toddle round the course? I say, Wentworth, when are you going to give me a game? You can't just play around with old bookworm here. There's no competition. You'll ruin your game. Come along! Name the day! I'll give you a four stroke advantage."

Wentworth smiled weakly but said nothing. That day he had a particularly bad case of 'the yips' and I beat him comprehensively.

There came to be something irritatingly ubiquitous about Sir Freddie Horner in Shellborough. As well as being a golfer he became a stalwart of the Shellborough Yacht Club, and managed to get himself on a number of local charitable and arts committees. Once there, he graduated rapidly to the post of chairman. Most people praised him for his geniality, energy and efficiency. There were some who found his style rather overbearing, but they soon learned that they and their objections were regarded as small-minded and envious, so they fell silent.

I remember a concert at the beginning of our annual Shellborough Music Festival in June. These events tend to be heavily patronised by Shellborough society. Though the quality of the music and the artists involved are generally above reproach, there is something about these occasions which makes me uneasy. Certain kinds of wealthy Shellburian attend in order to be seen, to reassure themselves and others of their cultural credentials. It is not that they don't care for the music, they just try too hard to show that they do.

You know them from the expression they adopt when they are listening to the concert: it is their 'I am appreciating Great Music' face. The head is tilted upwards; the eyes are half closed, and a faint, seraphic smile plays about their lips. I know the look well: it is similar to the one they adopt when they come into my shop and ask if I happen to have on my shelves the works of Mallarmé or Beaudelaire "in the original French, of course."

This particular opening concert of the Festival at the Shellborough Jubilee Hall was fuller than usual of such faces. A famous violinist had agreed to give a recital: people were congratulating themselves on having managed to get tickets, and on Shellborough being the kind of place that can attract a world class soloist. This mood of self-congratulation was enhanced when, before the virtuoso and her accompanist were applauded onto the stage, Sir Freddie got up to make a speech. He had somehow contrived to have himself appointed to the Chairmanship of the Shellborough Music Festival Committee.

215

The speech he gave was of course witty and accomplished, if a little overlong, full of that humorous self-deprecation which is the subtlest kind of self-promotion. I began to be irritated and looked around me to see how the rest of the audience was taking it. Most were enraptured, but several rows behind me, on the raised seating, I saw Wentworth frowning furiously. In the row above him and almost directly behind him was someone, a woman I think, with her hands covering her face. It was probably no more than a coincidence, but it gave me a shock.

Wentworth and I met at the interval in the queue for the glass of tepid Riesling. The music had not soothed him. "That bloody man," he said, "why does he have to bore us all to death with his stupid speeches?"

A large, rich Shellborough lady called Mrs Hawke-Proctor who was ahead in the queue heard his remark and turned round to give us a disapproving look. Just then Sir Freddie appeared and clapped Wentworth on the shoulder with a great show of good humour.

"Ah, there you are, Wentworth! Glad you could join us. What did you make of our celebrated soloist? The César Franck sonata was particularly splendid, didn't you think?"

Wentworth seemed visibly to contract under this onslaught of geniality. "Rather a hackneyed piece," he said stiffly, "but quite well done, I suppose."

"Now then, Wentworth, when are you going to give me that game of golf? You're not going to 'bottle out', as I believe they now say, are you?"

"I'm surprised you have time for golf these days, Freddie," said Wentworth coolly, "what with all your other multifarious activities."

"Ah, Wentworth! If only I could be a man of leisure like you, but I'm afraid it's just not in my nature. I have to make myself useful."

With that Sir Freddie went on his way, dispensing bonhomie and good cheer to all around him. Just before the second half began I looked round to see if Wentworth was still there. He had gone. More surprisingly, the woman I had seen in the row behind him with her hands over her face had somehow been replaced by the imposing form of Mrs Hawke-Proctor.

Wentworth and I still played golf together from time to time, but these occasions became more infrequent, mainly because when Sir Freddie was there, as he often was, he would always ask him to "give me that game you promised me." (Of course Wentworth had promised no such thing). Wentworth hated this. I once asked him why he didn't accept Sir Freddie's challenge and be done with it.

216

"I don't want to give him the satisfaction of humiliating me," he said.

"How do you know he would? You're pretty good at the game."

"Not as nearly good as Freddie: he used to be a scratch golfer. Anyway, Freddie never loses. I know what he's after. He wants me to get out of Shellborough, and he's doing his best to force me to go."

"But why, for heaven's sake?"

"I can't tell you that."

It seemed to me that Wentworth was becoming paranoid. I once even advised him to see a shrink, a suggestion which Wentworth treated with the utmost suspicion. "Did Freddie put you up to this?" he asked.

I noticed that his regular walks along the beach were becoming more and more strenuous. He would often arrive in my shop exhausted after one of these expeditions, needing tea and a sit down for nearly half an hour before he would make his way home, which was a flat above the main part of Shellborough at the top of the town steps. I learned that it was inadvisable to tell him to "take it easy" because he would invariably ask who put me up to it.

The conviction that Sir Freddie was "out to get him", grew, though I could never really pin him down as to precisely how this was being accomplished. He believed that Sir Freddie was watching him as he went on his walks, so he would make elaborate detours to avoid going past 'Crow's Nest', Sir Freddie's bungalow which was on the front at the north end of town. At last his belief that he was being spied on became so overwhelming that he abandoned his walks to the north of the town altogether. I recommended that he go inland and take his walks elsewhere, perhaps in the forests around Woodbridge, but he said he had no car and did not drive. Could not drive, or would not? I never discovered. There is no public transport to speak of to or from Shellborough, one of the disadvantages of living in a wealthy enclave.

Instead Wentworth would take his walks southward along the causeway to the Martello Tower and past the yacht marina in the estuary of the River Shell. This offered him some relief for a while, but then the old paranoia began to dog him again. Sir Freddie was a keen yachtsman, you see, and could spy on him using the telescope from the yacht club premises. He might even be following Wentworth's movements by boat. Nothing would convince him that this was absurd.

It was an evening in late September. I had shut up shop and decided on a stroll. It had been a warm summer but the evenings were now beginning to draw in. To the west there was a patch of

217

clear sky in which the sun was descending to the horizon, turning from orange to red. Over the town was a low, level roof of grey cloud. The houses beneath were bathed in the scarlet glow of the setting sun, artificially bright against the grey sky above. It was a sight of strange beauty; I would risk the possibility of rain.

I found myself walking in the direction of the Martello Tower at the end of the causeway. As I emerged from the protection of the houses I could see to my right the Shell estuary and, clustered around their clubhouse, the yachts. I heard the faint, eerie, tinkling sound of steel halyards frapping against aluminium masts in the evening wind. To my left, below the causeway, was the shingle shore threaded with dark lines of wooden groynes. Ahead was the Martello Tower, a squat quatrefoil hump of military masonry, its smooth curved walls sparsely windowed, all but eyeless; and, making his way towards it, head bowed, determined, a solitary walker. It was Wentworth.

He looked neither to right or left; he went joylessly on. He did not even glance up at the tower which was, presumably, the goal of his expedition. The sun threw his long shadow onto the shingle beach to his left where the brown waves crashed against the groynes. There was no-one but us about. At least he could not complain that he was being watched, except by me, of course.

But then there was someone. A figure had appeared on the ramparts of the Martello Tower. I moved closer to get a better look. Wentworth, head bowed, had not seen it.

As I approached I could see it was a young woman in a flimsy T shirt with a bare midriff. She had long red hair, somewhat matted, that wagged to and fro like a flag in the breeze and she was covering her face with her hands.

"Hello, bookworm, what are you doing here?"

I started and turned round. Sir Freddie Horner was standing only a few yards behind me. He was immaculately dressed in fawn slacks, canvas shoes and a double breasted yachting blazer, the insignia of the Shellborough Yachting Club embossed on its brass buttons. I studied his strangely red face, his fierce pale blue eyes, his hard, disciplined features, the cropped mane of white hair that shivered in the breeze.

"Spying on Jack Wentworth again?" I said.

"You don't believe that horseshit of his, do you?"

"I'm beginning to. And what about the girl?"

"What girl?"

"The girl on the tower. The girl with red hair."

"What bloody rubbish are you talking now?"

218

"Look!" I said, turning and pointing to the tower. There was no-one on the ramparts.

Something had rattled Sir Freddie. He took a step closer to me; a vein throbbed at his temples; his eyes raged. "I warn you, bookworm, don't try to stick your nose into things you simply don't understand. Do you hear me?" Then he turned and began to march off rapidly in the direction of the yacht club. Wentworth meanwhile had almost reached the Martello Tower, dogged, oblivious to all but himself.

When I got back to my flat I rang Dame Penelope Snell and asked her to tell me all she knew about Wentworth and Sir Freddie. She asked me why I needed to know.

"I think Sir Freddie is trying to drive Wentworth mad; or at least Wentworth thinks he is. I want to stop it somehow."

There was a long pause before she said: "I see. Well, I don't know the exact history, but I'll find out what I can. Expect a call from me in the next few days." She rang off.

A couple of days later – it was a Sunday – Penelope rang me up and invited me over to tea. "I can't say anything over the phone," she said. "This is strictly confidential, you understand?" It all sounded unnecessarily cautious to me, but she had been a civil servant.

That afternoon I drove over to her house in Alderness. It was one of those 'arts and crafts' half timbered villas which, along with its boating lake, and its white picket-fenced avenues, contrive to make Alderness look like a garden suburb by the sea.

Penelope received me in a very businesslike manner. Once the tea was poured, she immediately began to tell me what I wanted to know.

"It was the 1970s at the height of the Troubles. Freddie Horner was the head of an MI5 unit in Northern Ireland that recruited and ran a number of IRA informers, or 'supergrasses' as they were called. Wentworth was under him. One of their prize catches was a young woman in her twenties whom I shall call Bridget. She was the daughter of one of the top people in the Provisionals and the information she was able to give us was literally priceless. Now Wentworth was her 'handler', as we called it: her contact. Unfortunately he made the mistake of falling madly in love with her, and she with him."

I found it hard to think of the elderly, neat, rather buttoned-up Wentworth that I knew as an ardent young lover, but then I remembered myself at that age.

"She was a beautiful young woman apparently, rather skinny perhaps, but with flaming red hair and big green eyes. Well, somehow their liaison was found out by the Provos. The two of them were driving along a country road in County Armagh, not far from the border, on their way to a place where they sometimes stayed together. It was late at night. A roadside bomb was detonated and the car was thrown off the road. It was an IRA ambush. Wentworth was in the driver's seat and was able to get out, but Bridget was trapped in the wreckage. He tried to pull her free but failed. The Provos were on them. He got out of the car and ran. He managed to escape in the confusion with just a shotgun wound to the leg."

I could picture the scene in my mind: black night, the wrecked car smoking, torches flashing, shouts, gunshots. Above all there was the terror: the terror of being captured, the terror of leaving someone behind and not knowing what would happen to her, the terror of stumbling through lush unknown countryside in the dark, the terror of being hunted.

"Bridget's body was later found dumped in a ditch at the side of a road just inside the Ulster border. It was clear that they had meant her to be found. Her body had been scarred with cigarette ends, but the worst of it was her face which was unrecognisable. It was definitely Bridget, though. The red hair was unmistakable. Much later an informer told our people what had happened. She had been prized out of the car by the IRA men and dragged off to be questioned. The interrogation had taken place at the back of a chip shop in Armagh City. They had first tried lighted cigarette ends on her bare flesh, but got nothing out of her; then one of the pans of boiling chip fat had been used. You can guess how."

"Who betrayed them?"

"Officially it remains unknown, but the informer, who was not altogether to be relied on, did suggest that it may have had something to do with the fact that Freddie Horner fancied Bridget too."

"You mean Freddie betrayed them to the Provisionals out of sexual jealousy?"

"Nothing could be proved. We have only one man's fairly untrustworthy word for it. Horner was a very good officer; so was Wentworth for that matter. Their unit was disbanded; they went their separate ways. Horner in due course got his knighthood and Wentworth his O.B.E. They retired; then, by some malign chance, they both pitch up in Shellborough. So now you know. What are you going to do about it?"

"I have no idea."

The following morning I rang up Wentworth and invited him to play a round of golf with me that afternoon. I offered, as usual, to

220

pick him up in the car and take him to the club. He, as usual, refused, saying he would walk there. I met him in the car park and we entered the clubhouse together. I had more or less worked out what I was going to say to Wentworth as we came into the changing room. Sir Freddie was there, one foot on the bench, tying the lace of an immaculate golfing shoe. He was very smartly turned out as usual and his cardigan this time was blood red.

He looked up and said: "Ah, there you are, Wentworth! Now, you can't escape this time! I want that game you promised me."

"Sorry, Freddie," said Wentworth. "I'm playing with Martin."

Sir Freddie studied with distaste the scuffed golfing shoes that I was holding in my hand. "You don't mind bowing out just this once, do you, bookworm?" he said. I felt the force of his will almost physically. I hesitated. An idea came to me.

"No," I said. "I think you two have a matter to resolve. You might as well get it over with."

Sir Freddie's face turned a slightly darker shade of red. He came up to me and gave my chest a little push with his hand. "Don't presume, bookworm," he said in a voice so low that Wentworth could not hear. "Remember what I told you the other day." I left the changing room and spent the next ten minutes walking round the car park in a ferment of conflicting emotions.

When I entered the bar, several members were gathered at the window to watch Sir Freddie and Wentworth as they set off on their round of golf. The weather was fair, somewhat overcast, but there was no wind to speak of. There seemed to be a strange mood of febrile excitement about this event among the members.

"At last they've got it on," said Mason, the Secretary. "Sir Freddie's been trying to set this up for weeks. I gather they have issues. Wentworth was his subordinate when they were spooks, you know, and fucked up some operation of Sir Freddie's. Put a damper on his career by all accounts. He could have gone right to the top. Of course, Freddie is far too discreet to say exactly what it was, but one can tell he's still pretty cut up about it."

"I think you may have been given a rather partial précis of their relationship by Sir Freddie," I said.

"Oh? And what do you know about it?" Mason may not be the best golfer in the club but he likes to think he is the best informed and resents any competition for the title.

I did not give Mason the satisfying reply he deserved because Wentworth and Sir Freddie were just about to tee off and all eyes were on them. Wentworth went first and I'm glad to say his tee shot was excellent. It went straight down the fairway. Sir Freddie's shot was longer but he hooked it into the light rough. We watched them

221

play until they were out of sight and the honours seemed to me pretty even. Far away across that strange artificial landscape of the course a solitary figure stood watching. It was much too distant to identify.

Mason offered me a game and I accepted. I did not want to sit around in the club awaiting the outcome of the grudge match. It would be a way of keeping an eye on them, I suppose. It was a quiet, close day: voices might have carried far. Mason and I played silently. I looked to see what Wentworth and Sir Freddie were doing whenever I could.

"You're paying more attention to them than you are to the game," said Mason. Nevertheless, I was winning.

We had reached a hole adjacent to the seventeenth where Wentworth and Sir Freddie were playing when I heard a cry from the rough direction of their green. It was a shriek of despair and agony, high but not necessarily female.

"Did you hear that?" I asked Mason.

"No! And, do you mind? I'm trying to concentrate on getting out of this bunker here. Hey! Where are you going?" I began to run towards the seventeenth green.

I crashed through the belt of pine trees and gorse bushes that separated us from their green. Lying in the rough at its edge was a five iron, the club head stained with blood. I could see no-one. I called out. There was no sound except for the flag at the seventeenth hole gently flapping. I crossed the green to the bunker on its far flank and there I found them. I climbed down into the bunker for a closer look.

At first I could make out only a confusion of blood and sand with the odd arm or leg sticking out of it. They were quite still, the two of them, obviously dead and you could barely see their faces for sand and blood. Various clubs which had obviously not been used for their correct purposes were scattered about. The two dead men were locked together in a kind of embrace. Wentworth had his hands around Sir Freddie's throat; Sir Freddie was clutching at one of Wentworth's ears. It was at that moment that the sun chose to come out and throw the whole scene into even sharper and more terrible relief. I noticed that both their mouths had somehow become choked with sand which glittered in the sunlight, as did the half dried streaks of blood which striped their faces.

I felt a shadow on me and looked up towards the lip of the bunker. Above me and against the sun stood the outline of a thin young woman in jeans and a short brown t-shirt. She had red hair that was matted with dried blood. It flapped about her face in the breeze like a flag. Her bare midriff was showing, pale and scarred with the livid marks of cigarette burns. Her hands were covering her face. Then she began to lower them.

For a long instant I saw the dreadful confusion of molten flesh and, staring out of it, two burning green eyes, naked and lidless in their scorched sockets. They looked all too alive and full of rage. Then I wrenched myself away from their spell, turned and ran. I didn't stop running until I had reached the clubhouse.

Why had I, and no-one else apparently, seen Bridget? It doesn't seem fair. And will I see her again? Will she see me? I have to leave Shellborough.

SOURCES

All of these stories are original to *Terror Tales of East Anglia*, with the exception of 'The Watchman' by Roger Johnson, which first appeared in *The Best of Ghosts & Scholars*, 1986, 'The Marsh Warden', by Steve Duffy, which first appeared in *Midnight Never Comes*, 1997, and 'Wolferton Hall', by James Doig, which first appeared in *Shadows And Silence*, 2000.

FUTURE TITLES

If you enjoyed *Terror Tales of East Anglia*, why not seek out the first two volumes in this series: *Terror Tales of the Lake District* and *Terror Tales of the Cotswolds* – available from most good online retailers, including Amazon, or order directly from http://www.grayfriarpress.com/index.html.

In addition, watch out for forthcoming titles, *Terror Tales of London* and *Terror Tales of the Seaside*. Check regularly for updates with Gray Friar Press, and on the editor's own webpage: http://paulfinch-writer.blogspot.co.uk/.

Lightning Source UK Ltd.
Milton Keynes UK
UKOW032346051012

200126UK00001B/2/P